King's Gold

Or

Dramatic interruptions to a well-planned outback adventure

(2nd edition)

By

David Kentish

This book is a work of fiction, based on some actual persons and events. Names, characters, businesses, organisations, places, events and incidents either are the product of the author's imagination or are used fictitiously. Any references to actual persons, living or dead, events, or locales is entirely coincidental.

For information contact;
david.j.kentish@gmail.com or visit his web site
http://david-kentish.square.site
Book and Cover designed by David Kentish
First Edition: December 2011
2nd Edition : June 2017

ISBN 978-0-6487149-3-4

The story of King's Gold relies on the reader having some knowledge of some of Australia's history in regard to certain facts. By reading this introduction to the basics of Mr. H.B. Lasseter's background, you should have sufficient information to allow you to follow the details of the story.

History of Lasseter's Reef

Mr. H B Lasseter was born near Meredith, Victoria,. From 1925 to 1930 he worked as a carpenter, including a period of employment on the Sydney Harbour Bridge.

It was in 1929 that he claimed that he had discovered a reef of gold which was about 11 kilometres long and about 3.5 metres wide, somewhere near the border of Western Australia and the Northern Territory.

In 1930 an expedition led by a Mr. Fred Blakeley and accompanied by Mr. H B Lasseter himself, set out to search for the reef.

After two months nothing was been found that could be a reef of gold and the search was abandoned. Mr. Lasseter continued on, at first with a companion, then alone, when he disappeared.

It is thought that his body was found and buried in the Petermann Range but this has never been definitely proved, nor has the authenticity of fragments of a diary purportedly written by him and found with the body, which claim that he found the reef.

In 1931 a gold-rush occurred when groups of prospectors went to the area and, from time to time since, expeditions have gone out in search for the reef. None have been successful.

In Mr. Fred Blakeley's opinion the reef never existed.

A Mr. Gerald Walsh who also carried out some extensive research for the Australian Dictionary of Biography (1983) agreed with the opinion of Mr. Blakely.

Many searches have since found little or no evidence to support Lasseter's theory of the "Reef of Gold".

Disclaimer.

The story of King's Gold follows on from actual events that took place in Kalgoorlie, Western Australia in 2002 when there were reports of a gold robbery.

H B Lasseter's adventures as depicted in the various stories by other authors are part of Australian history, be they true or supposition.

The rest of the King's Gold story is purely fictional.
If you find that one or more of the characters sound familiar, then you may be right. That is your prerogative but not necessarily the intention of the author.

The towns, roads and other details are fact as far as they can be when telling a story such as this. That is necessary to give the story some visible credence.
If your name or the name of someone that you know is used in this story, then I do apologise as that was not my intention.

Happy reading,
David Kentish

Map

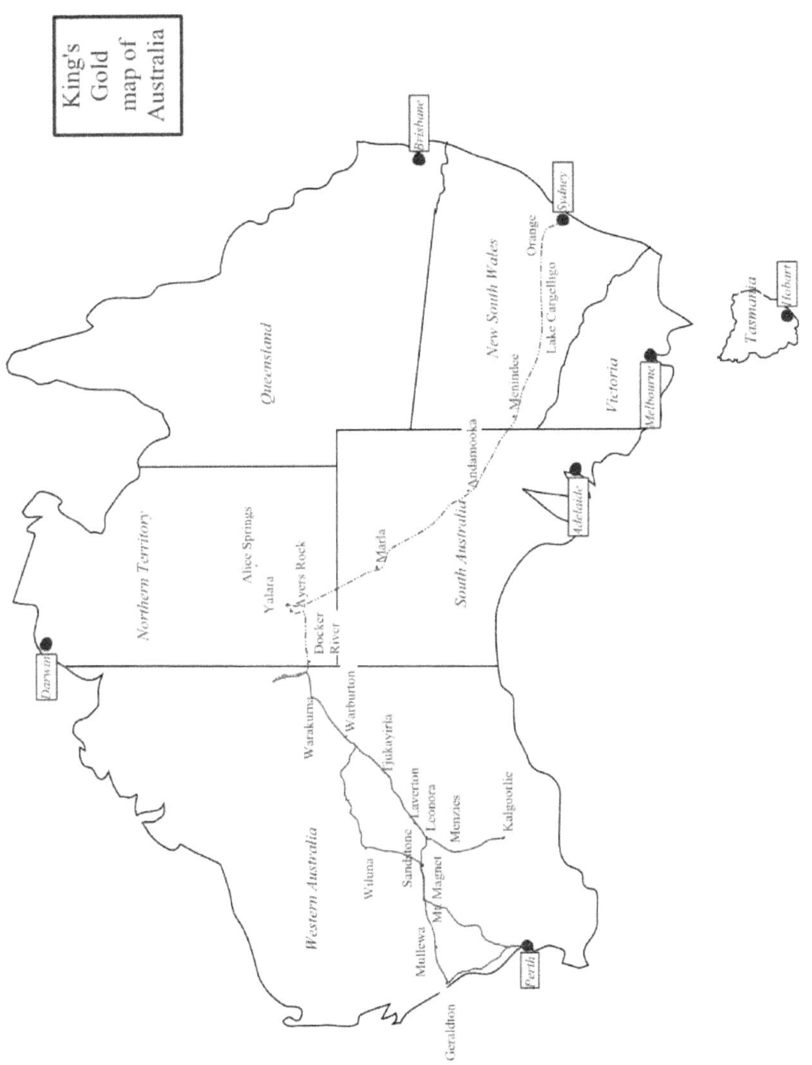

King's Gold map of Australia
Darwin
Northern Territory
Alice Springs
Yalara
Ayers Rock
Docker River
Queensland
Brisbane
New South Wales
Sydney
Orange
Lake Cargelligo
Menindee
Victoria
Melbourne
Tasmania
Hobart
South Australia
Andamooka
Marla
Adelaide
Western Australia
Warakurna
Warburton
Tjukayirla
Laverton
Leonora
Menzies
Kalgoorlie
Wiluna
Sandstone
Mt Magnet
Mullewa
Perth
Geraldton

Contents

Chapter 1

Kalgoorlie, Western Australia, 4th April

Kalgoorlie, Western Australia, 4th April

"C'mon hurry up!" It was a loud hoarse whisper from Angelo Botacelli through clenched teeth to Mick Dunraven. "We've only got two more dolly loads to carry out and we're finished here."

They had been busy at the job for six hours, since ten o'clock last night and they were both just about bushed and getting edgy. They have been running on adrenalin for the last few days and there was still some time to go before they would be able to relax.

"Yeah, aw right, aw right! Stop rushing me," responded Mick in his usual agitated manner, "just keep goin', and you'll make me stuff-up. Do you want that?"

"Just shut up and get on with it ya mug!" retorted Angelo.

These are the last two of fifteen dolly loads that they have moved from the old vault to the waiting van at the loading dock of the supermarket that adjoins the old bank building vault. Each of the loads is four, ten kilogram bars, of recently poured gold from the Middlemarch gold mine. This is one of the richest mines to operate in recent times in the Kalgoorlie area.

The mine owners and their local bank manager had decided to use this old vault for the short term storage of the gold. It was secure but hadn't been used for years and most people had forgotten about it.

The vault was built during the depression and was part of the old bank building. It was closed when the bank was renovated in the fifties. Because of its location, just away from the centre of town, they agreed that this was the best option to store the gold while they were awaiting the security gold transport company to collect it and deliver it to the Perth Mint for the final refining.

The local security company, NG Security, and their contractors have just completed the installation of some of the most sophisticated motion detectors and door locks. Surveillance cameras were part of their contract but because of several delays with the supply of them, there wasn't time to install the cameras before the consignment arrived.

So now they have a security system that is not complete.

The contractor failed to notify the owners or the bank manager of this deficiency.
It was, after all, a top-secret job and information was given out only on a "need to know" basis. They also had the bank's security team to carry out their periodical checks during the day and night. With all of this security in place, the mine and bank managers both agreed that this would be the safest place to secure the shipment.

Chapter 1

Kalgoorlie, Western Australia, 4th April

But one of the members in the team, who had the need to know, also had connections in Sydney, to whom they owed a large debt. Plans of the security system and other sensitive data had been shared with others over there. And that situation allowed things to happen very quickly.

Mick Dunraven has a lot of experience with sophisticated security systems. Following the detailed plans and the security codes which were supplied to him, it didn't take him long to locate the two master units and override them with the dummy load and various jumper leads. This gave the appearance that everything was functioning correctly and nobody was aware of any security breach.

The mortar between the stones on the old bank wall had been weakened with acid before Angelo and Mick arrived so their job was partly done. But they did need to remove enough stone of the outside wall and bricks of the inside wall before they could gain entry. This had to be done very quietly.

Removing the old granite stones was heavy work and they were not used to this. The acid had done a good job on the mortar and that came away easily. So with some scraping of the mortar most of the stones came loose very quickly. They only needed to remove five of the stones to create a hole large enough to crawl through.

Once these had been removed and laid on the floor of the dock, they started on the brickwork. Because the

acid had not penetrated to this wall, the mortar is still hard and difficult to remove. A hammer was out of the question, as it would make too much noise. So, they took turns in scraping the mortar away from the bricks with the scraping tool, until one came loose. When this was removed the next bricks came away much more easily.
After removing twenty or so bricks they had a hole large enough to crawl through.

It was here that they found a problem with their plan.

A steel mesh barrier about half a metre in front of them prevented any further progress. They were not told of this and it caused them some concern as it was going to slow them down.

"Bloody hell, Angelo! Why didn't some bastard tell us about this friggen steel mesh?" Mick complained to Angelo.
"Buggered if I know, Mick. Perhaps it wasn't in the original plans," Angelo replied. "Anyway I'll get the hacksaw and we'll have to cut through it."

By crawling out through the small hole they had made in the brick and stone walls, he went back to the van and took the hacksaw from the spare tools, which were supplied for them and returned to where Mick was sitting. Then he crawled back in through the hole that he had crawled out from. It all took some time, more time than they had allowed.

Chapter 1

Kalgoorlie, Western Australia, 4th April

"Bloody time's getting on, Mick. We'll have to keep the finger out if we are to be out of here before the security bloke turns up on his next round."

They took it in turns to cut through the steel mesh, which was tough. Just to make the job more difficult was the cramped area in which they were working. Jammed in between the brickwork and the steel mesh did not allow much room for movement. Once they cut a small section from the centre of the mesh, they bent the ends around so they had room to crawl through without snagging their clothing. Angelo would have liked to cut a larger hole but time just didn't allow it. He hoped that the small hole would not slow them down any more.

They previously had worked out a way of assembling some thick styrene foam panels to form an almost sound proof wall around where they worked. These styrene foam panels were painted the same design as the stone work so it would be difficult to notice at a glance even in the daylight. The lights on the dock which the old bank vault shared with the supermarket had been sabotaged by their local man and have not been working for several days so the place was in darkness.

While Mick was taking his turn at cutting the steel mesh, Angelo had driven the van out from the loading dock and travelled to the workshop and returned with it after a change of registration plates and different company markings. The plan was to not draw attention to the same company's van in the loading dock for an unusually long time.

By the time Angelo had returned, Mick had gained entry to the old vault. Mick shone his torch around and found that the gold was stacked on the far side of the vault floor. He worked inside the old vault carrying and passing the gold bars, one at a time, to Angelo who stacked them on the dolly.

"So far we are behind time with our plan," whispers Angelo. "Just pick up the pace a bit and we'll get Mr. Arnold's gold out of here for him."

Just to give Mick a break after each lot of four bars was handed to him, Angelo fitted them onto the dolly and wheeled it to the van and loaded the bars into the recess in the cargo bed. They continued with this process until all sixty bars had been removed from the vault.
Mick, who has just carefully reactivated the security system, crawled out from the hole in the vault's wall. Angelo had gone to do something else, leaving Mick with the load of four bars on the dolly just outside the stone wall. He was taking it to the van when he heard a sharp scraping noise.

He froze.

"The security bloke isn't due for another ten minutes and we should be finished by then." Mick thinks. "But I'll be buggered if I get caught now, so close to the end of this part of the job."

Chapter 1

Kalgoorlie, Western Australia, 4th April

"Angelo!" called Mick, in a loud whisper. But Angelo was out of earshot working on the panels.

There was no response.

"Bugger me! Where's the bastard gone now. Always piss'n off when ya need him most".

"Angelo what was that noise?" asked Mick, this time, a little louder. After a few seconds he decides that Angelo is out of earshot so he continues along the dock to the back of the van, which remained open not more than five metres away from him.

There was the noise again.

Once more he froze to the spot. He could feel the hairs on the back of his neck rise up and then he could sense someone behind him, watching. He swung around, nearly dislodging the bars from the dolly. His boot got caught in the cuff of his jeans and he almost tripped over. As he steadied himself, he saw a large ginger tom-cat run around and disappear behind the wheelie bins that were on the loading dock.

Just then Angelo appeared behind the panels near the wall of the old vault. As he approached there was the scraping noise again.

He froze too! Both of them looked as though they were statues, standing in that most unusual pose.

Chapter 1

Kalgoorlie, Western Australia, 4th April

Mick looked to where the noise was coming from and could find no cause. Just some wheelie bins standing on the dock.

"What the bloody hell is it? Nearly frightened the shit out of me! I thought the security bloke was coming," again, just a hoarse whisper from Mick.
"He's got ten minutes yet," replied Angelo looking again for the source of the noise.
He saw a sheet of corrugated iron on the back wall of the supermarket was loose and was being moved by the breeze each time it gusted.
"I think the breeze is moving a sheet of corrugated iron on the wall making the scraping noise. That's what it sounds like anyway."
"Why has the bugger just started doin' that, the breeze has been here all bloody night?"
"How the bloody hell am I supposed to know? Anyway I'll just finish replacing that last wall panel over the broken wall, so they won't suspect anything for a while. You get that last lot loaded and we'll get the buggery out of here."

Mick stood still, frozen to the spot for a few moments. He was sweating and breathing heavily from the fright he had just had but then he grabbed the handle of the dolly and pushed it to the truck. The load of four bars of gold just fitted neatly into the remaining space that was beside where Angelo had loaded the others.
The wall panels fitted so well to the old stonework that they'll not be noticed for some time.
Angelo used some construction adhesive to hold the panels in place so they would not move. They hoped

this concealment would give them at least a day or two start on their return trip with the gold safely loaded on their truck.

The rear door of the van was closed and the handle secured by Angelo. Mick walked around and got into the passenger side of the van. He was still on edge from his fright and still expected something to jump out and grab him.
Angelo climbed onto the driver's position, closed the door and turned the key to start the engine.

Nothing!

Completely dead!

Except for the barely audible click of the starter solenoid as it snapped into the start position.
"Well I'll be buggered. The bastard of a thing has started every time so far and I thought we were home and hosed." Angelo tried several times but each with the same result, so he turned the key off and got out of the cab again.
"For God's sake hurry up Angelo, the bloody security bloke is due on his next round. I don't want to get caught sitting here in the loading dock of some out-of-the-way-joint with a truck load of gold when the bastard turns up!"
"Aw, keep ya bloody hair on."
There was a pause as Angelo lifted the bonnet and fiddled with something beside the firewall in the engine bay of the van.

Chapter 1

Kalgoorlie, Western Australia, 4th April

"It's fixed. The battery terminal was loose." He quietly lowered the bonnet and pressed the catches home.
He hurried back into the driver's seat again, tried the key again and this time the starter worked and the engine caught.
They both breathed a sigh of relief as the engine fired on the first revolution. Angelo engaged first gear and they drove out of the loading dock, turning right into the street. They turned at the corner and headed south.
After he turned, Angelo could see the night security car in the rear vision mirror, coming down the street behind them. Although a fair way back, it did cause some concern for Angelo.
He kept his head and drove steadily. After a little while Mick saw him relax.
"The security bloke has just turned down the side street where we come from. See, I told you that we'd be okay," Angelo told him as he watched in the rear vision mirror.
"Whew! Thank Christ for that! It's too bloody close for me."

They drove south for three streets, turned left and continued on for about seven hundred metres. He turned off the street and faced a closed door of a workshop where Angelo held the van on the brakes as Mick jumped down and walked around the van. Using his key he opened and removed the padlock and then swung open the heavy door.

The door had a picture of a small scorpion painted onto it.

Chapter 1

Kalgoorlie, Western Australia, 4th April

He drove inside and parked the van alongside the light truck that was already parked there. Mick closed and secured the door after the van was clear. Now they were securely inside the shed they could not be seen by anyone outside. It gave them a better sense of security and they did relax just a little.

Geraldton, Western Australia, 2nd April

Geraldton, Western Australia, 2nd April

"G'day, Ted! How was the flight?"

"Hello Don. It was very smooth thank you. They served a pleasant little red wine with breakfast. It went down extremely well with eggs benedict."
Don grabbed the offered hand with a firm grip and a hearty shake of recognition and friendship resulted.

Ted Walsh had just arrived in Geraldton on the early morning flight from Perth. He left from his home in Wembley, a swank suburb of Perth just before 4:00 o'clock, half an hour before sunrise. Ted is meeting Don again after many hours of recent conferences on the telephone and e-mails.
"Glad you enjoyed it Ted. I got your consignment of three crates from the freight depot yesterday. All we need to do before we leave is make a few purchases and do a final check."
"Most impressive, my good man."

Don made easy work of picking up and carrying Ted's three bags and briefcase from the luggage collection area to the old Ford Ute, which he had waiting outside the airport terminal.
"Surely we're not taking this old vehicle on the trip to Central Australia, Don?" asked Ted as he climbed into the Ute, firstly moving some dusty junk from the seat, then wiping it so his white moleskins didn't get dirty.
"Nah mate, we've got ourselves the very best vehicle for outback travel, a Landcruiser tray back with a

closed in canopy that keeps out the dust. Do you remember seeing that last trip?"
"Yes I do and were you able to provide a solid compartment for our cameras and other electronic equipment, Don?"
"Yeah mate and I've also set up a shelf for your laptop computer in front of your seat so it's at your fingertips at all times."
"Bravo, old chap. That sounds marvellous."

Don started the old Ute and they drove out from the airport terminal, onto the main inland road and headed into town.
"You know Ted, I have difficulty in believing it's all finally coming together!"
"Yes, old chap it is marvellous isn't it?"
"Our planning has been going on since we met at that mining camp out from Meekatharra back in '89."
"Yes, by Jove, Don. I wasn't at all suited to that type of work, old chap. But now with father's money, that's all behind me. I'm glad I'm able to repay your friendship in a way that will leave a mark on both of us."
"Yeah, well I just hope those marks aren't only blisters and fly bites." Don replied with a wry grin on his face.
"Well, we both know of H. B. Lasseter's claims and the more recent information has really made all of that previous detail far more realistic."

Both men have had a long-time fascination with H. B. Lasseter's claims of "A Reef of Gold" in Central Australia. They have made extensive studies of recorded information and have recently found details of some of the crew who accompanied H.B. Lasseter on his last journey in 1931.

Don King has spent many years working on pastoral properties and in the mining industry around Geraldton and the Murchison area of Western Australia. He is a hard worker and able to turn his hand to anything that he has a mind to. His experiences have taught him the respect of the land that is necessary for survival in hard and difficult times.

In contrast, Ted Walsh is a man of good formal education, but tends to do only those things that suit him. He's not lazy, just particular at what he gets involved in. His experience in his father's jewellery stores in Perth and Kalgoorlie gave him to wonder at the fascination of gold and now he has gold fever. Ted has a very solid ally in Don. Finding this "Lasseter's Reef" won't be easy but if it can be done, these are about the best two men to do it.
With Don's mining experience, bushcraft and ability to make valuable paraphernalia out of almost nothing, added to Ted's education and experiences with the global positioning satellite system, quick assaying of rock and ore, electronics and computer science, the two make for a very formidable team.

As they approach town, Don turns right and heads north on the "Ring" road and in ten minutes drives in the driveway of his home. It is an older house that Don lives in with his wife, Macy, of twelve years and their two children. Fancy homes and possessions aren't their thing; they are more concerned with good education for the children, and an ample retirement fund.

Behind the house is Don's workshop. This is fitted out with some very good equipment. Metal working lathe; drill press; MIG, Oxy and TIG welders; pipe bender; sheet metal bender; compressor and air tools; a well organised shadow board with a comprehensive range of tools for all occasions. This is a workshop that any general engineering shop would be proud to have. It has taken him many years to put it all together and now he is able to do most mechanical jobs, most metal fabricating jobs, many wood working jobs. He also has the experience in using the tools and equipment that he has in his workshop. It truly is much more than a shed.

Parked next to the shed, in the lean-to are the Landcruiser and heavy-duty trailer he has been working on for the last six months. Every nut and bolt has been examined, every suspension component has been examined and many replaced. The mechanics of the vehicle have been stripped down and rebuilt with the care of someone who does a good job and enjoys doing it.
For an outback travel vehicle, it has everything. Two hundred and eighty litre capacity long-range fuel tanks. This should enable him to travel fifteen hundred kilometres between fuel stops. Fresh water containers with sufficient capacity for two people for six weeks. High frequency radio tuned to a private and several "Flying Doctor" frequencies. An EPIRB unit, in the case of total mechanical failure or any other extreme emergency. Three oversized batteries charged by the

vehicle's electrical system as well as two hundred watts of roof-mounted solar panels. Bolted in the back of the Ute is a one hundred litre, compressor fridge/ freezer.
The vehicle is finished in the "colour of the bush", green and brown, similar to military vehicles. Heat is the biggest problem to contend with in the bush, not rain, so Don has a double layered camouflage net that will cover the vehicle and an area seven metres all around. This provides ample shade once set up correctly.
This whole outfit has done many bush trips but Don is particular. For this trip is special. He has high hopes that it will be his most successful trip, certainly not his last.

Don drives down beside the shed, parks the old Ford Ute and turns off the engine.
Ted walks around the Landcruiser and is amazed at how much he sees changed since his last visit, just three months ago.

"By Jove, old man. You have been busy. This was all dismantled on my last visit."
"Yeah Ted, since you were last here, it was completely rebuilt. Then I spent several weeks out near Lake Carnegie. I've two leases out there and they show some promise. I plan to show these to you on the way if we have time."
He stretched out his lithographic map on the work bench and showed Ted where these two leases are located.

Chapter 2

Geraldton, Western Australia, 2nd April

"I think it best if we take the Gunbarrel Highway for this trip. There is that Cyclone Byron near Broome and if that crosses the coast and heads inland this will be the driest road. We'll need to keep an ear on the weather reports on the radio tonight."

They pawed over the lithographic projected map for several minutes. Each man with his own thoughts and expectations of what may transpire in the next few weeks. Both men began to show levels of increasing excitement at the prospect of achieving their goal. Don put his finger on the map at Geraldton and traced over the route that he had planned to take.
"I think we'll go this way, Ted. Out through Mount Magnet, Sandstone, then turn north to Wiluna. We can get our final fuel top-up there. Then out to Lake Carnegie, where I'll show you those leases, then continue on the Gunbarrel Highway to Warburton, fuel up again and then to the Giles Meteorological Station at Warakurna, cross the border into The Territory and onto the Petermann Ranges. When we are at Warburton, we can catch up with old Billy."
"Top stuff, old chap. You certainly have it all worked out and I know with your knowledge of the outback it will be the best route too."

Macy appeared at the Ute with steaming cups of tea and a few home-made biscuits for both men.
"Good morning Ted!" she said as she approached.
"Hello my dear, I didn't see you there. I thought you'd still be with your children on the way to school," said Ted.

Chapter 2

Geraldton, Western Australia, 2nd April

"No, I've been back for a good ten minutes before you arrived."
"Well it sure is good to see you, my dear girl." Ted said as he took her hand and gave her a kiss on the cheek.
"Thanks luv, for the tea. We've just been going over our route for the trip," mentioned Don.
"Yes, my dear. It's all very exciting stuff and you do make a good cup of tea," commented Ted.
"He didn't sleep too well last night, tossing and turning with excitement." Macy said with a big grin across her face as she indicated Don.
"I really can't imagine why!" replied Ted with a smile.

When the tea and biscuits were finished, Macy returned to the house while Ted and Don began the task of checking the machinery, equipment and stores. Don was satisfied with the vehicle and trailer now, so they spent time on the electronic equipment, metal detectors and the radios.
"Don, did you hear about that new electronic device that the Israeli army is using to detect minute amounts of metal fragments in their injured people?"
"No, mate I haven't."
"Well it's supposed to be very effective. I wonder if it would be any good to search for gold below ground."
"Perhaps when we complete this trip, you'll be able to find out some more about it, Ted. It certainly sounds interesting."

Then they moved their attention to the mining equipment. A short head-frame that bolts together and the diesel-powered winch was one of Don's favourites.

He uses this on his present leases and it is very successful with its remote control and automatic tipper.
The different picks, shovels, tungsten tipped hammer drills, drilling rods, air compressor, hoses and safety clips. Hard hats, safety clothing, boots and heavy leather gloves are in another trunk.
He included a case of dynamite and electric detonators. These were stored at different parts of the vehicle.

They knew it was one thing to locate the reef but to recover the precious metal from it was another job. They have put together enough basic equipment to cover both eventualities.

The miniature rock crusher and separation tables will separate the gold particles from the ore. Don's new mini furnace will melt the gold and he'll be able to pour ten kilogram gold bars. His updated license allows him to refine his own gold on site. This new system will save them a lot of time and money when they get into mining the "Reef".

The camp cooking gear was also important because to work hard you need to have a good diet. Don was not one to go easy on food when he was working hard and he does keep himself very fit. The barbecue plate, billy, camp oven, skillet, tripod and several pots and pans all have their own place in the vehicle. They need to get there in one piece so they will need to be packed correctly.

Chapter 2

Geraldton, Western Australia, 2nd April

Both men, satisfied with the equipment, walked back over to the workbench and looked at the litho. again. Each, with his own thoughts for a few moments stood side by side at the bench.
"Ted, all we need now is to buy the last of the stores. I'll get Macy to head to the supermarket and get them. I'll go to Mitrebox Hardware and get those extra screws and bolts for the shoring. While we're away perhaps you can put your bags on and your laptop in. That'll get us ready in time for lunch and we can be on the road by 2:00 o'clock."

While they were away on their errands, Ted had the opportunity to fit in his laptop computer after stowing his bags next to Don's. The laptop computer fits onto the special shelf Don has made for him in front of the passenger seat. He may need to use it while they are travelling. A map table folds down over the laptop shelf, so the map can be read when necessary. With Don's experience in the area, Ted thinks this may not be necessary. But he'll not say anything because Don does have a way of expecting the unexpected.
Once on site and the survey begins in earnest, the laptop computer is coupled to a set of transducers by electric cables. They drill a series of shallow holes in the ground and fit the transducers into them, let off a small charge and read the results of the rebounding shock wave as it returns from bouncing off the sub soil strata and underlying rock. This will help them locate the reef.
Ted has written the computer program himself and after a lot of testing and modifying, is satisfied of its value. They are not happy of the co-ordinates of

Lasseter's Reef that have been recorded in the past by others, because it's not been rediscovered yet.

They intend to change that.

Ted's mobile phone rang. Ted located the instrument on the dash and answered it. It was Don. "Ted, I've arranged for Cyril Coles, the marine surveyor to set the compass on the dashboard of the Landcruiser. Would you show him where it is and ask how we need to readjust if we move any metal gear around?"
"Not a problem, my dear chap. When is he due?"
"He's on his way, so he'll be there in five minutes or so, Ted."
After a short pause, Ted replied, "Don, do we really need this compass? After all we do have the G.P.S."
"Yeah, I know, but the G.P.S. is electronic and I do like to have an old faithful standby, Ted, you know that!"
"Too right, dear boy. I'll take care of it for you."
"Thanks Ted, see you in ten." Ted put away his phone.

It was three minutes later when a white sedan pulled into the driveway beside the house. The bloke who got out was short but not too fat and was wearing a black singlet, shorts and thongs. He walked towards Ted offering his hand as he approached. "Are you Ted Walsh?" He asked in a lazy sort of way.
"Yes that's me and who may you be sir?"
"My name's Cyril Coles the Marine Surveyor, Ted's got me to repay a favour and set his compass in the ute. He said you'd be here and show me where it is."

Chapter 2

Geraldton, Western Australia, 2nd April

"Jolly good show, old chap. It's right over here within easy reach."
"You blokes off on another prospecting trip, I take it then, eh?"
"Yes old man, we're heading out this afternoon."
"Where are you off to this time or is it a secret again."
"Oh come on Cyril, you know Don, he always plays his destinations and locations close to his chest."
"Yep he sure does." Cyril replied while casting his eyes around the shed, spotting the lithographic map. As he started to walk towards it, Ted hurried to walk ahead of him to fold the map and hold it in his hands.
"Oh! I see you're secretive too, then eh?"
"All for a very good cause, as you know Cyril."
"Yes but it's good to know who's going where and doing what."
"Cyril, curiosity killed the cat."
"And the satisfaction of knowing brought it back, Ted."

It was a good friendly banter between the two men and Cyril started to set up the compass. It was within two degrees of accurate so Cyril added a very small amount of steel to the pocket at the rim of the base of the compass to balance the effects of the metal of the vehicle and the load.
"Cyril, Don asked me to ask you, what we need to do to the compass as we shift the load or even unload the ute.
"Ah, I know Don is the eternal perfectionist and it will upset him no end, but don't do anything. If you were in the middle of the Indian Ocean it would be different, but inland would be near enough."

Geraldton, Western Australia, 2nd April

"I'm sorry to hear that. We do need to be very accurate with our surveying and we will not be satisfied if we are even a few seconds from the correct direction. So please show me what needs to be done."

Cyril was a little put out with this retort from Ted but knowing Don as he did, accepted it as fair comment.

"All you need to do is remove this small steel fragment from this pocket in the front of the compass base. That will make it as close as can done without this master compass here."

"Oh top stuff, old chap. We do appreciate your help in this matter."

"Great mate, I'll be off then. I've got two fishing boats to sort out today. Don just caught me at the hardware shop and reminded me that I was supposed to be here yesterday."

Ted shook Cyril's hand and thanked him for the job. Obviously Don has been owed a favour. This seems to be the case in these country towns, Ted mused.

After Cyril reversed out of the driveway, Ted put the lithographic back on the workbench again and smoothed it out. He was still studying it when Don returned in the Ute. Macy was right behind him in the wagon.

"By Jove, old chap. That Cyril is a character!"

"Yeah mate, he can be a bit funny sometimes. He always tries to get information from everyone who he works for. He doesn't know where we're going does he?"

"Well not from me anyway, old man."

"That's good to hear, Ted. I'd rather he didn't follow us."

Chapter 2

Geraldton, Western Australia, 2nd April

"Lunch is ready." Macy yelled from the back veranda.
"Okay, luv, we're there!" yelled Don in reply. Then to Ted he added, "We'll have lunch, then if everything is in order with you, we'll be able to get on the road soon afterwards.

Lunch consisted of cold meat and a salad. This was washed down with a cup of tea for Ted and a glass of water for Don.
While they were eating they were going over the final details of the trip with Macy. Don always keeps Macy informed of where he is going and when he intends to arrive. Don reckons these are the details that will get him out of trouble one day.
"Macy, I'll call you on the satellite phone when we need to but expect me to call at the end of the week. We will be monitoring the Flying Doctor in Meekatharra until we get to the border then we'll change to the Alice Springs frequency."
"Don, old chap, you certainly have the communications in order. Satellite telephone, a.m. and short wave radio receiver, H F Radios, Flying Doctor frequencies, mobile telephones, EPIRB. Where will it all end?"
"Well Ted, I see it this way. If we're going to get into trouble, travelling and working in the outback, I for one want to be absolutely sure that at least some one knows exactly where we'll be located."
"Too right old chap. You have my total support."

With the meal finished and the arrangements made, the two men returned to the shed. Don started the Landcruiser and reversed it out of the lean-to backing the trailer around in a turn and parked on the back lawn. Ted drove the old Ford Ute into the space where the Landcruiser had been. The Landcruiser then drove forward and Don alighted after parking on the driveway, ready to go. Don closed the doors to the shed and after locking them, took the keys into the house putting them on their usual peg.

He spent some time in a warm embrace with Macy and after giving her a final loving kiss turned and left. He had spent some time with the kids last evening, so they knew that he would be away for some time. The two kids didn't know where he was headed. He is just going prospecting again. That was enough information for them.

The two men got into their seats and made a few adjustments to the gear that was close to them so it would be more comfortable. Don drove out the driveway, tuning left into the street. At the tee junction he turned left onto the "Ring" road, heading south. He turned left again after several kilometres onto the inland road. They were now heading east.

"Well Ted, if there is anything that we've missed, it will have to stay behind."

"Such would seem to be the case, old chap."

Ted fired many questions at Don, asking have we got this, have we got that, is this in, is that in?

Don was able to answer in the affirmative for each item, so they were confident that everything that was needed for their venture was included in or on either the vehicle or the trailer, which follows behind.

Chapter 2

Geraldton, Western Australia, 2nd April

Heading east from Geraldton there are a few hills to negotiate and although the Landcruiser was slowing at each of them, it was taking them in its stride.
"This vehicle handles these hills rather well, when you consider the load which we carry, Don."
"Ted, I had that low pressure turbo fitted to the 4.5 litre, direct injection, diesel engine. I'm impressed with its performance both in power output and also fuel consumption. The transmission is heavy enough to have another 100 kW of power, so I know it's well within its safety range. It's producing about the same power as the American 7.5 litre V8 diesels."
"I'm glad you know what you're doing with the mechanics. Give me the electronics side of things any time."

Don got the vehicle to cruise at a safe ninety kilometres per hour.

They had been on the road for nearly an hour when Don asked Ted to turn on the a.m. radio receiver so they could catch the weather report on the cyclone up north. After tuning in to the local A B C radio station, which covers a large area of the state, they got the tail end of the news and all of the weather.
" *Tropical Cyclone Byron which crossed the coast south of Broome yesterday has deteriorated into a rain bearing depression and is heading in a south/ south easterly direction, causing widespread rain fall and local flooding.*"
"Now listen for the rainfall report and we'll see how wet it's going to be." suggested Don.

Chapter 2

Geraldton, Western Australia, 2nd April

"Ex tropical Cyclone Byron dumps 50 mm of rain on Newman, Port Hedland 75 mm, Nullagine 65 mm, Wiluna 15 mm, Agnew 3 mm."

"Well, those places are well north of here and Sandstone township missed out, so I think we will get some rain but that rainfall report suggests that the depression is petering out and it should be only light falls. But this is nature's weather and we can't predict it too closely," said Don.

"What's going be the worst scenario, Don?" asked Ted.

"Well, with three to ten millimetres, it'll keep the dust down. Fifteen to thirty we keep to the road only. Forty to seventy five millimetres the roads will be closed and we'll need to wait for a few days before proceeding."

They could see the cloudbank ahead of them but it was well to the northeast.

About five kilometres before reaching the township of Mullewa, Don could see some activity on the road up ahead. As they approached they came across a bloke standing in the middle of the road. He had a large lollipop-sign in his hand with the word "STOP," printed on it.

"What's happening up ahead mate?" asked Don as he drew level with the bloke.

"They've just sprayed the new formation with bitumen. We're waiting for those trucks to cover it with aggregate. Then it's gotta be rolled. Then you can go through" the bloke replied.

"My good man, how long is that to be?" asked Ted from the other side of the cabin of the Landcruiser.

"I dunno. P'raps 'arf an hour, mate," he replied.

Chapter 2

Geraldton, Western Australia, 2nd April

They sat in their seats for fifteen minutes as they watched the activity ahead of them. The tip trucks had their trays raised and the metal was cascading from the control boxes at the rear and falling evenly onto the new shiny black surface. Rollers were following closely to compact the metal into the warm, soft tar. Ted unpacked his digital camera and began taking a few photos of the work around him and of the lollipop man. These images will be downloaded into the laptop computer when the camera's full, or this evening, which ever come first. He intends to keep a good record of the trip, the search and the diggings.

By this time there were several other vehicles behind them. A few vehicles from local farms, a school bus, several cars and a stock truck with two trailers returning to town empty.
The smell of the fresh hot tar was appealing to Don, but Ted thought it offensive.
"Quite an outfit you got there mate, when you was comin' at me I thought it was the army out here again." The lollipop bloke said.
"Yeah, we do a bit of prospecting from time to time to keep us off the streets and this is a good outfit. But you probably get paid more than us just doing your job."
"I dunno about that" he replied, "I don't make much here, just enough to keep me an' the missus an' kids fed. I always wanted to go prospecting but never had the guts to get out there."
"You're not an orphan in that score, mate. Most people are in the same boat."

Chapter 2

Geraldton, Western Australia, 2nd April

After a further ten minutes the lollipop man turned his sign around and now it said "SLOW".
Don started the engine and drove forward slowly.
"Thanks mate!" He yelled as he went by the lollipop man. The only reaction from him was the raising of his thumb.
They drove past the workings and there were now several rollers on the job. At the other end of the workings there was a long line of vehicle lined up behind the other lollipop man. This turned out to be a sheila when Don got close, so he gave her a wolf whistle and got a big toothy smile for his efforts. Several of her teeth were missing and her mousy coloured hair was a real mess and this put a smile on Don's face too. She was another subject for Ted's camera.

After getting up to speed again for a few minutes, it was time to slow down for the township of Mullewa. They cruised down through the town at the required sixty kilometres per hour. This gave Ted a chance to take a few more photos to add to his collection.
They had come across many paddocks that had been ploughed by the farmers waiting for the break to the season in a few weeks. The rainfall to the north now was from a very late cyclone and was most unexpected. This is one of the reasons for the timing of this trip. Wet makes it difficult to get around the country and the heat of summer is not a good time to be out in the centre.

They had been driving through agricultural country until now but as they passed the little settlement of

Pindar, this soon turned to pastoral leasehold and is used for grazing only.
"This is the country that I prefer, Ted. Instead of hundred hectare paddocks they've got thirty square kilometre paddocks. Instead of ploughing and degrading the land this is just stocked to an acceptable rate to allow feed for the sheep or cattle all year round."
"You really love this country don't you Don?"
"Ted, I don't know of any other place on earth where you can be so free. You see all the troubles of the European, African and the Asian countries. But it can be a killer if you are not careful. No traffic lights, no "Go slow for School" signs, no noisy neighbours. Just clean, pure air, the way God planned it I'm sure. Yes, I love this country but I respect it too."
"Just put the map on the map board and I'll show you something," he said to Ted after a short pause.
Ted took the map from its holder and spread it onto the map board folding it so that it fitted. Don pointed to the area to the north of the present position.
"See that area up there, around Yuin Station, Gabyon, Murgoo, Nookawarra and Meeberrie stations and so on?"
"Yes."
"Well that's where I was bought up. I know most hills and hollows, most clay-pans, most watering points, where the best pastures are, where the kangaroos congregate. That's a special place for me. I can understand why the aborigines get attached to it. What irks me about the Abo's though is they say the respect the land but they don't tend to it. What I mean is, they allow it to be spoiled. You look as we come to some of

those communities further out. Many of them have wrecked cars all over the place. I haven't learnt to understand that part of it yet. Perhaps I will one day but I don't know."

The country east of Pindar was generally flat with some low rises that the locals referred to as hills. The scrub was showing the signs of the end of the summer. The sheep that wandered and fed close to the roadside were in good condition with near full fleeces as shearing would take place in just a few weeks.

"If you look closely around here Ted, you can see the remnants of some of the earlier gold diggings. This is about the western edge of the gold finds," remarked Don as they drove past an old low dry blown heap.

"They did things hard in the old days, old boy, didn't they?"

"That's for sure. All hand tools and a horse and cart if they were lucky!"

They were approaching the township of Yalgoo and on the left was the racetrack.

"I spend a few days and won a few dollars at that racetrack in my early days," said Don, "We'd come in from the station, along with many of the other station people and have a good time and a night-time dance for those who were still standing."

"I imagine things were fairly rough in those days, Don," remarked Ted.

"By other people's standards, I suppose so but not by ours. Remember, Ted, we didn't have picture theatres; videos, TV or whatever was available in the towns or cities. We did it rough, yes, but I think we all turned

out pretty well," replied Don after thinking about his answer for a few seconds.
"Remember that story about the American miner who mined that hill just south of this town and how he tunnelled half way through the hill and conned that local bloke to dig in from the southwest?" asked Don.
"Yes." replied Ted.
"Well it got the name of "Joker's Tunnel" and that's the turn off just up ahead on the right. It has a few tourists baffled. I hear it's now got a colony of bats and many crickets in residence."
" Is that the one where the mine was salted and the local bloke to whom you refer was fleeced for a small fortune only to find it was worthless and the vendor had left the country?" asked Ted.
"Yep! That's the one. You never can trust them slimy yanks." replied Don.

There were several goldmines that operated in this area. The larger operators built a stamp mill in the late 1800's in town to crush and process the ore that many other miners brought into town. Some residues of this activity can still be found at the old stamp mill site.
"Tell me, old man, is that an Aborigine's house over there?" asked Ted pointing to an older weatherboard house, with several old cars and other junk surrounding it, over to the right.
"Yes, that's the type of thing that I was referring to a while ago Ted," replied Don. "Those houses were built for the workers of the railway line that operated through this area up until the seventies. They now are rented out by the state housing authority."

Chapter 2

Geraldton, Western Australia, 2nd April

They continued on the road heading east past the town. The road deviated around several of the low hills then back onto flat ground again as they headed for the township of Mount Magnet.
Some of the larger mining companies had opened up new mines in the area and activity was visible at all points of the compass. Because there was so much road traffic and the lack of water, there was a lot of dust. Just by watching the dust clouds, you could see where the mines were. Some had their own processing plants and some of the smaller ones deliver their ore to be crushed by the larger operators.
They came upon the tee junction where the road from Geraldton meets the Great Northern Highway. Don pulls up and waits as several road trains carrying general freight north go by. When it's safe, he enters the highway and turns left, heading north.

The mining activity increases as they approach the town site. Some of the mines are within two kilometres of the centre of town.
There's dust everywhere. Dirty, brown dust that billows from the road as you drive by.

Don pulls into the roadhouse and parks the Landcruiser and trailer by the bowser and fills with fuel. Ted gets out to stretch his legs and get a drink from the shop.
"What's your choice old man?" asked Ted.
"I'll have a ginger beer thanks Ted," replied Don.
"Good, I'll get another to take with us on the road."
"That'd be great. Thanks. I need my fluids. It helps to keep me alert as I'm driving."

Chapter 2

Geraldton, Western Australia, 2nd April

Don had been into this roadhouse many times but it recently changed hands, so he didn't know the new owners. As he paid the fuel bill he asked the bloke behind the counter who the new owner is, but all he got was a shrug of the shoulders. He thought that that was not very friendly, so he and Ted walked out together to the Landcruiser.
"Not a very friendly lot are they?" mused Ted.
"No. They don't have a good attitude for that type of operation. Probably from the city. Perhaps they'll settle down after a few weeks and become friendlier. They'll need to, to stay in business," replied Don. "Anyway, we've got some miles to cover". They got into the Landcruiser again and headed east on the road that was sign-posted "Sandstone 157 km".

The road has just been improved because of the heavier than usual traffic caused by the mines' activities. Last time Don was out this way, it was little better than an outback road. Now it's more like a highway.

At the turnoff to Windimurra and Youanmi Downs, Don veered left to keep on the correct road. About a hundred metres further along he came to a familiar camping spot, so he slowed and pulled off the road and stopped at a level area where they could set up and camp for the night.
"The first thing we'll do Ted, is build a small cooking fire and make a cuppa tea."
"Brilliant idea, old chap. I'll even collect the wood, there's plenty lying around."

Chapter 2

Geraldton, Western Australia, 2nd April

Don took out the tripod and billy and set them over a cleared area so Ted could make the fire beneath them. The water in the lower tank was warm, so he used this to draw water from for the billy. When the billy boiled Ted made the tea, the way he had been shown by Don several times.
"How's that, old chap?'
"Good, Ted and I thought you weren't watching or listening last time." Replied Don with a wry grin on his face.

They sat on the ground leaning against the wheels of the Landcruiser drinking their tea and going over the events of the day. Both of them were tired. It had been a long day but they relaxed as the westering sun hid behind a cloud.
"Macy made us some stew, so we'll have that for tonight with fresh damper. How does that sound Ted?" But Ted didn't answer. Don looked over and his chin was resting on his chest. He was fast asleep. Don got the damper mix made and heated the stew in the camp oven. The damper went into the camp oven as soon as the stew came out. The enamel plates kept the stew hot beside the fire while the damper cooked.
After about fifteen minutes Ted woke up to the smell of hot stew, damper and billy tea. Don had boiled the billy again.
"By Jove old man. I must have been stonkered. I haven't felt that tired for a long while."
"It does you good just to get a short snooze in sometimes. But you'll get used to it as we progress."
They cleaned up their dishes and got their bedrolls out for the night. After half an hour of talking about

tomorrows activity, they crawled into their swags and were asleep before very long.

Perth, Western Australia, 2nd April

Perth, Western Australia, 2nd April

"Are you ready Betty?" Gordon called from the driver seat of the Red Mazda 4x4 Motorhome.
"Yes I'm coming Gordon, just doing some final checks on the pot plants."
"But Meg, next door is caring for those."
"Yes, I know, but I just needed to check anyway."

Betty had developed a wonderful garden in the years that they had lived in this house and she treated all of her garden and potted plants as if they were her children.
When she had completed the last of her tasks, Betty climbed in the door that Gordon had opened for her and seated herself in the passenger seat next to her husband.
The engine was running sweetly and this made Gordon very pleased because of the time and effort they had spent to get to this point of leaving on their dream trip around Australia.

They looked at each other and smiled. This has been the culmination of all those years of work. They are not only, business partners, husband and wife but also the best of mates. There was a very warm feeling in the front of the vehicle and both could sense the feelings of the other as they just sat there and looked at one another for a few moments. Betty had a big tear in her eye and she smiled at Gordon and said in a very controlled but quiet voice "Let's go dear."

Chapter 3

Perth, Western Australia, 2nd April

He engaged the gears and drove off down the street, turning onto the highway and headed south.

Gordon and Betty decided to retire after working 18 hours a day for the last 25 years at their hardware business. *The Mitrebox* was a very successful business that the two of them had worked so hard to develop. This was in spite of the increased pressure from the multi-national hardware groups that existed around them. Their investments, savings and the revenue from the sale of the business allowed them to provide an adequate income for their future and to realize their lifetime dream. This is to buy a good motorhome and travel around for several years and see as much of Australia as possible.

At one of the local dealerships, they found a vehicle, which was close to what they wanted so they purchased the unit and carried out some improvements. With their background in the building industry they were very competent at this job. Their son, Michael, who is a diesel mechanic gave the mechanicals a very careful inspection and carried out the few repairs that were necessary.

Because of their desire to be self-sufficient, time was spent on planning the vehicle to suit. Solar panels are fitted to the roof and connected to deep cycle batteries. A 200-litre fresh water tank was fitted under the belly of the vehicle to provide them with ample fresh water. Where they wanted to go, water was not always plentiful.

Perth, Western Australia, 2nd April

A 250-litre fuel tank was fitted alongside the water tank. This would allow them to travel about 2000 kilometres between fuel stops. Very handy for outback travel where you could spend months just wandering around and not find a fuel stop.
A 40-channel CB radio was fitted along with the VHF radio tuned to the various Flying Doctor frequencies. A spare antenna was stored in the vehicle. A 250 cc Suzuki motorcycle was stored in the rear compartment so they could have mobility at any point. The interior has a shower and toilet, table and seats, gas stove and oven, 150 litre 3 way fridge, gas freezer. The lift-up double bed stored most of the stuff that always accompanies people on trips. They had clothing for all occasions and weathers.
"You never, never know just where we might go," said Gordon.
The camp oven and outside cooking gear was stored in a below-floor level cabinet that was accessible from the outside. Gordon's laptop computer with portable printer, bird books, wildlife books and fishing books were in the overhead lockers above the table. Betty had insisted that if they're going away for the two years that she would also take the sewing machine. This is under her seat along with a folding table with materials and thread.

After many months of preparation, the rig was now ready for the road. Recently they did a few short trips up the coast for a few days at a time, they were satisfied that it was as good as they could get it for their purpose.

Chapter 3

Perth, Western Australia, 2nd April

They planned the first two sections of their trip as Gordon's mate had told him of his experiences on the road through the "Centre". This road goes from Laverton in Western Australia to Ayres Rock in the Northern Territory and on to Alice Springs. Because of the remoteness of the road they decided to go this way. With their very close association with the public in their business this would be a pleasant change not to see so many people. They were looking for some quality time together and solitude. From Alice Springs they were heading north and onto the Plenty Highway then travelling East onto Longreach in Queensland. Here they would visit the "Stockman's Hall of Fame". Plans from here were sketchy. They reckoned on talking to many others on the road and use the value of their experience. They intend to see as much of the country as possible. This included items of natural origin in the outback and as well as those items of a man made nature.

But first they would visit their daughter in the Perth suburb of Wembley. Diane has been married to Archie for 12 months and intends to start their family in about five years' time. Diane and Archie's house has a wide driveway and Gordon and Betty are able spend a few days with them while the motorhome is parked in their driveway.

Their first stop was at the fuel depot where they had maintained their bulk fuel account and were able to fill the main and auxiliary fuel tanks to the brim. On leaving the depot they drove by the wharf area and had their final look at this industrious areas of town on their way out, continuing to head south.

They reminisced on their way past the newer subdivisions to the south of town. They remembered 25 years previous they had settled here and what it looked like at that time. The town boundary had moved 5 kilometres south during that time with a doubling of the population. They remembered too, the strong south winds which were a part of life then but are taken in their stride now.

Gordon was adamant that they should be on the road early so they could get past Dongara before midday so as to beat the headwind. This they were able to do.

Just a few minutes before 10 am they drove past Dongara and decided to take the coastal road by Green Head to Jurien Bay and onto Cervantes. Then they would connect to the Brand Highway again and continue to Perth. During their years of business in Geraldton, they did many trips to and from Perth and it was always by the quickest route. Now that they had the time, they wanted to see the alternate picturesque route. The road was fairly new with the last section from Jurien Bay to Cervantes having just been completed in the last year. Probably by the time they return from this trip the final section from Cervantes to Lancelin may be completed too. This will open the area to the sprawling metropolitan area and land values will increase.

Chapter 3

Perth, Western Australia, 2nd April

After they turned off the Brand Highway and onto Indian Ocean Drive, the road crossed over the rail line that carries the mined ore from the sand mining operation just south of Eneabba. Gordon tells Betty that this ore is shipped out of the port at Geraldton. Presently the road travels close to the beach and they pull into one of the provided areas and stop for morning tea. Betty had prepared a thermos of hot water so shortly they were sitting outside of the motorhome with their feet dangling in the water, drinking their tea. The beach to the right of them was covered in seaweed and a couple of gulls were scrounging through the weed looking for a free feed. The smell of rotting weed was not very strong but it was still in the air.

After Betty cleaned away the tea things, Gordon soon had the vehicle back on the road again and continued to head in the southerly direction. They arrived late in the afternoon at their daughter's place.

But that was all several days ago.

They enjoyed their few days with Diane and Archie. Telling them of their plans with Diane and Archie joining in their excitement. It also gave Betty some time to spend purchasing the last few items to fill the pantry before they took to the road.

On the morning of April 2nd it was chilly with a breeze blowing. Gordon and Betty being satisfied that they had covered everything got ready to depart from their daughter's home and begin the trip of their dreams. It was a teary goodbye as they would not be seeing their daughter again for a year or more, depending on how they took to the travelling life.

With Gordon the wheel, they drove through the newly completed Polly Farmer Tunnel and over the Swan River by East Perth. This connected them with Great Eastern Highway where they turned to the east. When they reached Midland, they turned onto the Northern Highway. This took them out through the Swan Valley and past the vineyards. Traffic was light so they had a trouble free tour through the metropolitan area. This part of the trip was familiar as they travel this part of the road each time they travelled to and from Perth to Geraldton on a frequent basis.
At the intersection of Brand Highway, Gordon slowed and nearly did the usual thing and turned left.
"Now, Gordon we are not going that way!" called Betty in a firm voice.
"Yeah, I know luv, I was just pulling your leg. We usually turn left here and it was just a habit," replied Gordon. "Well, we'll travel north through New Norcia and continue north at the Moora turn off, then we can probably find a bush camp for the night just past Paynes Find."

Betty had the map on the clipboard in her lap. She was calculating their speed, fuel consumption and estimating approximately where their overnight stay would be.
Both of them would prefer to have an overnight stop in the bush away from the scrutiny of the passers by. There are a lot of different birds out here and they both

enjoyed searching for and watching the various birds. They keep a log of what birds they see, where and when. Sometimes it takes a little while to identify the birds, as many of the varieties are similar. But with the bird books that they are using they are satisfied that they can be fairly accurate.

The road climbs the Bindoon hill and the vehicle labours but Gordon selects a lower gear that suits the grade of the road. The trees are now much taller and different species than they saw back down the road. There are several sections of bush and some cleared paddocks too as they drive along the road taking in all of the scenery.

Just on the northern outskirts of the township of Bindoon, Betty asked Gordon to stop at a roadside vendor's stall to buy some fresh fruit. Gordon pulled up and parked the motorhome on the verge of the road and Betty went across the road to the stall. There were fresh potatoes, tomatoes, grapes, onions, garlic, pumpkin, carrots, cabbage and a variety of melons. Betty bought a few of what she needed and then headed back to the vehicle with the bags of fruit and vegetables.

When Gordon pulled up, the vehicle was just clear of the road but the left side was positioned near to the loose gravel at the sloping verge of the road. As Betty came around the back of the motorhome she slipped on the loose gravel and skated down the slope and ended up in the gutter about one and a half metres downhill. The fruit and vegetables spilled from the

bags. On the way down she fell heavily on her knees and elbows causing some abrasions.
She screamed.
Because this happened on the left side of the vehicle, Gordon could not see it happening but he did hear her scream. He darted out the vehicle as fast as he could to get to the aid of Betty who was sprawled on the ground at the bottom of the slope. She was lying down on her back with feet and legs askew up in the air. As he approached, she started to laugh.
"God I must have looked a sight," she got out between laughs.
"Are you all right, luv?" called Gordon showing his concern. "You've knocked some bark off your knees." A closer look showed that she also has knocked some bark off both elbows too.
Gordon helped her to her feet. She was a little shaky at first but after several seconds was able to stand by herself. Betty brushed herself down to remove the dust from her skirt and cardigan. She looked around and saw the fruit and vegetables scattered and started to collect them together.
"You leave those Betty. I'll help you into the bus and fix up these cuts first then I'll come down here and get this stuff".
Gordon helped Betty up the steps of the motorhome and put her down on the seat by the table. He got down the first aid kit and carefully cleaned out the wounds with some peroxide and allowed this to soak for a little while. As this was happening he went outside to collect the fruit and vegetables that were scattered around.

Chapter 3

Perth, Western Australia, 2nd April

There is more damage done to Betty than to these, mused Gordon as he took them back to the motorhome. He put the bags down on the floor then turned his full attention back to Betty again.
She seemed to be okay at this point but he was watching for signs of shock while he continued to cleanse the wounds and applied iodine, gauze and bandages.
"Thanks Gordon, You're good to me aren't you?"
"That's only because you're worth it," he replied.
"But I must look like an accident victim with bandages on knees and elbows."
"Yes, you do look a sight, but please let me know if you are getting cold." Gordon was concerned that shock may set in but at this stage she was okay. "Did you bang your head in that skating display you put on?"
"No Gordon, it was just my knees and elbows."
"And your pride?"
"Yeah, just a little," she replied with a wry smile on her face.

Gordon put the fruit and vegetables in the stores cupboard and then looked to Betty again.
"If you'd like, get back into the passenger seat and I'll drive to a good spot and we'll stop on level ground and we'll have some lunch."
"Thanks luv. Do that, it sounds like a good idea."
Gordon allowed Betty to walk unaided just to see how she coped and was satisfied that she was okay but still intended to keep a close eye on her.
Betty settled into the comfortable seat and Gordon drove away.

Chapter 3

Perth, Western Australia, 2nd April

"What did you get from the stall, Betty?" Gordon asked, testing still. She answered correctly and he was happy that all was okay still.
"How much did that cost, Betty?'
"Four dollars fifty," she answered. "I put the change in the back of my purse".
"And where did you put your purse?"
"In the bag with the grapes."
"Are you certain about that?" Gordon asked, showing some concern because he didn't find the purse when he collected up the fruit and vegetables.
"Yes I am. Why do you ask?'
"Because I didn't find your purse in the bags, when I collected the fruit and vegies from your crash site."
"Perhaps you'd better pull up and we'll double check".
Gordon found a farmers' little used gateway and pulled up and parked in front of the gate. He got into the back of the motorhome and searched through the bags that he had just put away but could not find the purse.

"It's not here luv, so we'll go back to the scene of your crash and pick it up". Gordon reversed back onto the road, turned around and travelled back the way he had just come. Luckily it was only about five kilometres they had travelled and they were back there again in about six minutes. Gordon pulled up in front of the stall, walked across the road and looked around the area where Betty had fallen down. After a short search he found the brown purse amongst the grass under a small bush near where Betty fell. It still had the notes and change in it. Just as Gordon was getting up, he found another larger, older purse. He reached into the bush and picked it up. Upon opening it he discovered a number of large notes with a few smaller notes and change. The change looked unusual and on closer inspection, Gordon could make out the Vietnamese characters. In all there was over five thousand dollars in the purse.

Gordon was stunned.

What to do?

He wasn't sure.

After a few moments of indecision he walked back to the motorhome and got in the driver's seat once again.

"Here's your purse luv. Please check it and see if it's all okay."

She took the money from the purse and checked it.

"Yep it's all okay, just as I knew it would be."

"Now here's a surprise for you," he commented as he passed the other purse to her.

"Where did this come from?"

"It was lying on the ground amongst the scrub not far from where I found yours." She opened it up and could not find any identification or cards in it. "How much is here, Gordon?"

"Just over five thousand dollars."

"What do you think we should do with it?"

Gordon had been thinking on this question ever since he had picked up the purse. They had some bad debts owed by a group of Vietnamese tomato growers a few years ago and lost over six thousand dollars due to their cheating. This amount was never recovered.

"Well I think this is payback time."

"I know what you mean but is it right, Gordon?"

"I don't know, but it's not right to cheat in a business deal either." He was referring to the past debt that he just recalled.

Perth, Western Australia, 2nd April

"You are referring to that group of Vietnamese growers who cheated us out of that six thousand dollars aren't you."
"Yes."
"I think we'd better drive on and think about this."
"Okay."
Gordon turned the motorhome around again and drove along the road to the north again. Both of them were quiet and busy with their own thoughts, going over the situation in their minds. On one hand they have the opportunity to recover some of the bad debt they were left with. On the other hand, is it right to take this money not knowing where it comes from? If they do hand it to the police, how will they track down the owners if there was no identification in the purse? If the purse belonged to a tourist, they would probably have returned back home to their own country by now anyway. If it was drug money, and this is a possibility, what if they short-circuit their system?

Oh how the mind works.

"I think that we should hand it in at the next police station, Gordon," said Betty after some time.
"And will that clear that bad debt?"
"No, but is it right to not hand it in?"
"I don't know," was Gordon's reply after some thought on the matter.

They drove on in silence again. Both were looking around them and taking in the scenery. Gordon knew that the next police station was in Moora and as they

approached the intersection, he continued going north with no hesitation.
“Do I take it that that is you decision, Gordon”?
Gordon just grunted. He was in two minds as to what to do but at this stage he considered it better to do nothing and kept on driving north.

The scenery was delightful and the undulating country was changing to hilly country and the gum trees were getting larger and the bush more prevalent. This took their attention from the purse problem and after a while they pushed it to the back of their minds. Betty caught a glimpse of several kangaroos in the lighter scrub just off the side of the road. A group of Western Rosella parrots in aerobatic flight flew across the road ahead of them just swerving away to miss the bus

They entered New Norcia from the south and the sight of the old brick Monastery buildings took their full attention. They had visited these before, as their nephew was apprentice baker here for a while.

They continued on to the north.

The hilly country was levelling out again and the cleared farms were becoming more prevalent amongst the blocks of natural bush. This is good sheep and cattle country and there is sign of many of these. Also some paddocks here were harvested for grain last season. A big flock of sheep were grazing close to the road in a stubble paddock.

Chapter 3

Perth, Western Australia, 2nd April

"There's a lot of sheep in that paddock, dear," commented Betty as she pointed out some of the larger ones in the flock.
"Yeah and they look in good condition too."

The last couple of seasons had been good in this area but this was not the norm for other areas around the state. Some farmers in other areas had such little rain that they didn't even put their harvesters into the cropped paddocks.
Gordon was beginning to get a rumbling sensation in his stomach and when he looked at the dash clock he saw the reason why.
"It's nearly two o'clock and we haven't had any lunch yet! I think we should find a spot to pull off the road," said Gordon.
"Yes okay dear, that sounds good to me. I'm feeling a little peckish too!"

The country that they were travelling through now was open farmland and the hills had given way to fairly flat but lightly undulating.
Just up ahead on the left side of the road, Gordon could see the wheat bins that are near the township of Pithara, so he slowed and pulled into it. They were able to get about fifty metres off the road on level ground and this was ideal for the purpose of having lunch.
Betty clambered out of her seat and made herself busy in the kitchen making some sandwiches. She showed no signs of stress or shock and this pleased Gordon no end.

Chapter 3

Perth, Western Australia, 2nd April

While Betty was attending to the lunch, Gordon walked around the vehicle and checked the tyres for pressure and heat. He also put his hand on each wheel hub to make sure there was no overheating of the bearings. Everything was going well.

"Lunch is ready". Betty called from the doorway.
"Okay, I'm there," replied Gordon. He made his way up the two steps and parked his backside on the seat. The sandwiches that Betty made are always very tasteful and these were no exception. They added a glass of orange juice to the sandwiches and this complete their lunch.
The subject of the found money was obviously on their minds but neither of them spoke of it again that day.
It was a very quiet lunchtime!

They had been stopped for half an hour when Betty said; "We'd better be going if we want to reach that overnight camping spot before it begins to get dark. I know you don't like driving out here after dark."
Gordon got the vehicle going on the road again and continued to head in the northerly direction. Just half an hour later they turned to the right at Wubin.
"You know Gordon, we have never been into that pub".
" I know that Betty, I hear that it does have some history too, from the days of the early settlement in the area. We'll get onto it one day, but not today or we'll never keep up with our schedule".
He continued driving over the flat country. As they neared Paynes Find, the country became undulating.

Chapter 3

Perth, Western Australia, 2nd April

The old gold mining slag heaps were visible from the road. This was a medium rich gold mining area and some mining is taking place today but on a smaller scale in comparison to that which happened in the late 1930's and 40's.

The road had been changed since last they were here and it now bypasses the settlement by a hundred metres. They see someone standing out the front of the service station so Gordon toots the horn and they both wave. They get a good wave in return and this puts a smile on their faces.
Half an hour's travelling beyond Paynes Find is a small but level campsite off to the left of the road. Gordon slows and pulls into here and finds that another motorhome is already set up for the night. He gets out of the vehicle but leaves the engine running as he approaches the other vehicle.
"Hello the motorhome." He calls loudly. After a few seconds the door opens and a man and lady alight and greet both Gordon and Betty, almost as though they were long lost friends.
They had not met before.

Wally and Sam have been on the road for seven months from their home in Tamworth and invite them to stay the night in the camp.
Once Gordon and Betty get set-up on level ground, they break out a cold beer each and join the other couple just before the sun sets.
There are a few light clouds high in the sky and the sun illuminates the underside of these. The colour of the underside of the clouds changes from a fluffy

white to light shades of pink. While they are watching the colours in the clouds darkens and just as the sun disappears down behind the scrub to the west they change to a purple colour.

They talk for an hour or so and then go their own ways to prepare evening meals. After the meal the two couples set up table and chairs between the two motorhomes and they sit and talk around the lantern. They didn't light a fire as the grass and scrub was very dry from the long dry summer and they don't want to be the ones who start a bushfire.
They show their respect for the land.

Yarns are swapped by both parties but Gordon and Betty keep their little find to themselves. No one else need know about that.

After an hour or two, Betty becomes sleepy and suggests that they call it a night and then head of to bed for some needed sleep.
Gordon watched Betty as she dressed for bed and noticed that she showed some stiffness in her arms and legs but he also knew that she would not complain about her discomfort.

He wondered what would tomorrow bring as they continued along their path of discovering this great country.

The first day on the road with all of its events made them both tired and sleep was not long in overtaking them.

Chapter 3

Perth, Western Australia, 2nd April

Chapter 4

Kalgoorlie, Western Australia 4th April

Kalgoorlie, Western Australia 4th April

"Constable, I'll be down at the *Miners Arms* for lunch. Should anyone want me, that's too bad. Should be back by 1:15 though," said Alec Webster.
"Gee, Sarge, ya usually have two pies with dead 'orse 'n chips at ya desk! What's the occasion?" asked Connie, the police station receptionist.
"It's been a while since I ate out and the work load's been fairly light today, plus, I reckon I'm owed some time, so this is when I'm going to take it," replied Detective Sergeant Alec Webster, just before he stepped out into the sunshine.

Turning left out the door he walked the two hundred metres to the pub in good time.

Alec was a big bloke but fairly fit. The workouts at the gymnasium and morning walks, when he has time to fit them in, keep him at a good level of fitness. Many of those who he has dealt with from the other side of the law will testify to that.
"Steak, eggs, chips and salad, thanks luv!" he asked the barmaid after he scanned his eyes over the menu board. "And I'll have a pot of Hannan's Lager to take with me now please."
"That'll be $7.50 thanks Alec," replied the barmaid. She sees Alec in the pub usually on Friday nights after the weeks work has been completed.

Chapter 4

Kalgoorlie, Western Australia 4th April

After collecting his change from the bar, he sat at the round table at the back of the room where he was able to view all the activity in the room. He watched a few people enter and order lunch but he was able to keep the table to himself. A few patrons were part way through their lunch and the aroma of the food caused him to salivate.
He had been sitting at the table for three or four minutes when the barmaid brought over his meal.
"Thanks luv". He said as she sat it down in front of him. "I hope it tastes as good as it looks and smells."
She smiled as she returned to her duties at the bar.

Alec was happy.
A good beer, a good meal, in pleasant surroundings, what more could a bloke ask for?

Alec only had time to half finish his meal before his offsider came rushing into the pub and sat down beside him on the available chair.
"Artie, can't you see, that I'm enjoying the first proper lunch that I've had since ever. Why does this always happen. Just enjoying the good tucker and some bugger comes in to stuff it all up," said Alec without looking up.
Then he glanced at Artie and saw he was a very pale colour.
"Shit man, what's wrong now? Someone stolen all the gold in Kalgoorlie or something? You look bloody terrible!"
Artie is Detective Senior Constable Arthur Herberts, his offsider.

Chapter 4

Kalgoorlie, Western Australia 4th April

“Alec we just got word from the banks’ security blokes. They want us to come and have a look at the old bank building next door to the supermarket.”
“What’s wrong with it, fallen down. It’d be about time, it’s been there since before Federation.”
“No Alec it’s not the building so much but what was inside”
“What, rats and mice and bugs? That’s all that’s usually in those old unused buildings,” Alec replied with his mouth half full of steak and chips.
“No! N.G. Security have informed the Boss that yesterday they stacked sixty, ten kilo bars of freshly poured gold in there while waiting for secure transport to take it to Perth Mint. Now it’s gone!”
“I don’t believe you! You’re pullin’ me leg mate,” exclaimed Alec in total disbelief. “There’s no security in that building and we haven’t been informed of any shipments like that. No mate, you’re pullin’ me leg.”
“Well what I’m telling you is true and the Boss wants you in his office five minutes ago!”
“Look, just two mouthfuls and I’m finished me lunch. I’m sure he can wait till then.”
“Come on Alec, he said NOW!”
“Okay, Artie. Okay, keep your shirt on. I’m coming. I’ll eat this on the way back. Did you bring the car or did you walk?”
“I’ve got the car.”
“Okay, you drive while I eat, then.”

They exited the pub in a hurry, causing some comment from the other patrons but they didn’t answer any of their questions.

Kalgoorlie, Western Australia 4th April

Alec climbed into the passenger seat as Artie started the engine and left the curb with a squeal, completed a "U" turn in the wide street and headed for the Police Station.
As Artie parked the car, Alec was finishing the last of his mouth full of steak.
They hurriedly walked into the station and headed for the Boss's office on the second floor. As they approached, they could hear an unbroken string of angry, loud words being spoken.
They entered without knocking as was their custom, to find the Boss, Detective Inspector Collin Watts, bawling out the bank manager, the mine manager and the security manager. His blood pressure was high as he had been at this tirade for several minutes and he was well worked up.

"You stupid bastards! How the hell do you expect us to do our job, when unprofessional clowns like you do something as stupid as that?" He paused for a badly needed breath, then carried on again. "There are procedures for this type of situation and you all know them very well. We've all done the exercises together and ironed out the bugs to get a workable system and then this is what you end up doing. I SIMPLY DON'T BELIEVE IT." He finally yelled.

At this point he had to sit down as he was shaking from the vehemous attack on the well deserving trio. After a short pause, he continued. "Now, just break this to me gently, what's the market value of the gold that's been so dastardly removed from your control."

Chapter 4

Kalgoorlie, Western Australia 4th April

The Middlemarch Mine Manager, who probably had the most to lose, replied. “Sixty bars, each weighing in at 10 kilograms, that’s three hundred and fifty three ounces times six hundred Australian dollars, comes to the amount of twelve million, six hundred and ninety eight thousand, four hundred and twelve dollars.”
“Phew! Twelve point seven, million dollars. You bunch of bloody stupid dickheads.” Replied Collin quietly. He now was beyond the stage of anger. Now it was just ridiculous but he had regained his self-control “So now, I suppose you want the Western Australian Police Force to catch whoever took the gold and return it to you in its former mint condition? Is that correct?” He asked quietly but with considerable force.
The three replied in unison. “Yes.”
The three managers knew that they had breached the procedures that had been so carefully worked out and practiced by the Police in conjunction with themselves and they stood before the Police Stations’ commanding officer.
“Okay, this is what is going to happen. These two professional policemen who are standing behind you will interview you. They will find out exactly what courses of action you took to make the consignment secure and determine how it got removed from your care. While this is being done, we will investigate the premises and find out what we can do, to point us in the direction of the offenders. This would be the largest gold robbery in Kalgoorlie’s history and at this stage you three are being held responsible. So I’ll require that you make yourself available at every opportunity to assist my team.” He paused. “Oh and don’t leave town!”

Chapter 4

Kalgoorlie, Western Australia 4th April

"Boss, we'll take these three into the interview room and proceed with a taped preliminary interview. Then we can be at the old bank building to form a picture of the robbery. I'll send in our forensics team to check around before anybody destroys any evidence," suggested Alec.

"Yes. That'll be the best action! Then we can fill in the details of the arrangements after our preliminary investigation," replied Collin Watts.

When the three managers were taken away, he allowed himself a few minutes to relax and gain full control of himself before he put in the telephone call to Police headquarters in Perth.

Once he had settled down he selected an outside line and dialed the Commissioner.

An efficient female clerk whose voice he did not recognise answered the phone immediately. "Detective Inspector Collin Watts. Double "l" and double "t". Give me the Commissioner please."

"One moment please sir," was the reply.

The phone was answered in just a few seconds.

"Collin, how are you today? Able to find enough to keep your men busy out there in Kalgoorlie."

"Yes, commissioner, we have just been landed with a beauty that I had to call immediately we got word. We have just been informed that we have been given the honour of recovering some gold that has been stolen."

"What, two small time prospectors in disagreement again?"

"No sir, this is big time. Twelve point seven million dollars' worth of gold was stolen last night from the vault of the old bank building. We are just beginning

our investigations and don't have any details as this time but I'll keep you informed."
"Bloody hell, Collin! That must have been a well organised, big operation. I'll inform all of the other states' commissioners along with the Federal Police. We may need some help if it's gone over a border."
"Thanks sir that will be helpful but we believe we can handle the investigation here at this point in time but like I said we'll keep you informed and ask if help should be required."
"Okay, Collin. It's your baby. Good luck." The commissioner hung up and the connection was closed.

Collin breathed a sigh of relief and then headed out of his office and entered the interview room.
"…So we came up with this plan to add the security to the old vault and use that for this consignment. We have found that the gold has been stolen, but we'll need your people to find out how and then recover it for us." The Bank Manager was telling Alec and Artie.
"One thing, though! I didn't see the cameras that were supposed to be installed. Seems a bit odd. I wonder…."
"Tell me what's on your mind?" asked Collin.
"Well, we had paid for the security system to included motion sensitive video cameras and recorders. But on our brief inspection, we didn't see them. You'll need to investigate some details about that."
Alec suggested, "I think, that while we drive to the old bank, you tell us a little more detail of the security installation. It sounds a bit suspect to me."

Chapter 4

Kalgoorlie, Western Australia 4th April

The six men left the interview room and made their way to the car park. They took two vehicles and drove out to the old bank building. Collin turned up in another vehicle a few minutes afterwards.

The forensic team were busy collecting fingerprints and taking photos of the crime scene.

The officer in charge of the forensic team, Senior Constable Ted Evens, met the team on the dock and explained what he had found so far.

"These blokes, two we think, were well organised. They must have had help with the job by someone in the know, because they didn't have the time for the acid to react with the grout of the stone of the walls to loosen them. It needs about ten hours to do that sort of job. The styrene panels were prepared in advance. And the security system has been tampered with. You can see the scratches on the terminals. So, I think some jumper leads and probably a dummy load was used to deactivate the system. But they would need to know the password to enter the system in the first place." He pointed to the control panel near the door to the vault.

"Tell me Ted," asked Alec, "What about the motion sensing cameras and recorders?"

"Well, what about them? I can see by the control panel that there is allowance for them but none are installed. The wiring is in place too. Were they supposed to be installed here?" asked Ted.

"You betcha there were," said Collin.

The team of police viewed the crime scene from all angles to determine the procedures that the criminals must have taken to firstly gain entry and then to remove the gold from the vault. After about fifteen

minutes Collin called his men to an impromptu conference.
"Okay what facts do we have so far that could lead us to determine what went on here?"
Collin had been talking to Ted and his team and now he tells the rest of the team how he sees what has happened.
"I see it this way," starts Collin, "Firstly; some one knew what was happening and spilled the beans. Probably someone involved in NG Security or the transport mob. They pass on the details of the layout, passwords, movement times etc. Then a couple of blokes come in from out of town, drive a van in, set up the styrene panels to kill any noise and take care of the visual factor. Then they removed the loosened stones and knock out the reinforced brickwork inside. Now, Ted says that the mortar around the bricks is weak and the bricks are soft, so that wouldn't be too difficult. But to do that in the time span, without noise to arouse suspicion seems very difficult. They'd need to have a van or something parked here for seven or eight hours and that would have been seen."
"All right, that sounds feasible at this stage, so now we need to do a door-knock of the area and find out who saw what. Alec, take as many of the uniform people as you need. This investigation takes priority over any others at this time," instructed Collin. Then turning to the three Managers he continued. "In the next hour, I want everyone who was involved, even remotely, with the setting up of this business to be at the station, so they can be fingerprinted and interviewed. If someone is reluctant or refuses, just call us, we'll sort that out and get them in. one way or another."

Kalgoorlie, Western Australia 4th April

"Artie, you'll check with hotels, motels, caravan parks, hire car companies, airlines and bus companies to see who moved into town in the last couple of days. Take a uniform or two with you if you think it's necessary." Collin turned to the manager of NG Security. "You'll come with me back to the station; I need some more answers from you." To the other two managers he said, "I haven't finished with you blokes yet, so keep close by."

Collin took one of the cars with the manager of NG Security, Burt Wellington, and drove back to the station and into the interview room.
"Now, Burt, you've had your "No Gremlins" Security business for a few years. It seems that you do have a few gremlins and I want to know who works for you, see their security clearance papers and their background details. Before you answer, think carefully, because the person I'm looking for, probably has contacts with the Sydney crime syndicates. So, anyone who bets or gambles or visits Hay Street frequently may be the one we want. Do you have someone like that on staff?"
"None that come to mind, but we do have good records on all our staff because of the security legislation. I'll give you the dossiers and your staff can go through them."
"That'll be good. You go now and have those back to me in 30 minutes. No more." Collin said with the voice of authority.

Chapter 4

Kalgoorlie, Western Australia 4th April

Before ten minutes had past, the receptionist was on the intercom to Collin. “Boss, I have the manager of NG Security on the phone, he says it’s urgent.”
“Okay, put him through.” When he took the call he continued, “Yes Burt, what have you found?”
“Collin, one of my men is missing along with my new Landcruiser.”
Collin was not really surprised of this information. His notion was that it was most likely source of the breach of security.
“Burt, give me his description and the details of the vehicle and where do you think he may be headed.”
The manager continued to give the details, as requested, to Collin.
“Okay, get that printed information into me now and we’ll set things in motion here. Oh, by the way, is that your new turbo-charged V8 Landcruiser?”
“Yes, it’s only a week old”.

Collin hung up the phone and then called in the officer in charge of traffic.
“Gordon, organise immediately a watch out for this vehicle and driver, consider him dangerous. I want roadblocks set up on the roads at Coolgardie and Kambalda by their officers. That’s the two most likely routes he’d take from here. I’ll contact them. We don’t know how much of a head start he has but I’ll tip only about thirty minutes. But that can be a fast vehicle so move. Move now!”

He was immediately on the phone to the stations at Norseman, Kambalda and Southern Cross. He

instructed them to set up roadblocks and gave the description of the suspect and car.
The officers there realised it was an urgent situation, because the Boss was on the line. He then talked to the officer at the one-man station at Menzies and told him of the situation and advised him to monitor the traffic but be careful.
Within ten minutes, the radio operator was on the intercom to Collin, telling him that the roadblocks were in place at both Kambalda and Coolgardie and that they were stopping all traffic and asking for sightings of the Landcruiser and driver.

There is a negative response to date.

Collin was pleased that his team was functioning so well. That only took fifteen minutes to become fully operational.
"Keep me updated at least every five minutes," Collin instructed the radio operator.
The receptionist was on the intercom again. "Boss, the NG Security Manager is here with those dossiers. Do I send him up?"
"Yes, immediately!" replied Collin.
Shortly Collin asked Burt to enter and he handed over the dossiers. On top was the one that most interested Collin.
He turned to his computer terminal and entered the man's name and was surprised that the person whose dossier it was, was not in the system. "Burt, do you know if he used any other name?"
"None that I'm aware of, Collin".

Chapter 4

Kalgoorlie, Western Australia 4th April

Collin continued to enter the man's description and in a few minutes came up with the details he had suspected. Describing the man to a tee, along with his picture. He turned the monitor so Burt could see. "Is this the man that we're talking about?"
"Yes, that's him alright. I'm at a loss as to know how he passed that tight security check that was done before we employed him. We'll need to revise those checks. I also will need to contact the Association and inform them of the defects in the screening."
"Okay, well, right now we have roadblocks in place so we expect some answers soon. Leave those dossiers with me and we'll handle things from here."
Burt left the station and returned to his office to begin sorting out some of the details, which he had been discussing with Collin.

Now that Collin had his office to himself again he further studied the details on the screen in front of him.
Albert Ronald Macintosh, also known as Ron McAlbert, of Five Dock, Sydney. Known to associate with crime syndicates. Arrested three times on suspicion of burglary but never convicted because of lack of evidence. Arrested twice for handing stolen goods but not convicted.
Collin sent email messages to his counterparts in Brisbane, Sydney, Melbourne, Adelaide and Perth asking if any more was known of this bloke and if there are any more details of associates.
The intercom came alive with the voice of the radio operator. "Boss! The V8 Landcruiser was sighted heading west towards Perth but west of Coolgardie.

We also have confirmation of that by two other motorists. He was driving fast too."
"Okay, we'll review the roadblocks shortly. We need to be certain we have him before we discontinue those."
He immediately phoned the station at Southern Cross. "You're aware of the situation with the sightings of this vehicle, put everyone on that roadblock now and assume he is armed. We'll send a team from here to assist you."
He broke that connection and called the station at Coolgardie. "I want your team to dismantle and pack up your roadblock and head west to assist the team at Southern Cross. Back up from here is on the way." To the radio operator he said, "Call Alec and Artie, tell them to leave their team with the task in hand, I want those two to be in Southern Cross as fast as possible. I'll call the airport to get the chopper warmed up. I'll give them details when they're in the air. Tell them this is priority one."

There was an email message just arrived from his Sydney contact.
"One Ron McAlbert had not been seen around for several months but prior to this, he frequented one of the nightclubs owned by the syndicate known as Arnolds. He had been on low priority watch because of his past. He left no forwarding address with his landlord, to whom he owed two months' rent. Nothing more was known of him except that in the weeks prior to him leaving, he became a more frequent visitor to the club. Our suspicion was that he was up to something but we don't have any details."

Kalgoorlie, Western Australia 4th April

He replied with a brief outline of the details of what was happening and asked if they could put a watch on the activities of the syndicate. He ended with the request for the Sydney Gold Squad Officer in Charge be notified and call him. He sent the same email to the Federal Police in Canberra.

He called up Alec and brought him up to date.
"Boss we're fifty kilometres from Southern Cross and have flown over the blokes from Coolgardie, so we'll be at the roadblock in ten minutes, have you had word from them about the suspect?"
Collin said that he hadn't but just then the intercom activated and the radio operator said, "Boss we've got a message from the blokes at Southern Cross, they have just sighted the Landcruiser approaching the roadblock and are ready to apprehend the driver."
"Did you hear that Alec?"
"Yes, Boss we got that, we'll stay on line just in case he turns around."
The radio operator spoke again, "The vehicle has been stopped and the driver is sitting in the vehicle. It can't move because they have one car parked in front and another parked in behind it. Five of our blokes with weapons drawn are approaching the vehicle. (Pause) The driver looks a bit stressed. (Pause) He's opening his window and is asking what's wrong. (Pause) They instruct him to exit the vehicle. (Pause) He seems a little reluctant. (Pause) Now he's getting out. (Pause) He's on the ground. (Pause) He's been hand cuffed."
"Please inform the team that Alec and Artie will be there in five minutes to take the suspect into custody."
"Will do, Sir."

Kalgoorlie, Western Australia 4th April

He spoke into the phone to Alec. Did you get that too Alec?"
"Yes Boss, like you say we'll be there in four or five minutes. I'll call you from the ground as soon as I have some details. Could you organise with the teams we left behind to debrief at six o'clock tonight? We'll be back by then."
To the radio operator Collin said, "Call off all of the other roadblocks and advise them of the arrest. Tell them well done for their quick action time. We've got a good result. Everyone is to resume normal duties."

The pilot landed the chopper fifty metres from the roadblock, which was about five kilometres east of town. The two detectives walked over to the roadblock crew and introduced themselves.
They had met several of the officers before.
"Well, it seems you blokes have done a good job. That's what we need in this force, some good results."
Alec turned to the suspect who was sitting in the rear of the patrol car. "Well, sunshine, looks like your little run has ended. Wouldn't you say, Eh?"
There was no reply from the sullen face in the rear of the patrol car.
"Okay, we'll take him straight back to our station and get some answers. Thanks for your help in apprehending this bloke, apparently he has been a bad boy around Sydney too."
He turned to the suspect in the car, "Albert Ronald Macintosh also known as, Ron McAlbert, also known as Richard Arnold Menzies, you are under arrest for aiding and abetting a crime. You are to accompany my partner and myself to the Kalgoorlie Police Station to

assist us in our enquiries into the theft of some gold. You do not need to answer any questions but you are cautioned that if you later rely on information in court that was not given at the time of questioning you're stuffed. Do you understand?"
He replied, "Yeah okay".
"You will now accompany us in a nice little helicopter ride, please move. Now!"

They had him strapped into the rear seat of the helicopter with restraints on his legs and his hands cuffed in front of him.
As soon as they were airborne, Alec talked to the pilot, "Dick, perhaps you'd better radio ahead and tell them of our arrival time and get me patched to the Boss again."
As soon as the Boss was on the radio, Alec gave him the details of the arrest and told him that he'd like to see all the team fifteen minutes after he gets to the station. Yes the six o'clock time should be okay, thank you.

The one hundred and eighty kilometres trip passed without incident and they transferred their prisoner to their car on arrival and sped off to the station.
After he was logged in, the prisoner was taken to the interview room. Here he was looking at three hard faced detectives, Alec, Artie and Collin. He could see from the look on their faces that they were not here to play silly games.
Without any preliminary banter, the tape recorder was started. "Interview commenced at five, forty four, April the forth, two thousand and two. Present are

Kalgoorlie, Western Australia 4th April

Detective Sergeant Alec Webster, Detective Inspector Collin Watts, Detective Senior Constable Artie Herberts and we are interviewing Richard Arnold Menzies," Alec said for the benefit of the tape and the suspect.

"Well Richard, or would you prefer Dick or Rich? Eh?"

"I'd prefer Rich," he answered.

"Okay Dick, why did you take Burt's Landcruiser and drive to Southern Cross? The girls here not good enough for you?"

"Not at all. The girls here are great."

"Why then, eh?"

"Gotta keep ahead of you blokes."

"And why would you need to do that?"

There was no answer from the suspect as he sat there, proud of himself.

"Tell me Dick, what do you know about some gold in an old bank vault that went missing earlier today?"

"Oh, is that what this is about, why didn't you say so in the first place. I don't know much at all really."

Collin asked the next question, "Precisely what do you know about it?"

"Two blokes knocked it off."

"Who are they?"

"I don't know." He could see that he was going to be incriminated with this crime so he was thinking that he may as well come clean to the Police but try to hold things up a little and give the others a chance to clear the area, where ever and whoever they are. "What I do know is that two blokes came from Sydney to collect something from that old bank building. I don't know what it was but I did think that it might be valuable."

Chapter 4

Kalgoorlie, Western Australia 4th April

"Do you think that these two blokes might know a man called Mr. Arnold?" Collin asked.
The other two officers looked at Collin because this was the first they had heard of the connection.
"I dunno, maybe."
"We take that as a yes. We do know about your past, Dick and many of those with whom you have associated, so don't try to be smart, because it'll not get you anywhere."
At this point Rich could see that the best he could do was stall for as long as he can.
"I think what happened here is that Mr. Arnold sent you over here a few months ahead of this operation and got you a nice job with the security firm. Then got you organised to have the wall of the old bank building treated with acid so as to loosen the stones to let the other blokes in to do the job. How does that sound to you?"
"Not bad, but you can't fit that on me!"
"No one is trying to fit anything onto you, Rich, we just want a few answers to some simple questions. Now you can do that can't you?"
"Yeah, I suppose."
"How did these two blokes leave town?"
"That, I can't help you with, because I don't know."
"Who, worked on the walls of the building?"
"You've got me there too, I don't know."
"Who else in town is in this with you?"
"I thought that there must be someone else from the group but I don't know who it would be."
"Okay that will be all for now, we'll be talking again real soon."

Chapter 4

Kalgoorlie, Western Australia 4th April

The tape recorder was switched off and the three detectives left the room. The suspect was taken back to his cell.

Collin was ready for the questions but he held up his hand and said, "I'm only going to say this once so I'll tell everyone together."
In the squad room all of the others on the case were assembled, including the forensic team. There was a lot of noise too, because of the excitement as this was the biggest gold theft case most of them had been involved with.
"Okay, everyone! Quiet down, quiet down for the Boss!" Alec yelled at the top of his voice so as to be heard above the din.
"Okay team, today we have had some things happen here that we've not previously been involved with on this scale. As we see it, a syndicate from Sydney is involved and have in town at least two people. One we have in custody, he is Rich Menzies from N G Security. We haven't been able to identify the other person yet. I've been in touch with Sydney Police this afternoon and have some background on the one we have in custody. It seems they organised to have the wall of the old bank building treated with chemical to dissolve the mortar between the stones. The security system was not completed and the passwords were sent to the syndicate. Two men came from Sydney; we haven't worked out how yet, and used a vehicle to remove the gold from the vault by gaining access through the stone wall at the loading dock of the supermarket. I want all of your reports in now so we can correlate them and see how many gaps we can

fill." Collin paused to let this sink in because some of this team were fresh from the academy.
"Has any one from the door to door got any information that they feel is significant?"
There were replies from about four of the team at once and yes there were several vans of the same make and model seen near the loading dock during the early morning. One early morning walker noticed a white Ford Transit van at the dock on his way out and when he walked back, he noticed another white van at the dock but the company name was different. One he hasn't seen before. One of the car rental places had a car left at their gate last night some time. It had been rented in Perth.

"All right. That's not a lot to go on so far, so have those reports on Alec's desk in fifteen minutes, and then you can all knock off. But I want details of that rental car. Who, where, when, why etc. and also find out as much as you can about Ford Transit vans in town. Get those to me first thing in the morning. You've all done well, goodnight."
He motioned for Alec and Artie to follow him into his office. They sat down at his desk.
"A beer?" he asked as he handed a stubby of Hannan Lite to each of the officers. "What a day! I just can't believe that those three blokes could make such a cock-up of the gold delivery. But thanks for bearing with me tonight; there wasn't time to fill you in of the details that I was able to find out from the officers in Sydney. I don't know any more than you do now after that debriefing. So what do you think, Alec?"

Chapter 4

Kalgoorlie, Western Australia 4th April

He took a little time to answer, "We do know basically how the job was done, what we don't know is by whom and where they are now. Do you think it's time to ask for public support while it will be fresh in their minds? We could have a reporter here in five minutes."
"Yes, I'm thinking along those lines as well. I'll call the A B C radio local bloke and the editor of the Kalgoorlie Miner. If we can get some information out tonight, I'm sure we'll get some good responses."
He picked up the phone and spoke to each of them in turn and suggested that it would be in their best interests if they would be in his office in five minutes.

They finished their drinks before the reporters arrived and disposed of the empties in the bin behind Collin's chair.
Both the editor and reporter entered and sat on the chairs offered them.
It often helps to be pleasant to these people so we can get what we want, thinks Alec.
Collin outlined the basics of what had taken place, making no mention of any names. He showed them a picture of a Ford Transit van and asked for them to put the question to the public to assist with information regarding any movements of a vehicle like this, occupied by one or two men in the vicinity of the old bank building.
The two men were very pleased to have the chance to get at this story. What a scoop! As they left the office they commented that it would be in the next news bulletin on the A B C radio and in tomorrow

morning's local Kalgoorlie Miner and the West Australian newspapers.
"Well, I'm off home now, it's been a taxing day," said Collin. "I suggest that tomorrow will be hectic as well. We'll need extras on the phones right away, thanks for organising that Artie. Goodnight."

Alec and Artie left the boss's office and returned to their own. There were several reports on the desk and Alec took several minutes to look at them then pass them onto Artie. He'd go over the details in his mind during the evening and something might jump out at him to fill in a gap or two.
"I'm off too, mate. See you tomorrow."
"Yes okay, goodnight Alec."

Alec was nearly home when he tuned the radio in his car to the local station just as the news bulletin came on the air:

"Early this morning two men robbed the bank in Kalgoorlie of over twelve point seven million dollars' worth of gold. The police have several strong leads and are asking for community effort in assisting them with their enquiries with some details. A suspicious white Ford Transit van was seen in the area. If anyone has seen a van of this description with company markings on the side, please contact the Kalgoorlie Police. Detective Sergeant Alec Webster, of the Kalgoorlie Police, who is leading the investigation. Our sources at Kalgoorlie Police station have told us that there were several roadblocks in the area today and one suspect is in custody. Detective Sergeant Alec

Chapter 4

Kalgoorlie, Western Australia 4th April

Webster thanks the public for their support in the apprehension of a stolen vehicle at the roadblock. Kalgoorlie Police can be contacted on ……….

"Well, how's that for service?" Alec says out loud as he drives into the driveway of his home.

Sydney, New South Wales 5th April

"And in summary of the report for the operation of the "IT" section of the company, please allow me to add; it shows that we are on track to complete our third year with a seven point five percent profit margin. This is three point two five million dollars up on the last years' figures. Which is in line with our forecasts of three years ago."

George had been on his feet presenting this report to the board of directors for the last half an hour and he welcomed the chance to sit down.

"Do we have any questions of George's presentation or the facts and figures which are included within that report?" asked Mick Jones the Chairman of the ten-member board of Macrodelphus Pty Ltd.
"Yes, I do have a question, Mr. Chairman," this coming from Mr. Leong Cheong who is the head of the Hong Kong office. "I'd like to know when the new K47s10 software that we have developed in Hong Kong would be introduced into your programming."
George replied, "That is currently being integrated into the new version of our ISP hardware/software package that will be released to the market ahead of the like Microsoft product. We are very excited of the prospects of this package and I will have a comprehensive report on that for the next meeting."
"Are there any further questions?"
There was none.

Chapter 5

Sydney, New South Wales 5th April

"Well, ladies and gentlemen of the board, that concludes the business of this session of the board meeting. I call the meeting closed. I wish you all safe travelling and we'll meet again in four weeks. I hope to have some more very exciting news for you to digest after this most interesting trip, which I'll be leaving on shortly."
The board members all stood together and walked from the room, carrying their reports and paperwork with them. Several had their secretaries in attendance.

Mick Jones is a slim man in good physical condition and good health. The electronics and software development business was his own brainchild, which he started from his back room at home some twenty years previous. Now, his company, which is headquartered in Sydney, has offices in five countries and over two thousand employees. Mick spends much of his out of office time at the controls of his Bell 206 helicopter.
After leaving the boardroom, he handed his portfolio to Sandra, his secretary and had her file them in his safe for his return.
"Oh, Mr Jones, your visitor is waiting in your outer office." She said.
"Thank you Sandra, is the helicopter ready?" She replied that yes, it was on the roof just waiting for his instruction to warm up. "Please have the mechanic start the pre-flight procedure; I shall be taking off at one o'clock."
He entered his outer office and was surprised to see a man asleep in the large chair that was provided for the visiting executives.

Chapter 5

Sydney, New South Wales 5th April

Dr. Ravin Goldcastle was a swarthy man of Middle Eastern appearance. He in fact had been recruited to the European office in Brussels. After attending Eaton University and attaining his PhD with honours in physics, he was an electronics engineer with the Israeli Army and has excellent qualifications in his field. Castle, as he is known, had been flying by Qantas for the last 23 hours after leaving Heathrow Airport. Jet lag had set in and he was having difficulty in keeping awake.

Mick touched him gently on the shoulder and in a very quiet voice asked if he was awake.

Castle stirred and slowly opened one eye.

"Oh, I see you've closed the meeting, Mr Jones." He stood and was unsteady on his feet but he offered his hand to Mick Jones. Mick greeted Castle for the first time but had talked to him several times on the frequent videoconference links. After the handshake Castle became steadier as he woke up.

"Castle, just give me five minutes while I shower and change, then we'll be on the way. I assume all of your gear is loaded onto the helicopter."

"Yes, Mr. Jones, it's all stowed in the cargo area and strapped down," Castle replied.

Mick retired to the rear of his office and continued onto the ensuite. The shower was pleasant and relaxing and he was out in four minutes. He dressed into his heavy cotton bush clothing because that's where they were heading. Taking his holdall, he returned to the front of the office and had Castle follow him to the lift, which takes them to the rooftop, where the helicopter is waiting.

Chapter 5

Sydney, New South Wales 5th April

The Bell 206 is a sleek helicopter, which is painted white with red on the tail rotor strut. Mick opened a small hatch, stowed his holdall and climbed into the pilots' seat on the left. He had Castle sit in the co-pilot's seat. Mick was busy for ten minutes as he completing his pre-flight procedure. Meanwhile, Castle settled himself into the seat and made himself comfortable and fitted his headset so they can talk during the flight.

"Victor, Hotel, Mike, Alpha, X-ray to Sydney tower." Mike spoke into the microphone of the radio to the air traffic controller at Sydney's Mascot airport.
"Requesting clearance for help take off from Macrodelphus Tower, over."
"Sydney tower to Mike, Alpha, X-ray, you are cleared for take-off. Ascend to and maintain a height of one thousand feet at three-three-five degrees for twenty miles to clear the control area. Then, maintaining this bearing, you will climb to two thousand six hundred feet and maintain this height till you've cleared the Richmond RAAF defence area airspace at thirty miles. As you approach Mudgee, you will change to a heading of two eight zero degrees. For the next leg of the flight, contact air traffic control at Orange, over," came the exacting reply from the tower.
"Mike, Alpha, X-ray to Sydney tower, thank you, over."
"Sydney tower to Mike, Alpha, X-ray, enjoy your trip, Mick. Sydney tower standing by."

After checking the weather this morning he had lodged his flight plan with the Air Traffic Controllers. They are aware of his course for the first legs of the trip but not of his final destination. He was determined to keep that to himself.

Castle was quiet during take-off as he could see that Mick was busy concentrating on his flying and he wasn't about to upset that. He watched the ground start to move under the machine as it lifted off from the roof of the tall building. There was a sudden movement as they flew over the edge of the building and Castle knew this was because of the updraught due to the turbulence around these tall buildings. He remembers that New York was much worse. As the helicopter traversed over the city, they could see the traffic backed up in two, three and sometimes four lanes. There was the police car in attendance at an accident that was slowing traffic.

"You have a fine city here, Mr. Jones". Castle said as the craft settled down to level flight.

"Thank you, Castle. Yes we love our city with its Harbour, Harbour Bridge, Opera House and waterways." Mick replied. "Traffic can be a bit of a handful at times but we get through the day without too great a difficulty." He had spotted the police car at the accident also and could see that Castle had noted this too. It was good to have someone around who keeps his eyes open and can see what's in front of him. Mick finds many people who don't have those qualities.

"Castle, I was reading in your report of this equipment of yours that you have done some work in the hospitals with it too."

"Yes, Mr. Jones. I find it very satisfying to know that the technology that is used to find infinite traces of

precious metals can also have such a place in the prevention of human suffering. Some of the injuries that I have seen those people suffering from would turn many stomachs. But I was able to assist in the recovery of many of them."
They were talking of the Mio-particle Accelerating and Magnetic Resonance Imaging Device or MAMRID that was developed by Dr. Goldcastle. This device, which is the size of two suitcases, can be used to find the most minute particles of shrapnel in the wounds of the Israeli soldiers and civilians who have been in the thick of things at home. Not only can this device locate the minute fragments it can gently remove them without the need for surgery. This system has reduced the amount of trauma, as operations were not necessary in several hundred cases last year. There is also the reduced risk of infection, which in poorly equipped hospitals can always be a problem. Recovery from this type of injury had also been slow but not when using MAMRID. During his research for the initial device, Castle was using many different metals as a medium for testing. He noticed some very peculiar activity when it was around even infinite amounts of gold. He needed to make some alterations in some areas of the prototype for it to be used in the hospital as even with someone walking past six metres away wearing a gold wedding band the device would sense the metal and malfunction.

He went to great pains to keep this information secret.

He had been reading some press information that detailed some of the work that Mick Jones and Macrodelphus were doing, not only in business but

also for the community and decided that here was a man and an organisation that was worthy of the MAMRID. Although he had not met Mick personally till today, he has had many conversations with him over the phone and video link about the device.
Mick had seen some of the injured people who had operations prevented by using this device and he was duly impressed. He was yet to see the equipment showing its capabilities in the discovery of precious metals.
Mick needed to see it in operation and invited Castle to bring it to Australia with him and together they could test out its various activities. They were headed to a well renowned site of some dispute, to test the capabilities of the MAMRID.

For the first hour of the flight, Castle was totally captured by the vastness and beauty of the Australian bush that they were flying over after they had cleared the suburbs of Sydney. Although the flight path took them through the gap between the higher hills, there was plenty of hilly ground to see. The eucalypt forest was extensive and he was not surprised to see so many homes nestled amongst the trees.
"This is what we refer to as the Blue Mountains," Mick said to Castle over the intercom. "The blue colour is from the evaporated eucalyptus oil from the trees. There is evidence that this mist is part of the reason why our bushfires can be so drastic. One chap told me that in summer a match burned blue when he was lighting his cigarette."
He pointed out a large area of burnt forest.
"That area was burnt early last summer. They believe that lightning was the cause. Because the area is so

inaccessible, it was almost impossible to contain. With a change in weather and the use of back burning from the highway, they did gain control but at a cost. Several fire-fighters lost their lives in the battle."
"My heart bleeds for those lost in any battle. This is so different from Israel. We just don't have that area of forest." Castle was so enthralled in looking at what was below him, that he was surprised that the helicopter change direction to the left. Then he heard Mick talking on the radio.
"Mike, Alpha, X-ray to Orange control," Mike spoke into the microphone attached to his headset.
"Mike, Alpha, X-ray this is Orange Air Control, over," came the reply after several seconds' delay.
"Orange control? Mike, Alpha, X-ray, I am just changing course from three-three-five to two eight zero at twenty six hundred feet and maintaining air speed of one zero five knots, over."
"Orange Control! Roger. Mike, Alpha, X-ray. Please notify us again at your next variation, over."
"Mike, Alpha, X-ray! Orange Control, rojor that, out."

"Castle, we are just to the south east of the town of Mudgee." He said pointing to a large town in the distance on the right. "We'll change course now and head towards Peak Hill. You'll notice a total change to the country soon. We should be over Peak Hill in about forty five minutes."

Shortly the forests of the Great Divide gave way to gentle rolling farmland. Dairy cattle, beef cattle, sheep and cropping could be seen from this height and yes, Castle agreed this is a total change from the heavily timbered forests. Because of the abundance of stored water, many of the paddocks below were under irrigation. The whole area looked like a patchwork quilt as the textures and colours varied, according to the stage of crop maturity.

The roads were easier to see and shortly there is a large river ahead of them.

“That’s the Murrumbidgee River down there, Castle, it flows from its headwaters in the Great Divide, just to the west of Sydney and will join with the Darling River about one hundred and fifty kilometres north of Peak Hill”.
Mick could see that Castle was interested in what lay before him and was pleased to help him with a commentary for what they could see.
Just as they crossed over the Murrumbidgee River, Mick called on the radio again.
“Orange control, this is Mike, Alpha, X-ray, over.”
“Mike, Alpha, X-ray! Orange air control, over.”
“Orange control, Mike, Alpha, X-ray, I am just changing direction from two eight zero to two-two-zero degrees, maintaining twenty six hundred feet at one zero five knots. I request landing at Lake Cargelligo to refuel, over.”
“Mike, Alpha, X-ray! Orange air control, affirmative. You can reduce your height to fifteen hundred feet. As you take off from Lake Cargelligo, change to Broken Hill Air Control on frequency two six five four, decimal three, over.”
“Orange control! Mike, Alpha, X-ray. Two six five four, decimal three, rojor that Orange, thanks for your help, over.”

Chapter 5

Sydney, New South Wales 5th April

Mick had arranged to pick up fuel at Stamford Plains, a farm close to Lake Cargelligo. He was involved in a project for the Australian Museum there several years previous and visits from time to time. Gordon Pearce whose company owns the property is in Melbourne at a conference, so Mick will miss meeting him this trip but plans to spend the night there on his return trip. Gordon's company owns several large farms in the area and has his own helicopter to travel between them. He muses that when his grand-father took up the land in the late eighteen hundreds they had horses for transport. Where it took a day to travel then, he can do that same distance now in fifteen minutes.

The flight so far had a tail wind but now this has become a side wind and the helicopter is buffeted but Mick has no trouble keeping on his course and the flight continues uninterrupted.

As they approach Stamford Plains there is increased activity as early shearing is about to start and many sheep are being moved closer to the wool shed, just five kilometres from the homestead and sheds where Mick's fuel will be waiting. He carefully skirts around the moving stock so as not to scare them and approaches the homestead from the south. He is able to use Gordon's helipad as the other helicopter is in Melbourne. Mick touches down with the gentle perfection of an experienced pilot and shortly shuts down the engine.
Before he could alight from the helicopter, he sees the fuel truck coming out to meet him. Castle jumps down too and they have a stretch to relieve some slightly cramped muscles.

Chapter 5

Sydney, New South Wales 5th April

The fuel truck pulls alongside the helicopter and the driver jumps out and introduces himself to Mick and Castle.
"G'day Mr. Jones, me name is Percy. Mr Pearce told me to have this fuel ready for ya."
Taking his hand to shake, Mick said, "Hello Percy, I'm Mick Jones and this is my associate Ravin Goldcastle. Thanks for your help! Do you have about three hundred and fifty litres of jet A-1 fuel for me?"
"Pleased to meet you blokes. Yep! I sure do. I've got more if ya need it too!" he replied in his typical outback slang.
"Thanks Percy, fill it for me please but I think three hundred and fifty litres should do the trick."
"Okay," he replied. He took hold of the static cable and clamped it to the terminal, and then taking the nozzle in his hand unrolled the fuel hose and coupled the nozzle to the helicopter's tank filling port. When he had released the air valve to let the tank breath, he began pumping the fuel into the helicopter. The electric pump on the tanker began to whine as the fuel began to flow. Having set the metre to shut off the pump at three hundred and fifty litres, Percy stepped back from the helicopter.

"How many sheep are to go through the shearing shed, Percy?" asked Mick.
"Well, we got all eighteen stands working this year so that should take us around three and a half weeks to shear the seventy five thousand head." Percy replied after doing some mental calculation.
Castle was stunned. "You mean all those sheep belong to one farm?"

"Well, that's off three hundred thousand acres," Percy replied.
"My God, you do things on a big scale out here," Castle commented.
"Yeah, and that's just with only ten percent irrigation this year due to the low rainfall," answered Percy.
As they were talking, they heard the pump change note, then stop as the meter reached its pre-set amount. Percy disconnected the nozzle and then the static line, rolling them both up and storing back onto the tanker.
"I must say Percy, you've got that refuelling down to a fine art," Mick said, complimenting Percy on his obvious skill.
"Thanks Mr Jones, I spent eleven years as ground staff with Ansett in Broken Hill. So, yeah, I've refuelled a few before. Some big jets too!" he mentioned.
"How's the condensate in your tanker?" Mick asked out of curiosity.
"Well, I checked it about an hour before you arrived and it was fine, but you should check yours before you start up again though."
As Percy was talking, Mick was on his way to check the condensate bleed valve at the base of the helicopter. The glass showed that all was clear. He thought that it would be okay but being one to never take risks was relieved now.
Mick shook Percy's hand thanking him for his help said goodbye and that they would see each other in a week on the return trip. Percy took the tanker and parked it in the shed, while Mick was doing his pre-flight checks.

"Mike, Alpha, X-ray calling Broken Hill Air Control, over"

Mike had changed frequency on the main radio and needed to inform Broken Hill control of his impending take off.
After several minutes there was no answer, so Mick called again.

Still no answer.

He put his head out of the window and asked Percy if they had problems with Broken Hill control? He replied that you'd need to get to five hundred feet first. Something to do with feldspar or ironstone or something in the ground. It interferes with the radio's signal.

Mick fired up the Rolls Royce turbine and in a few minutes was airborne. They both waved to Percy as he stood near the shed where the fuel tanker was parked. Mick turned to the south again to avoid the sheep and slowly climbed to five hundred feet above the terrain.
"Mike, Alpha, X-ray to Broken Hill air traffic control, over."
The response this time was immediate.
"Broken Hill to Mike, Alpha, X-ray, over"
"Mike, Alpha, X-ray! Broken Hill, requesting take off from Lake Cargelligo enroute to Menindee Lakes on a heading of two nine zero at fourteen hundred feet maintaining one zero five knots, over."
"Broken Hill! Mike, Alpha, X-ray, confirmed. Gloria's on UHF channel 38 these days. Call her when you're close then confirm with us, over," came the reply. Obviously Gloria had told the tower that she was expecting Mick and his colleague for the night.

"Mike, Alpha, X-ray! Broken Hill, thanks for that, news travels fast now. Out."

Mick had arranged with Gloria Matson at Menindee Lakes homestead that he was doing this trip and she insisted that they stay at their place for the night. Mick logged the time of departure as three thirty p.m. at Lake Cargelligo so that should get them to Menindee by five fifteen, just four hours and fifteen minutes since leaving the helipad at Macrodelphus Tower.
Castle noted that the farming areas are now behind them and the ground appears to be covered in a low scrub on the flats. He could see some watercourses that had some trees and larger scrub and some low hills where there was the occasional mob of sheep.
"We're in station country now, Castle. The land is not so productive out here so they must run less stock to the acre and have more acres to grow their wool on. With the seasons being like they have been in the last few years, even the feed from the low scrub in scarce."
"How big are these properties here?" asked Castle as he watched a mob of emus running along a fence line.
"Some are up to a million acres but most are around the five hundred thousand. Some of these properties have been in the same family for a hundred years or more and some have changed hands in the last few months."
"Life must be interesting out here then?"
"Life is what you make it Castle, but yes interesting is a good word. Harsh is better and some would say very difficult, dependent upon the season."

Chapter 5

Sydney, New South Wales 5th April

Castle has his first look at the water supplies in the outback and is impressed by the size of some of the windmills. Mick went down lower on several occasions to have a closer look at these and several of the other unusual features of the area.

In the distance, Mick could see the green trees around the lakes at Menindee and called Gloria on the UHF radio.
"Mike, Alpha, X-ray to Menindee, do you copy Gloria?"
After several seconds his reply came.
"Mike, Alpha, X-ray can only be my old mate Mick. Is that you Mick? Over."
"Yes, Gloria, we are about ten minutes away, do you have the kettle on?"
"Sure do mate, we have a helipad now just north of the homestead, I'll see you there".
"Roger."
"What's the "kettle on" for?" asked Castle.
"That's one of our traditions. You always have a cup of tea upon arrival. That's the standard greeting out here, so when you ask "is the kettle on, then you intend to visit."
Mick calls Broken Hill control to advise them of his arrival.

He flies in low several kilometres to the east of the township, directly over the old woolshed and sheep yards. These are not in use, as shearing here will take place in several months' time. The creek has water in it and the trees along the banks of the creek look green and healthy. Cattle are grazing in the dry paddocks to the north of the homestead but are used to helicopters and are not disturbed by the noise. Just to the north of the homestead, Mick showed Castle the extensive vineyards and the large machinery and packing sheds. Table grapes are grown here and some are exported to overseas markets. The quality of the product is very high and because of the climate they can supply many markets in the off-season, so it's a good cash crop.

Mick can see the new helipad about five hundred metres to the north of the homestead and put the helicopter down onto it. The surface is compacted gravel so there is very little dust.
Gloria is waiting for them in the Landcruiser. She is dressed in a blue long sleeved cotton shirt and white moleskin jeans and tan riding boots. A wide brimmed brown Akubra hat keeps her eyes and face shaded from the bright sun.

Mick shuts down the engine and does his post flight checks before alighting from the machine. Gloria walks over to the left door and waits for Mick to complete the shutdown procedure. He gets a big hug from her when he steps down. They have been acquainted for many years, in fact since university days. They had both attended university in Sydney where they attended several lectures and student functions. Both had achieved honours and received their degrees in the same ceremony.
"Hello Gloria, it's great to see you again. What's it been, five years?"
"Mm, yeah about that," she replied after some thought. "You're looking great, obviously keeping fit."
"Thanks, Gloria; you still appear to be in great shape. Obviously this station life of yours certainly agrees

with you." He replied. Turning to Castle he continued, "Gloria, I'd like to introduce Dr. Ravin Goldcastle. He's with me doing some research on minerals and metals."
Castle shook the hand that was offered by Gloria and noticed that it wasn't soft as you might imagine the hand of a lady but tough like the hand of a worker.
"I'm very pleased to meet you, Gloria. You have a fine property here."
"Great to meet you too, Dr. Goldcastle. What's your speciality?"
"Call me Castle, please as my friends do. Electronics in a medical situation. I've helped to engineer many of the apparatus used by surgeons to conduct some intricate operations and procedures," he replied.
A look of confusion flashed across her face. "What does a medical electronics technical engineer have to do with minerals and metals? Gloria asked.
"You'd be very surprised at the connection there, as so many minerals and different metals react in different ways to electrical impulses to achieve excellent results in various circumstances in medicine." He replied, keeping his answer intelligent and close to the point without giving away too much as to the circumstance of their trip. "It is a very exciting field, manipulating metals, minerals and electrical impulses to help humanity." He continued.
This answer seemed to satisfy her curiosity and she asked, "I notice you have a Middle-eastern accent, where do you come from?"
"That's a long story but I attended Eaton, where I earned my degree and live with my parents in Israel, where I was born."

Gloria accepted the explanation. "Well if you blokes have some bags, get them now and I'll drive you to the homestead and have that cuppa, Mick".

Mick and Castle collected their bags from the helicopter and Mick spent a few minutes to tie the end of the rotors to the tail spar to prevent any wind from doing damage to the gearbox.
They put their bags into the rear of the Landcruiser as Gloria held the door open and climbed in. Castle sat in the rear and Mick in the front seat next to Gloria.
She drove around by the packing shed and then on the track to the homestead.
"I see the grape vines are nearly ready for pruning. Gloria how was your season and when do you start that job?" Mick asked as he saw the vines that were closest to the packing shed.
"Well, we had an excellent season and were able to get the top price in both the Sydney and Melbourne fruit markets. The export market was a bit flat but still worthwhile. The pruners are due to start in three weeks' time. It'll take a team of seven to do the job in five weeks. That's a hundred and twenty acres of vines there, Mick, or if you like about eleven thousand vines. And I planted many of them by hand too." She replied, obviously very happy with the result from so much hard work.

She pulled up under a large peppercorn tree at the back of the homestead and they collected their bags from the back of the vehicle and walked along the crazy paving pathway to the back veranda. Mick opened the door and held it for Gloria and Castle to enter and he followed. Gloria led them to the dining room where the kitchen staff had a pot of tea, scones and cream waiting for them.

"Take a seat and I'll play mother," Gloria said as they stood waiting for her to sit first.

While she was pouring the tea, Castle was looking around the room taking in all its features. Several large landscape paintings adorned the walls. One had an old shearing shed and yards where men with dogs were moving sheep. Another was of an old house made of corrugated iron walls and roof, with rainwater tanks at the side. A horse and cart was near the front the building.

"I'm impressed by these paintings, Gloria," Castle asked as he took in the sights. "Are they of this property?"

"Yes the old house is the original homestead built by my great grandfather back in eighteen seventy five. Bush timber for the framework and corrugated iron walls and roof. The floor was dirt for the first ten years then it was concreted. I believe that it was not lined but that's like so many station homesteads of that period. My grandfather was born there. By the way," she continued, "It still stands out by the creek not far from the old woolshed that's in the other painting."

She had poured the tea and handed a cup to each of them. "Help yourself to the scones, jam and cream if you wish. The cook was just making these as you radioed in, Mick."

"By gee, they taste as good as ever. Is it Molly who is the cook? Is she still here?" Mick asked.

"Yes she's been here since I came home from graduating at uni. So that's nearly twenty years.

Arthur, her husband still prefers to ride a horse for the stock work. Better than those noisy bikes, he reckons."
Castle was busy with the tea and scones and was impressed with the relaxed atmosphere and the good fare. He mind wandered to those who he attended university with and how he was not able to make lasting friendships from those days. He envied Mick and Gloria for that.
Mick and Gloria continued with the chatter and reminiscing while Castle was occupied with his thoughts and observations of the room.
When they had finished, Gloria showed the men to their rooms and the bathroom and suggested that they could shower and be ready for drinks, which would be served on the front veranda in thirty minutes.

Apart from managing this station by herself, she still enjoys the pleasure of brewing her own beer. She finds it relaxing to make the brews and do the bottling, usually after a day of work. Sometimes it may stay a little too long in the brewing vat, but to date she hasn't had a disaster.
Gloria's husband, Tom, had died in an accident some ten years ago and their two children were attending university. She runs the station with the help of six men and three women. Contractors were used for most of the work with the grapes and the sheep. She found that it was the best way because the work was so diversified. Grapes, cattle, sheep.
Different skills were needed and most people could not be proficient at all of the disciplines.

Both men had completed their showers and dressed in clean clothes, repaired to the front veranda where

Chapter 5

Sydney, New South Wales 5th April

Gloria was sitting in a comfortable chair with two others drawn up close by. A small table held several big brown bottles of home brew on ice and glasses were chilled, ready for the men. A bowl of peanuts sat to one side

"By gee, that looks great Gloria. I think I could do with one of those." Mick had memories of one of his previous visits when Tom was still alive. They may have drunk a little too much, but, by golly, it was good.

"Castle, you attended Eaton so you'll drink beer don't you! This is one I bottled about eight weeks ago and it's a lager." She poured the bottle into three of the cold glasses.

"Good colour, good head, good effervescence." Then Mick tasted the beer, "a good taste and cold too. Well done Gloria, that's a top drop!" Mick took a few peanuts and sat back to enjoy.

"I agree," said Castle. "Better than those English beers we had at Eaton. They were mostly warm and very thick to the taste. This is a very pleasant beer. Thank you."

They sat back in their comfortable chairs and relaxed. The day was not all that hot but was now cooling. The sun was soon to set and this was visible from the front veranda. There was a light, high cloud and it looked like it was going to be a spectacular sun set.

The white clouds began turning pink as the sun went below them and touched the horizon just behind a small rise. "I've not seen a sunset like that for many years." Said Castle as he watched, totally enthralled in what lay before his eyes.

Chapter 5

Sydney, New South Wales 5th April

The sun dips below the horizon and the colour of the cloud deepened to blood red, then darker, even into indigo and purple. As they sipped their beers and chewed on a few peanuts they watched the sunset. It seemed to set in a very relaxed mood. The veranda light came on as Molly came out and announced that dinner would be served in the dining room in five minutes.

They finished their drinks and taking the tray that they were on with them, strolled into the dining room. Gloria took the tray and put it in the kitchen for Molly and helped by carrying out the carving tray of roast beef. Molly already had the hot vegetables on the table over the candles of the warmer.

"You two sit down please, I'll be with you in a minute." Said Gloria

They sat at the sides of the dinner table allowing Gloria to sit at the head of the table. Castle continued to scrutinise the two paintings that had taken his eye previously. He was totally absorbed by the amount of detail, which they depicted.

Presently, Gloria entered the room with a bottle of wine and took her place at the head of the table. She carved the roast beef and laid the slices onto the plates.

"Help yourselves to the vegetables, chaps. Everything that's on the table is grown here on the station. This soil will grow almost anything. Just add water and just a little of the right fertiliser."

What Gloria didn't mention was all of the time and hard work that goes with growing and tending vegetables, or anything else for that matter. Castle notices that she is a very self-sufficient woman, capable of achieving anything that she might set her

mind to. He felt that he was in good company. The three of them are very similar in so many ways but each to their own field of expertise.
Mick added a roast potato, some beans, pumpkin and onion to his plate. Then added a little of the rich gravy that was in the gravy boat. After adding a dash of pepper and a little salt, began eating. His first mouthful produced an excellent sensation of taste and texture.
"My word, Gloria, this would have to be one of the best roast meals that I have ever eaten."
"Oh, come now Mick, you've eaten meals from the top chefs from around the world, this can't compare with them surely?"
"Oh but it does," added Castle. "I totally agree with Mick. The meat is tender and cooked to perfection. Many chefs undercook their roasts but this is excellent."
"I hope you don't mind but I've done a little experimenting and I'd like your opinion on this wine. We pressed about ten tonnes of grapes from last year's harvest and had a wine maker come up from the Barossa Valley to make some wine. I've not opened a bottle yet and thought that this might be the special occasion that I was saving it for."
Mick replied, "Gloria, if it's quality anything like what we are eating, I think it will be superb. Yes please."
"Yes, please," agreed Castle.
Gloria uncorked the wine {proper corks too!} and poured a little into three glasses.
It was a light honey colour with the appearance of a fine sherry.
The three of them sampled the wine at the same time. It was a sweet cream sherry that was of excellent body, solid nose, and rich creamy taste.

"Gloria. That would also be THE best cream sherry that I have tasted. Those vines of yours have done you proud. If that is what you can expect from them in wine production, then you have just created another enterprise for this property." Mick exclaimed.

"I too agree with that. From this sample, I feel that you would be able to blend together some early picked fruits to create several vastly different wines to please so many palettes." Castle agreed. "Plenty of sunshine and picked at the correct stage of maturity you can achieve anything."

"Castle, it sounds as though you know something of winemaking too?" Gloria asked as she poured their glasses full.

"My parents spent many years on a Kibbutz in Israel. One of my father's jobs was as winemaker, where he would select grapes from their own vineyards for a variety of wines. If my memory serves me correctly he produced ten different wines from just one variety of grapes. Selective harvest time was his secret, then careful blending and maturing. I helped a few times by spending some of my holiday time with him and, yes probably picked up a little of his knowledge."

"I understand things have been a bit unsettled in Israel recently? Gloria asked

"Yes", replied Castle. "Having been away from there for a number of years, it breaks my heart to see the conflicts still raging. Sometimes when they seem to be coming close to a resolution, trouble flairs up and away it goes again. So many people have been hurt. So many people have been killed. So many people have been displaced. I hope it will end soon". He replied in a very sombre voice, as it was apparent that he was very upset by what was happening back home.

Mick took the opportunity to change the subject. “Do you remember Gordon Pearce from Stamford Plains down at Lake Cargelligo?” Gloria replied with a nod of her head. “Well he seems to be doing well also. We refuelled there earlier today. He was in Melbourne at a conference but I will meet up with him on our return trip. His team is getting ready for shearing. One of his men, Percy, told us of his flock size. It’s enormous.”

“Seventy five thousand head, I believe,” replied Gloria. “One of the largest flocks of sheep in Australia going through a single shed. Takes good management to achieve that. We’ve only forty thousand here but with four thousand head of cattle and the grapes, we are kept pretty busy.”

“How many on your workforce then Gloria?” asked Castle.

“We have six full time experienced men, three jackaroos, two jillaroos, two cooks, a gardener and just me,” replied Gloria.

“In other words,” smiled Mick, “a small township all by itself.”

“When the contract workers come for pruning and harvesting and so on, where do they stay?” Castle was intrigued by the size of the operation.

“We have quarters for a further twenty and powered bays for twenty caravans as many of the contract workers prefer them. We use a contractor from Mildura who supplies most of our seasonal workers but some also travel around in their caravans following the seasonal work. We always enjoy having them here.”

Chapter 5

Sydney, New South Wales 5th April

By this time Mick was getting tired and he knows that his next day of flying will be tiring also, so he suggests that they should get some sleep.
Castle and Gloria concurred with this. Gloria was also an early riser, usually rising before the sun. Castle generally works on into the night but knows that he will have a change of work hours on this trip with Mick.
"I'll give you blokes a call as I get up if you like, that way we can breakfast together before you go," suggested Gloria.
"Sounds fine to me Gloria. Thanks for an excellent meal and great company," said Mick as he gave her a hug.
"Yes, thankyou Gloria, I did so enjoy the meal and listening about you and your property," agreed Castle.

They all headed in their separate directions. The beds were not too soft but very comfortable and Castle was asleep about fifteen seconds after Mick.

Great Northern Highway, Western Australia, 3rd & 4th of April

The sun broke over the hill.

Gordon knew this, because it peeped through the chink in the curtain and hit him square in the eye. It took him a few moments to recognise his surroundings. It slowly came back to him as his mind set itself into action for the day. He recalled the incident where Betty injured herself and wondered how she was feeling this morning. He sat up in bed and viewed a magnificent sunrise. There were clouds in the sky to the east and the sun was reflecting off the bottom of these to produce a splendid colour show. He immediately woke Betty and she was appreciative of him, as she would not have been happy to miss that sight. They watched for several minutes as the sun disappeared behind the cloud to show an overcast day.

"How are you feeling, this morning, dear?" asked Gordon, "after your escapades of yesterday."
"Fine thanks dear, just a little stiffness but I think I may even survive," she replied with a smile.
Betty got dressed and began arranging breakfast while Gordon dressed.
"Just a cuppa and cereal, okay for you Gordon?"
"Yes thanks dear, that will be fine."
They sat down at the table as the kettle began whistling on the gas stove. Betty made the tea and then they both enjoyed their first breakfast "on the road".

“Well, dear let’s make a toast to many more of these peaceful and glorious mornings!” Gordon said as he raised his cup in a toast.
“Hear, Hear. Many many, more.”

Betty cleaned up the dishes when they had finished breakfast while Gordon checked under the bonnet. He knew that if he kept on top of the maintenance of the motorhome, it would last the distance for them.
The other couple were ready for the road at this time and the good byes were said after the exchange of addresses. Gordon and Betty intend to visit Wally and Sam when they are in Tamworth.
Both vehicles started within minutes of each other and were left idling for several minutes to warm up. Wally and Sam left the campsite first and Gordon & Betty were on the road several minutes later and heading north again.

After a few minutes of driving they see the sign “Sandstone 130 km” on the right. Betty knew they were going through Sandstone, a small mining town, and asked if they were using that road.
“No dear, I heard that road is rough, so we’ll go up to Mount Magnet and head east from there. It will add twenty or so kilometres to the trip, but we’ll save in the long run because of the better road.”

The road they are travelling on is The Northern Highway, the traffic is quiet but there are a few road trains travelling south. With the light breeze coming from the northeast, it not only causes a head wind but also increases the draft from these trucks and Gordon does have to be careful as they go past. The vehicle does sway little as these large trucks drive past them in the opposite direction.

After about an hour of travelling through the scrubby pastoral country, they come across a well formed road from the left. The sign indicates to Yalgoo and Geraldton. Just then they can see the town of Mount Magnet up ahead. The cloud of dust that was visible for several kilometres is now very close as it is caused by the large trucks, which are carting the gold bearing ore from the mines to the treatment plant closer to town. There is a hive of activity here with vehicles running all over the place. Mining vehicles of all sizes are driving around town. Some of them are a little disrespectful of the traffic laws and Gordon slows down to avoid a collision with a Landcruiser that came at them from the left. It got into the same lane with just metres to spare.
"Boy! You need to keep your eyes open here, dear."
"Yeah, they seem a little haphazard in their driving techniques. They would need to sharpen their ideas when they drive in the larger towns or the city." She replied.

Near the centre of town, Gordon pulls over to the opposite side of the road and enters the service station. He parks at the bowser to fill with fuel. While he pumps the diesel into the tanks, Betty goes inside to buy an ice-cream and drinks and pay for the fuel. When Gordon has filled the tank, he walked in behind Betty and gave her a little dig in the ribs. She let out a soft scream. The person who was serving her never even batted an eye.

Gordon asked, "I see things are pretty busy in town. How's business?"
The counter person just shrugged his shoulders and muttered "Not bad". As he didn't have anything else to say, Gordon and Betty left the shop after paying for their purchases.
"Bit of a surly sod, isn't he dear?" said Betty.
"Yes," replied Gordon. "You'd think his manner would be much more pleasant when dealing with the public. Perhaps, he hasn't been here long and is still learning the ropes."
They get back into their motorhome again and headed north for a short distance when they turned right and headed east on the road that was sign-posted "Sandstone 157 km".

This was another well-maintained bitumen road, wide enough for three vehicles. Gordon assumed it was well used by the mining industry.
After several minutes of travelling, Gordon pulled off to the left onto a flat area where they stopped and had their ice-cream and cool-drink.
"This will be smoko today!" Betty said. "We can splash out now and again as we won't be in towns much."
"Too right, dear," Gordon replied. They walked into the bush for a little way and got a closer look at the scrub, which was woody with spiny narrow leaves and spines on the stems. The leaves were a grey-green colour and quite hard to the touch.
"Looks very uninviting," thought Gordon. "Must be tough on the sheep if this is what they have to feed on."

There were signs of sheep and also kangaroos on the ground. They had narrow paths through the thickets of scrub. Gordon showed Betty where the leaves had been eaten and new shoots sprouted for a more succulent meal for the stock.
After a short time looking around, Betty suggested that they should move on so they could have lunch in Sandstone and visit the mining museum, which was located right in the centre of town.

Back on the road again and they have a short hold up as they approached and area where the local contractors are carrying out some road repairs. A section of the road has subsided and more foundation and seal was being applied. They were faced with a person holding the “STOP” sign. He was part Aboriginal with a great head of fuzzy hair. Gordon had his CB radio on scan and at channel 22 he could hear the chatter of the vehicle drivers and foreman as they carried out the work.
“Okay, send them down after the caravan, Joe”. Gordon could hear on the radio. Then he sees that there is a caravan approaching from the opposite direction. As it goes past his position, the chap holding the “Stop” sign rotated it to show “SLOW”. Gordon was able to move forward again, as did the several vehicles behind him. As they drove through the repair section they were on the right hand side of the road and could see the new work on the left.
Nearly finished now, Gordon thinks to himself as he sees the rollers driving over the new aggregate on the fresh tar.
When they had driven past the sign at the far end of the road-works, they were able to speed up again.

Chapter 6

Great Northern Highway, Western Australia, 3rd & 4th of April

Gordon drove at a steady 80 kilometres per hour and was able to take in the sights as well as Betty.

After about 50 kilometres from Mount Magnet, they could see a building of to the right where a gold mine was in operation. There was no dust coming from around the area of the buildings.
After they past the turn off to "Windsor Station" the road became almost dead straight. The land was almost flat here and several of the claypans had puddles of water visible. The roadside showed the odd puddle too, so Gordon thought that there might have been some rain during the night. In some places beside the road there are damp patches and just a hint of fresh green grass in its early stages of growth.

Just after midday the pulled into the town of Sandstone. The old stamp mill was visible near the centre of town and they made their way towards this. As they approached, they could see the buildings of the museum. They stopped in the parking area and entered the building and got talking to the local who was in attendance for the day.
He turned out be a real "Character".

Dick, who said he had been in the area since he was a teenager, had worked on many different mines and some of his own workings as well, from time to time. He told them of the days when bullocks and horses were used to pull the wagons of ore to the stamp mill. Many of the smaller miners would dig the ore from their lease and deliver this ore to the stamp mill where it's crushed and the gold separated from the ore by the amalgam process. The company who ran the stamp mill would pay the miners on the quality of the ore after it was assayed. Usually there was a difference between the company-assayed value and the government-assayed value and this caused many arguments between the private miners and the company. In later years, the government, to protect the interests of all parties, particularly the small miners assayed all of the ore.

Dick told them of several large finds in the area but usually most miners would pack up and leave after about six months. The work was very hard as the digging was in the white quartz and ironstone country. "Real shin cracker stuff," he said.

In the early 1920's some of the more affluent miners and merchants began using motorised vehicles. This was the start of another era.
Since the 1950's, the town has been very quiet. Now most of the mines fly in their workers for three weeks and fly them out again for a week off. This seems to be the standard practice for the mining industry.
"Sure kills the smaller towns and I hear some of the larger towns are suffering too!" Dick told them.
After paying the entrance fee, they took a self-guided walk through the museum and saw many of the aspects that the attendant had told them.

They had seen all they wanted to see and by one thirty, left the museum and Betty made lunch for them in the motorhome.
Just after two o'clock, they headed out of town to the east. The road is now gravelled, but not very dusty.

Great Northern Highway, Western Australia, 3rd & 4th of April

As they drive along they could see many of the older workings that they had learned about in the museum. The information they had got from there has given them a new understanding of the history and the hardships of those who participated.
Occasionally they could see a well-used track off to the side which led to a working mine. Most of these were small shows, judging by the size of the buildings.

They approached the intersection with the Goldfields Highway just south of Leinster and headed south. Gordon didn't go into Leinster as this was a mining company town and didn't hold much interest for them.

Back on the bitumen road again and the driving is easier for Gordon.

After about one hundred kilometres on the black top road, Gordon finds a cleared area just off the road on the top of one of the low hills and pulls in here. It was just after four o'clock and he was ready for a cuppa. He parked on a good level site and switched off the engine. Betty made herself busy preparing the cuppa. Gordon set up the table and chairs beside the motorhome and Betty bought out the cuppa and scones.
"By gee, love. I didn't think you'd have time to make these!" exclaimed Gordon.
"Well, I actually didn't just make them, they have been defrosting on the bench since smoko this morning, dear," she replied.
"Well, they taste just as good as ever, dear."
While they were enjoying their cuppa, a caravan pulled into the same area and set up some distance

away. Gordon and Betty waved to the couple as they walked around their vehicle. They were greeted with a friendly smile and wave.
While the other couple was setting up their camp it started to rain. Not very heavy but just enough to send everyone running for shelter. The light rain lasted for about an hour and made the ground around the vehicles muddy.

Gordon and Betty spent the rest of the afternoon in their motorhome catching up on the diary and Betty wrote a letter to their daughter telling of their travels to date.
Just on dark, Betty prepared their evening meal and they had this while they listened to the radio. There was a weather report, which told them that because of the ex-cyclone, there was some rain in the area into which they are heading. Provided there isn't much more rain, there won't be any problems with road closures.

Gordon and Betty headed off to bed as they talked about their experiences of the day. She was obviously still a little stiff as her movements caught Gordon's eye as she dressed herself for bed. They lay down together and for a few minutes talked about the museum but eventually tiredness overtook them and they slept soundly.

Sunrise the next morning saw them both awake and taking in the colourful sight. Most of the clouds had cleared and those remaining gave the sun a brilliant welcome to the day. The clouds were bathed in shades

of purple, which turned red, to orange, to gold and then to yellow.
It was another brilliant day in paradise.

The birds are flitting around amongst the bushes darting in and out as they search for their food for the day.
The ground had dried out overnight due to the southerly breeze and the dirt area that they had parked on would be safe enough for them to drive on. The last thing Gordon wanted was for the soft ground to bog the motorhome as getting it un-bogged again would be a big job for them by themselves.

After breakfast they got going on the road again, heading south. The headwind was light but the crosswind from the large trucks was buffeting the motorhome and Gordon needed to take extra care when these passed them.
After half an hour's driving they came to the town of Leonora. Gordon pulled into the roadhouse and filled the tank with fuel again. Betty was inside and she paid the fuel bill while Gordon worked out the fuel economy. He was pleased with the seven point five kilometres per litre. It was equal to what others had told him, they were getting.

They spent a short time looking around the town, found a letterbox and posted the letter that Betty had written to their daughter. Gordon was convinced that if it weren't for the pastoral area, the town would become a ghost town. Many of the accommodation units were empty and he thinks this is because of the fly-in-fly-out system.

They have a cuppa in the motorhome before they head east on the road towards Laverton, another mining town.

The ground here is relatively flat and to the south they can see a low flat area, which would become a lake if there were sufficient rainfall.
About ten kilometres before the town, they turn off to the left and onto what is the beginning of the “Great Central Road”. They didn’t need to drive into the town so kept on travelling. After a few kilometres, this becomes unsealed but still a very good road. It appears that a grader has been here a short time ago. There are a few puddles in the table drain and there is evidence of water run-off from the road. This would have been due to the rainfall in the last few days.
The weather is still fine and the remaining puddles will evaporate in a day or so. There are some short grasses growing here as well. They will provide feed for the kangaroos, sheep and camels, Gordon thought.

The sign up ahead said that they were entering the Cosmo Newbery Aboriginal Reserve. Gordon had taken great pains to make sure he complied with his permits to travel through Aboriginal lands. He has the permits in the glove box for the land councils for here and also the Northern Territory, where they are necessary. They can traverse through and camp beside the road but cannot visit any of the settlements or landmarks. He’d like to talk to someone about that a bit later on and find out some more detail.

The ground here is undulating and shows signs of heavier rainfall in places. Obviously they had patchy rain out here from that cyclone which degenerated to become the rain-bearing depression. He hoped it wouldn't interfere with their trip.
There were several freshly killed kangaroos beside the road. They are obviously last night's roadkill.

He saw a rise that had a patch of heavy scrub behind it. There was a track leading off to this. Gordon turned off and after several hundred metres; they came to a good campsite. It has been used by travellers frequently but was fairly clean. There were only two old car bodies here. Crashed or broken down then abandoned by their drivers.
They stopped here for lunch. While Betty was preparing the meal, Gordon was out looking around to see what he could find. Always little bits of useful stuff can be found in these places. Nothing of note could he find. Even the old relics of cars had been stripped of anything that could have been useful. He set up their table and chairs in the open again and they enjoyed the peace and quiet in the open whilst having their lunch.

Several birds came close to them while they were eating and this had them engrossed for an hour or so. They watched the birds flitting around the scrub, taking insects from the branches and leaves. There was a nest that the birds were flying to and from. With their powerful binoculars they could see in details what was happening. There were several chicks in the nest and they were keeping the parents busy with their constant requests for more food.

Chapter 6

Great Northern Highway, Western Australia, 3rd & 4th of April

The sun was on its way to the horizon when Gordon suggested they should move from here because of the conditions of the permit. They began driving again and in about ten kilometres they came to a turn-off with a sign that pointed to Yamana.

Betty was able to pinpoint their position on the map with this road and worked out that they have sixty kilometres to travel before they would be clear of the reserve and could stop for the night.

"Keep an eye on the right hand side, dear, there should be a turn-off soon to Peegull Waterhole and Caves. That could be a good place to camp for the night."

"Okay, dear, I'll do that," replied Gordon.

He had forgotten that there were caves out here in the Great Victoria Desert.

After several kilometres, near a ridge in the road, they came across the turn-off and after a short drive down a bush track came to an area at the edge of the breakaway.

It was getting late, so they set up the motorhome for the night. Betty prepared the evening meal of lamb chops, mashed potato, green peas, broccoli and kumara.

Gordon had a quick look around the area and was satisfied that they were alone and it was safe to stay.

After the meal was completed, they turned on the radio and were able to tune into the ABC just several minutes into the news bulletin there were details of a robbery

Great Northern Highway, Western Australia, 3rd & 4th of April

"Early this morning two men robbed the bank in Kalgoorlie of over twelve point seven million dollars' worth of gold. The police have several strong leads and are asking for community effort in assisting them with their enquiries with some details. A suspicious white Ford Transit van was seen in the area. If anyone has seen a van of this description with company markings on the side, please contact the Kalgoorlie Police. Detective Sergeant Alec Webster, of the Kalgoorlie Police, is leading the investigation. Our sources at Kalgoorlie Police station have told us that there were several roadblocks in the area today and one suspect is in custody. Detective Sergeant Alec Webster thanks the public for their support in the apprehension of a stolen vehicle at the roadblock. Kalgoorlie Police can be contacted on ………

"That sounds serious, Gordon. I wonder about these things. Is it a tax dodge, insurance fraud or is it a real robbery?"

"Well, perhaps we'll never know. They don't seem to report on those details if it's only a small amount but that was a large haul of gold."

"If it is a real robbery, I wonder if it's related to the mobs that you hear about," said Betty

"It is intriguing though, after our talk with Dick at the museum at Sandstone, yesterday," said Gordon after thinking on the matter for a few seconds.

At the completion of the news was a brief weather report and it seems that the rain has departed for the time being so they shouldn't have any hold-ups with the weather after all. Just plain sailing to the border and we'll see what happens from there.

After several games of cards, they retired to their comfortable bed for the night.

After Betty had nodded off to sleep Gordon began to wonder what lies ahead of them. He began to fantasize about the gold robbery that they had heard about in the news bulletin and could only imagine how it may have happened.

But then, he thought, tomorrow is another day and I look forward to it. Presently he was asleep too.

Mount Magnet, Western Australia, 3rd & 4th April

Don woke to the smell of smoke from new wood on the fire and rain in the air.
As he gazed towards the fire, he was very surprised but not disappointed to see Ted was up and busy. There was extra wood beside the fire and the billy was sitting in the flame.

"Well, Ted, it sure is good to see you up before the sun. How often does this happen in the city?" chided Don.
"And good morning to you too! It has been known for me to rise before the sun. Anyway you're still in the sack, so what grounds do you have to chide me anyway, old chap," Ted retorted.
Don extracted himself from his swag and rolled it up and stowed next to Ted's on top of the Landcruiser. At the tucker box he took out bacon, eggs and bread. He began cooking while Ted was making the tea. They sat down to a hearty breakfast and watched the sunrise. There were clouds to the east but just enough breaks in them to show the sun. The undersides of the clouds were red, but this soon changed as the clouds blocked the sun.
"Well Ted, "red sky in the morning, shepherds warning", it seems like we may have some rain today. I hope it doesn't rain too much for our travels but the pastoralists do need the rain. It would make a good season for them."

While Ted was washing the dishes, Don dismantled the fire to let it go out. In summer he would have covered it with sand but with rain imminent, he considered it safe to leave.
When everything was packed away, Don warmed up the engine of the Landcruiser and in a few minutes, they broke camp and began the second day of travel.

"I just want to spend a few minutes in Sandstone and see who is on duty at the museum. If it's Dick, I have a few questions for him. He was prospecting around Docker River and the Petermann Ranges years ago and may know some details."
"Every little snippet of information will help us to build a picture of the events when Lasseter was in the area," Ted replied.

They could see some evidence of some of the mining operations from the road with dust coming from several of these.
"You can see how dry it is, Ted but with some luck we might see some rain later today."
After a few minutes Don continued.
"I did some prospecting out in this country, years ago but didn't get much colour, or any much of any other indication, yet the big companies can cover a lot more country and get better returns."

They stop at some older mine workings and Ted takes some digital photos to add to his collection. He didn't get the chance to download them into his laptop computer last night so the camera had only several shots left. Perhaps he'll be able to do it tonight when they stop.

Just after the Wondinong Station turn-off, Don sees the road-working signs beside the road. Obviously the road gang hasn't started work yet. He slows down and is wary of the road because there may be some damage. There is a patch of road that has subsided and is partly repaired. There is a group of road working machines parked nearby.
Ted takes another photo of the machines as they travel by.
Several kilometres after they had past the road-works site, Don reckons he sees the bus taking the gang to their worksite.
"There is the road gang heading out to the job now. They must be camped at Sandstone somewhere." Don suggested.
"I thought that they would camp near their job, old chap?" Ted said.
"That used to be the way it was, years ago but things have changed in the last ten years and the they find it's cheaper to house the gang in towns and bus them to the site. Further outback of course that is different again." Don replied.
"How far do we travel before we reach the outback, old chap?" asked Ted.
"That's a good question, Ted. I don't think that there is a border or anything like that but rather it's perception. What someone would perceive where the true outback begins is probably different for the next person, so I think it starts where ever you think it does."

As they approach Sandstone they can see the old stamp mill and Don heads for it as the museum that Dick might be at is there too. They park the vehicle and walk into the building. No one seems to be there

for several minutes but then there is a voice from the back room.
"Don King, what brings you out this way again? More prospecting or working your lease?"
"That sounds like Dick Manton to me!" exclaimed Don.
"Yep sure is." Dick said as he came through the adjoining door. He proffered his hand and gave Don a hearty handshake.
"Dick I'd like you to meet a friend of mine, Ted Walsh. He's accompanying me in a new venture."
They shake hands with Dick giving Ted a scrutinising look.
"By gee, Ted, I've seen you before. Was it back in '89 in Meekatharra? You were the emergency radio operator."
"I say, old chap. You're right and you were always in trouble with the boss for damaging equipment." Ted responded.
"Yeah, they had some light duty gear that wasn't safe that they wouldn't replace it with solid stuff, so, it got broke. Then we had some proper equipment to work with." Dick said.

The three of them spent nearly an hour reminiscing on old times at the gold mine at Meekatharra in 1989.
Don asked of Dick, "When you were out in the Petermann ranges did you meet an old aboriginal named Billy?"
Dick thought about this for a while and scratched his head occasionally during this process. What do these blokes want with old Billy, he must be nearly ninety by now? I'll bet they're up to something! No, he

thinks, Don's not the type for shenanigans. Neither is Ted.
"What do you want to know about old Billy-The-Lid for? He'd be over ninety now if he is still alive." Dick asked.
"We're gathering details of Lasseter's last months and trying to track down as much information as possible". Don replied.
"Yeah, that part I understand but why is this information so important?" Dick questioned.
Ted answered in his educated voice, "Well you see, old chap, we're on a fact finding mission to determine if the reports of Gerald Walsh in 1983 have a solid ground of fact. Many of the reports conflict and it is important that the facts are found to correct any of the misinformation that has been reported on."
Dick looked a little confused. He'd never heard of Gerald Walsh but said "Okay, yeah old Billy came to my lease a few times and told me some stories and I thought that that is what they were, just stories or old bloke's rambling's. I never put much faith in what he said. But now that you say that, there was something that he told me that does make sense and it was that Lasseter wore a chain around his neck with a large rough nugget fixed to it. He claims that it was taken from the reef of gold."
"Thanks for that, old man", replied Ted. "That was mentioned in one of the reports but not in the last. We need to speak to old Billy and we think he is still at the Warburton Aboriginal Community."
"Dick, it was great to catch up again after all these years. We've gotta be going now, but we'll catch up with you again soon. We're off to my lease at

Carnegie, to work that for a while and see if it shows any promise." Don told Dick.

He put a twenty-dollar bill into the donation box.

They shook hands and walked out the door. Just as the men got into their vehicle a motorhome came into the carpark. Ted got several photos if it and they pulled out on their way to Wiluna.
"I've taken a shot of that motorhome, Don. They seem to be coming very popular with the retired fraternity."
"Yeah mate. It seems to be becoming a bit of a hobby, this travel and the need of everyone to see all parts of Australia." Don replied. "I might get one of those ourselves one day and show the family the rest of this great country of ours."

They left the motorhome and the museum behind and made good time on the dirt road. It was mostly on flat ground with some hills off to the left just before the Sandstone-Meekatharra road. Then they came along the dry shore of Lake Mason. Don had been out this way several times but never called into the homestead at Lake Mason.
After three and a half hours they came to the tee junction at the Goldfields Highway just a few kilometres south of Wiluna.
Once they arrive in Wiluna, Don pulled into the roadhouse and the attendant comes out unlocks the grid's door, then the bowser and begins filling the tank with fuel.
Don and Ted go into the building and they talk about the prospect of rain. The weather report says that the Cyclone Byron which dumped 50 mm of rain on

Newman yesterday is now a rain bearing depression with light falls expected in this area late today and overnight.
"It'll make a good season out here for the stations," says the attendant. "Be good for a change, not having so much dust around. It gets ya down after a while."
After paying the fuel bill, Don and Ted take off in the Ute and trailer again and head out on the Wongawol Road towards Carnegie Station.

Just past the turn off to the Aboriginal Community, there are a number of wrecked cars. The community buildings can be seen in the distance and there appears to be more wrecks there too.
"See those wrecks, Ted, that's what I was talking about yesterday. I just can't understand their lack of respect of ownership. Those Landcruisers would only be several years old."
"I understand how you feel, old man, but they have a long culture of not having owned anything. Their home was made of sticks and bark and when they moved on they'd simply leave it behind. The tools they used are very basic and there is no cost. No cost, because they didn't have a currency until they were indoctrinated into white society. Most of them are, obviously, having great trouble integrating into white society".
"Mmm. Yeah, ya might have a point there Ted," Don said after considering Ted's diatribe for a few seconds.

The road was rising ever so slightly to the east. There is a range of hills to the south and it is in here that Don has his gold mining lease.

He turns right at Windidda Road and continues on for about forty kilometres then turns right and heads up into the hilly area. The track takes them alongside a creek.
"That's Miningarra Creek there Ted." Don informed him. "That's another of the aboriginal names used in the district."
About fifteen kilometres along this tight, windy, rough track they come to some buildings. There is a campfire burning slowly outside of a lean-to that covers a caravan.

The dog races out to meet them. It was barking as it ran towards them and Ted was wondering if it would chew right through the tyres of the Ute it looked that fierce.

As they drive up an old man comes forward to greet them.
Don's pulls up near the larger shed and the old man walks up to them. Both Ted and Don get out of the vehicle and the old man greets them. The old dog has lagged behind but is approaching at a slower rate than when he darted out to meet them.

"G'day Bert," Don turns to Ted and says "Ted, I'd like to introduce you to Bert Memory. Bert this is Ted Walsh, who I was telling you about last trip out here."
"Please to meecha, Ted." The old man said in a drawling, rough voice. "I heered lots aboucha. Dis bloke 'ere tells lotsa stories, so I reckon you'd be a good bloke too, eh?"

"I'm pleased to make your acquaintance too, Bert. I reckon Don's an alright chap, too, so we should get along together well."
"Had any rain lately Bert?" Asked Don.
"Nah, none since August, den when we only got fifteen mils. But the wireless says some more's comin' today."
The wind that was picking up was from the northeast and there were some heavy clouds out that way.
"Anyhow, I got the billy boiling if'n ya want a cuppa, Don".
"Thanks Bert, we'll just unload some supplies for ya, and be there." replied Don.

Don untied some ropes off the trailer and took out a large box. He took this box into the caravan that Bert was using for his accommodation. It was spotless. The old man kept a very clean show and this was one of the reasons that Don employed his services. Don provided tucker and accommodation for Bert, in turn for Bert acting as caretaker for Don's lease. Bert was about seventy and too old for any more mining or manual work. Bert's old one eyed blue heeler helps by keeping away unwanted visitors. He looks pretty vicious but really is quite harmless to those he knows.

Bert filled the three enamel mugs with hot tea straight from the billy and the three men sat on a plank near the caravan to drink it. Don told Bert of their conversation with Dick Manton. Bert knows Dick and reckons that the story may be true.
"Bit of a sly old bugger is Dick. Don't tell him too much of wot you're doing or he be dogg'n ya!" said Bert slowly.

"You'd be proud of what Ted said to him Bert, I think he was thoroughly confused. Or he thinks we're going to spend some time here on this lease." Don told him.

The sun had gone down behind the hill and the temperature was dropping rapidly and the rain was very close. Don and Ted took down their swags and set them on the floor in the shed.
"Be safer in here tonight Ted. It'll be raining soon and I prefer not to get wet while I'm sleeping."
After setting the swags up, Ted went back to the Landcruiser and connected the camera to his laptop and downloaded all of the photos he had taken so far. After he had shut down the computer, he took some shots in the fading light around Don's mine area.
"I'll get a few more in the morning after you've shown me your workings, Don."
Don had told Ted that he'd show him the underground workings of this small lease that he had and where he anticipated putting the next drive. He had drilled the line and the colour from it looks promising.

Darkness and the rain fell at the same time. The darkness was more complete than the rain, which was light but saturating. The noise on the iron roofs was like good music, soft and gentle. It continued while they ate their meal of damper and beans. It was still raining when they went to bed but Don heard it slow soon after. He didn't want too much rain or it would be difficult getting out tomorrow. To delay a day would upset his plans for the return trip and he was determined to keep to them.

Chapter 7

Mount Magnet, Western Australia, 3rd & 4th April

Ted and Don woke at the same time just before dawn and packed their swags ready for loading later in the morning. After they had eaten Bert's cooked a breakfast of sausages, eggs and toast, Don took Ted into the mine. At the entrance there were the usual gates that were locked to keep out wild animals and unwanted visitors, then the room where the hard hats and headlamps were kept on charge. They each took a hard hat with headlamp and checked the batteries. Don turned on the light switch and when the generator started, the lights down the decline glowed with a soft light. The shoring was in good condition and Ted was satisfied it was safe to continue.

Don pointed out to Ted where he got the last lode of high-grade ore and Ted took a couple of pictures of it with the flash. About fifty metres in and ten metres down, there was the start of a drive to the left. "This is where the drive is going to be, Ted. This is the line of test holes I put down and the ore sample which you tested for me came from."

"That was an awesome sample. You should do well with that drive. Does anybody else know of it, Don?" asked Ted.

"Only you and me. Old Bert of course but he is solid. The fewer people know of course the better. We don't want any claim jumpers out 'ere, mate," Don replied.

"No, old chap, we could do without those. Do you need much fracture in this ground, Don?"

"That's one of the beauties of this ground is that it only needs two or three half sticks per face and I can blow out four or five tonnes at a time. I keep the drive about four foot wide and just six foot high and triangulated until the load begins. So it makes for fairly comfortable mining, Ted." Don replied.

Ted could see that Don was on top of things here and after several photos they turned and walked back to the entrance of the main shaft. This was a little larger than the new drive. About seven foot high and six foot wide, while being fairly square on the sides.
Some of the timber for the shoring was local bush timber but further down the main stope it was rough sawn jarrah and karri. This had to be trucked in and was the most expensive part of the mining operation. Don used a small rubber wheeled cart to carry the ore back to the main shaft and then winched it back to the main shaft entrance with the electric winch. From there it went through his small crusher and through the new process he and Ted developed for separating the gold from the ore. For a small show like this, it was very efficient and a suitable one-man operation. The furnace for melting the gold to bullion was in the shed where they had slept last night. Ted had been very helpful to Don in the design of much of this equipment and he wouldn't take any payment for it. This current project with Lasseter's Reef was to be all the payment Ted required. If they made a profit from it, that would be even better.

As they emerged from the mouth of the mine, Bert called out that the billy was on and would be ready in five minutes. Don waved his thanks. He and Ted returned their hard hats to the small room, put the batteries back on charge, turned off the lights and locked the gates before heading back to the caravan.

Mount Magnet, Western Australia, 3rd & 4th April

The weather had cleared and the sun was shining brightly but the southerly breeze was chilly after being down the mine.
"Looks like the rain is finished for the time being, old chap," said Ted.
"Yeah, I think we'll have some fine weather for a few days, Ted."
They took their enamel mugs of tea and sat on the same plank again.
"We'll be off soon after lunch, Bert. We're going out towards Docker River for a few days. We hear there's something interesting out there. We'll fill you in on the details when we get back," Don said, then continued, "we should be back by this time next week. Could you service the generator and crusher while we're away? We'll have a job for 'em when we get back."

Don and Ted spent some time unloading and re-sorting some of the gear on the Ute and trailer. Some was to stay here and they needed some with them on this operation.

Each could sense the growing excitement and anticipation of the other as they got closer to the Peterman Ranges. This was going to "something".

Bert had damper and stew for lunch around midday and called the two of them over when it was dished up. There was nothing left on the plates when they had finished.
"Thanks a lot for that, Bert. We'll be off and back again next week, like I said. Take care of yourself now," Don said. He had a bit of a soft spot for the old

man, whom he had known for many years. The difference in age didn't mean anything except perhaps as a father-son relationship.

They tied down the last few things on the trailer and headed out of the minesite. The old dog followed them for a while then stopped and watched for a few minutes before heading back to the old man.
"Never mind me old dog, they'll be back next week. You can be sure 'bout that." The old one eyed dog looked up at the old man and wagged his tail as though he knew exactly what he had said to him. He then went to lie down in his favourite spot, just under the edge of the caravan. He lay down with his paws out in front of him and rested his head on them, looking and watching and waiting.

The road was moist in places but with Don's careful driving, he was able to keep the vehicle in the centre of the road. Had he gone off to one side, the camber of the road would have caused the Ute to slip sideways and they would have fallen into the table drain and gotten bogged.

It was like driving on ice.

The hilly section was fine but some of the road on the flat area was a bit slippery. There were some small washaways but because of the steady soaking rain, there were no washouts of any consequence to interfere with the trip.

Don turned right when he came to the Windidda Road, which continued southeast. This road would take them around the south end of Lake Carnegie near Prenti Downs station then back up the east side of the lake to the Gunbarrel Highway, east of Carnegie Station.

The road around the south end of the lake was wet but by keeping to the centre of the track, Don was able to keep going. Both the vehicle and trailer tyres were collecting a bit of mud. This mud, along with some grasses and other debris, builds up on the tyres causing them to become larger. They needed to stop several times to remove the mud from off the wheels and tyres. If this job was not done frequently the mud would build up and jam the tyre into the wheel arch and stop it from turning. For this job, after parking on dry ground, they each took a spade and scraped the mud away, being careful not to interfere with the brake lines etc.
This slowed them down and they made camp on some high ground about fifty kilometres to the east of Carnegie Station.

Ted helped with the gathering of firewood again and soon the cooking fire was right for Don to cook the steaks on the grill. He wrapped spuds in foil and buried these in the coals, made a small damper in the camp oven and cooked some carrots and peas in an old pot in the coals.
Just on dark, the meal was ready and Ted had turned on the radio just to hear what was happening around the world. Just before the news bulletin, there was an announcement of some sketchy details of an early morning gold robbery in Kalgoorlie, Western Australia.

"Bloody gold! Everyone wants some, Ted," Don exclaimed after hearing the report.

"My good man, we are all after the same thing in this world. The only difference is that there are some people who actually still prefer to get theirs the correct way. And that is by hard work and carrying out a legal operation at all times," retorted Ted.

Don looked sideways at Ted after this outburst. He knew that Ted had some skeletons in the cupboard, but that was years ago when he was a young fella.

"I'll bet it's on the way to Sydney by the fastest way possible. Didn't say how much they stole, but I imagine we'll get told in due course? If they think it's worth reporting, of course." Don reasoned.

After the dishes were cleared away, they listened for a while but as no further reports came through, they turned off the radio, then lay a ground sheet under their swags, and crawled into them.

"We'll need an early start in the morning Ted; we're a little behind now because of the mud on the road." Don told him. "I'd like to be on the road again by sun up."

"Don't worry, old chap. I'll keep good time for you. Goodnight!"

Don didn't answer as he was asleep already and Ted was asleep within several minutes.

Great Central Road, Western Australia, 5th April

The sun was well up into the sky by the time the two men woke up. They had been working hard and for a long time yesterday at the old vault and they had slept soundly for more than twelve hours.

"G'day Mick! Did you sleep okay?" Angelo asked just a little sarcastically.
Mick was busy wiping the sleep from his eyes. Early mornings were not his thing. It usually took him some time to get out of bed and today was no exception.
"Yeah. G'day, I think I must have died, I don't remember a bloody thing," replied Mick.

They both lay in their swags and watched several birds which were flying about close by and one perched on the dishes from last night's meal, catching some flies that were there attracted to the remains of last night's meal.
"Mick, it seems that you need more rest. Stay there for five minutes while I get some wood for the fire so we can cook breakfast."
"Five minutes! Thanks a bloody lot! How about 30?"
"No can do! Five minutes, then out of the sack, mate or I'll chuck water over ya."
"Yeah, okay, okay. Keep ya bloody hair on."

Angelo scouted round and found enough firewood to cook a gourmet meal.

There were still some coals in the fireplace, so he added a little paper, then kindling. Soon there was smoke and shortly after there was flame. Angelo added larger pieces of wood until he had a roaring fire going. He stood back and watched the fire burn with a feeling of satisfaction of a job well done. Those days in the boy scouts had paid off after all.

As the wood had burnt down he roused Mick out of his swag and returning to the fire put sausages, eggs and beans on to cook. They were ready before Mick was.

"Hurry up, Mick. The bloody tucker is ready before you are. Come and get it now before it gets cold."

"Give us a minute, will ya!" Mick came round the front of the Landcruiser doing up his fly. "A man's gotta pee."

The meal was dished up by the time Mick arrived. He took the plate and mug of tea and sat on the ground leaning against the front tyre of the Landcruiser. Angelo rested against the back tyre and they ate the meal in silence.

"This is the only time I can get any peace to myself," Angelo muses to himself.

Mick finished his meal and re-filled his mug with more tea from the billy.

"Rinse it out when you've finished there, Mick, put it on to heat up, then you can do the dishes."

"And who the bloody hell said you could be father," Mick retorted.

"Just do it, ya mug."

Angelo walked round the Landcruiser to see that everything had survived last night's activity. The roo bar was bent back a bit but that's nothing to worry

about. The tarp is well tied and everything looks to be well secured.
He is not happy about having to have such a slow trip back to Sydney with the gold aboard. But there is always that contingency plan of Mr Arnold's. The plan is to telephone from Warakurna Roadhouse, near Giles Meteorological Station and if there is any heat on, find a good spot and bury the gold. The vehicle has a GPS instrument in the glovebox. Record the location and another team will be out to recover it, when the heats off.
Angelo didn't want his to happen, as he wanted to arrive in Sydney with the gold and complete the job they'd set out to do.

Mick had finished the dishes and put everything back into its place ready for travelling again. Angelo lifted the bonnet of the Landcruiser and checked the engine oil level and the radiator fluid level. Both are okay, but he heard that it is a good practice to check them daily out here.
They climb into the cab of the Ute with Angelo driving. He starts up and they head back to the road and turn onto the Great Central Road again and head east again.

Mick turns on the radio but the reception is bad.
"Angelo is the radio antenna all the way up? He asks.
Angelo puts his head out the window and sees that it is only part way up so extends it to its full height.
The only station that they are able to tune to is the ABC. Just after Mick tuned in, the eleven o'clock news was just beginning. There was talk of oversees

problems and deficit with trade and possible elections next year and a report about a bank robbery.
Both men we not really listening to the news but when Mick heard the words "bank robbery", he increased the volume so they could hear more clearly.

"Early yesterday morning two men robbed the bank in Kalgoorlie of over twelve point seven million dollars worth of gold. The police have several strong leads and are asking for community effort in assisting them with their enquiries with some details. A white Ford Transit van, which was seen in the area, has been found burnt out. If anyone had seen this yesterday, please contact the Kalgoorlie Police. Detective Sergeant Alec Webster, of the Kalgoorlie Police, is leading the investigation. Our sources at Kalgoorlie Police station have told us that there were several roadblocks in the area yesterday and one suspect is in custody. Detective Sergeant Alec Webster thanks the public for their support in the apprehension of a stolen vehicle at the roadblock. Kalgoorlie Police can be contacted on...

Angelo had stopped the vehicle and they were both sitting still in their seats listening to the report. Their mouths wide open and eyes like saucers. They are both sitting there in wonderment, totally enthralled in the news.
"I wonder who the mug was that got caught?' queried Mick after a few minutes.
"I have no idea," said Angelo, "But we are perfectly safe because of the way things were worked out. None of the locals have seen us or knows what we look like or who we are."

"Anyway, if he squeals, I'm outa here."
"I don't think that will be necessary, Mick. Mr Arnold and I have a foolproof plan. We are as safe as houses," Angelo replied.

He got the vehicle going again and each had his own thoughts for the next half an hour. They didn't watch the countryside or see the turn-off to a waterhole and caves or see the lake that they went past.
After a time Angelo got his road sense back and began watching the road. It's good with Mick being quiet, he thinks.

Makes a change too. Peace.

In the distance he sees an amber flashing light. Just a pinprick at first but slowly it gets bigger as they approach it. Then there are the signs. "Roadwork Ahead". "Slow Down". "Be Prepared To Stop". Up ahead he can see a line of ten or so vehicles. They are all parked on the road. They see a man in khaki with a safety vest, walking from vehicle to vehicle
"Bloody cops!" exclaims Mick.
Then he sees a person holding a "Stop" sign. Between themselves and the sign there are several Landcruisers, a coaster bus, two cars and a large motorhome. He pulls up behind the last vehicle. It's a Landcruiser just like theirs but white in colour.
"Mr Arnold said to blend in with the tourists, so make it look as though that is exactly what we are doing," Angelo cautioned.

Mick was sitting on the window ledge trying to get a better look at what was up ahead. He was looking for any blue and red flashing lights or cops in uniform. He could see none of these.

Angelo spots him and says. “Mick for Christ’s sake get down and sit in the seat. Look like a tourist with plenty of time to spare. Keep this activity up and you will make us look suspicious.”

After a couple minutes he continued, “Well, did you see anything?”

“Just workin’ blokes around with trucks, graders and rollers. Looks to me just like a regular road working crew doing repairs,” replied Mick.

As Angelo watches, he sees one of the crew walking down the line of traffic on the driver’s side. He didn’t tell mick until he was at the door.

“G’day, mate! What’s going on up ahead?” Angelo asked. Mick was startled and nearly jumped out of his skin.

“G’day mate. We’re just doin’ a bit of repair to the damage done by the rain the other day. We gotta wash out and it looks like it’ll take us another hour before we get it clear enough for you to get through, So if ya wanna boil the billy, or have some grub or sumpthin, go for it, mate.”

“Thanks, mate, we just might do that.”

He switched off the engine and suggested to Mick that they could get out and have some lunch, even boil the billy and look just like the other tourists. Mick, still recovering, was not happy. But then when is Mick ever happy.

They could see some people from several of the vehicles up ahead taking advantage of the situation as well, so they didn’t feel quite so uncomfortable when they made a small fire from some local wood and put

the billy on to boil. To Angelo's amazement, Mick made some sandwiches while they waited for the billy to boil.
They ate their lunch while they waited.

None of the other people came to talk to them and both men were quite happy about that too. Mick even put the stuff away after lunch. Angelo was wondering what had caused this change in Mick. He wouldn't say anything just now, as it might cause an argument and this was not the time nor the place for that to happen.

Angelo got to eye off the motorhome, which was parked about four vehicles up. He had heard about these but had never had the chance to see on up close.
"Mick, I'm just going up to that motorhome for a look. Be back in ten minutes. Don't leave the vehicle."
"Okay, mate," came the answer.
Angelo walked up to it and had a look at the outside. Just then the bloke from inside came out and seeing Angelo said, "G'day mate, looking at getting one are you?"
"I keep an open mind about things and always looking to see what's around."
The motorhome bloke extended his hand and continued, "I'm Gordon and my wife Betty is inside. We're on the first couple of days out of Geraldton on our way to Brisbane. Where are you headed?"
"Me mate an' me are just travelling around looking at several things and heading back to Sydney." Angelo answered, giving nothing away. "I got to thinking the other day that this would be a good vehicle to take the missus and the kids on a trip. How much do they cost."

"The price depends on how much detail you want inside. Ours is basic and I did the fitout of the inside myself. The total cost is about forty thousand."
"Thanks, mate. I'll keep that in mind."

They hear a whistle sounding from up ahead and when they look up they can see that the sign is now showing "Slow".
They say "See ya!" to each other.
Everybody heads back to their respective vehicles and after starting, the line slowly moves forward.

They travel for several kilometres almost nose to tail. They drive by the fresh roadwork and see where the road had been scoured out by the water flow. The machines are standing by the roadside waiting for the convoy to pass before continuing again. After a while the signs indicate that they could speed up, so Angelo puts his foot down to keep up with the vehicles ahead but out of their dust. He was happy of the break because he must keep to the timetable and not get to Warakurna Roadhouse at Giles before the eighth, that's in three days, so that he can make the telephone call.

The small settlement that they see up ahead turns out to be the fuel stop at Tjukayrla Roadhouse. They don't stop but Angelo notices that Gordon and his missus in the motorhome have pulled in. They drive straight past and continue for about forty kilometres before he decides that it would be a good idea to make camp for the night. There are a few hills off to the right. There is a track that winds to the north. He turns the Ute off the road and turns into this track. The track is well used but not for some time as there are no new tyre tracks and after several kilometres he stops and finds a good place to camp near a small dry creek-bed.

Angelo studies the map after suggesting that Mick could get the fire going. He works out that they are about one hundred kilometres from Warburton. So far the plan is coming together well. We fit in, just like the other tourists, the vehicle looks just like many others on the road. He feels satisfied that everything has been planned well and is progressing just as well.
He puts the map away and after getting two beers from the fridge, walks over to Mick, who has a good fire going and hands him a beer.
"Bloody lifesaver you are, mate," said Mick as thanks for the beer.
"No worries, mate. You've got a good fire going there," Angelo said and then continued after taking a swig at his beer, "we're doing quite well. I just checked the maps and we are right on target with our travels. I like the vehicle because we look like half of those on the road."
"I'm still a bit edgy but I must admit that so far so good," Mick replied.

They took a couple of boxes off the Ute and sat on them in a little more comfort. Mick has taken to the domestic duties well, much to Angelo's satisfaction. He gets out some steak from the fridge and greens from the tucker box, mixes up a damper mix and proceeds to cook their evening meal.
Angelo watches and even allows another beer, which he gets from the fridge. Handing one to Mick, he said, "I wasn't sure how we would get on together in this

job, Mick but I'm pleased to say that I'm impressed with you."
"Thanks, Angelo. We are a good team in spite of our differences before."
"We just need to keep doing what we are doing right now and the rest of this job will be a breeze."

The meal went down a treat and both of them being satisfied, crawled into their swags about an hour after sunset.
They didn't think to listen to the radio for any news of the police reports.

Kalgoorlie, Western Australia 5th April

Detective Sergeant Alec Webster was early at the station this morning. He knew that he would have a big job ahead of him today.
He picked up the local paper from the front step. There was the story on the front page. In a bold heading, "GOLD ROBBERY". A picture of a white Ford Transit van, a photo of the Boss and himself and quite a story:

"Early yesterday two men robbed the Miners Own Bank in Kalgoorlie of over twelve point seven million dollars worth of gold. The police have several strong leads and are asking for community effort in assisting them with their enquiries with some details. A suspicious white Ford Transit van was seen in the area. If anyone has seen a van of this description with company markings on the side, please contact the Kalgoorlie Police. Detective Sergeant Alec Webster, of the Kalgoorlie Police, is leading the investigation.

Under this story was another, "SUSPECT HELD".

Our sources at Kalgoorlie Police station have told us that there were several roadblocks in the area today and one suspect is in custody. Detective Sergeant Alec Webster thanks the public for their support in the apprehension of a stolen vehicle at the roadblock.

The story goes on to tell of the efficiency of the local police and how they apprehended the suspect and flew him back to Kalgoorlie in the helicopter. It went on at some length but there was no mention of the suspect's name. Alec was pleased with this. "Keep them guessing a bit."

On page two, there is a story of the roadblocks, several motorists' reports of being stopped and questioned.

He folded and put down the newspaper. Leaning back in his chair he began thinking of the events of the previous day trying to glean some detail that he may have missed. Before the team arrived he reads through the reports from yesterday's activities. There was some little thing that was bugging him but as yet he couldn't put a finger on it. After reading the reports, the doubt was still there.
"There's something here somewhere, I just can't find it yet." He said to himself.

At about the same time the rest of the staff turned up and got to work.
He worked out the workload for each of the groups. They all needed to go over their reports from yesterday to see if there was any significant point, which may have become clearer overnight.
Some of the team actually thought about work in their time off. He'd find out just how much shortly.

Artie had entered his office and Alec said, "Artie, get the team together for a briefing in fifteen minutes. I

want to hear any developments from them and to brief them on today's work."
"Okay, Alec. Be back in a sec."
Artie visited each room and office and passed on the instructions.

When the fifteen minutes were up Alec joined them in the squad room. On the white board he started to list the main points of what they knew for fact.

1. Incomplete Security system.
2. Sydney's "Arnold" crime syndicate, including the detained suspect Albert Ronald Macintosh also known as, Ron McAlbert, also known as Richard Arnold Menzies
3. 60 bars of gold = 600 kg.
4. Ford Transit van
5. Acid on mortar.
6. Styrene foam wall panel.
7. Hire car.

"Okay, everyone listen up!" He waited several seconds before continuing because of the noise of the group. "Righto! Firstly, well done to all the teams who were involved in the roadblocks yesterday. The reaction time to the initial orders confirms your training has been okay. Well done to all those who assisted in the apprehension of the suspect. We didn't get much out of him last night and no one has come forward, at this point, to post bail. What I need to know is; does anyone have any more to add to their report of last night? Something which may not have been complete in their reports. Any little detail that you may think is insignificant may be an important piece of the puzzle to assist in apprehending the offenders." He paused for anyone to speak up. "Anyone?" he paused again. "Oh well, just think about it some more and keep your minds open to any little snippet that may come your way. Let Artie or myself know immediately."

Alec continued, "Your assignments for today. All leave is cancelled for the duration of this investigation. Senior Constable Ted Evens and his team will do a more in depth test of the chemical used on the mortar, find it source, where it was purchased, by whom." He paused to take a breath. "The boss is in contact with Sydney Gold Theft Squad and is continuing to question the managers of the mine, bank and security. There is nothing more from that angle at this stage."
"Four uniforms in two teams will continue with the door to door. I want more information on that Transit van. Times in, out and details of company markings on the side, etc."
"Styrene foam panel. After forensics has finished with it, I want any details posted on this board and then I want someone to find out the details; who makes them, who sold it, who bought it, who delivered it etc."
"Artie and I are going to look at the suspect's digs just as soon as the warrant is ready."
Just as he finished that detail, Artie entered the room.
"I have the warrant here, Alec, the magistrate just signed it." Artie said.
"Sixty bars at ten kilograms per bar is six hundred kilograms. That is not a light load to shift. Think about how it may have been shifted and look for evidence to back up your theory."

"Are there any questions?" after a brief pause, "No? Okay let's get at it. All reports on my desk as soon as anything comes to light or by six o'clock tonight and no later."
Before anyone could leave, Connie entered the room.
"Here Sarge, I thought this might be handy so I brought it up straight away." She handed a sheet of typed paper to him. He read the message.
"Okay, listen up! A new development! A Ford Transit Van has been found in the old reserve ten kilometres south of town. It has been extensively burned. A patrol car is at the site to secure the area." He looked up at the team and continued, "Artie and I will take care of this right now and have the van brought in for you to look at, Ted. We'll let you know when it's here."
"Okay, that's all! Let's go, get 'em."

The team filed out of the squad room and an air of excitement was evident by the chatter.
"Artie, come with me but first call the tilt tray truck bloke to send a truck out to the reserve. We'll get out there and see what's happening."
Artie used his mobile phone to call Connie to get the truck while they walked out to the car. Alec drove while Artie completed his call. Several minutes later, Connie called back to say that the truck was on its way.
"This could be the breakthrough that we were looking for Artie; I couldn't help but think that there was some little thing that we have overlooked. Perhaps this will help."

Chapter 9
Kalgoorlie, Western Australia 5th April

It only took them seven minutes to reach the reserve and several more to locate the patrol car where the van was found.
They pulled up beside the patrol car and Alec talked to the officers there. "Who was it that reported the vehicle?"
"We usually call around here in the morning to wake up the inebriates and found it about half an hour ago. When we reported it in, we were told to wait until you arrived."
"Good work, mate. Has anything been touched?"
"Not by us and I couldn't see any footprints around either so it looks like a clean crime scene to me."
"Alright, thanks for that. We'll take over from here; you can resume your normal duties."
The patrol car left the scene and Alec and Artie had a look round for footprints. There were a couple of them but they were very feint and blurred.
"Nothing of substance there, mate." Alec said.
They looked into the vehicle without touching anything. The arsonist had done a fairly good job but they kept their hands off anything so that the forensic team would have the best chance. There was some white paint left on the rear panel and Alec felt sure that it was the vehicle they were looking for.

The truck arrived and Artie spoke to the driver, telling him to load it without touching anything. He'd need to take it to the police yard and offload it again. He stressed that nothing must be touched, not even the brake, if it still worked.
They watched while the driver tilted the truck's tray and payed out the winch cable. He attached it to the

pintle hook on the front of the chassis rail. Then he operated the winch and the burnt out van was being dragged up the tray until it reached the end of its travel. Then the tray was lowered to the transport position. There was a tie down bracket at the back and Alec allowed the driver to secure the vehicle by tying onto this point.
“Okay, mate, we’ll follow you in to the police yard and be there while you unload it.”
“Righto.” Yelled the driver and off he drove.

The police yard was at the rear of the police station so security was not a concern. The truck driver attached another winch cable to the vehicle after untying it and winched the van off the truck and left the yard.
“Well, I wonder how long it’ll take the grapevine to spread the news of the burnt out van.” Artie said.
“Now, that’s a good point, Artie. We should have some feelers out to hear what’s being said about town. You never know what we might find.”
With that Alec used his mobile phone to make several calls.
“That has set the cat among the pigeons,” he said to Artie. “If there is word around we should know who is talking and who is asking very soon.”

He made another call to Ted and told him that the van was ready for him at the yard.
“Okay, Artie, now let’s have a look at Rich Menzies’ digs and see what we can find.”
It took them several minutes to find the old cottage in the older part of town. It was clad in horizontal corrugated iron on the walls with the same on the roof

as were many of the older style cottages in Kalgoorlie. They didn't need a key, as the doors had no locks.
"There can't be much of value here, Alec. No locks," said Artie.
"Yeah, that'd be right. And this bloke works for a security company. Looks a bit odd to me. You look in the rooms on the left and I'll take the right. Look for anything which may be of interest."
They carried out a thorough search for the next half hour but could not find anything, which may be useful. Not even a passport.
"It looks like we drew a blank here Artie, let's get back to the station."
As they walked into the station, they paused at the front desk and asked Connie, "Can you add our lunch order to the others please. Yep! Same as usual. We should be in the office for a while."
Alec called in at the Boss's office on the way to see if there were any further developments from the Sydney end.
"Alec, they gave us what they knew about this syndicate yesterday and I've spoken to Australian Federal Police. They have no knowledge of "Arnolds", so this is a state only crime. I've had further talks with Bert from NG Security but no further developments than yesterday. It seems that the first few hours are the most important in getting the details. How are your teams going?"
"We've recovered a torched transit van, which will be covered with forensics shortly, door to door is still going on and the team is all revved up. I expect we'll have some more details by the day's end."

Alec returned to his office just as lunch was delivered. He sat down and ate his pie and chips straight away, because he knows he will get disturbed if he doesn't. The uniforms, who were doing the door to door, have just come in, so Alec asks the team leader, a senior constable, into his office to debrief. He tells him that no one saw the Transit van during the evening. Just two sightings in the morning. One at four thirty when a resident saw a white Transit van with "Bakewell" markings and the other at five fifteen when a walker saw a white Transit van with "Peters" marked on the sides.

"Okay that's good. Now, for the follow up. You'll get out to their depots now and find out all the details of those deliveries. Drivers; times in; times out; rego numbers etc. Look at the vehicles to determine if you think they may have been involved. I need a complete picture of events at that loading dock." Alec told them.

The senior constable left his office and headed out the door to gather the required information.

Alec finished his chips after he had left and threw the packet into the bin.

"The bins. Has anyone checked the bins?"

He phoned Ted of forensics to see if he was still at the scene. He was just getting into his car. And yes they had checked the bins but could find nothing of evidence there. Another dead-end, thought Alec. But if you don't cover all angles etc. etc., he thinks.

Artie enters his office and says, "Alec how's this! AVIS rented a car on the first of this month. A Holden Commodore V8 Executive, rego 1AYT 7794. It was booked from their Sydney office and the bloke walked in and paid cash for it, as well as a thousand kilometres of travel. It was picked up from the Perth airport. They don't have a description of the driver as the keys were picked up from the counter just after the flight from Yulara arrived. It was full of Japanese tourists who all wanted to hire cars. They have a signature but it could be anything." Artie informed him. "Now, for the disappointing part. That car was detailed here in Kalgoorlie yesterday afternoon and hired again this morning and is on its way to Perth via Esperance."

"How well do they do their detailing between hiring's?" Alec asked.

"I asked that, and they tell me Kalgoorlie is one of the few agencies that do a thorough job of cleaning and they think that any evidence which may have been there would be wiped. Sorry, mate."

"On the off chance, do you think it worthwhile to ask the Esperance boys and girls to apprehend the vehicle and carry out a forensic check?" Alec asked, clutching at straws.

"I don't think so. It would be bad for PR and there is only a slim chance of evidence and where would it lead?"

"Yeah, I thought so too, but I wanted to hear your point of view."

Alec got his head down and read the reports again. Then he stood in front of the window going over the details in his mind. Nothing more came to light.

Several minutes later, Ted came in and gave him a brief forensic report on the van.
"The Ford Transit Van was painted white. Now here is some interesting detail, the "Bakewell" sign was overlaid with the "Peters" sign. Just about all burnt off but just a couple of shreds. The licence plates have been removed. The chassis and engine number have been ground off. I'll need to do some more work on those with "BM4 acid" to bring up the original numbers. To our surprise, there are some fingerprints on the underside of the driver's door handle. We're attempting to match those at this point. In summary, I am satisfied it was the vehicle which took part in the robbery." Ted reported.
"Thanks, Ted that helps a lot. We'll get these blokes, you'll see." Alec told him confidently.

Ted left Alec's office and went back to join the team to continue with their investigation.
Alec was on the phone to one of the people he had phoned before, to ask if they had heard anything. He was annoyed by the negative answer.
Just as he was hanging up the phone, the uniformed senior constable entered his office.
"Sarge, we have some information from the local distributors for "Peters" and "Bakewell". They don't use Ford Transit vans; they use eight tonne pantecks. Usually Isuzu's or Mitsubishi's. They have no knowledge of any white Transit vans being used for deliveries during after-hours."
"Thank you! That is a very positive piece of information. If you have finished with the door to door around the loading dock area, have your team out on

the road to the old reserve south of town. I want a door to door done, asking for details of the sighting of the transit van in that area in the last twenty four hours or any vehicular activity in that area in the last two days. Did anybody see the smoke from the burning vehicle? Have a report to me by six o'clock. That gives your team one and a half hours." Alec paused before continuing, "By the way, that was good work, keep it up."

Alec took the details that he had received in the last hour or so and headed to the Boss's office.
"Boss, we have a few developments, which I feel are positive and I like to bring you up to speed on the investigation so far." He told of the details of the signs on the van, the engine and chassis numbers, the wrong vehicle in the loading dock, the hire car and the lack of information on the street. He told of what was happening at the time and said that he would like to show him the results of today's investigation after the debriefing at six o'clock.
"That sounds to me like you have your hands full. How is the team handling the investigation? Do you think we need to bring in a team from Perth central head office to assist or take over? Are you confident to carry on the investigation from here?" Collin Watts asked.
"No and yes Boss. I feel that the team has something to get their teeth into here and are even enjoying a big investigation. I feel that we have the expertise to not only do the groundwork but also to run the show from here. Artie is doing well and we always have you

around to bounce things off if we need to." Alec replied.
"Okay, then. That's fine. I was on to the Commissioner just now and he was getting ready to send a team from central to take over the investigation. I told him that I would reassess the effectiveness of the operation this evening and let him know of my decision by six thirty. Now, if you are as satisfied by day's end as you sound now, I'll inform them that we can handle it. BUT. Think very carefully. If the brown stuff hits the fans, it'll be your and my head to roll." Collin told him.
"Yes Boss, I understand that and thanks for your confidence in the team and myself. We won't let you down." Alec left the Boss's office and made his way to the squad room. He began writing on the board the details as of the investigation to date.

He was just finishing when the uniformed senior constable entered and told him that so far, they have not been able to find anyone who saw anything, out of the ordinary, happen out at the reserve or the road leading to it. It seems like a dead end.
"Okay, that's all you can do today, get your team in here in five minutes for a debriefing. Thanks."
The different teams began entering the room and the noise level increased as they are all talking about what they had done for the day and suggestions of what they may be doing tomorrow. Generally a lot of speculation but everyone was in good spirits of not a little tired after their days work.
At six o'clock Artie called for everyone to quieten down and listen to what Alec has to say

Chapter 9

Kalgoorlie, Western Australia 5th April

"Okay team, Thanks for your efforts today. We have been able to gather more information. It seems that someone torched the van but we still have some work to be done there. Any more to report Ted?"
"Yes Sarge, the acid has worked on the engine block and we have the last seven digits of the engine number. With Fords, that is also the chassis number. Unless, of course, the engine's been changed. So we are trying to search for it on the licensing files. We'll keep working on it tonight for a while and have the details for you in the morning. Tomorrow we'll continue to work on the chassis number just to make sure they correspond."
"Senior, tell us the results of your DTD's today."
The senior constable spoke of what transpired from the door to door questioning today and finished off with saying that they will start tomorrow to do more DTD on the road to the reserve. Many people whose houses are on that road were not in today.
Artie told the team of the hire car details. Then went on to tell the team of the multitude of phone calls that flooded in following the reports on radio and the newspaper. These are being followed up but the process will take some time, to evaluate and cross check all details before adding them to the "to do" list.
The Boss was standing in the back corner and heard all of the reports. He was happy that they had everything under control and would tell the Commissioner, "thanks for the offer but no thanks".
"Okay team, that's the way it stands at this time, thank you everyone for a good days work. Don't think this is going to be easy. It is going to take every one of you to keep on your toes. I expect each and every one of you

to give us one hundred and ten percent on this case. Also to keep in mind, even the tiniest piece of information that you hear around town, or during questioning people, may be of the greatest importance, so record everything and we'll sort thought the combined information and find which is relevant." He pauses for a breath. "You've all done some good work today, we thank you for that. Keep it up tomorrow and I think we may have a result. Thank you. See you all tomorrow." Alec completed his debriefing session, then he and Artie left the room to join Collin in his office to finalise today's debriefing.
"Alec, it seems you have made some headway today. Are you sure you and the team can do the job?"
"Yes, Boss. It's frustrating that more than half the questions are still unanswered but I'm sure we are on top of it. Did anyone post bail on Richard Menzies yet?"
"That is a very unusual situation, Alec. No one has come forward at this stage. I would have thought that a syndicate like Arnolds would have a top brief in here and get the bloke out. Perhaps he is expendable and just a decoy. Now that is something to be mindful of."
"Yes, very unusual," replied Alec.
"Alright Alec and Artie, I'll inform the commissioner that we're ok and he can call off his boys. I'll see you in the morning."
"Goodnight, Boss." Both of them said in unison. They walked out of his office and back to Alec's.

Alec and Artie have a beer each and talk over the day's events. Neither of them can draw any further conclusions to the data, which is at hand. We'll need to see what tomorrow brings.

Peegull Waterhole, Western Australia, 5th April

Betty was out of bed before Gordon, this morning. Her leg and shoulder were aching. She had this same pain yesterday morning but said nothing to Gordon about it.
"He'd only worry and he doesn't need to worry about anything else," she thinks.
The pain wasn't too bad but enough to stop her resting. She couldn't find a comfortable position while lying down so thought it best to be up and comfortable. Gordon was still sound asleep, so she made herself a cuppa and took it outside to watch for the sunrise.

The harsh scrub was the home to many birds and several species of these were flitting around searching out bugs, seeds or moisture as she stepped down from the motorhome. Looking up into the sky she could see that there were just a few wispy clouds and it looked like the sun had set fire to them from below the horizon. The effect was spectacular. She couldn't contain herself and went back inside to rouse Gordon, so he could absorb the spectacular sight as well. He had just woken and being surprised to find her bed empty was about to get up anyway.
"Gordon, come quick, you've just got to see this sunrise. It's the best one we've seen on this trip so far." She exclaimed joyfully.
"Yes dear, I'm on my way." He replied.

Chapter 10
Peegull Waterhole, Western Australia, 5th April

Betty poured his tea while he dressed quickly and they both spent the next ten minutes watching another beautiful sunrise.
When it was fully daylight, Gordon took a stroll around the area while Betty prepared breakfast.

The waterhole was a natural phenomenon within the rocks and the cave was beyond that. The opening looked safe, but he'd need a torch before entering. He went back to the motorhome and Betty had breakfast ready. After they had finished breakfast they gathered up a few items and went cave exploring. Gordon carried a strong torch and a large coil of light rope. He secured the end of the rope to a rock just inside the cave's entrance and payed out the rope as they went. Betty was in charge of the torch. The floor was littered with rocks and sharp boulders. The roof was just above head height, so it was comfortable walking for a hundred metres.

Then it got interesting.

There was a colony of small bats. As Betty swept the area with the beam of the torch, they became unsettled and some of them began flying around. One came close to Betty and she let out an involuntary scream. This startled Gordon, herself and the bats. Most of the bats released their hold on their roost and began flying around.
Gordon called Betty to his side where he held the rope. "Crouch down, switch off the light and be still and quiet and they will settle again," he told her.

After a few minutes the faint squeaking sound that they had heard diminished and there seemed to be no movement on the cave. Betty turned on the light again to find the bats have attached to their roost again.
“Okay,” Gordon whispered to Betty, “we’ll keep as quiet as we can and keep going. The roof is not as high here so, we’ll have to bend down as we walk.”
It was difficult walking like this. Betty’s aches and pains had diminished as she began some activity and she was pleased about this.
After fifteen metres, Gordon called a halt because he had come to the end of his rope.
“We can’t go any further, dear because that’s the end of our rope. We’ll rest here for a few minutes, before we make our way back along the rope to the entrance.”

While they sat down Betty played the torch carefully around and they had a good look at the cave. The rock was white, limestone thinks Gordon. There were a lot of red vertical markings. These would be where water has washed down from the rains and left a soil stain. From Gordon’s limited knowledge of caves, he thinks this may be a relatively young one. There are no stalactites or stalagmites or shawls. They would need a lot more water. He had heard of dry caves in the past and assumes this is one too.

They began their way back to the entrance with Betty in the lead with the torch. Gordon was coiling the rope as they went. He had heard of cave disasters where explorers had got lost and knew the rope idea was not new but very effective. They stopped at the section where they could stand again and quietly walked

through the sleeping bats. They were very small, smaller than a house mouse but with wings that wrapped the body twice around. There was a bend just as the daylight began to show and Betty saw something on the wall at about shoulder height. This was a group of Aboriginal paintings. They studied these for a while, but not knowing a lot about aboriginal art, were not able to appreciate the value of what they had found.
"When we get to the next stop dear, we must ask about these paintings and find out their significance. I think it would be a wonderful education for us."
"Oh! I agree dear. These are marvellous paintings. They are so clear and sharp. You'd think they were painted last week," Betty agreed.
Gordon had found the end of the rope and they made their way into full sunlight. By the time they walked out, their eyes had become adjusted to the bright light.
"Put the kettle on again dear, I'll get this gear stored way and after smoko we'll be on the way again."
Gordon stowed the rope and put the torch back in the bracket. He checked the levels of the engine so they were ready to go straight after smoko.

While Betty was clearing away, Gordon packed up and stored the small table and chairs. They were on the road just as the eleven o'clock news began on the radio. The headlines include talk of overseas trouble again, balance of trade and elections again soon. Then there was the report of more details of the gold robbery that they had heard about yesterday.

"Early yesterday morning two men robbed the bank in Kalgoorlie of over twelve point seven million dollars worth of gold. The police have several strong leads and are asking for community effort in assisting them with their enquiries with some details. A white Ford Transit van, which was seen in the area, has been found burnt out. If anyone had seen this yesterday, please contact the Kalgoorlie Police. Detective Sergeant Alec Webster, of the Kalgoorlie Police, is leading the investigation. Our sources at Kalgoorlie Police station have told us that there were several roadblocks in the area yesterday and one suspect is in custody. Detective Sergeant Alec Webster thanks the public for their support in the apprehension of a stolen vehicle at the roadblock. Kalgoorlie Police can be contacted on...

"That was fast work by the police to get that bloke so quick!" Gordon exclaimed. "I wonder how long it will be before they get the rest of the gang. It seems there must be more of them to move that amount of gold."
"What is the weight of gold, dear?" Betty queried.
"I think the bars are about ten kilos each, so twelve point seven million dollars worth of gold must be between half and three quarters of a tonne." Gordon replied after spending several seconds to do the guesstimating.

They were still discussing some theories about how they would shift that weight of gold if they were the robbers when they came up to some signs on the side of the road.

Chapter 10

Peegull Waterhole, Western Australia, 5th April

"Looks like some more roadworks up ahead." Betty said.
Gordon could also see a line of several motor vehicles stooped in front of a chap with a safety vest displaying a "Stop" sign. There were several Landcruisers, a coaster bus and a car. He came to a stop behind the vehicle in front and waited.

Several minutes later, the man who was holding the sign made his way towards them, stopping to talk to each of the drivers as he came to their windows. He arrived at Gordon's window, which he had rolled down in readiness for him.
"Hi folks. You're going to have a delay of about an hour or so while we repair the road surface here. You can get out and walk about if you like but please keep away from the machinery. When you hear a whistle, look at my sign and you can probably move on then." He told them.
"What's happened here, mate?" asked Gordon.
"With the recent rains, we've had a washout. The road surface was washed about a hundred metres downstream. We've been carting road base here for several days but now it's time to fix it. Even better than before."

Gordon switched off the engine. It was too early for lunch but Betty suggested that if she was to make some sandwiches now, they could have them later. Gordon agreed that it was a good idea.
He got out of the motorhome and watched as several other vehicles approached and pulled up. The bloke

with the sign walked out to their vehicles and shortly he could see the occupants walking around.

Gordon was talking with several of the other drivers and asked if they knew of the caves back down the road. They thought they were discovered by the explorer Gregory but didn't know much in the way of detail but if he was to ask at the next roadhouse, the people there may be able to fill in some more detail for him.
Gordon was checking the front of the vehicle when he noticed a well-built man with Mediterranean colour and a roman nose near the back of the motorhome. He seemed to be interested in the motorhome so Gordon approached him.
"G'day mate, looking at getting one are you?" Gordon asked
"I keep an open mind about things and always looking to see what's around."
"I'm Gordon and my wife Betty is inside. We're on the first couple of days out of Geraldton on our way to Brisbane. Where are you headed?" Gordon said shaking the man's his hand
"Me mate an' me are just travelling around looking at several things and heading back to Sydney." The man answered. "I got to thinking the other day that this would be a good vehicle to take the missus and the kids on a trip. How much do they cost?"
"The price depends on how much detail you want inside. Ours is basic and I fitted out the inside myself. The total cost is about forty thousand." Gordon told him

"Thanks, mate. I'll keep that in mind." The man replied.

Gordon heard the shrill sound of a whistle. Turning around he saw the sign rotate and display the "Slow" message. He turned to say goodbye to the other chap but he had already turned and was walking back towards his vehicle. Gordon got the motorhome going again and saw in his driving mirror the bloke he was talking to, had climbed into a mustard coloured Landcruiser with a cover over the back. Those vehicles seem to be everywhere he thought.

As they drove forward, they could see the new work, which was being done to the repairs of the road. The heavy road-working machinery was parked just off to one side, ready to recommence once the traffic had cleared. It was going to be a far better road after the work was completed, Gordon thought. The culvert will also help the flow of water, instead of tearing up the road surface.

Gordon drives past the signs that indicate the end of the roadworks and the vehicles in front speed up. Gordon gets up to a comfortable eighty kilometres an hour and several of the vehicles from behind overtake them. In the distance he can still see the Landcruiser.
"Funny bloke that, Betty. We were talking and then when the whistle went, I turned to say goodbye to him but he had already turned and was walking away to his vehicle."
"Takes all sorts, dear." Betty replied, quickly.

Gordon knew this was true but it still seemed unusual. He was quite pleasant to talk to.

They ate their sandwiches while driving and after half an hour they saw the buildings and movement up ahead on the left. The signs suggested that it was the Tjukayirla Roadhouse, so Gordon slowed the motorhome and drove in. he didn't need fuel so he parked away from the bowsers. Both of them went into the roadhouse building, as they wanted more information on the caves.
They asked at the counter but there was no one there who knew much detail of the caves.
Someone said, "Go out the back and see the old bloke under the tree. He has been here for generations, he'll know."

They walked around the back of the building.

The ground was dry and dusty again and under a large wattle tree sat and old aboriginal man cross-legged. He was blind in one eye and was wearing a bright red beanie on his head.
"G'day mate!" Gordon started. "We're told by the folks inside that you might be able to help us with some information about the Peegull Water hole and Caves back down the road?"
"Mebe," came the answer.
Gordon, understanding that this man must get these questions frequently, elaborated, "We had a quick look in the cave this morning and saw some Aboriginal paintings in there. It looks to be good quality and in

good condition. Can you please tell us of the tribal significance of the paintings?"
"Well, bloke. It like dis. My people 'ave bin in dis land since da Dreamin' Time. Many time we make our mark in da good seasons. When da bad season come we go 'way to 'nudder place. We only come back when good season. Doze painting, it represent our good time and good season. I put my mark dere many time since me been young fella."
"How many years between good seasons?" asked Betty.
"Oh. Some time it be many years, some time he comes together. I doan know."
"How far away do you have to go for the ochre for the painting?" Gordon questioned.
"Dat a secret for my people and we not telling but it on sacred area not far away." The old man told them.
"Well, thank you for your time. We find it very interesting out here and try to find the information so we can understand your culture better." Gordon told the old man.
"Dat's okay, fella. It good you unnerstand our culture so we can unnerstand each udder."

They left the old man to chase away the flies and to dwell in his own thoughts.

Some smaller aboriginal children were playing with a football beyond the old man. They were having some discussion about who marked the ball. One of the boys ran over to the old man and it seems he settled the dispute. He must be the chief elder of the tribe, Gordon thinks.

Betty and Gordon make their way back to their motorhome and start off again heading east.

There was a row of hills well to the south of the road that Betty works out to be the Rowe Hills. Ahead on the right is Sharps Bluff. Before they get that far, Gordon finds a small track leading off to the left. He turns off the road and follows this, travelling very slowly and found a small turning area. There are signs of an old campfire. They set up their motorhome on the level ground and prepare to stay here for the night. Gordon sets up the table and chairs in the open facing the sunset. The sky has been clear all day but a few light clouds are showing just above the horizon. It should be another great sunset today and Gordon wasn't going to miss it for the world. He takes two beers from the fridge and he and Betty enjoy these while settling onto their comfortable chairs.

It was another great sunset and after the "sunset picture show" had ended, Betty prepared their tea, while Gordon calculated their position.
"As far as I can work it out, Betty, we are eighty kilometres from Warburton. That small creek that we turned off the road at must be Bakers Creek. It runs south east into Bakers Lake but that's probably dry at this time."

They played a few hands of cards after dark, but both were tired after their day's activities.

It's not every day that you get to explore caves out in the middle of the Great Victoria Desert.

Chapter 10
Peegull Waterhole, Western Australia, 5th April

Before Gordon drifted off to sleep he could not help but wondering about the bloke in the mustard coloured Landcruiser with the cover on the back, who spoke to him earlier in the day while they were stopped at the road-works. For some reason he just didn't seem to fit.

Carnegie Station, Western Australia. April 5th

The stars shone brightly and the eastern sky was not even lightening when Don was up and had the fire going.

He roused Ted.

"Wakey, wakey, Ted. You'll need a good breakfast today, mate. It'll be a hard drive."

Ted answered as though he had been awake for hours, "That's fine old man; I'm ready for whatever you send my way." He crawled out of his swag and after folding it, put it on the top of the Ute with Don's. He was already dressed.

Don had the billy on the fire. The sausages, eggs and bacon were nearly cooked.

"Ted there's leftover damper here, would you prefer as it is or toasted?"

"As it is, old chap. It'll probably be quicker that way," Ted replied.

Ted handed Don the enamel plates and he put the breakfasts on these. The two men sat down on the ground and ate the hearty breakfast. The tea was ready for them as they finished and this was necessary to wash down the fatty taste of the bacon.

The fire was dismantled so it was safe to leave and the cooking and breakfast equipment was washed and stored.

Carnegie Station, Western Australia. April 5th

The eastern sky was a brilliant red as the sun made its presence known. There were not many clouds but the effect was astounding.
They were on the road before sunrise proper and driving into the sun. Driving into the early morning sun was something that Don had done for many years and he always cleaned the windscreen before he started out for the day. He preferred to play it safe.

The road had deteriorated to a two-wheel track after an hour or so. Sometimes the scrub on either side of the track nearly touched in the middle above their heads. The going was slow due to the many wash-outs. Closer to the ridges of the many hillocks, the ground would give way to a rocky outcrop and this needed to be negotiated slowly because of the rocks on the road. There were many deviations, which had been put in by the travellers to go around the boggy patches of road.

"When Len Beadell put these roads in during the fifties, they were good roads. That's why this is known as the Gunbarrel Highway. That's what it was, a highway. The only problem is that I don't think it's seen a grader since," Don was able to get out between getting buffeted from side to side by the vehicles' motion.

They stopped every half-hour to check to see if anything had come loose. Several times it was necessary to tighten the ropes, as they had become slack because of the movement.

Chapter 11
Carnegie Station, Western Australia. April 5th

Because of the frequent scrub brushing against the side of the vehicle, it was necessary for them to remove the various radio antennas, so as to prevent damage to them. Likewise, the mirrors were turned in to prevent them from becoming damaged.
Occasionally at the top of a rise, they would get out of the vehicle, climb on top of it and look to see if they could find any landmarks. They were able to get a good view of the surrounding country from near the top of Mt. Nossiter, without deviating from the track. They knew where they were because Ted was frequently plotting their position with the GPS instrument. This was connected to his laptop computer at these stops and the information used to create their own map. Ted had many megabytes of this information stored.

By ten o'clock, Don was in need of a break. Don had driven as far as Mt. William Lambert. They stopped and were able to get off the track near a cleared area on the side of the hill. Ted boiled the billy on a small fire while Don checked the vehicles and equipment. One of the pieces of mining equipment had worn a small hole through the floor of the trailer and Don was repacking this with a piece of timber under it to spread the load. The sides of the vehicles were brushed clean of any dust or yesterday's mud.
"One thing about this track Ted is that it wipes off any evidence of yesterday's activities."
"That is for sure, old chap, looks quite clean again."

Ted had downloaded the GPS to the laptop and had a map of their travels on the screen. Don came to look at

this and estimated that if they keep up their current speed of travel, they should be able to be at Warburton by eight o'clock tonight.
"Well, I won't be driving after dark, so we'll be in Warburton tomorrow morning. It would probably a better time to see old Bill anyway," Don says.

Ted walks around looking at the ground. There are a few stones here the size of tennis balls and some smaller. Mostly they were very rough in shape and some of them are not symmetrical at all. The edges are not sharp and they appear to be most unusual. He has the position logged, so he takes a few samples and puts them away after marking the bags there are in. When they return to the mine, he'll find out a bit more about them.

"Okay," Don says after being stopped for fifteen minutes, "time to move on again".
They climb back in the Landcruiser and get back onto the track again.

After another forty-five minutes, Don hears a different sound and pulls over immediately. Just in time too, as another vehicle with exhaust trouble, travelling in the opposite direction comes out of the next turn at speed. He seems unperturbed about his speed and when he sees their vehicle, skids to a halt and switched off the engine straight away. The driver and his offsider jump out of their battered, late model, red Range Rover and walk to where Don is parked.
"Phew, that was close. I didn't know anyone else used this road." The driver exclaimed. Don took one look at

this bloke and his first impression was that he must be high on adrenalin. Or something else.
"Well that seems pretty obvious to me," Don replied sarcastically. "Looks like you want the whole road to yourself. Anyway, what's the big hurry? You should show a bit of respect for other road users, you know."
"What's the matter, mate are we too good for you?" the other driver replied.
"Look, I'm not going to get into an argument with you, mate, but just have some respect for others. Anyhow what's that patch of oil on the ground under your sump?"
"Been like that for a day or two now. I'll just chuck some more in and away we go. Nothing is going to stop us."
"Before it gets any worse, I'd have it fixed if I were you. This is not good country to break down in. Too far for the RAC to come to the rescue. Be best if you just left the vehicle and get a ride out."
"No mate. We know what we're doing."

Don and Ted got back into their vehicle. The other driver added oil and then tries to start his engine. The battery was nearly dead. The engine fired as the battery died. It rattled like it was out of oil and sounded like the exhaust system had detached before the muffler. They took off down the track in a cloud of dust and noise, going three times the safe speed for that road.
"Well, there goes a problem for someone. Tonight, we'll call Carnegie Station on the radio and check to see if he's got through. You never know, we might just save someone's' life.

Chapter 11
Carnegie Station, Western Australia. April 5th

Back on the road again and Don finds twenty kilometres an hour the best speed for the road conditions. The bush is less now and they can see a good way across the country from time to time.

"I say, old chap. That other driver was awfully rude, eh?" Ted said to Don.
"You betcha, he was. The unfortunate thing is that, that sort of people get through these situations but they don't understand or care about other road users," Don replied. "I still think he was on something, he couldn't stand still. He was hopping from one foot to the other while he was talking to us."
"Yes! His passenger kept out of the discussion but he looked a little bewildered by it all."
"I just hope that they don't cause any harm to come to anyone else with their stupidity."

They cross David Carnegie Road and see the wheel tracks of the red Range Rover coming from around the corner.
"I wonder what those blokes were doing out there, there's nothing for miles, just this same desert. Little Sandy Desert to the west and Gibson Desert to the east," Don queried
"Well, old chap, by the look of the two men in the vehicle may suggest they were up to no good. Perhaps they have a drug manufacturing facility out there," mused Ted.
"Perhaps we'll never know, but it does make you wonder."

Carnegie Station, Western Australia. April 5th

The track improved for fifty kilometres and Don was able to catch up on some time till he approached the western slopes of Mt. Gordon. This caused them to slow again due to the rocky outcrops on the road. "We'll stop here for a late, short lunch break, Ted. Then make for the Lake Breaden area for the night," Don exclaimed.

Ted made sandwiches and boiled the billy while Don checked the loads and vehicles. They had their lunch, then back on the road again. Their next half-hour stop was at the Len Beadell Monument. They paused here for a few minutes to read the inscription of the work he had done in the area for the British Atomic Commission in the fifties. The roads were put in initially so vehicles could recover the spent rockets and junk from the launchings at Woomera to the east. Prospectors, mining companies, pastoralists and travellers have used the roads since that time. This has become known as one of "the" roads to drive on in the outback of Australia.

After another hour and a half of driving, Don was tired and they decided to stop for the night on some flat ground between the dry lakes.

Ted collected some of the dry bush wood that was in the area and made a small cooking fire while Don, once again, checked the equipment and vehicles. The heavy-duty trailer, which he had made, is standing up to the rough driving conditions very well and Don is pleased with this result.

Carnegie Station, Western Australia. April 5th

Ted downloaded the details from the GPS to his laptop and confirmed their position to be at the narrow neck of Lake Breaden.
"That is two hundred and fifty kilometres for the day, an average of just twenty five kilometres per hour, Don. Goes to show the degree of difficulty of driving on this road. Had you have travelled any faster it would have been very unpleasant in the vehicle," Ted told Don.

Ted also downloaded the photos, which he had taken for the day. They included those of the two blokes in the red Range Rover.
"Pity we can't see the rego number," Don said. "We would have more information for the people at Carnegie Station."

He fitted the antenna to the VHF radio and was talking to the manager of Carnegie Station. Don was told that he saw that vehicle go through late in the afternoon in a cloud of dust and noise. He was thankful for the information and he had already called the police in Laverton to check that they reach there. Don signed off and put the set on standby.
He unpacked the satellite dish and had it set up in less than five minutes. He put a call through to Macy at home. She and the kids are fine and everything is great. Cyril Coles called to see if he could find out where they went, but she didn't say. Don told her of their experiences so far but neglected to mention the red Range Rover. That would only cause her grief. There were no messages for him or Ted and after a few minutes he disconnected the call. He dismantled

the satellite dish and packed away all of the gear which he had used.

“That’s modern communication for you, Ted. All done in just a few minutes and as good a reception as if you were in the house next door.”
“Yes, old chap. Things have come a long way since the pedal radio,” replied Ted.

By this time it was approaching dark and Don cooked up a quick meal on the fire, which Ted had started. They finished this off with a glass of port, which Ted had bought with him.
They sat at the fire talking of the day’s events and planning tomorrow’s before they headed off to bed. They unrolled their swags, crawled in and were asleep before Ted could find the Southern Cross and its pointers.

Kalgoorlie Western Australia, 6th April

Alec and Artie entered the back door of the station at the same time. Both were at work early this morning as they had feeling that it was going to be an exciting and busy day.
The morning paper was on the counter was they entered showing some details of yesterday's events on the front page. It told of the burnt out van and asked for further assistance to be given to the police to assist with their investigation.

Alec had a note on his desk, which annoyed him no end. The suspect who they had been holding had been bailed during last evening, against the discretion of the station's senior officer.
A solicitor from Sydney arrived on the seven o'clock flight from Perth and had Rich Menzies out of the cells in fifteen minutes. But, one thing in Alec's favour was that Rich Menzies was required to visit this police station every day.

The team was already for Alec in the squad room and he was quick to tell them of the new information and the news of the bailed suspect.
Ted, the officer in charge of forensics, handed Alec a report. He had done some work since last they spoke.
"My report shows that the engine number of the Ford Transit van corresponded to the chassis number. We found that the vehicle was purchased from one of the wholesalers in Perth three weeks previous. It was

registered and carried Northern Territory license plates. I had spoken to the dealerships' principal and found that the purchaser was one Rich Menzies. The transfer papers had not been completed and he does not show up as the registered owner of the vehicle on the police database."

The senior constable in charge of the DTD began the reports after Alec had asked for them.
"We had started work early this morning in the attempt to contact many of the people who were not in yesterday. We've already had some positive results. The van was seen driving down Hannan Street on the morning of the forth of April at about seven o'clock, turning left into Mile Street. We are checking with people in Mile Street and already have some detail of a rarely used workshop there."
"Great work. Okay give me the address of the workshop and I'll get a warrant to search it." Alec said with much gusto.

After getting the address he sent Artie off to the magistrate to get a search warrant.
Flipping through the telephone reports from last night, Alec found another piece of information. "Listen to this. One of the security blokes from NG, who are under contract to the bank, reports seeing a white van turning from Lane Street onto Hannan Street on the morning of the forth of April at about six o'clock just at the end of his shift. He had been on two days off, fishing or something, and was unaware of the robbery."

The door to door was to continue now with more personnel to dig up more information about the van sightings.
"Okay, team keep up the good work. It looks like we are going to get these blokes today. Keep the information flowing. Thank you.

The meeting disbanded and the teams began their day's work.

About fifteen minutes later, Artie arrived with the search warrant. Alec called in Ted and the three of them drove out to the address to investigate. They found an old workshop with a wide door facing the street. It had no markings on the building except for the picture of a small scorpion painted on the door.

"That's interesting, Artie, do you know of any local group who uses that insignia?"
"No Alec, that's a new one to me too."
As the sliding bolt was padlocked, he took hold of the sledge hammer, and swung at the door. After several well-aimed swings, the door finally gave in and they were able to gain entry.
In the workshop were some hand tools, pre-cut pine boards, a tin of nails, tins of engine oil, containers and some camping gear. The sort of thing that you would find in any bloke's shed but nothing of any great significance to this case.

"Not much chance of fingerprints here Sarge," said Ted, "this old timber really soaks up the body oil. But

we'll bag up the rest of this stuff and have a close look at it."
Artie took a camera from his vehicle and took some photos of the shed, inside and out. He also took a few a close-up shots of the insignia on the door. After an hour they left the workshop.

Once back at the station the digital photos were downloaded and put onto the database. This is accessed by the other local stations and officers. Fifteen minutes had passed when Alec got a call from the officer in Menzies.
"Alec, I just bowsing the database on this case and saw the new information of that insignia on the door of your workshop. We've got one here too. I don't know if this is significant but I thought it was worthwhile to let you know."
"Thanks for that! Have you had a close look at the shed?" Alec asked
"Yeah, but the door is locked. Do I break it down or get a warrant?"
"Get a warrant as fast as you can, do a preliminary investigation, don't touch anything and let me know, just as soon as you can. Please treat this as most urgent! Thanks for being on the ball," Alec said as he hung up the phone.
Turning to Artie he said, "Drop what you're doing and get up to Menzies as fast as you can. Let me know what's up there in that shed. I'll bet that is what we've been waiting for."

Artie left the station and was on the Goldfields Highway to Menzies in ten minutes. The one hundred and thirty kilometres should take him less than an hour to complete.

Senior Constable Ted Evens, the officer in charge of forensics, entered Alec's office.
"Sarge, we found some good fingerprints on the tools but there is no match with anything on the Western Australian database. Can you access the Sydney or AFP database for a match?"
"Thanks Ted. There's the terminal, I'll log in for you and away you go." Alec logged into the Sydney database and left Ted to do the search and see if he could find a match.

Alec spent some time going through the reports from the telephonists yesterday and last night. Most of the reports either have been followed up with no result or are currently being followed up. He found an interesting report on someone seeing a small truck driving up Mile Street and turning right into Hannan Street at about seven o'clock on the morning of fourth April. The person making the report, a Mr Leppington, knows most of the people who use the workshops in that street and the two men in that small truck were from out of town.
He phoned the senior constable in charge of DTD.
"Senior, I am reading the reports from last night and see there's one from a Mr Leppington. Have you read that?"
"No Sarge, we've been a bit busy this morning. Is it interesting?"
"You betcha." Alec told him of the context of the report. "I suggest that you should get some more

information from Mr. Leppington. I reckon that it'll be a good lead there."
"Okay Sarge, I'll do that myself. I'll call him now and get onto it straight away."
"Good one, Senior." Alec felt confident that the senior constable could get the required information from Mr. Leppington. It'd be interesting if there was a tie in of the transit van and the small truck but he couldn't see it yet.

The desk phone rang and Alec answered. It was Artie on the other end of the radio with the message being relayed to him by the radio operator.
"Alec, you'll love this. The insignia on the door is an exact copy of the one we found yesterday. Inside we found a small Mazda two tonne truck, which has a false floor but is empty. Ted is going over it for prints now. There has been another vehicle parked inside here, alongside the truck. There is also some oil containers, an old fridge in the corner, some pieces of old mining equipment and some camping stuff. The old mining gear hasn't been here very long. Looks like a recent storage place."
"Alright Artie, have a very good look at everything and log it down. Get all the pictures and details that you can. Before you leave the scene, seal it off and tape it up. Anything which you think may be used as evidence, bag it and bring it in too." After a short pause, "Is there anything else, Artie?"
"That's it for now; see you in about three hours."

Alec made directly for the Boss's office.

Kalgoorlie Western Australia, 6th April

“’Morning, Boss. I think we may have some positive leads in this gold robbery. We’ve just found a small truck in a shed in Menzies, which fits the description of a truck seen at the intersection of Mile and Hannan streets on the morning on the fourth. We haven’t worked out how this all comes together yet and Artie will be away another two hours yet.”
“Alright Alec, That’s good news. As soon as we get Artie’s and Ted’s information, let’s have a meeting and go over the evidence and brainstorm the details. We will probably come up with some details to work out their modus operandi.”
“Yes Boss, it seem to me, at this stage anyway, that the two blokes who knocked off the bank, drove to the Miles Street shed, changed vehicles, drove to Menzies, changed vehicles and got away. What I can’t understand is why go to Menzies? The shortest way to Sydney is down to Norseman and across the Nullarbor.”
“Alec, from what evidence that you presented so far, I would have to agree with your assumptions. Let’s get that brainstorm session under way and we’ll see what we can deduct from that.”

Alec went back to his office via the front desk and said to Connie, “I’ll be in for lunch today Connie, could you add mine to the order please.”
“No worries, Sarge. What about Artie, will he be in?” she asked.
“He’ll be back but a bit late for lunch. He’s out at Menzies gathering information. He’ll get his on the way back”

Once in his office, Ted had just found a match for a set of prints on the hammer found at the workshop in Miles Street. "Sarge, the prints on the hammer are a positive match for a Michael Shaun Dunraven from Sydney. He has form for petty crime. Arrested five times but not convicted of any crime. They believe that he has been involved in shoplifting, car theft, handbag robbery, illegal credit card use, breaking and entering, possible robbery with violence, possible bank hold-up. He seems to be a pretty slick customer."
"Good work, Ted. Now we can start putting some names and faces together. I'll get onto Sydney and see what they can tell us."

One of the junior officers who had been working with the telephones came into Alec's office.
"Sarge, I've been doing some checking and it seems that both the workshop in Miles Street and the shed in Menzies have been rented for the last two months by a Mr. Maurice Westerly. He lives in a caravan park in town."
"Very good work, constable. Have you anything on the styrene panels yet?"
"Not yet Sarge but one of the others has been calling all the hardware shops in town. I'll get her to come to see you if you like."
"Yes please. Just as soon as you can, I'd like to be up to date on all of this information now. You can bring in Mr Maurice Westerly, so he can assist us with our enquiries."
"Okay Sarge, I'm on my way." He was quite pleased with himself to be the one to give the Sarge good information.

Kalgoorlie Western Australia, 6th April

Just two minutes later, one of the female officers entered his office with the details of the inquiries into the styrene panels. She took a seat opposite Alec at his desk.

“Sarge, many styrene panels have been sold of the same size lately. Most of them to the ice company. Some to the fridge repair bloke and some to the fibreglass fabricators. Three weeks ago, a small man bought two sheets from Mitreknot Hardware in Miles Street. They don’t have any further information on the man; he paid cash and carried them away in a small truck. That’s all I’ve been able to gather at this stage.”

“Excellent work, constable. This small man in the truck is of extreme interest to us at this stage. Go down to Mitreknot Hardware and talk to the salesman who made the sale, the storeman who loaded the truck etcetera and get as much information of the truck, the bloke, the panels as you can.”

“Okay, Sarge. I’ll get onto it right now.” She got up from the chair and walked out of the office just as Alec’s lunch arrived.

He spent some time reading all of the information, which had just come to him and devoured this with his lunch. By the time he had finished eating, Artie had returned and was in the chair opposite at Alec’s desk.

“I’ve left the officer at Menzies doing a door to door, to find out any movements of vehicles around the shed up there. He’ll let us know of his results this afternoon. I told him it was of extreme importance. I’ve lifted some good fingerprints off the door lock and Ted is looking at those now.”

“Excellent, Artie. We’ll go to the Boss’s office in an hour or so and have a brainstorming session with the details that we have at hand and see what we can come up with. The boss thinks it’s a good idea.”
“Alright, I’ll have some prints done of the photos that we took of the truck and insignia and we can view those together as well.”

Ted entered the office with an air of excitement.
“Sarge, those prints which Artie just gave me, match those taken from the hammer of the Miles Street workshop. They belong to the same bloke, Michael Shaun Dunraven from Sydney.”
“Hey, great work guys! It seems some of our loose ends may be getting tied together.” Alec exclaimed.

The front desk called to say that Mr Maurice Westerly was ready in the interview room. “Artie, come with me. This could be interesting.
They entered the interview room and found Mr Maurice Westerly to be a small, man with a dark tan. They introduce themselves and began asking some questions after making the man comfortable with a cup of coffee.”
“Mr Maurice Westerly also known as Maurie West. Maurie, we’re hoping you can help us with our enquiries into the recent bank robbery. Have you driven a small truck around town in the last few months?”
“Yep!” was his answer.
“Maurie, we know you have rented two workshops, one in Miles Street, Kalgoorlie and one in Main Street, Menzies. What do you do with these workshops?”

"I let them out to a bloke who paid me in cash." He told them
"We have information that leads us to believe that you have been using some styrene foam sheets lately. Can you tell us what you've used these for?"
"I got them for the same bloke who uses the sheds. He paid cash for them too!"
"Perhaps you can tell us about this bloke. Who is he? Where can we find him to talk to him?"
"He told me his name was Albert Macintosh. He always called me so I don't know any more about him."
"Where did you leave the truck when it was last used?"
"It was parked in the workshop in Miles Street just a couple of days ago."
"Is that the shed with the scorpion painted on the door?"
"Yeah. Funny that. It was painted on only last week. I don't know nothin' about that."
"Okay Maurie, that will be all for now. Thank for your cooperation, we may need to talk to you again soon, so please make yourself available by not leaving town." Alec completed the questioning and they left the room.

"Okay Artie, now we'll collect Ted and go to the boss's office for our brainstorming session. This new information is starting to make sense."
As they were passing the front desk, Richard Arnold Menzies was reporting in for the day.
"'Afternoon, Dick." Alec said in a friendly voice. "Just a quick question. What happened to the plates that came off the transit van?"

Dick looked almost frightened. It seemed to him that these coppers knew more than was good for him. He didn't answer but it wasn't necessary. Alec already had his answer but he didn't know how the Northern Territory plates would be used.

They got settled into Collin's office and began by bringing up all the details that they had at the time. "Righto, people. It seems to me that we have a highly organised team at work. They set out several months earlier and get a mole into the local Security Company who does some background work. That's Richard Arnold Menzies. He hires a couple of sheds from a local who likes the cash. He buys a van in Perth for the main part of the robbery. Here we also see that he bought a small truck from out of town. That's the one that you found at Menzies, Artie. So far it all fits together to that point. Put your minds into gear. They have just arrived at the shed in Menzies and offloaded the bullion onto another vehicle. Now here's two questions; what vehicle and what direction are they taking?" Collin put the scene together rather well and the small team began to work out the next details from what was already known.

"I've been out here in the goldfields for ten years and as you know, there's just three ways to go. The type of vehicle depends on the direction. If I were going to backtrack and head across the Nullarbor, I'd have another small truck. This would fit in with the many vehicles on that road. On the other hand, if I was to travel overland to Sydney, I'd have the most popular vehicle that your see in that part of the country, a

Landcruiser, probably with tarp over a frame on the back of it," Alec started out.
"That's fine. Now think which would you choose; go across the Nullarbor or across the desert?" Collin asked.
Ted said that he would get to Sydney by the quickest route possible. The Nullarbor.
Artie agreed with Ted. The fastest way would be the safest.
Alec was standing by the map of Australia on Collin's office wall and said, "Well after you think about it, that is what we would first think. How about this scenario? They headed across the dessert via the Great Central Road to Yulara then on the Plenty and Donohue Highways to Boulia and down to Sydney from there. Ten to fourteen days at tourist speed. In fact become tourists."
None of the others liked this scenario because of the time delay.
"If they had gone by the Nullarbor, they would be almost in Sydney as we speak. But if they had gone through the centre at tourist speed they may be close to the Western Australian/ Northern Territory border," Ted pointed out.
"Well in either case, they are out of or soon will be out of the state. This then becomes an investigation for several states or the Australian Federal Police," Collin pointed out.

None of them liked the idea of having another police service take on their job. They were proud of what they had achieved to date.

“We must answer ourselves this question in the next ten minutes. When do we call in assistance?” Collin put to the small team.

They were consumed with this question for a few seconds.
Alec was the first to speak; “I think we should do it now and cover the escape routes as we know them. Until we have a description of the vehicle, it is going to be a big job of searching every vehicle that uses those roads.”
“I think that by the look on your faces that you all agree with that, so I’ll get onto the other states right away. Until I get details of who will be doing what, keep up with your investigation. We need all the help we can get on this”.

The team left Collin’s office and he contacted the relevant authorities. He also called the Commissioner of Police in Perth Central and advised him of the day’s events and their decision to ask for assistance.

They entered Alec’s office and found a fresh report lying on his desk. The officer in Menzies has some unsubstantiated reports of a mustard coloured Landcruiser with a tarp over the back near the shed in Menzies around ten o’clock on the forth. It was seen leaving the shed and heading north on the Goldfields Highway.
Alec was onto the radio operator immediately and got connected to the officer Menzies, who was on patrol in his car. “We need that information substantiated as soon as possible, do you need any assistance?”

"No Sarge, there's only fifteen houses in town and I'll have those covered in an hour."
"Okay, but don't let us down, this is most impartment." The connection was closed.

One of the traffic patrol officers who is involved with escorting oversized loads around the goldfields district, phoned into Alec's office.
"We were escorting a wide load towards Leonora on the morning of the forth and there was a mustard coloured Landcruiser. It went past too fast. It collected a white roadside marker post and the driver nearly lost control of the vehicle on the shoulder."
"Good work, constable. Any other information, rego etc." Alec asked.
"Yeah, Sarge, the bloke on the CB radio didn't sound like a local. Easter-stater, I'd say. The rego was 1BAT.44776. I recorded it because I was going to send him a brochure on *SAFE DRIVING IN THE BUSH*. I haven't been back to the station yet to follow up on it, Sarge."
"Okay, thanks for the details, we'll follow up for you and get some details." Alec put down the phone.

Before he was able to ask Artie to get onto it, he was at the terminal searching for that registration number. After several minutes, he had an answer.
"Alec, that rego number belongs to a Mazda 2 tonne truck. The same one that we found at the Menzies shed. The engine number matches."
"Bingo!" Alec shouted excitedly. "So it seems they went via the desert. Now we need to work out a plan

of attack and try to get these blokes before they cross the border. Let's try and keep this thing local."

He immediately picked up the phone and dialled the boss's number. He told him of the new development. "So now we have a description: mustard coloured Landcruiser Ute with tray back and canvas cover. Two men, one by the name of Michael Dunraven, the other as yet unknown."

The team was assembled in the squad room and Alec and Artie brought them up to speed with the latest information. All the reports of today's activities were brought in and each of the officers in charge of each section gave a brief report.
"The boss will be holding a press conference shortly to put this new information out so the perpetrators can be apprehended. Thank you everyone for your work today, now we are getting close." Alec concluded.

By now the news of the robbery had spread to the national television and newspapers and the local reporters had a monopoly on the news as it unfolded. The local reporters from the regional and national television stations, local and national radio and newspaper were at the press conference, which lasted fifteen minutes. They were all asking many questions but Collin gave them the necessary detail and asked if they could request that the public be on the outlook for the vehicle and not to approach it as the occupants may be armed and are to be considered dangerous.

Kalgoorlie Western Australia, 6th April

The boss called Alec and Artie into his office after the conference had concluded and they covered all the points of the day's activity.
"Boss, we'd better get the boys at Laverton, who cover that area, to keep a tight watch on the road traffic. Can they set up a road block?" Alec asked him.
Collin picked up a clip board and studied it for a few seconds then replied, "Problem there, Alec. These officers are out on their monthly patrol. But there is the Aboriginal Liaison Office at Warburton, we will advise him. I'll get Laverton to set up that roadblock and suspend other patrol duties. If they can set this up tonight or in the morning, early, then we may have a chance."

Collin considered several options before he continued, "Alternatively, if I send you two out there to the border with four other officers from here, you could be there by eight in the morning if you average ninety kilometres per hour. The Laverton team would be your back up." He watched their faces as he talked. He knew it was a big ask. "It's a pity the helicopter is out of town. It'd mean non-stop and fast driving on bad unsealed roads. Can you do it?" he finished.
"Yes, boss. Give me the two new V8 Landcruisers and I'll get a team together. We'll need to organise fuel as those roadhouses close at five o'clock. We'll just have to get some sleep as best we can." Alec replied. As he was speaking he looked at Artie and who was nodding his head in agreeance.

Alec raced back to the squad room, as the team he wanted would still be there. After he asked the question he had to turn down five volunteers, as there were too many. He selected his team and they immediately collected the gear they would need. Flak jackets and automatic firearms were issued at the direction of the station commander.

They were ready to leave by seven thirty.

The two vehicles drove out of town with sirens wailing and lights flashing in the attempt to cover the twelve hundred kilometres distance in time to apprehend the bank robbers before they reached the border.

It was going to be a close call.

As they drove towards Menzies they picked up the local news report on the radio.

"There has been some new development in the saga of the Gold robbery in Kalgoorlie on the fourth of this month. The white Ford Transit van which was discovered by police had been extensively burned but gave police some clues to the identity and modus operandi of the bank robbers.
They changed vehicles after the robbery and were seen in Menzies later that day in a mustard coloured Landcruiser Ute with a dark green tarpaulin covering the back. Police are asking that anyone with information of the vehicle to report to them immediately. Do not attempt to approach the vehicle or the occupants as they may be armed and are to be considered extremely dangerous. They are expected to be travelling east on the Great Central Road".

"That sounds good to me. Not all of the information but enough to be of great use," Alec said.
The first three hundred and fifty kilometres was on sealed roads and they travelled at speeds up to one hundred and forty kilometres per hour. This will allow them to slow down on the bad sections of road and still maintain their arrival time.

The high frequency radio call signal sounded and the boss's voice said, "Alec we have a vehicle from Laverton to assist you. They will be waiting at the roadhouse to travel with you. Good luck."
"Thanks boss. The more help, the better chance we have. I just hope that we've picked this right."
"So do I." The boss signed off and the radio was quiet.

They drove into the roadhouse at Laverton right on eleven thirty. The other team was waiting and all vehicles refuelled ready for the next section to Tjukayirla Roadhouse. Their ETA there was one o'clock in the morning.

The going was tough on the unsealed section. Although most of the road was good, at the crests it was very rough and several times the vehicles became airborne. Sleep was not possible and every hour they needed to stop for a change of drivers, as it was hard work driving at that speed at night on these roads.

They lost count of the number of kangaroos that were hit by the vehicles. Fortunately there was no other traffic to contend with.

After refuelling at Tjukayirla Roadhouse the road conditions became worse and they were forced to slow to seventy kilometres per hour. The road was just too rough to maintain a higher speed with the degree of safely that was required.

Bakers Creek, Great Central Road, Western Australia 6th April

It was a cloudless sky this morning and the temperature was climbing by the time that Gordon handed Betty her cup of tea in bed.
"Thanks dear, that doesn't happen very often!" exclaimed Betty, a little surprised.
"I know, but there were no clouds to give us a colourful sunrise, so I thought I'd let you sleep for a while longer."

Gordon had been up for some time, looking around the campsite. There was a small dry creek-bed within a hundred metres and he was looking in the sand at the colourful stones. Most of them are quartz and Gordon suspects that there may be some gold in the area. He has no experience with the gold industry with the exception of several prospectors who would come into his hardware shop for a few items but he began to fantasize. He had heard of several people doing well with metal detectors but had never taken the time to get involved himself.

By the time he returned to the motorhome the sun was well up, so he made the tea for Betty who was just stirring. She was sleeping a little more comfortable lately. The injuries of her fall were healing. She considered that she must be getting old, as the pain and discomfort from such a small fall had caused so much discomfort that had lasted for these last few days.

Bakers Creek, Great Central Road, Western Australia 6th April

While Betty was having her early morning cuppa, Gordon spent some time checking the motorhome's mechanicals. He laid a ground sheet under the vehicle and had a look around. There appears to be no problems. The dual wheels at the rear of the vehicle had no stones between them. He was concerned about this because there were a few large stones on the road near some of the creeks and stones between dual wheels can cause unwanted and unnecessary problems.

"Breakfast is on the table, dear," Betty called from the motorhome's kitchen, "or we can have it outside on the table if you'll set it up for us, please."
"No worries, dear. I'll have it ready by the time you bring the stuff outside." Gordon responded.
They enjoyed their cooked breakfast of bacon, eggs and toast once a week and Gordon was pleased that she had chosen today for the meal.
During the meal they talked about the cave visit yesterday and the old aboriginal man and scenery that they had driven past.

After they had completed their meal, Gordon packed away the small table and chairs while Betty did the washing up. He closed the windows and had completed his chores at the same time as Betty. After warming up the engine for several minutes, he turned the motorhome around and headed back along the track to the road. Turning north-east again, Gordon had the sun in his eyes and needed to shade them for the first fifteen minutes of driving. The windscreen had collected a few bugs yesterday and he had failed to clean them off. He made mental note to himself that tomorrow morning he must not forget to clean the windscreen so he can see more comfortably.

The dirt road here was undulating and then become hilly. The surface was still good, although not as comfortable to drive on, as it had been earlier. The country seemed to be dry but this was before the winter period, which was about to break in four or five weeks. This would be pretty country to travel through then, thought Gordon.

After about an hour and a half of driving, Gordon pulled into a small clearing beside the intersection of the Gunbarrel Highway. The sign-post said Tjirrkarli Community. The dust caused by the movement of a vehicle recently still hung in the warm dry still air. Obviously, someone had just come down the road. From the wheel marks that it made Gordon could see that it headed east towards Warburton. Betty made them a cuppa and they drank this while walking around the bush looking at the various shrubs and grasses.

"I hear this can be very pretty country after the rain. There are many everlastings and other small flowers that can form a pretty carpet," Betty said.
"Yeah, that's right, dear. We'll need to come back this way after the rains so we can compare the different seasons," replied Gordon.

While walking around they could see some unusual marks in the sand.
"What do you think made the marks in the sand Gordon?" Betty asked.

Bakers Creek, Great Central Road, Western Australia 6th April

"I don't know for sure," Said Gordon as he bent down for a closer inspection, "but I would say that they may be camel's hoof prints. I've never seen them before, but from what I've read this sure looks like them."
"Well if that's the case, dear, there must have been a good many of them pass this way recently. There are tracks everywhere. Like twenty or more." Betty told him after she had a closer inspection.
They wandered around for a while and they could see where some of the scrubby plants had been eaten off.
"They must like this country, with the abundance of feed for them." Gordon said. Betty mumbled her agreeance with him.

They are back on the road heading east again and in the distance up ahead they could see the beginnings of some hills. Betty checked her map and said, "There are a lot of hills shown on the map to the east of Warburton, Gordon. It'd be good to camp out there amongst them for the night."
"I don't think our permit allows us to deviate that far from the highway, Betty, but if you like we'll check with someone at Warburton just to make sure and then we can make up our minds. How does that sound?"
"That'll be fine dear. You always seem to know the right thing to do." Betty replied.

Having made that comment, she cast her mind back to the first day of this trip and what they had talked about when he found that purse with the money. She still wasn't sure that they had done the right thing. But then again we did have that trouble back in Geraldton with the business and what is done is done! She cast these thoughts from her mind and sat back in the comfortable seat and watched the passing scenery. After travelling for another half an hour, they could see that they were approaching a settlement.

“Warburton coming up, Betty. We’ll stop here for a fuel top up and talk to someone in authority about those hills for you.”
They drove over Warburton Creek that crossed the road by way of a floodway and made their way on the sealed road to the service station. Gordon could see that the diesel fuel bowser was enclosed in a steel cage. As was the avgas pump so he parked close to that. There was no bowser for petrol. The bowser was locked with a padlock and Gordon thought that this was rather unusual so he walked over to the roadhouse. When he was inside he asked the girl behind the counter if she could pump some diesel for him as he wanted to fill up the tank.

“No wurries, luv. I’ll get lazy Max for yu.” She replied. She turned toward the door leading to the back of the shop and yelled at the top of her voice MMMAAAXXX.” He obviously didn’t hear so she yelled again a little louder. “MMMAAAXXX, some bloke wants diesel!” Just a second or two later, “Okay” came the reply from well outside.

Shortly Max, wearing grubby mechanic’s overalls, walked in from out the back and seeing Gordon at the counter motioned for him to follow. He unlocked the cage and then the bowser and began pumping diesel fuel into the motorhome’s fuel tank, from which Gordon had removed the cap.

"My wife's a bit taken with those hills out to the east, do you know if the permit allows us to drive out there." Gordon asked him.
"Mate. Now, you wouldn't wanna take this luvly vehicle on dem roads. Day are just not for dis vehicle. You'd get stuck in all the creek crossings. Now if you had a rig like that one," he pointed to a Mustard coloured Landcruiser Ute with a canvas cover on the back which has just pulled up off to the side, "ya won't have a problem. Nah, mate stick to the road. Even that gets interestin' at times," he said in his broad outback drawl. "As for the permits, ya could ask Nick up at the Community Centre. Nick's the local Aboriginal Liaison Officer with the local cops. There's not much that goes on around here that he don't know about."

The pump's nozzle trigger switched off and Max withdrew it from the fuel tank opening and hung it up on the bowser. "There yu go, mate, she's full. Just pay Maureen in there eighty-five bucks and you'll be sweet. Now don't forget about Nick and dem hills will ya. Or ya missus'll be onto ya!" he said with a smile and a wave as he walked around the outside of the building towards the back, once again.

Gordon said thanks and walked back into the roadhouse and passed the girl a one hundred-dollar bill.
"Max said eighty five dollars, Maureen." He said to the girl behind the counter.
"No, he didn't, mate. Just get it right." She said with a cheeky grin. "He woulda said eighty-five BUCKS, luv. But no worries, mate she'll be right."

Gordon grinned as he felt that he had been part of a constant joke between the two of them. He passed her the cash acknowledging the joke. Betty had come inside as well and they lashed out and bought themselves an ice-cream and a can of soft drink each.

He told her that they would need to go to the police station to get information about the hills. He saw two men from the mustard coloured Landcruiser enter the building and saw one of them was the bloke he had spoken to, while waiting back at the roadworks. Gordon acknowledged him when he glanced his way and the man gave a brief nod as he saw Gordon. He didn't come over to them but stayed with his mate at the counter talking to Maureen.

With their ice-creams and drinks finished, they walked out to their motorhome and drove back onto the road again and turned off at the sign which pointed to the Community Centre. This was several hundred metres along the road.

Parked in the carpark was another Landcruiser Ute but with a heavy-duty trailer attached behind. This looked somewhat familiar to Gordon but at this time he couldn't place the connection. Must be from Geraldton though, he thinks, possibly one of his old customers. He swung around on the road and parked beside the other vehicle. As he was getting out of the driver's door, two men were coming out from the front of the building. He recognised the shorter of the two but the taller bloke looked a little "well to do" in his opinion.

Bakers Creek, Great Central Road, Western Australia 6th April

"Betty, that's Don King. He was a good customer of ours at the *Mitrebox*," Gordon exclaimed to Betty.
"Of course it is dear. I don't know who his mate is, though but he's coming this way so we'll probably soon find out."
"Hello, Don. Good to see you again," Gordon said extending his hand in warm greeting to Don.
"G'day, Gordon and Betty. I bet you're having a great time relaxing while you're travelling now that you've sold that business of yours. Oh, by the way, this is a partner of mine, Ted Walsh. Ted this is Gordon and Betty from Geraldton. They used to own the *Mitrebox Hardware* shop just down the road." Ted shook the hands of Gordon and Betty, saying he was pleased to meet them, in his polished voice.
"Don, we've never had such a great time as we are having right now. Without those pressures of the business we are relaxed, our blood pressure is way down and we are totally enthralled with this country out here. We even spent some time down the cave at Peegull, the other day. It was quite an adventure for us," Gordon told them.
"Well you've certainly picked a great time of the year to see this part of the country. Usually it's pleasantly warm days with cold nights for sleeping. Gets a bit hot later on though," Don told them.

While Gordon was talking to Don, Betty and Ted had wandered off to the motorhome and she was showing him the inside. He took some photos of it "for future reference Madam" he'd said.
Very pleasant chap thought Betty as they stepped out of the motorhome again.

Bakers Creek, Great Central Road, Western Australia 6th April

"Perhaps you can help us Don; we're interested in going through the hills to the east of here. What do you know about them?" Gordon asked of Don.
"Gordon, don't take this vehicle through there, it very rough country. You'd only get a kilometre or two before turning around but ask Nick inside, he has more local knowledge than I do. He was born and grew up here, and knows this area like the back of his hand." Don told him.
"Okay, we'll do that. Thanks for the tips and it's been great to catch up with you again, Don, Ted." Gordon said as he shook the hands of both men.

The two men turned and went to their own vehicle. Gordon and Betty walked into the Community Centre and stood by the front counter. While they were waiting, they looked around the room taking in all of the posters of missing and wanted persons. After a minute or so, an Aboriginal chap in police khaki uniform came in from the backroom.
"Good morning, folks. How can I help you?" he asked them in a more educated voice than they both expected. He looked exactly like the locals but spoke very well and pleasantly. Obvious he is not only well educated but wants to be helpful too.
Gordon could see by his name badge that this was the "Nick" whom he was told to come and see. "Good morning, Nick, I'm Gordon and this is my wife Betty. We're wondering if we are permitted to travel through or near the hills to the east of here. Betty would like to have a closer look, even stay around there for several days." Gordon said.
"Hello Gordon and Betty," came the reply.
"Unfortunately, your standard travel permit doesn't

allow you to deviate from the main road. So, I'm sorry to be the one to dampen your enthusiasm, but you'll need to keep to the main road, unless of course you have obtained a Miners Permit. This does have some bearing on where you can go but you'll still need to get permission from the local Aboriginal land council before you can proceed." Nick told them.
"We knew about the permit to travel through here and we've got those but we don't have a miner's permit," Gordon told him. He turned to Betty, "do we need to go to the trouble of getting a miner's permit, dear?" He asked her.
After some consideration, Betty replied. "No dear, I think we can give it a miss this time. Perhaps later on we'll ask a few more questions and get a bit better organised, before we leave," she told Gordon with a degree of sarcasm in here voice.
"Yes dear". Gordon knew when it was best not to continue with that line of conversation. It helped to keep the peace. Anyway, it was a valid point, he agreed. They should have found out more about things while planning the details of the trip.
Never mind. We're here now and we'll keep on going.
"Thanks, Nick for your assistance. Do you police this area by yourself?" Gordon asked.
"No, Gordon, I'm just the Aboriginal Liaison Officer. The Sergeant and the others are from Laverton but I expect them to be here tomorrow afternoon. This is a big district that we have jurisdiction over and each month the team is out of town for three or four days at a time." Nick told them.
"Well keep up the good work, Nick. We may see you again one day," Gordon said.

Chapter 13

Bakers Creek, Great Central Road, Western Australia 6th April

"'Bye Nick," Said Betty. The two of them turned and walked out of the police station back into the sunshine again.

It was lunchtime and Gordon drove the motorhome back into the main area of the town and finding a parking area near a park, deciding to have lunch before travelling on.
They watched the local kids playing in the street and the park. School must be out for lunch Betty thinks.

Looking around town, she could see that it was similar to the other towns, which they had passed through, but there seemed to be a higher level of cleanliness here. There were a few pieces of paper being buffeted by the gentle breeze but there was no evidence of rubbish, which had been lying around for a long time. Obviously, someone has been busy keeping the township tidy. It was refreshing to see.

With the sun high in the sky, they headed out of town travelling in a north easterly direction. The Great Central Road mostly follows the valleys though the hilly area and Betty could see some of the details of the hill and valleys which she had wanted to. It was a pity that they could not get amongst the hills proper and from what she could see; they are missing out on some great scenery.
"Looks like you'll be able to get your wish anyway dear," said Gordon as he changed into a lower gear to climb the hill.
"Yes dear," Betty replied. Then checking her map said, "This is the western edge of the Whitby Range. It's quite attractive with those small trees and scrub. In

the valleys you can see the heavier growth so there must be better soil type or even more water for the plants down there."
"Probably a bit of both I would think. There are probably some different birds in this bush too. There seem to be different species as we travel along," Gordon replied.
The road deviates around some of the higher hills and Gordon and Betty are busy looking at the scenery.

The camels have been here since they were imported from Afghanistan during the nineteenth century. They were brought here to assist with the exploration and the opening up of pastoral properties and other interests of that period. Over the years many of the camels had escaped or been let out to fend for themselves. They have developed into many different herds and spread across a wide area of the deserts of Australia. There are several of these herds in the Gibson and Great Victoria Deserts areas. Some of them have been near the roads and have become accustomed to the traffic. Cars, buses, trucks and utes are common to them and they consider them to be just other occupants of the area.

Betty and Gordon had seen sign of a group of camels earlier in the day, so they weren't surprised to see a herd of them alongside the road as the came around a sharp bend just over the brow of one of the low hills.
"Look at all those camels!" exclaimed Betty. "There must be thirty in that herd." She began counting while Gordon stopped the vehicle at the side of the road.

Bakers Creek, Great Central Road, Western Australia 6th April

"I can count thirty two animals all together and there is just one bull amongst them. But aren't the calves beautiful, dear? There are four very young ones."

Gordon was taking in the scene in front of them and yes, he was surprised to see so many camels in one heard.

"I wonder, dear, if these could be the camels that we saw the hoof prints of this morning near the start of the Gunbarrel Highway?" Gordon suggested.

"Well that could be the case, Gordon, we don't know how old those hoof prints were. If they were a day or two old, then this could quite well be that same group," Betty answered as if she had some knowledge of camels and how far they can travel each day.

Betty took out her old camera and began taking a few photos looking out from inside the vehicle.

"Do you think it would be safe to get outside and get some photos a bit closer to them, dear?" Betty asked

"I think it would be wise to stay in the vehicle, dear. You know what they say at the animal parks and so on. 'Always stay in the vehicle.' I think it has something to do with recognition. They recognise the vehicle because they see so many of them. But they rarely see humans walking around and that just might upset them, particularly the bulls. And I don't think we would want to be around an angry bull camel," Gordon answered with some authority.

"But I don't want to hurt them dear, just take a few more photos."

"Yes dear but I am sure that if you were to get out of the vehicle, the old bull would at least become inquisitive and when he is in that state he may do

something unexpected. I think it best if you stay here and we'll watch them for a while."
"Okay dear. I'll do as you ask. You're probably correct anyway. What you are saying seems sound anyway."

They sat in the vehicle for some time watching the camels as they were feeding close to the roadside. Occasionally one or two would wander over to the other side of the road to feed over there.
"They are marvellous animals aren't they Gordon? So majestic in the way that they move. Their big long legs, moving forward at such a leisurely pace."

As they watched one of the calves began bunting its mother in the udder.
"Oh, look. That one is bunting the older one!" exclaimed Betty.
"Just wait and see what happens here."
Then they could see that the calf was suckling from the cow.
"He is just having a feed, dear," Betty said as she saw that the calf was suckling from its mother.

Most of the herd had walked forward of the vehicle now and Gordon started up again and they moved forward very slowly. They were passing some of the slower members of the herd as it had spread out over several hundred metres alongside the road. Gordon was careful not to go too fast or they may baulk and walk in front of the vehicle.
"You can see how easily you can have an accident with these animals, dear. They just walk across the road at will. No road sense at all. I suppose that some

must be injured or even killed with the road traffic." Gordon said.

They came to a small level clearing, several hundred metres ahead of the leaders of the herd and Gordon pulled over.
"Think we can have a cuppa here Betty before we go too far and then we can watch these animals come towards us."
Betty boiled the kettle on the gas stove inside the motorhome and soon they were drinking their tea with some of the scones which are left over from the other day.

The camels were slowly heading their way with more of them crossing over the road. There were several other vehicles on the road but each of them had slowed to a crawl as they drove past.
By the time that the herd had reached their vehicle, they were all on the other side of the road.
"There is something to write in your diary, dear. It's not every day that we wait for a herd of camels to pass our vehicle. They are a marvellous sight aren't they?" Gordon said with some conviction.
"Yes dear, they certainly are. Now I can see the power that they could unleash on us should they become excited. Thank you for letting me watch them for so long a time. It was an experience that I will not forget."

Gordon got the motorhome going again and they travelled along for another hour looking at the scenery change from time to time. The occasional hill and valley showed them the various types of vegetation.

Mostly the vegetation is mulga with the occasional wattle tree in bloom. Sometimes the wildflowers showed themselves in the hollows where there is a greater degree of moisture in the soil.

Gordon had set the vehicle's trip metre when he refuelled and this was showing one hundred and ninety five kilometres.
"We'll try to find a good camping sight within the next five kilometres dear and set up for the night." Gordon suggested to her.

They both kept a look out for a level site on the left side of the road. After a few minutes Betty pointed out a shallow clearing with a good access just ahead. Gordon slowed the vehicle and they pulled in and set up for the night.

The trip tomorrow, if they don't stop for any sightseeing, will take them over the Western Australian / Northern Territory border. Then they can travel onto the Docker River Settlement. They have heard some of the stories of the Docker River settlement and they were looking forward to see if the place really lives up to its reputation.

Great Central Road, Western Australia, 6th April

The sun was well up by the time that Angelo woke. It was quite comfortable in their padded swags and they both overslept again.
This seems to be becoming a habit.

Angelo was the first to wake and he let Mick continue to sleep. There was no hurry as they were going well and he needed to keep mindful of the telephone call to Mr Arnold before they crossed the border. That call would need to be made on the seventh and that's tomorrow. To do this, they would need to call from the Warakurna Roadhouse near the Giles Meteorological Observatory. The mobile telephone does not work out here in the bush and they were not equipped with a satellite service, so they needed to use a public telephone. It would be a more secure option anyway, thinks Angelo.

The Warakurna Roadhouse was about seventy-five kilometres from the border. Mr Arnold would give him the directions for the next leg of their return trip. Of course, should the police suspect them, he would know immediately and would be able to advise them and work out the best action from that point.

There are several options available for the return trip. The best route was via Alice Springs, up the Stuart Highway seventy or eighty kilometres, then onto the Plenty highway. Continue onto the Queensland border.

This then changes to the Donohue Highway to as far as Boulia. Then there were several options once again, each with its own advantages.

Angelo was considering some of these options when Mick woke up with a grunt.
"Wakey, wakey, sunshine. It's a beautiful mornin'! The sun is shinin', the birds are singin', the bugs aren't bitin' and it's time you were out of bed, ya lazy bugger," Angelo exclaimed.
"Shit, mate what are you so bloody excited about? You'd think you were on friggen holidays or something. Lay off me will ya?" retorted Mick in a sleepy voice.
After a minute or so Mick extracted himself from the swag. He was fully dressed, but for his boots.
"I can see you're not going to waste any time today, Mick."
"Sleep in ya clobber and save time. Sounds like a bloody good idea to me. Anyway, what's your problem?"
"I've been going over the details of the return trip and I thought it might be a good idea if we get a couple of ideas out in the open so if something happens, we know what we are doing."
"Sounds bloody good to me. You've treated me like a bloody mushroom, so far. I've been kept in the dark and fed bullshit. It's about time you included me in the plans of this heist," said Mick being quite earnest.

Angelo told him of enough of the details to satisfy his curiosity to as far as Boulia.
"We'll phone the boss again from there and then we'll work out our plan of approach from that point. We

can't make any firm plans on the route that we'll take from there. This depends on whether the cops have a lead on us or not. The boss will have his finger on the pulse and will know what they are doing even before they do it," Angelo told him.

"Okay. That's bloody fine so far. But what happens if the cops are already onto us. What smart-arse plans do you have then?" asked Mick.

"After I phone him tomorrow, that'll be the seventh and then we'll know what the cops know. I don't think they have a clue of what happened, who did it or where we are. But on the off chance that they do, and it looks like they might be closing in at any time, we'll just bury the boxes. The GPS will record the location and we can come back later when the heat's off and pick them up again."

"Sounds a bit like a bloody fairy tale to me. But if you blokes have got this all worked out, then that's fine by me. Just by doin' the job gets me off the hook with the boss. If he can recover the boxes then, that's up to him. That part of the job is nuthin' to do with me," Mick replied and then continued. "What do we do if the cops catch up to us after we've buried the boxes?"

"They won't have anything on us! There'll be no gold on us. So, there'll be no evidence. No bloody worries mate!" exclaimed Angelo.

Mick took all this in and after a while said, "That's fine then, just as long as I'm not going to get caught with this bloody lot."

That seems to have satisfied Mick's curiosity for the time being, thinks Angelo. "I'll get the fire going for breakfast and you can cook if you like, Mick," Angelo suggested.

"Yeah, okay. Bacon and eggs again? Is that all right with you, Angelo?" Mick queried.

"Yeah, that's fine with me, Mick," Angelo said, as he was on his way to collect some more firewood. They wouldn't need a lot of firewood, as there were still coals in the fire from last night's cooking. He gathers an armful of medium sized sticks and placed these by the fire and fed a few onto it to get it going. Mick soon had the billy on and the pan on the flames and appeared to be happy to do his part.

In a few minutes, their breakfast was ready and Angelo handed the plates to Mick to place the meal onto. While they were eating, the billy boiled but Mick left it boiling until he had finished his bacon and eggs.

"Can't allow that spoil this tucker, mate!" exclaimed Mick.

He made the cups of tea and they settled back on their boxes, leaning against the wheels of the Landcruiser.

"Ya know, mate," Mick mused, "I reckon I could get used to this lifestyle. Out here in the big open spaces. No pressures, no phone calls, no bloody TV, no missus, no noisy neighbours to bug ya. Just peace and quiet and relaxing." He let out a satisfying sigh as he finished that sentence.

"Yeah mate, I was looking at that motorhome yesterday and it looks like a good idea to me. I could get one of those and bring the missus and kids out here. That would get them away from some of the problems they've got in Sydney. Things were bad when I was a kid there but I reckon it's got worse. I know the boss makes lotsa cash from the drug trade but I know it harms the kids and I don't want my kids getting mixed up in drugs. I've seen too many

druggies around and I don't want my kids to get into it."
"Be a big change, Angelo. What would you do for income? Have the kids and missus help with a bank job or two?" Mick asked with a grin on his face.
"Don't be bloody stupid! She doesn't know what I do and she never will," Angelo snapped.

He wasn't going to tell Mick but he has a good deal with the boss on this job. He gets to keep a million for this job. Something Mick definitely does NOT need to find out about.
They had finished their tea and Mick was using the last of the hot water to wash the plates. Angelo spends a few minutes under the bonnet of the Ute checking the fluid levels and the belt tension. Everything looks as it should be.

After Mick had stored the cooking and eating gear away, they climbed into the Ute and Angelo turned the key. The starter whirred away but the engine would not start. He released the key and after a few seconds tried again. Still, it would not fire.
"Bugger the thing. Of all the times and places for this type of bloody thing to happen," yelled Angelo, getting frustrated with the vehicle.
"What's the matter with it, do you think?" asked Mick.
"Well I know it needs the glow plugs to heat up in the cold, so perhaps it needs some more time on the glow plugs before I start the bugger," Angelo replied.

He held the key to the glow-plug position and after fifteen seconds turned it to the start position. He held his foot down hard on the accelerator to give it more

fuel. After several seconds the engine fired but was running rough for a while. Angelo sat there with an expression of relief on his face as the engine began to run smoother as it got a warmed up. He could see that there was a big cloud of dirty smoke at the left side of the Ute, near where the exhaust is.
"She's running a bit rough. Probably a bit of dirty fuel we got somewhere," commented Angelo. He looked at the fuel gauge and saw that it was on the quarter full mark.
"There will probably be a mechanic at Warburton so we'll need to get him to check it out for us, before we put more fuel in," Angelo said.

Angelo drove down the short track and back onto the main road again, heading towards Warburton.
After several kilometres, Angelo says, "It is lacking in power, so there must be a problem there somewhere. I'll just have to take it steady till we get to town." He drove along the road at a speed slower than normal. He could only get it to go about seventy-five kilometres an hour. There was a cloud of black smoke behind them whenever he tries to drive faster.
It seemed as though it would take all day to get to the roadhouse at Warburton. After an hour's driving they came to the intersection of the Gunbarrel Highway.

"So far, so good Mick. Now we have just forty kilometres to go till we get there," said Angelo.
"That'd be a bloody relief," replied Mick. "It seems like we'll never get there at this speed."
"Yeah. I hope it's a simple job when we get there too! I don't want to waste time, it'll put us behind on our

schedule and that could create a problem," continued Angelo.

Ahead in the distance they catch a glimpse of another vehicle going the same way. Mostly they could see its dust. This was heavier in the hollows where the breeze hadn't blown the dust away. It was a large vehicle and Angelo thinks that it would be incredible if it was that motorhome which they had already seen on several occasions.
As they approached the settlement, Angelo could see the entrance to the roadhouse and pulled in. He needed to get the fuel system problem sorted out first, so he pulled around the corner and parked off to the side. The motorhome, which they had been following, was at the diesel bowser getting fuel. Angelo switched off the engine and put his hand to his back pocket for his wallet.

It was not there.

"Oh, shit! What else can go wrong? Me bloody wallet's missing! Have you seen it anywhere, Mick?" he asked.
"No mate, you had the bloody thing for the last fuel stop, so perhaps you've lost it somewhere."
Angelo got out of the vehicle, and stood by the door. He scratched his head while he was thinking of his movements and where he may have placed the wallet since he last used it. No, it was always in my back pocket, he tells himself. It had never slipped out before but there was always a first time.

I t may have come out of his back pocket.

It could be under there seat.He flipped the lever, which allows the back of the driver's seat to swing forward. There was a lot of stuff down there on the floor. There are bits of rag, old bits of paper and an old map. He shuffles these around and found his wallet on the bottom of the pile amongst the dust and grime on the floor. The vibration from the road must have mixed up all of the stuff that sits on the floor under the seat.
"Found it, Mick!" he exclaimed.
"Thank Christ for that. I was beginning to think that we might have to barter some gold for fuel to get us through."
"Don't even think about it! Don't ever say that word! You'll get us bloody stuffed, ya silly bugger!" exclaimed Angelo.
"Yeah, okay, okay. Keep ya bloody hair on. I won't be the one to spill the beans," retorted Mick.

They watched as the motorhome moved and park away from the bowser. After several minutes they walked into the roadhouse. Angelo saw the motorhome couple, Gordon, he thinks his name was. He couldn't remember what the ladies name was but he nodded to them as he entered.
They came up to the counter and Angelo asked, "is there a mechanic around? I've got a bit of a problem with me Landcruiser that I need some help with."
"No worries, luv. I'll get lazy Max for yu!" she replied. Then she turned around and facing the open back door yelled at the top of her voice, " MMMAAAXXX!" After several seconds, there was a feint reply from out the back. "Yeah, I'm comin'."
Presently a bloke in dirty overalls come into the shop

through the back door and approached the two men at the counter.

“What can I do for you blokes?” he asked.
Angelo replied, “We seem to have a fuel problem with the Landcruiser out the side. It’s been going great guns but this morning it was a real bitch to start. Took several goes on the glow plugs and then ran very rough for a while. When we got going, it was down on power and the best speed we could get was just seventy kilometres an hour. Each time I tried to go faster, it just pumps out black smoke.”
“Awright, mate. Let’s ‘ave a look at it and see what we can find for ya!” replied Max. “Bring it around the back and park in the empty car bay. I’ll get onto it in five minutes.”

Angelo walked back to the Ute and after having difficulty starting it again, drove it around to the vacant car bay and switched off the engine. There were several other vehicles in the workshop in various stages of repair. He could see two other mechanics working on one of them. One of the mechanics was Aboriginal.
A few minutes later Max came over to Angelo who had the bonnet locked in the open position.
“First we’ll look at the filter.” He opened the drain cock at the base of the filter and black liquid oozed from it. “Well, mate, it looks like you’ve picked up some dirty fuel somewhere. When was the filter changed last?”
“I dunno, mate. I only got the Ute last week and was told it was just serviced. Being the honest bloke that I

am, I took his word for it. Why, is there a problem?" Angelo responded.
"Sometimes some blokes forget about the fuel system on these. Usually we just need to flush out the fuel lines and fit another filter and you're away," Max told him.
"How long do think it'll be before we can be on the road again, mate?"
"Better give us about an hour and a half, I reckon," replied Max.
"Okay, mate, we'll go and have lunch while you do the job. You do take credit cards don't ya?" asked Angelo.
"Yeah mate! Gold, diamonds, real estate, cash and even credit cards," replied Max with a wry grin on his face.
Angelo was taken aback with this reply and it showed on his face.
"Don't worry, mate. She'll be jake," Max said with a smile. This bloke seems a bit testy, he thinks. I'll have to keep an eye on him.

Mick and Angelo walk into the roadhouse and ordered themselves a hamburger with the lot for lunch. They take a seat near the front door and wait for their order to be made ready. Angelo could see that the motorhome couple has gone but there were another couple of blokes at the corner table.
He was wondering if one of them should stay with the vehicle but after giving this more thought, reckons it is packed pretty well and there is next to no chance of anyone finding their contraband load.

Their meal arrives and they also get a bottle of cool drink from the fridge to have with their lunch. The hamburger was so big that they had to cut them in four before they could eat them.
"That's value for money!" exclaimed Mick between mouthfuls.
"Yeah. Tastes better than your bloody cookin'," responded Angelo.
"Piss off! You'd die of starvation if I didn't cook for ya, mate."

They lounged around in their chairs for several minutes after completing their meal. Then Angelo suggests that they might go out the back and see how Max is progressing with their Ute. As they entered the workshop, there was two mechanics working on their Ute. "How's it goin' mate?" asked Angelo.
"Yeah, not bad, mate. Your tank had some black sludge in the bottom. We've drained that. With ya travelling, the pump has picked it up and stuffed the filter. We've blown out the lines and just fitted a new filter. Then we'll check out the fuel pump's final filter before we prime the system. Give us another ten minutes and she should be sweet mate," the mechanic told him.
"Okay, we'll be back shortly," Angelo told him. They went back into the roadhouse again and sat down to wait for the job to be completed.

They were surprised at the number of people coming and going at the counter. Angelo thought that this was only a small place. But then looking at the people coming and going he could see that about half of them were tourists. This made him feel a bit more at ease,

knowing that they were fitting in with the travelling fraternity that are usually referred to as tourists.
"That's about ten minutes, so let's go and see how the mechanics are going," he told Mick. They once again walked out to the workshop. The younger of the two mechanics was just getting in to start the engine. Mick and Angelo walked around to the front of the vehicle to talk to the other mechanic. Just as they got there, the engine turned over and after a few seconds fired and ran for a minute before it was turned off again.
"That should've fixed ya problem, mate," the mechanic told him. "We'll try it several times more just to make sure that it'll get ya home safely." They stared the engine and it fired first time. They let it run for several minutes, then turned it off and repeated this procedure several times just to satisfy themselves that it was working correctly. Angelo was happy that it sounded as it should and when the mechanic told him, he drove it out to the diesel fuel bowser. The mechanic then filled the tank.
"Just leave her parked there mate and come with me inside and ya can fix up the bill." He told Angelo. They all walked up to the counter. Max came in from the back with a box and a sheet of paper in his hand.
"Here's another filter for ya. I reckon you'll need to change it after you've gone about two hundred kays. Any shit, which gets stirred up, will clog the new filter, so this is insurance for ya," Max told them.
He gave this to the girl behind the counter who after a second or two said, "That'll be two hundred for the job and a hundred and ten bucks for the fuel, thanks luv."
Angelo passed over his credit card and she completed the transaction. She handed him the bill and the receipt and then after saying their thanks, turned and were

about to walk outside when an Aboriginal police officer in khaki uniform came in the door.

Mick froze for a split second. Angelo faltered in his step but both men kept on walking. When they had reached the Ute and got in, they both took their next breath.

"Shit! Me heart is just about to tear itself out of me friggen chest. Why do they always arrive like that? Out of the blue," Mick said a little breathless.

"Buggered if know, mate. But I don't need it to happen again. I nearly shit meself too!" Angelo replied.

Angelo was in the driver's seat once again and he drove carefully out onto the road. They drove passed a park where some kids were playing and then when they cleared the last building, they both seemed to relax.

"That has stuffed up our schedule now, so instead of having plenty of time to spare, we are running behind. Have a look at the map and tell me if we can get to Warakurna before dark?" Angelo asked.

After a while with his addition of the road distance and the calculation of their speed he answered, "If ya stick to ninety kays, you'll be there by an hour after dark," Mick reckoned.

"Well that's okay. If we camp a bit over half way, we should be okay. I've gotta make that call to the boss in the morning. The earlier the better," Angelo responded.

He was powering up a rise when he noticed that the vehicle had lost power again.

Chapter 14

Great Central Road, Western Australia, 6th April

"Seems like that little fuel problem is still with us, Mick! She'd got sluggish again. I'll keep it goin' for a while, then we'll stop and change over the filter." Angelo said as he thought about their situation.
"That mechanic back there said something about a sediment or water trap. Should you empty that out first, mate?" Mick asked him.
"Okay. We'll pull over and drain that first and see what happens from there." Angelo slowed the vehicle and pulled clear of the road. He got out and lifted the bonnet. He knew which thing was the fuel filter, as he watched the mechanic while he was working. Under the filter is a small cock. He turned the handle and saw more black liquid flow from it. When the flow stopped, he closed the cock and operated the priming pump for several strokes. He got back in and started the engine. It seems to be running well so after a few minutes he drove off again.
"That seems to have solved the problem, Mick. We'll save the filter until we absolutely need it. That way we should have a good chance of getting through."
"I hope that's the end of the fuel problems, mate. Or it'll take more time to get to ya phone call. If the cops are onto us, it'd be good to find out as soon as possible, so we can do something about it," Mick announced.
"Yeah, that's right," Angelo responded.

The road was now relatively flat so he didn't need to power up so much and the Landcruiser was running quite well.

They continued driving for another half an hour.

Chapter 14

Great Central Road, Western Australia, 6th April

The sun was getting low in the west and Angelo decided that it was time for them to stop for the night. He had seen several camels in the distance and didn't want to run into any of them by night driving. They hadn't covered as much ground as he would have liked to but this seems to be the best option.

They were in a low depression and this seems to be a good place for a camp. After he had pulled off the road and driven along a rough track for several kilometres, he pull up to standstill.

Angelo began gathering some wood for a fire. Mick was getting the meal prepared. Before he started cooking, Angelo handed him a beer. They sat on a box each and sank the beers without talking. Angelo got off his box and got another beer each for the fridge.
"There's one thing missing from this unit, Angelo," suggested Mick.
"Yeah, what's that?" asked Angelo.
"Table and chairs, ya silly bugger. All we've got to sit on are these storage boxes. Not exactly the most comfortable. And where I eat me meal me legs get burned from the plate that rest on them. I'll have to consider going on strike until we can get this sorted out, mate," Mick said with a cheeky grin on his face.
Angelo looked at him, thinking he might be just a little bit serious but when he saw his grin decided that he was jesting and took the comments in that manner.
"Yeah, bloody good idea. Let's tell the boss that we won't drive any further until we have chairs and a table for our mess room."

After their day it was a good note to finish on.

Great Central Road, Western Australia, 6th April

Mick cooked the meal as the sun was setting. They used a torch to see the last of the meal as darkness had fallen before they had finished eating.
Mick washed the dishes and Angelo dried them and put them back into the storage box.
"The whole day has been a stuff-up. I'm hoping that tomorrow will be uneventful," Angelo said as he turned on the radio and tuned it into the ABC for a news bulletin. It was a little before time and there was music playing, so he sat down on his box again. As the news items began they both tuned their ears to the voice of the newsreader…

"There has been some new development in the saga of the Gold robbery in Kalgoorlie on the fourth of this month. The white Ford Transit van which was discovered by police had been extensively burned but gave police some clues to the identity and modus operandi of the bank robbers.
They changed vehicles after the robbery and were seen in Menzies later that day in a mustard coloured Landcruiser Ute with a dark green tarpaulin covering the back. Police are asking that anyone with information of the vehicle to report to them immediately. Do not attempt to approach the vehicle or the occupants as they may be armed and are to be considered extremely dangerous. They are expected to be travelling east on the Great Central Road".

"Bloody hell!" exclaimed Mick. "That was not supposed to friggen happen. I wonder how the bastards found out that much information in such a bloody short time."

"That van was supposed to have been totally burnt so that that wouldn't happen!" exclaimed Angelo.
"Always the same; rely on someone else and that's the results that ya get. We should've torched it ourselves. That's what I wanted to do but the boss said no, his local man was supposed to take care of it. I wonder what else he has stuffed up."
"Now they know our vehicle and where we are headed. It's only a matter of time," said Mick rather annoyed.
"At least they haven't given out our rego number. We'll change to Northern Territory plates just before we go over the border. That'll help us a lot," surmised Angelo. The only thing is where did these plates come from? Could that dickhead of a local bloke stuff that up too?
"There's a brown tarp in the back, mate. Should we fit that on to cover up the green bastard?" Mick asked hoping to find some solution to their problem.
"Yeah, that's a good idea. We'll get that out and fit it on in the morning. It won't take long, Mick," Angelo told him.

They talked for a while longer covering some of their options but because of the new developments and anguish they were feeling, they both had trouble falling sleep.

Things now were not going according to plan. Firstly the fuel problem that caused them to lose time. The bloke in Kalgoorlie was supposed to have serviced the Ute so that sort of thing would not happen. Next they heard on the radio that the cops know what vehicle they are using for the getaway. Well if you could call it a getaway car. That's usually in a fast car that you dump and torch and take another.

But we have a couple of unplayed cards up our sleeves yet. In the morning we'll change the tarp and fit the Northern Territory numberplates. When we call the boss we'll certainly tell him what sort of dickhead he hired to do the jobs in Kalgoorlie.

Lake Breaden, Gunbarrel Highway, Western Australia, 6th April

Don knew the importance of their meeting with old Billy-The-Lid at Warburton today. He could hold some very relevant information for them to assist with their chances of locating the gold reef that Lasseter reported. There are several discrepancies in the reports that are around and he and Ted are certain that old Billy-The-Lid can help them fill some of these gaps.

He was wide-awake well before the eastern sky began to lighten. He dragged himself out of his swag and after putting on his boots, collected some small sticks to get the morning fire going.

His movement around the camp must have stirred Ted, because he was soon up and around. Ted rolled up both swags and put them onto the Ute. He could see that Don had the fire going well and could also see that he was deep in thought.

"Penny for them, old chap?" he asked Don.

Don looked at him but didn't seem to see him. He was deep in his thoughts of their meeting today. But then he realised that Ted was talking to him.

"Sorry, mate. What did you say?"

"I just said 'penny for them' old chap. You seemed to be deep in thought and I was wondering if I could help sort out whatever it was that was consuming you so," Ted replied.

"Oh, yeah! I was just thinking about how well old Billy could help us today. We've got to be careful how

we ask the questions, because I don't want to offend him in any way."
"I'm sure you will apply all the tact that is necessary, old man. I've seen you with these people before and I'm satisfied that you have the necessary tact to handle the situation in the best possible way," Ted told him.
"Yeah, I've been with this community before but that was quite a few years ago and I don't remember old Billy that well. I hope that with the mention of Lasseter that it will spark his memory. If his memory of that experience was pleasant, we'll be fine. If he was abused or anything like that, we could have a difficult time ahead of us," Confided Don.
"But, old chap, you've got some information and when you put that to him, I'm sure it'll jerk his memory into action."
"I believe that you could be right," he added and after a pause, "again."

The eastern sky was now beginning to lighten and the billy was starting to sing. Ted had taken some sausages from the freezer last night and he had these ready for the pan. Eggs too and the bacon was in the pan waiting for him to put it onto the fire.

"If we go back over the data that we already have, old chap, then we can probably have old Billy fill in the gaps. We do know that Lasseter claims to have been out here in 1897, when he discovered the reef of gold. He reports that it is eleven kilometres long and three and a half metres wide. From 1925 to 1930 he worked as a carpenter, on the Sydney Harbour Bridge. His mate, John Bailey accompanied Lasseter in a further expedition, later in 1930. After about eight weeks

Bailey returned to Sydney but Lasseter continued on with another assistant. It is claimed that Lasseter died or was killed but there is no positive evidence of this. Also there is no proof that his entire journal has ever been found. We find out, just a few weeks ago, that a local Aboriginal, named Billy-The-Lid was part of Lasseter's team in that 1930's expedition. We think that Billy-The-Lid must have been in his early twenties at this time so that would make him about ninety-two or three now. Now the other interesting note is that Lasseter was reported to have been wearing a rough gold nugget on a gold chain around his neck. He claims this to have come from this reef of his. But there is no mention of this in the official records," recited Ted.
"Yeah, that's right. And remember when we saw Dick Manton back there at Sandstone, he said that old Billy-The-Lid had told him of it. Now if this nugget did come from the reef, then perhaps Billy-The-Lid can help us with a more accurate location," Don completed the saga.
"Whoa, old chap, don't burn the sausages." Ted exclaimed.

Don was more occupied with their venture than he was with the job at hand and he quickly removed the pan from the fire. "Not too bad mate, only a little dark on one side. Anyway, charcoal is good for the digestion." He dished the meal on to the two plates and both men sat down to eat their meal.
"A couple of things we don't know for certain are; what was Billy-The-Lid's job with Lasseter and how long was he with him?" pointed out Don.

Lake Breaden, Gunbarrel Highway, Western Australia, 6th April

"Well old chap, I think the answer to those questions will be submitted to us by one Billy-The-Lid. I just hope he is lucid enough to answer the questions that we have for him. After all, he is over ninety," Ted offered.

By the time they had broken camp and were on the road, the sun was just showing on the eastern horizon. Driving into it for the first half an hour was difficult at times. They were on the edge of the Baker Range and the road was undulating but quite drivable. Near Mount Samuel, the road turned south for the next thirty kilometres and then southeast for fifty kilometres. The last section also is the main access road to one of the Aboriginal reserves and was in much better condition than the previous section of road had been. Don was able to get up to ninety kilometres an hour. They reached the intersection with the Great Central Road at about ten o'clock.

"We won't stop for smoko here Ted, I think we'll press on to Warburton and make contact with old Billy-The-Lid. We can have a break after that," Don told him. He continued onto the better-formed road and the last forty kilometres into the township of Warburton was without incident.
"I think we'll start at the roadhouse and ask there if someone can tell us where Billy-The-Lid can be found."

Don drove into the parking area near the roadhouse and he and Ted went inside.

Chapter 15

Lake Breaden, Gunbarrel Highway, Western Australia, 6th April

"G'day, mate! Wot can we do for ya?" was the question that was fired at them from behind the counter by the female attendant.

"G'day," replied Don. "We're looking for an old Aboriginal bloke about ninety, called Billy-The-Lid. Do you know where we can find him, please?" Don asked kindly.

"Please, huh? We don't get much of that aroun' 'ere mate. What's yer business with old Billy?" was the unexpected reply.

"It seems we have a common friend and he has asked us to call on him and say 'G'day', on our way through," Dan said.

"Ya could try at the local Community Centre, just around the corner. They would have the best idea, mate. Say that Maureen sent ya."

"Okay, thanks for your help Maureen," said Don, "you've been a great help, See ya later."

They traipsed out the door again and in their vehicle drove around the corner as indicated by Maureen.

"She's a real card, eh mate." Don said to Ted as he pulled up outside the Aboriginal Community Centre building.

"It takes all sorts old chap," replied Ted as he stepped from the Ute.

They approached the counter just inside the foyer and the girl behind the desk asked if she could help them. When Don said that they have come to see Billy-The-Lid, the girl's face lit up into a beautiful smile.

"What do youse blokes want with grandfather?" she asked playfully.

"We came past the museum at Sandstone and me mate there, Dick Manton, asked me to call in and pay his

respects to the old man," Don told her. "How is he anyway?" He thought it best to ask that question too, so that they may have some idea of his health.
"I've heard him talk of dat bloke. Him be well for a bloke of ninety-five. He is still chief elder of our community," she told them.
"That's marvellous news, my dear. But where would we need to go to find the old gentleman?" Ted asked her.
"He no gennleman! He my grandfather. He cumin to town for a meetin' in the afternoon. He be here this morning in about half an hour," she replied maintaining that same grin on her face. Obviously she is very proud of her grandfather.

Just then an old Aboriginal chap walked in the front door.

"Here he be now. He's come early today. Just wait a minute an' I'll see if he can see you now." She left her seat and caught up with the old man as he struggled to walk down the corridor. He was having some trouble with his walking but appeared to be in good health for a man of his age. He stopped when his granddaughter approached him. She told him of the two men and after looking at them, motioned them to come into one of the rooms. He went in first and they walked down the corridor and the girl ushered them in.
"Thank you my dear," said Ted and she replied with that marvellous grin once again.

The old man was sitting in a comfortable chair in what appeared to be a waiting room. The walls were covered in local artist's work of painting, sculpture,

handicraft and bushcraft items. It had a very Aboriginal feeling to it. There were several seats in the room with a table of magazines in the centre of it.
Don began the conversation while still standing, "Hello, Billy-The-Lid, I am Don King from Geraldton. I have a friend in Sandstone, Dick Manton. When we told him we were coming out this way he insisted that we call in and offer his respects to you. This is another friend of mine, Ted Walsh."
The old man shook the proffered hands in warm greeting to the two men. "I is glad to meet you blokes," he said. "Dick an me go back over twenny years when he had a gold show just over da border. We used to chat about all sorts a things. He very interesting bloke."
"Oh, I can agree with that. We've had a few interesting times with him over the years. He had been a good friend to me too. We had some fine times in our younger years," replied Don. He cast his eyes around the room and said, "You have a fine building here, Billy and I'm told that this is a very successful community. Are you still the chief elder in the community?" Don asked him.
"Yeah, I chief elder with some other good people, too. We had a problem with the drinkin' and da substance abuse but with help we have stop that now. We are havin' not many problems now," the old man told them.
"Billy, Dick told us that in your younger days you helped many people who were prospecting in this area. Do you remember those days?" Don asked.
The old man's face was a mass of lines but they could see that he smiled at the mention of this.

"Yeah, I bin helpin' some blokes do dat. Some blokes, day take my advice an odders day don't. Some give good memories an' some day are bad memories."
"Were you one of the men who helped Len Beadell when he was putting in all of these roads?" Don asked the old man.
"Yeah, I bin helpin' Len for many years. We good mates. He listen many times but sometimes he not listen to me. Sometimes he have trouble and I help him get out of trouble. Yeah, day were intrestin' times," mused the old man.
"I'll bet Len had some good laughs with you around the campfire, eh Billy?" Don suggested.
"Yeah many good laughs wid Len."
"Do you remember when you helped John Bailey and Harry Lasseter when they got lost?" asked Don fishing for information.
"Yeah, day was silly men. Day could not find water but I showed dem how. Many times I showed dem how to find water. They did not learn very good."
"Dick tells me that you saw Lasseter with his gold nugget around his neck. Do you know what happened to it Billy?" Don pushed the questions to him.
"Yeah I knows all 'bout that gold nugget," Was the reply that the old man gave them. It indicated that he knew a lot more about Bailey and Lasseter than was previously thought and it might take some time to persuade him to reveal this information to them.

The old man smiled then opened the front of his shirt. There on a gold chain was a rough gold nugget about the size of a matchbox.
Both men looked in awe at the sight of this memento of the days of Lasseter. It took both of them by

surprise and it was a few seconds before they could follow on with their discussion.

"By gee, Billy, I'll bet Harry was happy with your work when he gave that to you?" asked Don with a surprised tone to his voice.
"Yeah, he very happy. I saved him from the death by thirst the third time. He silly man in some ways but smart man in odder ways. He good wid da horses and camels." The old man looked like he was talking in his sleep. His eyes were almost closed and his breathing deep and slow. He seemed to be enjoying the talk that he was having.
"For many years I keep dem secrets but you seem good fellas an' I like talkin' wid ya. Lasseter said he had more gold in the Kaltukatjara area. But he had trouble to find it again. After Bailey left he come west from the Petermann Ranges and after many weeks we find his old place. He very sick and nearly blind. My people keep him alive for many weeks but he die before he get da chance to get back to da big smoke town."
"Was his blindness caused by the sandy blight?" Don asked the old man. After him spending time with Len Beadell, he would have known of this problem.
"Yeah, many years later Len had same problem, but my people able to help him this time," the old man answered this question after giving it some thought. Just like he was still thinking in his native Pitjantjatjara language then translating this to English.

Don kept on leading the old man to tell more of his story, "What was Lasseter like when he gave the chain

to you? Was he nearly dead or was he very bright, Billy?"
The old man needed a little time to recover the memory of this. "Yeah, he was on the bed of his death but looked bright like he is excited. He gave the chain to me and said 'Keep this as a gift for the help that you've given me, Billy. You have done more for me than my people. You believed in me when they didn't." Next morning we wake up an' he dead."
"While you were with him, Billy, did he say where he got the nugget that's on the chain from?" Don asked while he pointed to the nugget that was proudly worn by the old man.
"Yeah, we spend lots time there and he diggin' for the yella gold. I not diggin', just him. He not allow me to dig. He say I too good to dig."

It took them a while to understand this 'too good to dig' but they took it that Lasseter held this man in very high esteem and would not let him dig on that principal.
Now Don prepares himself for the big question. He hesitates and draws a deep breath. "Billy, we think that Harry Lasseter believes you to be a great man not only with your people but for all people. And from what you're telling us we feel that you are a great man too. We see what you are doing here with your people and the visitors that are here too. There are just two questions that we have for you. Can you show us where Harry's body was laid to rest and can you show us where the nugget was found?"
The old man opened his eyes to read the faces of the two men. The younger of the two was doing all of the talking but the older man was more intelligent. He

knows that Lasseter's secret must come out sooner or later and he was satisfied that these would be the best men to tell.
"Yeah, I have the maps which Harry kept. Day are still in a nudder room here. I will give these to you but I ask you to please an old man. Don't start diggin' the place all up till after I'm dead and gone. I know dat the yella gold must be dug up, and I want to know you'll help my people. Also, help my people to understand the white man's value of this gold and let them share in it with you," the old man asked in a deep and serious voice. He knew that the recovery of this gold was going to upset the normally tranquil settings around where his people were. It is a big area. From Uluru in the east and west to Lake Throssell. From Yuendumu in the north to the Southern Ocean. Those are his homelands.

"Billy, we will do as you ask and have respect for you and your people." He extended his hand to shake with the old man to seal the agreement. The old man slowly stood and willingly took the proffered hands of both men and the shake was one of solid trust.
"Don't write it down, just work with these wishes and everything be okay," the old man told them solemnly. "I tell the odder elders at da meeting today of what I have said and all will be okay wid dem too."
"Yes we agree to do as you ask and will keep to that agreement that we have just made with you," Don told Billy.
"Yes Billy, both of us will see that each other keeps to that agreement. You have no fear of that," Ted added to allay any doubts that Billy may have had.

Lake Breaden, Gunbarrel Highway, Western Australia, 6th April

The old man slowly walked into the corridor and then entered another room. He motioned for the two men to follow. The room was similar to the previous but there were several filing cabinets. The walls were again decorated with local art and artefacts. This was the office of an important man in the community.
The old man took a key from a draw in the desk and opened a filing cabinet. There he found another key and took this to open a drawer under the solid desk. He removed from this desk a cardboard cylinder. In it were several old but carefully tendered maps.
They were old military lithographs of the area and there were markings on them. Billy spread them on the desk. He pointed to several of these marks close together and said, "This is where the nugget came from." And pointing to the mark left most on the map said, "This is where he be diggin' last before he be dead. I think this where you'd be interested in diggin for Harry Lasseter's yella gold. We buried his body there too!"

Both men studied the map and were surprised with the final location. It was about a hundred and fifty kilometres from where it was reported to be. They were studying the map and working out their approaches when they were interrupted by the girl who they had met before at the front desk.
"Grandad, the meeting be startin' in ten minutes," she told him.
He replied in his native tongue and she left the room. He turned back to the men and said, "I must attend meeting for last time. New chief elder elected today. I retiring," he told them with a smile on his face. He

handed the maps to Don who rolled them up again and inserted them into their cylinder.

They walked from the room and made their way to the foyer where the girl was once again sitting at her desk. Several other people were in the room and it was bustling and buzzing with excitement.
"Is this a big day for your people?" Ted asked the girl.
"Yeah. Very big day. New elder to replace grandad to be elected today. Our council very good. People very happy. He tell me that you special people too. I will let you know details of our new council."
"Thank you very much. Here is my card. I'd be very grateful if you could post me your newsletter and anything of interest from time to time," Don told her as he handed his card with his address details on it to her.
"That not be a problem, Mr Don King of Geraldton. I can do that for you. Will I see you again? My name is Millicent," she asked him with that big smile again.
"I'm pleased to meet you Millicent. Yes you will be seeing us from time to time. And we'd be happy to see you and your people."

The two men felt as though their feet didn't touch the ground; they were both so elated with their discussion with the old man.
"So you see, old chap. It pays to keep honest. See where it got us?" Ted said.
"Yes Ted and now the interesting stuff starts. We need to visit the Police Officer and get a miners permit for that area. Then we need to get an approval letter from the local Aboriginal Council before we can go in there to prospect but I don't think that will be a problem."

They asked Millicent if the policeman was around. She said yes and pressed a buzzer and disappeared to another room. Presently a khaki uniformed Aboriginal Policeman enters from a back room. From the name badge on his chest they could see that this was Nick.
"Good day," he said, "How can I be of assistance?" he asked them in a voice that was well educated.
"Good day Nick. You can help us by issuing us with a miners permit for this area, please," Ted asked him as he pushed a piece of paper over the counter with the location details on.
"Oh yes. I've just had a talk with Millicent about you blokes. It seems old Billy-The-Lid is getting soft in his old age."
"Oh, come now. I don't for one minute think that you think old Billy would get soft in the head," Ted responded.
"No! You'd be right there, mate. He has been the backbone of this community since the sixties. I just hope that the new council can live up to the task that he has set out for the community. It'll be tough going but if everyone does their little bit, it will work out well," Nick told them.

They completed the necessary paperwork and Nick issued them with a permit to prospect in the area as specified.

"Just sit down for a while and Millicent will have your documentation ready for you."
"Thanks a lot Nick. We expect to be around for a week or so, then we'll be away for a short time then we'll be in touch with you before we come again next time. I think in view of what is going to happen out there, that

you be aware of what's going on." Don paused for a breath and then continued, "I understand that this office is manned by more than just you?"
"Oh no! This is just an outpost. Our office is in Laverton. The sergeant and the other two constables are on their regular run. I'm just the Aboriginal Liaison Officer. But they'll be back tomorrow afternoon if everything goes well."
"Thanks for your help Nick. We'll be off and see you on our way back." Both men turned from the counter and walked out the front door of the Community Centre.

A Mazda motorhome had pulled up near their vehicle and a man and a woman were walking towards them. They were familiar to Don but it wasn't until he was up to them that he recognised them.
"Hello Gordon and Betty, fancy meeting you our here," he said
"Hello, Don. Good to see you again, too," Gordon said extending his hand in warm greeting to Don.
"I bet you're having a great time relaxing while you're travelling now that you've sold that business of yours. Oh, by the way, this is a partner of mine, Ted Walsh. Ted this is Gordon and Betty from Geraldton. They used to own the Mitrebox Hardware shop just down the road." Ted shook the hands of Gordon and Betty, saying he was pleased to meet them, in his polished voice.
"Don, we've never had such a great time as we are having right now. Without those pressures of the business we are relaxed, our blood pressure is way down and we are totally enthralled with this country out here. We even spent some time down the cave at

Peegull, the other day. It was quite an adventure for us," Gordon told them.
"Well you've certainly picked a great time of the year to see this part of the country. Pleasantly warm days with cold nights for sleeping. Gets a bit hot later on though," Don told them.

While Gordon was talking to Don, Betty and Ted had wandered off to the motorhome and she was showing him the inside. She was excited to be able to proudly show off her motorhome to someone else who was interested. She spent a few minutes showing Ted the details of what's where and how and why. Ted took some photos from several angles so he could reconstruct a complete image of it later.
"You never know, I may purchase one of these myself and these photos will be great for future reference, Madam. Then I can build in the features which you have," he told her.

A very pleasant lady, thought Ted as they stepped out of the motorhome again.
"Perhaps you can help us Don, we're interested in going through the hills to the east of here and what do you know about them?" Gordon asked of Don.
"Gordon, don't take this vehicle through there, it very rough country. I was through there about ten years ago. You'd only get a couple of kilometres before turning around but ask Nick inside, he has more local knowledge than I do. He was born and bred here, and knows this area like the back of his hand," Don told him.
"Okay, we'll do that. Thanks for the tips and it's been great to catch up with you again, Don, Ted."

Chapter 15

Lake Breaden, Gunbarrel Highway, Western Australia, 6th April

Ted and Don said goodbye to the couple who walked on into the Community Centre's front door.
They drove back to the roadhouse and then parked at the diesel fuel bowser. Not far from there was a mustard coloured Landcruiser parked just off to one side. Ted took some photos of this to add to his collection. As they pulled in, it was driven around to the back of the building. Don walked to the roadhouse and asked if someone could pump some fuel for him as the bowser was in a padlocked steel enclosure. The girl behind the counter turned towards the back door which was open and yelled "MMMAAAXXX, diesel." From the back of the building came a reply, "okay, keep ya hair on I'm comin'."
About half a minute later a mechanic enters the building from the back and walks over to the counter. "Max, this bloke needs diesel," she told him as if she was angry with him.
"Aw. Okay mate, just follow me and we'll have this sorted out for ya," Max said to Don.
Once at the bowser, Max unlocked the padlock and began pumping fuel into the main tank. "Looks like you're on a mission with all this gear mate?" he asked after having a look over the equipment, which is mostly covered by the tarpaulins.
"Yeah, mate we're doing a bit of prospecting out this way. Been doin' it for years," Don told him.
"Gold eh. Keeps people poor, that game, I reckon."
"Well, I don't know about that Max. We're making out okay so far and ya never know what's around the corner. We've a few irons in the fire and it gets interesting from time to time." He wasn't going to

elaborate anymore because this would be a great gossip place. And gossip would not do them any good.
"We've got a couple of clowns in here now who've got a problem with their fuel system. Musta picked up some dirty fuel somewhere. Hasn't a clue when the filters were changed. Bit sus I think. The vehicle looks heavy too. It must have a good load on. But not to worry, the boys'll have it going in no time."
"Is this place good for business? It looks like you're pretty busy," Don asked him.
"Yeah not too bad, we took out the lease from the Community but they had bad managers before. They were very hard to get on with. But yeah we're doing okay. Sometimes the missus, that's Maureen at the counter, gives me a hard time but she'll get over it later," he told Don with a grin on his face.

After a few minutes the tank was full and Max hung up the nozzle, he said to Don, "There ya go mate, she's full. Just pay Maureen in there a hundred and twenty bucks and she'll be sweet."
"Thanks Max," Don replied.
"He'll do well here, old chap," said Ted, "a bit rough around the edges but he seems to be good with people."
"Yeah, he's that alright," agreed Don. He parked the Landcruiser away from the bowser and they walked into the roadhouse. They paid Maureen for the fuel and ordered themselves a burger and drink.
"No worries, luv. It'll be ready in ten. Just take a seat an' I'll bring it over to ya," she told them.

They selected a table with two seats in the corner away from the main thoroughfare. They could see the two

men from the mustard coloured Landcruiser sitting together at a table eating their lunch.
"Max says he is a bit suspect of those two blokes. Got a big load on their Landcruiser and its got fuel problems."
"That would be a bit difficult out here old chap. You'd need to have some mechanical knowledge and some spares. But if they come from Sydney they probably don't think of these things," Ted replied. "Pretty desolate if you break down out of town."
"Yeah I reckon," said Don who had his mind back to their plans for the future.

Their meal arrived and they were astounded with the size of the burgers. "That's a meal for ya," Maureen had said. They spent the next half an hour with their lunch and Ted glanced at his watch and said, "I say old chap, it's after three. Do you wish to set up camp in the camping area or do you want to push on today?"
After some thought on this matter Don responded, "I think the camp-ground sounds a good idea to me. A rest and a hot shower would be great. Then we can be on the road at first light and start on the project that we came out here for."

They enquired at the counter and booked into the campground and paid for the night. While they were setting up camp, they were surprised at the number of other campers and caravaners in the park.
"This seems to becoming a very popular place here Ted!" Don exclaimed.
"I must say that I am surprised with the number of travellers that we have seen here today. Certainly a busy tourist spot," Ted replied.

When Don headed off to the showers, Ted downloaded all of the digital photos to the laptop. He filed them away into their relevant files. Prospecting, vehicles, people, places and sundries. He was building a library of images, some of which could be of interest later. Particularly, those of the inside of that motorhome of Don's friends. That is a nice bus, the way it's laid out and finished. That was well set out and well finished. Good quality fittings too, from what he could see. He then set up the programs that he would need to tomorrow's initial prospecting study. He didn't want to do anything with the hardware in the park because he didn't want to have to answer any questions from the other people around.

After their showers, they decided that a short break followed by a meal would be the ideal way to relax for a while. The next week or so is going to be hard work. As they were preparing their camp, they caught snippets of the news on a radio from another camp.

"…….. saga of the Gold robbery in Kalgoorlie on the fourth of this month. The white Ford Transit van which was discovered by police had been extensively burned but gave police some clues to the identity and modus operandi of the bank robbers.
They changed vehicles after the robbery and were seen in Menzies later that day in a mustard coloured Landcruiser ……. covering the back. Police are asking that anyone with information of the vehicle to report to them immediately. Do not attempt to approach the vehicle or the occupants as they may be armed and are

to be considered extremely dangerous. They are expected to be travelling east ……..

Around the camping area there was a lot of talk about the robbery and someone said that they 'saw the vehicle in town today.' Then someone else said 'every second vehicle on the road fits that description.'
It was a pleasant evening and they were able to crawl into their swags before ten o'clock.

Lake Menindee, New South Wales, Australia, 6th April

Mick and Castle arrived at the kitchen door at the same time after being woken by the noise from the kitchen. Gloria was busy with the frypan and the smell of bacon with eggs and toast was strong.
"Good morning boys," she said as she watched them enter the room. She motioned towards the large dining table and said. "Take a seat. This will only be a few minutes and it'll be ready."
"Good morning, Gloria. That sure smells great but I think Castle may have a different view."
"Oh, I've thought of Ravin. His beef sausages and eggs will be ready at the same time as your breakfast, Mick," she retorted.
"Many thanks for your consideration, Gloria. I appreciate your thoughtfulness. Sometimes it can be a little difficult being away from one's own culture," Ravin Goldcastle responded.

Gloria removed the pans from the wood stove-top, transferred the food onto the warmed plates and then placed these onto the table in front of the men and one for herself.
"Well, it tastes as good as it smells, Gloria, it's wonderful, thank you," Mick said between mouthfuls. Castle was busy with his breakfast but when his plate was clean he said. "Yes Gloria that was an excellent meal. It's a great change from some of the food that I've had to endure in the last few weeks."

"My pleasure," she said to both of them. Then she asked, "What's your destination today Mick?"
"Today our first stop will be Broken Hill where we'll fuel up, then on to Andamooka, Marla and into Yulara this afternoon. That should give me my eight hours flying time for the day. Castle is going to see some country that will remind him of home, on the way and some very interesting topography as well," Mick told her.
"I wish you well in whatever it is that you two are about. I won't ask what you're doing as I know you'll tell me when the time is right Mick," she said, sounding very understanding.
"Yes, Gloria. I'll let you know how it goes and what we achieve from this trip at a later time. The details can be very sensitive at this stage. It is very exciting in many ways," Mick told her.

Gloria cleared away the breakfast dishes and the men returned to their rooms and packed their gear and then brought the bags to the back door. When Gloria was ready she brought the Landcruiser to the back gate and the men placed their bags in the back and got into the vehicle. Gloria drove out to the airstrip.

Mick could see some of the cattle along the track and said. "These cattle look to be in good condition, Gloria, considering this is the end of a hot dry summer."
"Yes, I'm proud of these cattle. I'm breeding into my herd some Droughtmaster and Brahman. The market seems to want that type of animal at this time and they do bring better prices. My biggest surprise is that these crossbreeds are so quiet that it is almost difficult to

handle them. They can be difficult to drove, sometimes," Gloria responded.

As they moved along the track they could see several hundred of them scattered around several smaller paddocks. She had taken the long way around because she was proud of her cattle and wanted to show off a little.

After several minutes they arrived at the helicopter. Castle took the bags and stowed them in the cabin. Mick began his pre-flight checks from the ground, then from the pilot's seat. "Clear props!" he yelled as he hit the starter that caused to gas turbine to ignite and the Rolls Royce 250-C30P came to life. The main rotor slowly began to rotate and increased in speed. While the engine was in warm up mode, Mick jumped down and taking Gloria away from the noise of the engine spoke to her for several minutes, "thanks for your hospitality, Gloria. It was great last night, catching up on so much time. When this little job is completed we may come back and see you again on the return trip. That is if you'll have us," Mick said with tongue in cheek.
"That won't be a problem, Mick Jones as you well know," she responded in a mock scolding voice.
They hugged each other and then Mick took his seat at the controls of the machine. Ravin was already seated.

Mick brought the engine up to operating revs and with the manipulation of the controls had the helicopter airborne in a few seconds. The lift-off was reflective of his skill at handling the helicopter. Smooth and clean. Mick checked the dash mounted clock and saw that it was 0730 hours. They returned Gloria's waves as she watched them climb into the air.

As the elevation increased they could see away to the east from where they had come yesterday. The buildings of the homestead became smaller as they gained altitude and headed out on a setting of two ninety four degrees.
"We'll be in Broken Hill by eight o'clock, Castle. So I'll call up and confirm our arrival so we can refuel without any delay." He took the microphone from its cradle in front of him and spoke into it, "Mike Alpha X-ray calling Broken Hill tower, over"
After a few seconds came the reply, "Mike Alpha X-ray, Hill tower, we have you on our screen, over,"
"Hill tower, Mike Alpha X-ray, my ETA is 0800 hrs and I request that I can land near the refuelling station as per my request last week, over."
"Mike Alpha X-ray, Hill tower, stand by, over." After a minute the operator came back again. "Mike Alpha X-ray, Hill Tower, not a problem Mick. There are no other aircraft in the vicinity at that time so proceed directly to the helipad by the fuel location near the intersection of taxiway zero two three and three two one, your refueller will be there for you, over."
"Hill Tower, Mike Alpha X-ray. Many thanks for your support. Mike Alpha X-ray out."
After replacing the microphone, he turned to Castle and said "Well that's our fuel organised. All we need to do is sit back, relax and enjoy the view until we get there.

The ground was undulating with a low scrub cover. There were also a few lines of hills running about

northeast/southwest. Ravin had noted this and asked the question. "Mick, I see that most of the hills, with the exception of the Great Dividing Range run in this direction. How much of the country runs northeast/southwest?"
"Castle, it's common of the mainland for many of the hills to run that way. I'm not a geologist and I can't answer the 'why' of your question" Mick replied. "But I would think it has to do with the way the land folded while it was young and the wind direction. Of course a lot has happened here since the last ice age. And many scientists believe that this is one of the oldest parts of the earth."
"Yes I can see from the hills that they are worn down to hillocks in many cases by wind and water erosion. This must have been a very wet place at one stage in the past," Ravin countered.
"Yes the wetter areas are now confined to the coastal belts. The rivers, which run inland, are being over used and things will need to change before we have some sort of stabilised water supply. It needs to be shared by everyone not just the few who are in a convenient location."
"We learnt that lesson back in nineteen fifty two when we were setting up our desalinated water supply back in Israel. The kibbutz system was the best for that time but things have progressed since then," Ravin reflected. His father was one of the developing engineers on the water project and had told him of many of the difficulties before he had retired.
"Perhaps we could learn a lot from your people about how to make the best use of the water which is available instead of wasting so much," Mick replied.

Chapter 16

Lake Menindee, New South Wales, Australia, 6th April

On the horizon they caught their first sighting of the mine workings and buildings of the town of Broken Hill. They became more defined as they approached. The airport appeared on their right quarter and Mick made his way towards it. As they flew over the parked planes he could pick out the helipad near the refuelling station and he exercised a perfect landing. After turning off the engine he jumped out as the rotors slowed to a stop. The refuelling attendant was waiting for the exhaust to cool for five minutes before he attached the static line. Then he connected the fuel nozzle to the helicopters' inlet and began pumping fuel. While he was doing this, Mick walked around the machine and checked the container for condensate. He flushed this out and replaced it again. He swept his eyes over the entire machine, just looking to see that everything was as it should be. He ended his walk near the refueller and said, "We were out at Stamford Plains near Lake Cargelligo yesterday and we had Percy refuel us. He tells us that he used to work as a refueller here before the Ansett problems. Did you know him?" Mick asked.

"Know him! That bastard! Yeah, I bloody knew him! That bastard's lucky to be liven', mate. He thought he was God's gift to women. Tried messin' with me missus, she said. Several other blokes at the airport said the same thing. The union got him shifted out of here, and then we heard he had retired to work on a sheep station. Till now I didn't know where." The refueller was red in the face and he showed all the signs of someone who was very upset. Mick could almost see the steam emitting from his ears.

"Sorry to hear of your problems," Mick said simply. No sense in following this line of conversation he

thought, so he changed the subject. "How is the job this year? Are you as busy as you were with mining company aircraft?"
"Nah, mate. That's all but closed down now. Not much mining stuff goin' on around here. Tourists look like taking over the joint now," he replied.
"Oh, well then. The important thing is that you've got a job."
"Yeah, that's right mate."
The pump had switched off indicating that the tank was filled. "Well, there ya go mate two hundred and ninety two litres." He handed Mick a clipboard, "just sign here mate and you're on ya way."
Mick signed the slip and took his copy. "Thanks for your service. We'll be back again next week, so we'll see you then, eh?"
"Yeah, sure mate. No worries," came the reply.

The refueller took his pumping and hose trolley away with him. After carrying out his pre-flight checks, Mick fired the turbine again and they were once again airborne.
Mick altered his direction and flew north and close to Silverton just to point out some of the features to Ravin.

Then he got back onto his two hundred and seventy degree heading for Quorn in South Australia. After about fifteen minutes, Mick pointed out the border. "We are now leaving the fine state of New South Wales and are entering the state of South Australia," he told Ravin.
There was not much to indicate the different states from the air. But on the highway there is a pub, which

helps some motorists to cover the distance. It also hinders some others.
After half an hour of flying they needed to increase elevation as the ground begins to rise as they approach the Flinders ranges.

Mick pointed out to Ravin that the flight path takes them to the south of the South Flinders Ranges and bypassing the higher hills which are over six hundred metres in elevation.
"After we have passed Quorn, we'll descend again and there should not be much turbulence then. It could be a good opportunity to begin setting up some of your equipment. We can land for a short time if necessary but we'll have to limit the stop to not more than ten minutes," Mick told him.
This would give them a head start once they arrived on site at the Petermann Range.
"That's great, thanks Mick. It does take some time to set up and I feel ineffective just sitting here while you're doing all the work," Ravin responded, "but if it's alright with you, I could begin at once."
"That'll be okay but if we experience any turbulence you'll need to be strapped in," Mick told him.

After removing his seat belt, Ravin climbed between the two front seats and positioned himself on the rear seat. The two rearwards facing seat had been removed and his equipment was stored in this location. He began unpacking the equipment. This was all stored in two suitcases. The main computer and console fitted into one of these and the cables, transponders and other ancillary equipment were stored in the other. The laptop computer was mounted in its own case with straps to be attached to the bulkhead of the helicopter. This would hold it firm in the case of turbulence. The main computer system was in two separated compartments and these were strapped onto the floor just behind the bulkhead immediately behind the pilot seat. After half an hour there was some turbulence and Ravin had to stop his setting up and strapped himself into one of the rear seats.

They must be over Quorn now as Mick was changing heading and Ravin could see the main compass swing to a heading of two-ninety-three degrees.

Then Mick said, "This heading will take us to Andamooka, Castle, where we'll need to refuel again. If the wind stays as it is, calm, we should be there by eleven o'clock."

Ravin was busy again with the setting up of the equipment. He had the transponders duct taped to the inside of the rear side doors. This should be okay but if not then they will need to be fitted to the underside of the belly of the helicopter. He wouldn't be able to make this decision till they booted up the system and carried out some preliminary testing. He continued with his work and had everything tied down with Velcro straps or by using the cargo straps that are in the cabin. There were several 12-volt power sockets available to him and each of the components was plugged into these.
"Mick, I'm ready to boot up the system in a few minutes, do you wish to land while I do this in case I cause an electrical fault?" Ravin asked.

After giving this some thought, Mick replied, "What size circuit breakers are you using, Castle?" he asked.
"Just ten amps maximum and these are quick trippers, Mick," he replied, "and the transponders are on five amp slow blow fuses."
"That's fine, because I have a separate circuit for those outlets there and they are covered by a fifteen amp main fuse. But as you say, to be on the safe side, let's land while you do the necessary work." He immediately began descending and found a suitable landing site, which was about ten kilometres to the north of South Gap Station homestead.

The machine settled to the ground with a flurry of dust. Mick was quick to feather the main rotor to reduce the chance of dusting the intake of the engine. While the engine remained on low power, he indicated that Ravin could boot up the system. Ravin closed the main circuit breaker for each unit in the system and each of them started according to plan. He checked out the system monitors for operational details. Each circuit has its own amp-metre and volt-metre so that they can be continuously monitored. Everything is running at its ideal rate. All of the amps were well within the safe range and the volts showed the same. He then switched the monitors over to automatic. The main computer will now do its own monitoring and notify the operator should anything need attention. Ravin had built in a fail-safe system so that if one component should be close to eighty percent of maximum, then a warning would alert the operator at the screen.
He was satisfied that all was safe and ready for operation.

"The only thing which I have not tested is the response of the transponders. That will be difficult to do until we reach the work site. But I do think that I will get a better result if I attach the transponders to the underside of the belly. Is there some suitable place for that?" he asked Mick.
Mick knew his machine fairly well but consulted the handbook just to be sure. After looking at the book for several minutes he replied, "I think we can attach them quite safely to the skid struts, right here at the base of them," Mick said pointing to where the skid struts are attached to the main frame of the helicopter.

Ravin used several cable ties and duct tape to secure each of the six transponders. When he was satisfied of their transmitting direction he told Mick, "That seems fine to me Mick. The cables can enter the cabin via the door opening. The sealing rubber is flexible enough to allow that."
Mick agreed with his suggestion and in just a few minutes they were ready for take-off again.

Carefully, Mick gave full power and they were in the air before any dust could get into the engine intake. He resumed his previous heading, which took them parallel to the western edge of the dry Lake Torrens. Mick pointed this out to Ravin who could see much resemblance to parts of his homeland.

For the next hour, Ravin carried our various tests to the MAMRID system to satisfy himself that every component was functioning correctly. Everything was fine with the exception of the reading, which he was getting from the outboard transponders. His feeling was that they would get a better response from them but their outside location may be suspect. He would need some time over the test site before he could be one hundred percent certain of the full operation of the system.

As they approached Andamooka, Mick pointed out many of the opal mines and workings in the area. Little hillocks of light coloured spoil were beside nearly every hole that appeared in the ground. This is where the shafts were drilled for mine entrances on for ventilation shafts.
The entire area was littered with these.

Mick noted the location of the airfield and altered his heading towards this. He could see where the refuelling station was and landed on the helipad area, which was located nearby.
Mick cut the fuel and ignition of the engine and allowed the rotors to wind down before they got out.
"This is the outback now, Castle. We'll need to pump this fuel by hand."

The fuel for the helicopter, Aviation Turbine Fuel, was stored in two, two hundred litre drums. A rotary hand pump was nearby and Mick used the tool beside the drums to remove the large bung. Into this he screwed the hand pump. Then operated the handle and allowed a small amount of fuel to spill onto the ground. This would clear any foreign materials from the inside of the pump. After removing the cover of the fuel-filling valve, he connected the hose from the drum pump to the valve and began pumping. After a few minutes

Ravin relived Mick on the handle. Mick checked the condensate container and conducted a general inspection of the exterior of the craft.
After fifteen minutes the first drum was empty. Mick, having removed the bung from the next drum, unscrewed the pump and transferred it to the full drum. The same process here was repeated until, when ten minutes later, the tank was full. Mick disconnected the nozzle from the fuel valve and after draining the pump removed it from the drum and replaced the bung tightly. There was about forty litres still in the drum and one of the local pilots could have that for his own use. He had already paid for the fuel and these two drums were marked "Macrodelphus Pty Ltd Use Only". There was no one in attendance and as the paperwork had already been completed, they were able to take off again.

Mick fired up the turbine again and in a few minutes, they were airborne once again. Mick set the helicopter on a course of three-one-five degrees. In two hours and thirty minutes they would be at their next fuel stop. This will be at Marla, which is also a Stuart Highway Roadhouse.

They have a light airstrip behind the roadhouse for general use. This services the local station people, flying tourists, mining aircraft operators and the Royal Flying Doctor Service.
Mick had been on this heading and for some unknown reason was having second thoughts about it. He had another look at his flight plan and the area that he was about to enter was the Woomera Prohibited Area. This was clearly marked on his map and he was astounded

that he had not noticed this when he laid out his flight plan. He quickly calculated a heading, which would take him outside the perimeter of the restricted area. Directly below he could see Mattaweara Lagoon and he had a GPS fix on this location so he plotted a course that would take them over William Creek settlement then back to Marla. Three-four-zero degrees would get him to over William Creek then he would need to turn onto a three-zero-two heading. He noted the adjustment on his flight plan and also updated his logbook to show the alteration. It would also add eighteen miles to his distance. He was still within the safety margins of fuel. He was angry with himself for missing that important piece of navigation. He was not sure if there would be any activity at Woomera at this time but he had heard of some unusual timing of activities in the area. He had no intention of becoming a statistic in one of the operations, which do occur there from time to time.

This was the longest leg of the journey and below he could pick out water courses because of their tree lines. As they altered course near William Creek the Old Ghan Rail line was below them. Then further on there were a couple of smaller lakes out to the north. While they were flying, Ravin was at his monitor watching the results of the transponders. He made several adjustments to the program and was getting a clearer picture of their signal. He also spent some time looking at the ground, which was going past under them. He knows that the deserts of the Middle East were desolate. He had no idea that the country out here would resemble parts of Israel. He even saw a herd of camels following their bull as he wandered amongst the low scrub. He persisted with the transponders, as he was not happy that they were operating as efficiently as they should. He felt that he had gained the optimum performance from them in their present position but he was not satisfied that it was correct. When they land next time, he'll spend a few minutes to find a better location for them.

At about forty minutes from their scheduled stop at Marla airstrip, Mick pointed out to Ravin the colourful hills to the east of Arckaringa Station homestead. "There's the Painted Desert out there, Castle, just to the east of the homestead buildings." There were several old breakaways in the area and the colours, which showed in them, ranged from deep purple to golden to white. Mick enjoyed looking at this area but unfortunately can't afford the time for an excursion on this trip. He will need to keep a tight schedule.

Presently they were approaching the Marla Airstrip and Mick began losing altitude. He landed on the helipad, which the roadhouse team had provided. With the approach of the helicopter, one of the attendants came out to assist with the refuelling. Before Mick was out of his seat, the female attendant had the static line attached in readiness for the filling operation to begin.

Ravin and Mick stepped down from the helicopter and enjoyed the opportunity to stretch their legs. It had been over two hours on that part of the trip and there was not enough room for activity in the cabin. While Mick was attending to the exterior inspection, Ravin determined that he would need to alter the position of the transponders from their present location. By having them point in a more downward direction, it would improve the effectiveness of them. He was able to cut off the cable ties and old duct tape, change the position and reattach them without much effort. By the time he had completed this operation, the refuelling job was completed.

It was a long time since breakfast. All they had had to eat was a few muesli bars each. They headed off to the roadhouse for a snack. On offer were all sorts of fatty stuff and Mick was not impressed with the array so asked for a fresh salad sandwich. Ravin, having seen the presentation was dying for an Australian meat pie. He heard that these were great tucker. He placed his order and took a bottle of drink from the fridge. When their snacks arrived they sat at one of the tables in the air-conditioned restaurant.
They had completed their snacks and returned to the helicopter and were in the air again by three o'clock.

"Castle we are getting closer,' Mick said, "but it seems to take forever, doesn't it?" he commented.
"Yes, Mick. You have a very big country here. I had no idea of the size in relation to my country. You look at maps but really don't comprehend the size of a continent like Australia," he replied.
"Yes, Castle, many people make the same comment. We see some funny things out here. Especially with people who didn't comprehend the distances and times that are needed to be travelled between cities and other points of interest," Mick commented.

Ravin was checking his transponders again and after a re-calibration of the program was satisfied that they

were as efficient as he could get them at this time. When they were over the test site, he could carry out any fine tuning measures to suit his purpose.
"Castle, this is the eastern edge of the Great Victoria Desert that we are flying over now. Tomorrow we'll be closer to the western edge of it, near when it joins the Gibson Desert of Western Australia," Mick told Ravin as they were flying over some inhospitable country.

The ground was rising now as they approached Mount Woodroffe. At fourteen hundred and forty metres in height and was the highest peak in South Australia and they would pass within forty kilometres of it.
There were several other peaks around. They did look unusual as they just popped up out of the ground. Mt. Connor, thirty kilometres to the north east of them and later they could see the famous Ayres Rock with the outcrop of the Olgas further off to the west.

Mick called the airport at Yulara, "Mike-Alpha-X-ray, calling Yulara tower, over."
The reply came back immediately, "Yulara tower to Mike-Alpha-X-ray, go ahead, over."
"Yulara Tower, Mike-Alpha-X-ray. I request permission for helo landing, over."
'Mike-Alpha-X-ray, Yulara. Welcome back Mick, we still have your favourite spot for you. Look for helipad, zero one five near taxiway zero two four. Please hold your approach until Qantas flight Q278 on runway zero two four had departed, over."
"Yulara, Mike-Alpha-X-ray. Thank you, out."
Mick could see the Qantas flight at the end of runway zero two four and kept to the south of this. After it had

cleared the runway on its departure, Mick headed directly for the helipad, which he has used frequently. Once on the ground he shut down the engine and carried out his post flight checks. When these were completed they exited the cabin and Mick showed Ravin the tie down points. The rotors were tied to the main structure of the helicopter and then it was tied in four places to anchor bolts in the tarmac.
“That will keep it safe from wind damage. Not that there is usually much out here. Now we’ll get ourselves a taxi and we’ll be staying in the Yulara Resort Hotel for the next few nights. Do you think you can handle that?” he asked Ravin.
“Thanks Mick, I’m sure I could put up with that inconvenience just for a few nights.” He replied with a smile to his voice and face.

The Yulara Resort Hotel has a five star rating and one of the top hotels in the Northern Territory.
Their rooms were adjacent and sumptuous. Ravin had not spent a night in a room like this before and he felt very privileged to be able to do so.

After showers they joined each other at the restaurant and consumed a meal that was excellently prepared and presented. A bottle or two of good Australian wine complimented their meal.
It had been a tiring day and both men turned in early for the night.

East of Warburton, Great Central Road, Western Australia. 7th April

Betty was enthralled at the sunrise this morning.

There were a few wispy clouds to the east and the sun came up behind these, causing them to glow pink. The shadows of them were a grey colour. Several pink and grey galahs flew overhead and she could see that the colouration in both the sunrise and the birds was very similar. Gordon was standing beside her, as he was not going to miss this sunrise. He reckons he has missed so many from working indoors for the last forty years that it was about time to make up for that discrepancy. The sun began to rise from below the scrub and the bushes created a silhouette with the sun's light shining through from behind.

The sun had risen into the sky now and the clouds had changed to their wispy grey, white colour.
"Well my dear that's another one to chalk up for this trip. I am absolutely amazed we can see these sunrises and each one is different and spectacular in its own right," Gordon said to Betty as they were standing hand in hand facing the sun.
"Yes, dear. This is becoming a bit of a ritual with us isn't it? Up before the sun so that we wouldn't miss any of the spectacular sights," she replied. They turned in unison and walked back to their motorhome. Once inside Betty prepared breakfast while Gordon sat and watched. She said that it's best this way as he is always getting in her way.

Chapter 17

East of Warburton, Great Central Road, Western Australia. 7th April

When they had completed their breakfast, Gordon studied the map while Betty was clearing and storing the dishes.

"If we get on the road before seven thirty, we can be through Giles and into Docker River before smoko. That is provided we don't get delayed by more camels again," he told Betty as he worked out the distance and time for that short leg of the trip.

There was a light dew during the night and Gordon needed to wash the windscreen to remove the bugs that had accumulated over the last few days of travelling. As they would be driving towards the sun, he wanted to be as safe as possible this time.

They were ready for the road by just after seven thirty. Gordon eased the vehicle onto the road, as there was a windrow of gravel on the edge of the construction, which he needed to negotiate.

Gordon was still pleasantly surprised of the condition of the road. He had been told that, six weeks after it was graded, that it would be difficult to drive on due to the corrugations. He didn't know when it was last graded, but the condition of the road was good. He had also been told that he should expect to have the road deteriorate when he crossed the border. Anyway, we'll see about that shortly.

As they approached Giles, they could see the Rawlinson Range.

"There's the Meteorological Station with the Warakurna Community nestled at the base of the hills. What a pretty setting for them," Betty exclaimed.

They bypassed these and kept to the main-road. As they reached a crest in the road, they could see the hills to the east of them.
Betty pointed out the tracks of some camels that had reappeared along the side of the road. With the winding road it was difficult to see very far ahead but Betty thought she caught a glimpse of a few camels up ahead.
Gordon slowed the vehicle due to a hill that they were climbing and at the crest, the road veered to the right. They could see some camels, again, up ahead.
As they approached the rear of the herd of camels, Gordon slowed down so as to not disturb them.
Up at the front of the herd the big bulls were having a difference of opinion and were sending up a cloud of dust right at the road edge. Around the corner comes a Landcruiser at speed. Even with the sun behind them they should have slowed well before reaching the camels so they could avoid a collision. The car swerved to miss several animals but didn't seem to slow down. It just kept coming.
By this time Gordon was getting concerned for the safety of the driver and passengers, if there were any. Many of the herd were on the road now, as they had been disturbed by the fighting bulls and also by the approaching vehicle. The Landcruiser struck a glancing blow to one of the cows but continued on. The cow was only slightly injured but Gordon could see her bellowing then she began to move off the road. The vehicle was still approaching Gordon but it seemed to have slowed. Everything looked to have slowed to slow motion as he watched this car getting closer to them. Another cow stepped out into the path of the car just fifty metres from the motorhome. The

car was going too fast and could not stop before the collision. It hit the cow in the hind legs. The cow's back end was thrown up into the air and the animal spun around by the force of the collision. The car was obviously out of control now and heading directly for the motorhome.
"Betty, hang on we're going to crash," he yelled at her.
His foot hit the brake pedal. He didn't swerve, as this would have caused them to tip over.
The cow's body had broken the windscreen of the Landcruiser and the driver could not see ahead. The wheels were locked up as the brakes were applied to the extreme.

The two vehicles collided head on.

Gordon and Betty were flung to the extremes of their seat belts movement then came to a sudden jolt as they were restrained by them, thus preventing further unnecessary injury. The Landcruiser had buried its front bumper into the front of the motorhome. Both of these are strongly built vehicles but the damage was enough to cause the Landcruiser's radiator to burst. Gordon could hear the fan on his vehicle scouring into his radiator and managed to switch off the engine before too much damage was done. Betty was sitting in her seat and Gordon could hear her moaning. He was okay except for a bruise where the seatbelt had stopped him. He unbuckled himself and moved over to Betty.
"Betty, can you hear me, dear?" he asked.
It was a few seconds before she answered. "Yes dear I can hear you alright. I think I'm okay. A bit bruised.

But everything seems to work alright," she replied in a pained voice as she moved her hands, arms, legs and ankles. "Perhaps you'd better see to the others."
"Yeah, I'll do that, just as soon as I'm satisfied that you are alright, dear."
"Well, I think I'm fine, dear, so do go and help the others."

Gordon fixed the parking brake and climbed down from the motorhome and sprinted over to the others vehicle's driver's door. The lady driver's head had hit the steering wheel. She was dazed and bleeding from several cuts to the head. The steering wheel had come back and looked like it had pinned her to the seat. He felt for a pulse in her neck and found this was strong but fast. He called out to her but she didn't answer. He assumed she was unconscious. He walked around the back of the vehicle to get to the passengers door and there was a teenage girl who had been in the passenger seat. She had not been wearing a seatbelt and was thrown forward onto the dashboard of the vehicle. She was bleeding from the mouth and forehead where she had come into contact with the windscreen. In a glance he could see that she also had a broken leg. Her pulse was strong but fast and Gordon recalled his first aid training and began working out a plan to help these people out of the vehicle in case it should catch fire.

After checking out the two occupants of the vehicle, he walked around the vehicles to determine if there were any other dangers. He could see none and discovered that this was a diesel-engined vehicle so the danger of explosion was minimal. He checked out the battery, which is at the front of the vehicle and saw that it was not causing any short circuits. They were safe from that problem.

Just as he was completing his inspection of the vehicle Betty joined him. She was a little dazed but otherwise seemed fine.
"Betty can you get out the emergency triangle and set it up a hundred metres back down the road, please. That will stop anyone from running into us," Gordon asked her. The road behind them was straight for nearly a kilometre, so there was no danger here as other road users could see them.
She walked off to get that job done. She would be satisfied of Gordon's expertise at first aid and would be back to assist him in a few minutes.

In the back of the Landcruiser, Gordon found a rolled up foam mattress and removed this and put it on the ground beside the vehicle.

Another vehicle pulled up and parked just down the road.

Great Central Road, west of Warakurna, Western Australia 7th April

Angelo was up and about before daylight. He was a bit apprehensive about today. There were some jobs to do on the vehicle before they set out and then the phone call to the boss. He was hoping that there was not bad news. They'd had a good run so far, well with the exception of the fuel problem and it was be good to stick to the plan.

He walked over to where Mick was asleep in his swag and gently poked him in the ribs with the toe of his boot. "Wakey, wakey, Mick me lad. Time to be up and at 'em."
"Yeah, I thought that it was too friggen good to bloody last. You got somethin' on yer mind?" Mick asked him. He could see the lines of concentration on his forehead.
"Yeah Mick, I think we'll change that tarp like you said but I also think we'll change the plates over as well. Nobody's about here and it seems the best option now. When we get into Warakurna, I gotta phone the boss. Then we'll know what the cops know and can alter our plans if we need to."

Mick extracted himself from his swag and being fully dressed after putting on his boots, rolled up the swag and stored it in the back of the Landcruiser Ute. He knew it was his job to get the meal so he set about doing that.

Chapter 18
Great Central Road, west of Warakurna, Western Australia 7th April

Angelo had his head buried under the bonnet of the Landcruiser. There was still some dirty fluid draining from the bottom of the fuel filter and he was concerned about this. He closed the drain cock and then operated the priming pump. He started the engine at the first try and was very pleased with this. As he turned off the engine, Mick told him that his breakfast was ready.
They ate in silence, indicating that the tension was starting to show again as they neared a difficult part of the plan. Both of them were keeping their thoughts to themselves.

With the meal completed, Mick continued with the clearing away of the utensils. Angelo located and unloaded the brown tarp and the Northern Territory licence plates.
Mick gave him a hand to fit the brown tarp after the green one was removed. Angelo changed over the licence plates and dug a hole to bury the Western Australian license plates.
He proceeded to dig a larger hole and then filled it in again after laying the folded green tarp in the bottom.
"It's a pity we don't have some company's logo to stick on the side, mate. It might throw the buggers off our scent," Mick said.
"Yeah. We did that in Kalgoorlie, I think that might land us in the shit if there's cops out here."
Having said that, he cast his mind back to yesterday and wondered if that black cop in Warburton was onto them. The mechanic gave us the third degree. I wonder if he was suspicious? Angelo thinks.

Great Central Road, west of Warakurna, Western Australia 7th April

Several vehicles go past on the road about one kilometre from their camp. Both men could hear the sounds and see the dust of them but the vehicles were unsighted.
"Road seems bloody busy this morning," Mick says as he cocks his head to hear the vehicles better.
"Yeah, I reckon they must have got out of bed before us. Well that's less traffic for us to worry about," Angelo replied. He checked his watch and saw that it was just seven o'clock.
As Mick was putting away the last of the breakfast stuff, Angelo started the engine. Once again it started first try. Perhaps this is a good omen for the day.

They are on the road and travelling east again heading for Warakurna. The information tells him that there is a public phone there.

The road is corrugated now and they are forced to travel at about seventy kilometres per hour to get the most comfortable ride. Angelo was driving again and it took them just an hour to make the distance. As they approached they could see some buildings with one that looked like a dome.
"That's probably the Met. Station," said Mick pointing to it.

Angelo turned off the main road and entered the area of the roadhouse. He parked by the fuel bowser enclosure and switched off the engine. He let Mick organise the fuel while he made his way to the phone. He was connected and soon was talking to the boss in

Sydney. The two hour time difference meant that the boss was already in the office and waiting for his call.

Mick could see him from the vehicle and watched his face to see if he could read it. From what he could understand of Angelo's expression, he reckoned on bad news. This is not good, he thinks. He followed the attendant into the roadhouse and paid the fuel bill, then sat in the vehicle until Angelo returned.
"For God's sake Angelo, tell me what's bloody going on. Don't keep me in suspense any more, ya bastard."
Before Angelo spoke he drove out of the roadhouse area and back onto the main road.
"Yeah, okay, okay, keep ya bloody hair on, it's complicated." He replied. After taking a deep breath, he continued. "It seems that the cops are onto us comin' on this road. Our man in Kalgoorlie said two cop cars left Kalgoorlie last night in a hell of a hurry towards Menzies. The robbery is on all the TV and radio news right across the country. They know about this vehicle and the WA plates. So it was a good thing that we changed to NT plates and from a green to a brown tarp. It just might help. The boss's man in Kalgoorlie has been charged but is out on bail. He doesn't know anything about us so we should be okay. The news reports say that we are dangerous and possibly armed. So it's just as well that we aren't. We've gotta bury the boxes in two or three stashes and record their locations in the GPS, our memories and on paper but so that no one else could decipher it. The boss said 'Don't be stupid and put an X on the map'.
"Friggen hell, Angelo. How the bloody hell are we going to get out of this one, with our skins?" Mick

asked in a very agitated manner. His blood pressure was up and his face was getting red.
"Bloody hell Mick, just settle down will ya! Everything's gonna be okay. We just gotta do a few things different from the original plan. That's all! No big deal! We just gotta find a few locations away from the road so we aren't spotted to dig some holes. Then we'll bury the boxes and we're sweet. Simple," he told Mick it was simple but he knew it wasn't quite that easy.

Angelo drove out from the service station and back onto the road and was travelling east again. The surface has improved a little and now he was doing about ninety kays.
"Look, Mick, keep an eye out for some feature that will be easy to locate from, like those hills over there," Angelo said pointing to a row of barren looking hills to the right and left.
They had been on the road for about forty minutes when they came upon a stand of Desert Oak trees. Angelo stopped the vehicle. "How about that for a location? The only forest in the desert. I reckon we'll make one deposit here somewhere."

In just a few hundred metres he found an old two-wheel track leading off to the left, he followed this. It continued for about two kilometres and put them well out of view of the road.
Taking the GPS from the vehicle he located an area close to several trees that was good digging. He recorded this location in the GPS and also wrote it down in a notebook.

Great Central Road, west of Warakurna, Western Australia 7th April

South 25° 05’ 17” East 128° 30’ 12”

He marked on the map with the word ‘Desert Oak Forest’.

They broke out a shovel each and began digging. The red earth was firm but easy enough to dig. They spent ten minutes to make a hole about a metre square and the same in depth.
Not being used to this activity they rested several times to catch their breath.
After shifting their load, they removed seven of the boxes and lowered them into the hole. Then they filled in the hole using the soil that they had removed from the hole which they had made and spread the thin, narrow leaves all over the area to make it look like there hadn’t been any disturbance. It wasn’t perfect but at a passing glance it would be difficult to recognise that a hole had been dug here.

Both men stood back and admired their work. “Well, then. That’s the first of them. Let’s hope the next one is as easy as this one, Mick,” Angelo said, feeling happy with the result so far.
“What about termites, won’t they eat out the boxes and cause the ground to collapse?” Mick asked in concern.
“Nar, ya dummy! There’re made of treated pine. The termites don’t like to eat ‘em.”

Back in the Landcruiser again, they made their way back to the main road on a parallel track and turned to the east once more. In about another five kilometres they came to a creek crossing. It was dry. Checking the map, Angelo was certain that this is Giles Creek.

Angelo turned off again following a set of animal tracks between the spinifex, scrub and some boulders that were strewn around. He headed away from the road about twice the distance as before. The ground here was not as easy to dig and it took them nearly half an hour to make a hole the same size.
More resting was needed here and before they had finished the digging their muscles were beginning to burn.
The next seven boxes were removed from the bed to the ute, carried over and laid into the hole and back-filled with earth again. There were a few large boulders close by and these were rolled over and placed on top of the shallow mound of new soil. Angelo used the GPS once again to plot the exact location of the boxes.

South 25° 06' 27", East 128° 33' 15"

On his map he printed 'Giles Creek'

After a short rest again Angelo got Mick to drive the Landcruiser for a while and he dragged a dried bush over the tracks on the soft sand to obliterate them. He'd heard of this done before and it seemed like a good idea. A good breeze would soon cover their tracks anyway. He let Mick drive back to the main road and then turned east yet again. Mick was not used to driving on dirt roads and Angelo could see he was not happy but would let him go until he complained.

Chapter 18

Great Central Road, west of Warakurna, Western Australia 7th April

He took some time studying the map between bumps and reckoned that if they travel up the Sandy Blight Junction road they would find a good place for the next drop. That was in about thirty kilometres from the last drop.

The view of the hills had taken Angelo's eye and they were nearly up to the back of the Mazda Motor home before they realised that it was not moving but stationary. It was parked near the middle of the road and it looked like another vehicle was parked close to the front of it.

Mick's first reaction was "Bloody cops. They've got this poor bastard pulled up."
He quickly pulled up about a hundred and fifty metres from the rear of the vehicle and they sat watching for a short time. They could see several people moving around but no sign of uniforms. Angelo picked up a pair of binoculars and studied the situation for several moments.
"No mate they've had a prang with another vehicle. We'd better get up there and see if we can help."
"Bloody hell, Angelo, we can't stop here. If there's been a prang that means cops."
"Mick, settle down. The cops are a hundred miles away. It'd take them at least two hours to get here. We've gotta help these people."
"Okay, then but one of us needs to stay close the bloody vehicle and be ready to piss off quick if we need to."

"Alright, that sounds good to me. But go past and park the other side of them so we can get out quickly if necessary.'

Mick drove up slowly and once they were around the motorhome they could see the damage and the injured people in the vehicle.
"Shit, mate. It looks bad," Mick said as he parked the Landcruiser at the side of the road. "I'll stay here and you go and help the bloke from the motorhome. He looks like he knows what he's doing."

Angelo paced back to where Gordon and Betty were working out a plan of action.

Warburton, Great Central Road, Western Australia 7th April

Just as the eastern sky was showing signs of light, the stars were beginning to dim and the birds began to sing, Don stirred in his swag. He rolled over and then thought that it was a good time to get up and get started for the day. As he thought about the discussion with Billy-The-Lid, yesterday, he became excited with anticipation for what he expected to be able to find today.
He extracted himself from the swag just as Ted opened his eyes.

"G'day Ted. I can sense it's going to be an interesting day today. One that we'll not forget for a long time," Don told him.
"I say old chap. It seems that you may be a little excited. You have that childish grin of anticipation on your face. Just like you were about to have your thirteenth birthday party," Ted paused, then continued, "but I understand your anticipation, because I feel in a similar mood. Quite elated in fact!"

Both men looked at each other a little sheepishly for a moment then set about starting the day.

While Don was attending his needs in the ablution block, Ted had sausages and eggs with toast cooking in the campers' kitchen. This was well set out with gas cook top, electric kettle and fridge.

Chapter 19

Warburton, Great Central Road, Western Australia 7th April

They sat down to eat their meal just as some of the other campers were stirring.
"I think we'll get out of here before these blokes start asking too many questions. They always want to know where you've been, what you've seen and where you're going. We can really do without their questions at this time," Don exclaimed to Ted, who nodded his head in agreement.
Don cleaned away the breakfast things and stowed them once again in the back of the Landcruiser ute. With their swags and other gear stored again they were ready to get on the road at seven o'clock. Ted opened the compound gate and closed it after Don had driven through, then he got into the passenger seat beside him.

Once back on the main road they headed out in a north-easterly direction. To the right were the newly grassed playing fields with lights on tall poles. The place was very quiet in the early morning with the exception of the bird-calls. The locals were well known for their lack of early morning activity.
The unsealed road was rough with some loose shingle on the surface. The old creek was dry but they could see where the water level had risen to by the debris still in the shrubs and trees.
"I say old chap, this would be interesting country to travel over in the wet."
"Yes Ted, I think you would need a helicopter for a few days until things dried out a bit. The road the other side of town was the typical red dirt and that does get very interesting when wet."

Chapter 19

Warburton, Great Central Road, Western Australia 7th April

The road gets a little undulating as the road bypasses most of the low hills to the southeast. After about an hour's driving they come to an outcrop of white rock beside the road. Don stops the vehicle and reverses back and parks beside it. They take their knapping tools and chip away small sections of the rock. It is quartzite material and in the fractures there is an ironstone residue.

"This is typical of some gold bearing deposits, Ted. I'd like to dolly this up 'n pan it off to see if we can get some colour."

Ted was collecting some samples while Don returned to the ute and brought back the dolly pot, pan and container of water. Some of the samples were put into the dolly pot and Don dollied it up for several minutes until it was reduced to a fine powder. The dolly pot was emptied onto the pan and Don worked this with a little water. By swilling it from side to side and gently working in a circular motion he was able to separate the heavier particles from the majority of the material. Most of the lighter material and the larger lumps, he removed from the pan with his thumb. As Don worked the pan there was a few specs of fine gold at the tail of the sediment in the bottom.

"Yep, Ted, it does show some colour. But it is very low-grade ore. But it is encouraging because there must be a greater concentrate in the vicinity. Maybe the land has dropped since this formed or this was pushed up from below. Or maybe this is just another of those floaters and shouldn't be here at all. We could check it out with your seismic array but that will take several hours to set up. What do you think?"

Chapter 19

Warburton, Great Central Road, Western Australia 7th April

"Don, I think we should push on to the location as shown us by Billy-The-Lid. That should be our primary objective, surely!" Ted replied.
"Of course you are right. We can come back to this sometime later. It easy to locate, being so close to the road but log it into the GPS for future reference, Ted."
"Consider it done, old chap."

Don packed away the gear he had been using. The undulating country has given them some respite from the dreary road. They frequently drove past groups of camels just off the road. Some of these groups were five animals and some were as large as fifteen. There was no movement from them as the vehicle went past and Ted asked Don to stop where they were close to a group.

Ted took his camera and standing on top of the vehicle got some shots of the animals.
"Incredible animals! Soft footed so they don't damage the environment. Long necks so they can feed off the tops of the scrub. That leaves the lower feed for the kangaroos and emus. Don, I think I'll start farming camels when we get this show off the ground," Ted said as he got down from the roof and took some more shots from the ground.
"I think you might get a surprise about camels, Ted. These are wild and I hear they are not pleasant to be around in close quarters. I think I'll stick to mining gold. It'll be less unpredictable," Don replied.

When Ted was in his seat Don drove off again.

Chapter 19

Warburton, Great Central Road, Western Australia 7th April

Ted was consulting the map of the area and some of the explorers had noted the number of gnamma holes that were around in this area. There was one at the side of the road just up ahead and he got Don to stop at it. This was marked on his map as "Tjulum Rockhole". He had never seen one before and was inquisitive. Don pulled over in an area where the road had been shifted. The ground was very hard and of solid rock. In this rock were several holes. Possible natural holes where the softer rock had been eroded away or been scraped out by animals or humans. Rainwater had collected there. It was evident from the many footprints around, that it was frequently visited by dingoes.

"By Jove, old man, that water looks a very dirty green. These animals must have a very strong constitution to survive on that putrid stuff."

"Yes they sure do. But they don't look that healthy, judging by the ones which I've seen."

They were back on the road again in several minutes. Cresting a rise in the road Don pointed out the Rawlinson Range to Ted. "That's where we'll find Giles Meteorological Station and Warakurna Roadhouse. It must be about forty kilometres to go, so we'll be there in about half an hour."

The road material was constantly changing. Generally on the flats it was constructed of the natural red dirt. On the slopes it was made from gravel. The ridges of each rise were rough where harder rocks have a stratum. The road graders had difficulty when grading these because of their different degrees of hardness. But it made for interesting driving.

Chapter 19

Warburton, Great Central Road, Western Australia 7th April

They left the highway and entered the Warakurna Roadhouse and Don pulled up next to the diesel bowser cage to get fuel. After several minutes an attendant came out to unlock the cage and pump some fuel for them.

"Got a bit of excitement here last night," the attendant told them. "We had three police cars come through early this morning. They had an early breakfast then on they went again. Wouldn't say what they were doing but it sounded urgent. Got a call from their boss in Kalgoorlie last night to expect them and have stuff ready for them. He said they had to keep going."

"How often do you get the police out here?" Don asked.

"We get the regular visits from the Laverton Police each month but I've never seen the likes of this before. Zoomed in, got fuelled up, took breakfast and zoomed out again," he replied in an obviously excited voice.

"Well, that sure is something to brighten up your day," Don told him with a great smile on his face.

The attendant hung up the bowser nozzle when he had finished and locked the cage again. Don followed him inside and paid for the fuel. The inside of the roadhouse was very clean with a few of the local artefacts displayed on the walls for sale. Don avoided the temptation to buy any prepared food but it looked good.

They drove out and got back onto the main road again. Presently there was a panorama of hills in front of them. As they worked their way through these low hills they came across a stand of Desert Oak trees. They were in a fairly tight forest on the lower ground.

After several kilometres they were back into open country again.

They had to slow for a couple of very short, deep and sharp creek crossings. Then they came to a wider creek and Ted checked the GPS and told Don that it was Giles Creek.
"By Jove, old man, those hills are quite impressive. I had no notion of their scenery. I know the map shows hills and ranges but these are spectacular," Ted told him as he waved his hand around pointing out the various hills.

Up ahead Don could see the road winding around the hills. They came to a straight section and at the end of this he could see a vehicle ahead. But there was no dust. As he got closer he recognised the motorhome of Betty and Gordon. It was parked on the road near the middle at an angle.

Don slowed the vehicle.

As they approached he could see another vehicle close to the front of the motorhome and a mustard coloured Landcruiser ahead of that.
"I don't like the look of this Ted," Don said sternly, as they neared the back of the motorhome.

Then they became level with the front and they could see the damaged vehicles and the injured people in the Landcruiser. There was Gordon, Betty and one of the men from the other vehicle standing about them. Don drove just a few metres past then pulled to the left, parked his Landcruiser and at a quick pace, walked back to the accident site.

“How can I help, Gordon?” he asked as he got close. “How many people are hurt?”

Yulara, Northern Territory, Australia, 7th April

Mick Jones was in the shower before the eastern sky became visible through the windows of the balcony to his room. He preferred to get started in the early morning. He considered this was his most productive time of the day. After he had dressed he attended to several phone calls and cleared up a few of the difficulties that come with his position in the company. As founder, chairman of the board and the CEO, he was constantly in demand to solve some of the more difficult situations. He preferred to do this early in the morning. He found that he was able to get a better result at this time of day when others had obviously failed.

Donning clean slacks and shirt he made his way to the dining room. As he past Castle's door, he heard the door opening, so he stopped and waited for Castle to come out.

"Good morning, Castle. I trust that your room was up to standard and that you slept well?" he asked as Castle stepped from the room.

"Good morning Mick. Yes thank you. The room is excellent, equal to any that I've stayed in before. The bed is comfortable and I did have a relaxing sleep," he replied.

"Excellent news! Leave your gear in the room; we'll be back here again tonight. I've booked in for just one more night," Mick told him, "but for now, let's get to the dining room for a top order breakfast."

"I'm with you on that one, Mick."

They made their way to the dining room, which is on the second floor. They were the only guests in the room at the moment. There range of food for breakfast was enormous and it took both of them several minutes to decide on their meal.
They both returned to a table with plates filled with a steaming meal. A waitress brought coffee to the table. They were quiet while they consumed the meal and as they began their coffee, other guests started arriving. The two men kept up a quiet dialogue between themselves. Mick said that he wanted to keep to themselves at this stage and not encourage others to approach them. With a quick glance around the room, Mick did not recognise any faces.
Mick asked the waitress to prepare them a lunch, which they could take with them, as they would be away from facilities all day. She returned with this after five minutes.

With their hunger well and truly satisfied the two men made their way to the lobby and had the concierge call them a taxi to take them to the airport. After a few minutes of waiting, one arrived and soon they were being driven down the main road and to the airport.
It was the same driver who had driven them from the airport last night and, after asking where he had got up to last night, he completed his description of the history of the area. Castle was taken with the telling of this information as it gave him a better understanding of the people and this land, which he had come to like.
Presently they were at the gate to the aircraft compound and the taxi driver left them there.

Yulara, Northern Territory, Australia, 7th April

Mick and Castle made their way to the helicopter. Mick immediately began his pre-flight checks and had the attendant fill it with fuel. After fifteen minutes they were ready for take-off.
Mick, using the radio, checked with the control tower for clearance for take-off. This was granted after a delay because of the arrival of another Qantas flight full of tourists.
As the helicopter gained height, Ayes Rock came into view.
"I can see why there are so many tourists out here, Mick!" exclaimed Castle as he could see the rock with the different light on it. "You have here a magnificent natural spectacle that would be amongst the top 'must sees' for any tourist."
"Yes, we are very proud of the 'Rock," said Mick, "the light does make it so different each time that I see it. It is truly magnificent as you say."

Mick past to the east and south of the rock so that Castle could get a good look at it then he set a course for the west. In a few minutes the Olgas came into view.
"Definitely and place of contrasts, Mick," he said as he pointed to the Olgas.
"These two formations here are different material. The Olgas are of a conglomerate while Ayers Rock is a solid sandstone boulder. The aborigines call them Uluru and Kata Tjuta," Mick told him.

Mick maintained a heading of two hundred and seventy degrees, due west.

Chapter 20

Yulara, Northern Territory, Australia, 7th April

"We came past near Mount Woodroffe yesterday. That's the highest peak in The Northern Territory. That's now behind us and you'll notice that we are losing altitude as we head west. We'll get down to just under six hundred metres above sea level near the border. Just near that is where I expect to be able to test out your equipment, Castle," Mick told him.

Castle made his way to the back of the cabin and switched on his equipment. In a minute or two everything was booted up and carrying out self-diagnostics. There was a lot of information on the screen and he was making some adjustments to the display to sort out the hash from the data.

"Mick, you'll need to reduce airspeed to fifty knots. This is just too much information for this system to decipher," he said in the intercom.
Mick reduced his forward motion to just fifty knots and said, "How's that, 'Castle? Does that improve your information?"
There was no answer from Castle for a moment or two as he again adjusted his system. The displayed data slowed down and he was able to pinpoint the different minerals as they flew over them.

"Yes Mick, I think we have some good information now at that speed." Castle switched on some more equipment. This is based on GPS technology and allows him to pinpoint these minerals and elements for future reference. All the data is being stored on two of the five hard drives. After half an hour he'll need to transfer this data to DVD's.

Chapter 20

Yulara, Northern Territory, Australia, 7th April

"We are over the border now, Castle does there appear to be any changes?"
"No Mick, still much the same. Give me half an hour of this and we can land and then I can examine the results and pinpoint the locations of the different elements and minerals."

Mick changed course and was following the dry watercourse of Giles Creek. In the distance ahead he could see the Great Central Road. Twenty miles before the road he hears an excited call from Castle.
"Mick there is a big change to the data. There appears to be some heavy mineral deposits back there just twenty seconds ago."
"Hang on Castle, I'll go around and cover that area again a bit slower and see if that improves your data."
He banked the aircraft in a tight right turn and once that was completed slowed his forward movement to just ten knots.
"Wow, you should see this display. What a wide variety of minerals there are here. And in abundance too! Later we may be able to determine the recoverable percentage."
Mick banked and turned again to get back onto the previous course. This caused them to fly over the same area a second time. This showed the same data on the screen.
"A lot of heavy mineralisation in that area, Mick. I'd like to investigate that area more closely from the ground after this sweep, if that's okay with you."
"Yes that will be fine Castle."
They were above the road now and following the creek to the northwest.
After two minutes there was a massive blip on screen.

Chapter 20
Yulara, Northern Territory, Australia, 7th April

"Stop! Stop the aircraft! Mick this is incredible!" Shouted Castle in obvious excitement.
Mick stopped to a hover and backed up a little until Castle told him to hover over a specific area.
"The reading I have here is beyond any that I've ever had before. It seems that your Mr Lasseter may not have been wrong after all," Castle said as he pinpointed the location in the system.
"Castle we'll go back to near the road and put down. There you can sort and store your data. It seems that we'll need to send out a ground party to determine how successful this find really is."
Just by the road is an area suitable for landing, so Mick puts the aircraft down and slows the engine to an idle.
Castle had already begun the process and after fifteen minutes he presented Mick with a screen full of sorted data.
"As you can see Mick, the data shows the elements and minerals. The first column is the GPS location, which should be accurate to within two metres. The second column of data is the elements and minerals depicted by their atomic numbers. We can see from this that the most abundant item here is feldspar. Then silica and so on down the list that's sorted in number of 'hits'. The most exciting is this one here. It was about the last entry before we switched to data download. It shows the atomic number for gold. It appears to be in high grade and in quantity. But it is in a very small area. It is a bit baffling."
"Castle, I'm impressed with this information. I think we'll need to have a ground team come out and carry

out a further investigation and determine the extent of what you have found," Mick told him.

It took several more minutes to complete the download of data to the storage discs.
While this was happening, Mick was consulting his charts and decided that he would fly northeast adjacent to the road in an easterly direction. Going across the lay of the land my give different results. This was a good time to test the different angle of interpretation. He told Castle of this suggestion and he agree with Mick.

After half an hour on the ground, Mick advanced the throttles on the engine and they become airborne again.
Castle was getting very similar data on the screen. He was excited at the apparent success of his system.
"Looks like we have a motor vehicle accident up ahead, Castle. I'll need to go around them a bit for a look." Mick approached the vehicle on the road. There was a motorhome and several Landcruisers, one with a trailer behind it. It appears that several people may be hurt. He set down the helicopter off to the side of the road so the air wash would not affect the people on the ground.

"Mick! Mick! We got the same reading again. A big blip of data on the left side as you flew over the road. There must be a large concentration of minerals right under the road," Castle told him.
"Okay, Castle, we'll certainly check it out later. For now let's see if we can lend a hand with these people here."

"I'm with you, Mick," said Castle as he removed his headset, shut down his system and climbed out from the helicopter.

As Mick approached the group of people, one of them came towards him.
"Hello, I'm Gordon, we've had an accident and have two injured people. If you've got a first aid kit, please bring it with you to supplement ours."
"Okay, we'll do that." He motioned for Castle to go back and get the kit, which he did, and was beside Mick again in a minute.

Tjukayirla Roadhouse, Great Central Road, Western Australia 7th April

The road did have some good sections in it so it wasn't all bad. It just seemed that way sometimes. Alec and his team in their three Landcruisers were making good time. He checked his watch by torchlight: two a.m.

His mind keeps him busy "If we keep up this speed we should be on station just inside the WA border by 7:30 in the morning. With any sort of luck we should be in time to set up a roadblock before too much traffic passes by. Sure there would be some traffic from the east, which we would miss but they aren't of a concern to us. Hopefully the getaway vehicle and the crooks in it have camped somewhere along here and we'll pass them in the night. Let's just hope they are not camped too close to the road and see us go past. Surprise is always the best way to catch these types. It worked with their mate at Southern Cross. Pity the boss couldn't get the helicopter. The ride would have been much more comfortable. It was on another job and out of town for a couple of days. Pity just the same. This is bloody hard work driving in the dark under these road conditions."

Bang!

"That's another kangaroo, which got too close to the roo bar at the front of the vehicle. I don't like hitting them but is very difficult not to when they are so unpredictable in their movements. I told the driver not to swerve, as that would be just too dangerous for us. Brakes are okay if it's essential, but just keep the vehicle straight. The driver is slowing down now so it must be my turn to drive for the next hour. Well I'm certainly awake enough for it."

Alec had been sitting in the seat behind the driver. As the vehicles all came to a stop, doors opened and people get out, stretch their legs and changed position. By keeping fresh drivers behind the wheel, Alec reckons on maximising vehicle and passenger safety.

So far the practice is working well.

It was another driver change and a half before they reached Warburton. The boss had been busy and had the roadhouse open up for them to refuel. It usually closes around five in the afternoon and opens again at eight in the morning. The management found that few people drive at night and it was no commercial value in night trading.
It took fifteen minutes for the three vehicles to refuel and to have the windscreens cleaned. The occupants were not in uniform and it was hoped that this might prevent tongues from wagging. The roadhouse personnel were told not to broadcast that police are out here in force, that they had a special job to do and would be back this way again later in the day.

The eastern sky began to lighten at around five, so the next hour or so they would be driving into the sun. The fronts of the vehicle were inspected to determine if any had been damaged in the collisions with the kangaroos. There was some superficial damage but nothing to prevent them from completing their mission.

"Okay people, saddle up," Alec called as the last of the windscreens were finished.
Everyone climbed back into the vehicles and off they travelled again, heading out of town in a north-easterly direction.

Unfortunately there was no improvement in the road's condition. In fact in several places it was very bad, particularly at the dips and crests. At one of the crests, the leading vehicle became airborne so those following slowed down at the worst of the problems.
Alec decided to have an extra driver change during this period as they were all getting tired and this was the most difficult of driving.

Driving into the sun with the hills on the horizon was interesting to say the least. Some of the crew even gave it top marks for a great sunrise.

The sun was just up into the sky when they pulled into the Warakurna Roadhouse for fuel and breakfast. It had been a very long and arduous night for all of them. They welcomed the fifteen extra minutes it took them for a short breakfast break. Lunches were already packed for them to collect as well.

With full tanks, clean windscreens and full bellies they headed back to the main road again.
Alec checked his watch. "Just six o'clock, right on time. Now for the border and we'll have our roadblock

set-up before eight o'clock," he told the team in his vehicle.

Now that it was daylight they could take in some of the scenery, which changed frequently around them. None of this team had been out here before and most of them agreed that it was very picturesque.

The stand of trees that looked like a forest took the interest of several men and there were even a few camels to be seen well off the road.
"Shit, I'm glad we didn't hit one of those buggers last night. I think they would hit a bit harder than kangaroos," one of the team said out loud, pointing to the group of camels.
Everyone in the vehicle agreed that it was indeed good fortune.

Just on seven fifty, they arrived at the border with all its signage.
"Welcome to the Northern Territory", "Thank you for visiting Western Australia", "Have a safe trip", "Return soon." Was the wording on some of the signs.

The area at the border was relatively flat with the hills being several kilometres away.
Alec looked around for a good site for the roadblock. Keeping in mind that these may be desperate men; he wanted to block off any possible escape. They moved back down the road again and found a suitable place. The hills come right down to the road just west of the Sandy Blight Junction Road intersection. After changing into uniforms, they set up two vehicles on

the road facing in opposite directions. The other is parked just off the road out of immediate sight.

"Now it's just a waiting game. See who comes along."

Alec has sent two men to get some sleep in the vehicle away from the road. The team would take it in hour about turns to sleep. They were close enough to assist if and when it became necessary.
After about one and a half hours the first vehicle, coming from the east, was a Landcruiser. The woman driver was extremely nervous as two of the police team approached the vehicle. They asked for her driver's license, name and address. There was some camping gear in the rear compartment of the vehicle and the passenger, a teenage girl, was in the front seat. Both were wearing seatbelts.
When Alec was satisfied everything was in order he showed her a photograph of a vehicle similar to the getaway vehicle and asked her if he had seen it in the last two days.
"Gee, there are so many of those around here. Some with canvas covers and some without. But no, I don't think I've seen the one you're looking for," she replied.
"Thank you, madam, for your assistance; you are free to be on your way," Alec told her.

The lady was on her way and seemed to be in a hurry.
"She seems to drive fast for these conditions senior," Alec said to the senior constable standing alongside him.
"Well, she is local and perhaps she's used to the roads Sarge," he replied.

"Yeah, you could be right."
There was no more traffic for some time and Alec was getting to wonder if they were even on the right road.

After they had been at the roadblock for about two hours they could hear the sound of a helicopter in the distance away to the west several kilometres.
"Pity we didn't have one of those last night, Sarge. We'd all be in better shape this morning," Artie said as he walked up beside Alec.
"Yeah, yeah, I know but it was out of town on another job. One day we'll get a police chopper and not have to hire it when we need one," he responded.

The discussion got Alec to thinking. He took Artie aside and sounded out his musings. "What if they had arranged to have a chopper meet them here and take them out? Is that a plausible possibility?"
"Well we could send a car down the road and check out the chopper. That will answer the question."
"Yeah, that's a good point. It'll leave us one vehicle and three men down."
"A quick call on the radios and that will have them back here in quick time, Alec."
"Okay, Artie. We'll leave the two sleeping. Take two blokes with you and check out the chopper. See what's going on. Don't do anything if it's suspect and keep on the radio. Okay?"

Detective Senior Constable Arthur Herberts took two constables with him and they drove west along the road towards the sound of the helicopter.

Chapter 21

Tjukayirla Roadhouse, Great Central Road, Western Australia 7th April

The road was windy and hilly and rounding one of the bends, they come to a red triangle warning sign placed on the road. He told the driver to slow the vehicle, not sure of what was around the next corner.

What they did see was most unusual and unexpected. There was an injured camel on the road, looked like two broken hind legs. He could see several parked Landcruisers, facing towards them. There seemed to be a bus or perhaps a motorhome parked on the road. It looked like the vehicle they had stopped at the roadblock parked in front of the bus. Alongside this appeared to be several people laying down and being cared for by several other people. And a helicopter parked off to the side.

Recognising the scene as a motor vehicle accident he said "Okay people, we have an MVA with possible injured." He paused for a while, deciding the best course of action. "Constable radio the Sarge and tell him we have here an MVA. Please stand by to provide backup! Driver, park just in front of the Landcruiser ute with the trailer, you stay with the vehicle. Constable you come with me and we'll approach and determine the next course of action."

As the vehicle pulled to a stop, they got out and walked towards the scene.

They didn't see the other man near the mustard coloured Landcruiser.

East of Warakurna, Great Central Road, Western Australia, 7th April

Because Don and Ted were actively involved in the mining industry, their first aid training was up to date. Even though they arrived several minutes after the other vehicle and about five minutes after the accident, they took charge of the operation to remove the injured from the vehicle.
It was a difficult job because the driver was jammed in her seat and the crumpled front of the vehicle had her pinned.

Gordon said. "Thanks for your help Don, my first aid is a bit rusty so take charge please."
He could see that the driver was jammed into her seat by the steering wheel. The passenger was cramped onto the dash.
Don asked Ted to bring the first aid kit and several pine boards. They will do for a splint, he said.
He pointed to Angelo and said, "mate, you can go and help Ted."

While he was waiting for Ted to return he closely inspected the steering wheel and the seat mountings. "Gordon we'll unbolt the seat, it'll only take several minutes and she'll be free. I'll get some tools." He hurried back to his Landcruiser passing Ted on the way. "Splint and bandage the girl's leg, Ted before we move her. It'll reduce the stress for her."

Presently he had the tools and was unbolting the seat, while Ted was applying a splint to the girl's leg to support it.
They were all surprised to hear and then see a helicopter approach and land near them. The pilot and passenger alighted and approached to vehicles. After several seconds of taking in the scene the pilot said, "hello people, I'm Mick Jones and my associate Ravin Goldcastle. Our chopper is at your disposal if you need to evacuate these people to hospital."
"Thanks, Mick. I'm Don King and my offsider Ted Walsh," he said motioning to Ted. "These are Gordon and Betty from the motorhome and this bloke who is helping is..?" he didn't know the bloke's name and hoped he would offer it to them.
"Oh yeah, I'm Angelo." Angelo told them.
"Mick, Ted has the passenger ready to be removed from the vehicle; we've splinted the broken leg. We'll put her onto that mattress and attend to her other injuries. In the meantime I'm unbolting the seat so we can remove the driver. She's trapped and probably has some internal injuries."

The girl was carefully removed from the dash and laid onto the mattress. Ted attended to her scalp wound. He could not find any other broken bones but she was badly bruised from having been thrown about in the crash. By this time Don was removing the last bolt from the seat. Angelo was in the back holding the seat forward to release the pressure on the bolt. As the seat moved a fraction backwards the driver gave a painful moan.

East of Warakurna, Great Central Road, Western Australia, 7th April

"I think we have some internal injuries here, so getting her to a doctor quickly is paramount. In the mean time we can keep applying pressure to the stomach region." He took several pillows from the rear of the vehicle and gently pressed them into the woman's stomach area as the seat was moved back. He hoped that by keeping this pressure applied it would prevent excessive internal haemorrhaging.

With the help of the others, Don removed the woman, still in the seat from the front of the vehicle and placed her on the road.

She had other injuries that Don was attending to, when another vehicle approached from the east.

"Mick, can we fit the lady into your chopper in this seat? It could be the best way to transport her in view of the internal injuries."

"Don, I'm sure we can make it fit. I've got some cargo straps, which will tie it down. But the girl will need to be on the floor on that mattress."

The police Landcruiser was parked on the other side of his Landcruiser and Don could not see it but he saw two-uniformed policeman approaching.

"G'day, mate! We have everything under control for the injured," Don told the policemen. "We're just about to load them onto the chopper to take them to the nearest medical centre, probably at Yulara. You can help us get them on board."

"Yeah, we can do that. Is the driver able to answer some questions?" Artie asked.

"No, mate, she's still unconscious. We haven't had a peep out of her since the prang happened," Gordon told him, "but I can help you with some accident details after they've gone. I was driving the motorhome."

Don walked back to his ute to collect a tie-down strap from the side box. On the way he walked passed the police vehicle.

While this discussion was taking place, no one saw Angelo leave the area and walk to his vehicle. Mick Dunraven was extremely agitated and this showed by the foul look on his face.
"Bloody hundred miles away? Ya bastard. Ya don't know what you're friggen talking about! Now we got bloody cops crawling around. What are ya gunna do now mister friggen smart arse?" Mick exclaimed in a very agitated voice.
"Look just settle down, Mick. They are probably just driving through and don't even know about us. Just keep ya bloody hair on, stay calm and we'll be okay," Angelo said quietly as he tried to quieten Mick down.
"Listen here Angelo, I've had as much as I can take from you bastards. These bloody cops being here is the final straw." Mick turned as he finished speaking and picked up something from his bag on the front seat. When he turned around again he had a gun in his hand. It was a nine-millimetre Glock automatic.
"Bloody hell, Mick, I said no guns! The boss said no guns! Waving that bloody cannon around here won't get you anywhere! Put it away and let's just drive out of here." Angelo was surprised that Mick had a gun.

He recollected that Mick was agitated at the start of the job but settled down in the last few days. The arrival of the cops must have set him off again. He hoped he wouldn't do anything stupid that would put the job in jeopardy.

While they were talking beside their Landcruiser Ute they heard another vehicle approach from the east. They looked up in time to see two more police vehicles coming into sight.
"Hostage, Angelo! I'm gonna take a friggen hostage! We'll get on the bloody chopper and get clear! Simple!" Mick told him. His voice grew in pitch as he was talking and Angelo feared that Mick had lost his marbles.
He tried to tackle Mick and take the gun from him but got a blow to the head for his trouble. It was a hard hit and he sagged and sat on the ground by the wheel of their ute. He was very groggy and unable to stand. He sat there for what seemed like ten minutes.

Don could hear them talking but could not make out the conversation but did notice that it was heated. He walked back with several tie down straps in his hand. As he passed the other ute he saw Angelo on the ground and stopped to assist him.
Mick Dunraven made his way over to the others by the vehicle and before anyone understood his intentions they were unable to stop him from taking Betty away. He encircled her with one arm and with the gun in the other waved it around and immediately got everyone's attention.
"Okay, ya bastards. Listen to me. The lady gets dead if ya don't do as I say! Understand?" Mick yelled at them. "I'm gonna take that helicopter and get outa here. The old dear comes too and the pilot."

Chapter 22

East of Warakurna, Great Central Road, Western Australia, 7th April

The other police vehicles pulled up just then and the officers began clambering from them. They didn't hear Mick yelling or know the situation.
Mick fired a shot into the air to support his argument.
Artie's first reaction was to yell to everyone, "everyone on the ground. Lay as flat as you can."
He carefully moved over to where Alec and the other police were and told them of the recent events. They began by surveying the scene. They noticed the vehicles and in particular the mustard coloured Landcruiser ute with the brown canopy and Northern Territory plates. Alec remembered the details of Mick Dunraven on the flyer from the Sydney Police.

"Artie, I think this is one of the blokes that we've been looking for. They have changed some details on the vehicle to make it more difficult to identify. But what's set him off? Did you try to apprehend him?" Alec asked Artie.
"That's the funny thing, Alec. He wasn't near us. He stayed at the vehicle the whole time and didn't assist. I didn't even give him a thought. He just ran over, grabbed the lady and yells out," Artie tried to explain, "but where's his accomplice. He was here a while ago."
"Over there by his vehicle, on the ground." One of the constables said, pointing to the mustard coloured Landcruiser. "He's not far away and looks groggy, we could nab him, he's out of sight of the gunman."

Alec spent a few seconds taking the new situation in and planning the next move.

East of Warakurna, Great Central Road, Western Australia, 7th April

While this was happening, Angelo told Don who had just walked over to him, "I think you can help me". Angelo took the GPS from his pocket and handed it to Don. "I'm okay. Keep this. The stored locations will be good for you. Keep out of the way of Mr Arnold. Don't tell the cops about it. And don't ask any questions."

Don was completely puzzled but did as he was asked. He put the GPS into his ute and walked back to the crash site. He had been aware of a commotion there but was unsighted and didn't understand what was happening. When Don got near, Ted told him what had happened and he exclaimed, "By Jove Don. When we were in Warburton, that vehicle had a green tarp on the back and had WA plates. Now it's got a brown tarp and NT plates. Something there is just not right."

"Ted, why would someone change those details on their vehicle! Are you certain of that?" Don asked him.

"By Jove, old chap. As certain as I've been about anything before," Ted responded, paused and continued, "what about that report on the news. Could that vehicle of the gold robbery have been coming this way?"

"Possibly, but I would think it an unlikely getaway route. But then I don't know the criminal mind," Don answered. He wasn't going to tell Ted about the latest development of the GPS unit until they were away from the crowd.

The other police officer who was in the second vehicle with Alec has been trained as a sharp shooter with the Police Tactical Response Group. Alec was some distance away from him but he was able to catch his eye. He used hand signals to indicate that Senior

Chapter 22

East of Warakurna, Great Central Road, Western Australia, 7th April

Constable Richard Morrow should take out Dunraven with the rifle.

Richard was unsighted of Dunraven and was able to crawl away to the police vehicle and retrieve the weapon. By keeping to the gutter of the road he was able to get into a position where he had a clear shot at Dunraven but not without some risk to his captive. He sighted in on the target and awaited the order to fire.

Mick was becoming more agitated and Betty was looking fairly ill and frail as he held her. Being a bit rough with her, Dunraven was trying to emphasise his point and get something to happen.

Alec called out to him. “I’m Alec Webster and I’d like to talk to you about this situation! What is your name so we can talk?”

Mick Dunraven yelled back at him, “Not if you’re a bloody copper, I won’t. Just get the pilot to get this thing started so I can get out of here.”

Alec replied, “What is your gripe with everyone? Obviously someone has done something to upset you! Can you tell me what that was and maybe we can sort this out.”

“Ya sound like a bloody copper and I said I won’t talk to you. Just get this thing started,” he fired another shot into the air just over their heads.

“Look we can help you here with whatever you want but first let’s talk about what’s troubling you. Can you tell us what caused this upset?” Alec was careful with his words. He could not afford to get him more riled than he already was.

“Why don’t you bloody coppers just clear off and leave me be? I just wanna get out of here.” Mick Dunraven replied in a very agitated voice.

His voice seemed to steady a little and Artie reckoned that he might have begun winning in turning Mick Dunraven around. "If we leave, will you be prepared to let the lady go? She looks pretty ill to me and I'm sure you don't want to hurt her," Alec called.
After a few seconds to mull over this suggestion Mick Dunraven replied, "Yeah, okay! You bloody coppers piss off and when I see your dust on the road, I'll let her go. But the chopper's gotta be goin' first," Mick agreed.

Alec could see now that he was making some headway and didn't reply to him for several minutes.
"I can't get the pilot to start the chopper till you've let the lady go. So let her go first, and then we can get the chopper started for you. Where do you want to go?"
"Look just stop stuff'n around and let me get goin' outa here. I'll let the lady go after you leave and the pilot can start the chopper. I wanna go back to Sydney."

Suddenly, Betty passed out and sagged in the arms of Mick. The unexpected weight caught him off balance and he stooped to let her fall to the ground. At this point Alec signalled to Richard to fire.
Richard had a good sight of Mick but this altered as he bent over to let Betty down to the ground. He followed with the rifle but was not able to get a suitably positive sight.

He waited.

Chapter 22

East of Warakurna, Great Central Road, Western Australia, 7th April

Mick Dunraven stood up, his arms empty and a baffled look on his face.

He was in perfect sight again. Richard fired two shots in rapid succession. The first hit Dunraven in the upper right arm. The second hit his left hand. The automatic flew out of his hand as he fell to the ground. Dunraven took a few seconds to recover from the shock of being shot. He began to crawl towards the gun, which had landed some three metres away.

In a few seconds several of the police officers were on their feet. They soon covered the distance to Dunraven and pinned him to the ground.

Once he was secured, the others ran to be beside Betty. As it turns out she had merely fainted and was not hurt. After a few seconds she came to but was shaken by her experience. Gordon was at Betty's side and he began taking good care of her.

Angelo had been arrested and was handcuffed in the custody of two policemen.

While two policemen were holding down Dunraven, another was attending to his wounds. The first bullet was still in his arm but the second shot had merely grazed the skin.

Alec said to him, "Dunraven this must be your lucky day. You're lucky that Senior Constable Morrow is such a bad shot. He missed your head. No bones broken and you'll be looked after in the prison ward."

Alec decided that they would need to get the injured people to medical attention as fast as they could so he agreed with Mick Jones to have the chopper fly the motor vehicle accident people to Yulara medical centre. The injured Mick Dunraven was well bandaged and able to travel in one of the police vehicles back to Kalgoorlie.

The ute, which Angelo and Mick had been driving, was unloaded and searched. The officers found six boxes hidden under the false floor of the tray. When one of these was opened they found bars of gold, which the Middlemarch Gold Mine stamp on them. Obviously they had been taken from the old bank building in Kalgoorlie several days before.

Artie walked over to Angelo and said, "We found your gold, mate but it's not all there! By my information there should be another fourteen boxes if there are just three bars to a box. Where is the rest of the gold?"
Angelo replied, "I don't know what you're talking about. We only had six boxes." He reckoned that if he put them off the scent they might not look too carefully around here and leave that other bloke, Don, alone.
Alec looked closely at Angelo for a few moments and some doubt crept into his mind. He felt that the whole deal with the gold robbery was a bit suspect. In his mind he could see that it was possible that the rest of the gold could even be still in Kalgoorlie or on another route out of town. But he pushed Angelo a bit more.
"I don't believe you, Botacelli! I think that you've already offloaded the rest somewhere. Where is it?" Alec asked him.
"Get a hold of yourself copper. We only had six boxes and that's all there is to it!" Angelo responded vehemently.

Chapter 22

East of Warakurna, Great Central Road, Western Australia, 7th April

"Okay, then we'll leave it at that for the time being, Botacelli. But I haven't finished with you yet."

Artie walked over to where the other officers we treating Mick Dunraven.

"Is he up to answering any questions?" he asked one of the men.

"I don't think so, Sarge. He's just rambling. I think the shock has got to him," came the reply.

East of Warakurna, Great Central Road, Western Australia, 7th April

The police vehicles had left on their return trip to Kalgoorlie after statements had been taken from everybody. The crashed car was pushed off the road to await recovery. The helicopter was on its way to Yulara with the crash victims. The mustard coloured ute was being driven by one of the police officers. They seemed to believe that it was still carrying all of the gold from the robbery.

Betty seemed to have fully recovered and she said that she did not want to leave Gordon by himself. With the help of Don and Ted, they were able to make the motor home sound enough for Gordon and Betty to get to Alice Springs where they would need a few more permanent repairs.

She made them a snack while they were working and they sat in the motor home when it was ready. This break gave them some time to discuss the events of the morning.

With the engine of the motorhome running, Betty and Gordon said their thanks and farewells to Don and Ted.
"We'll probably cross paths again in the future Don, so until then, keep well and thank you for everything," Gordon said. He climbed into the driver's seat and manoeuvred the vehicle back onto the road again, then headed down the road for Yulara and then onto Alice

Springs with his arm waving out the driver's window and several sharp blasts of the horn.
After Gordon and Betty had departed, Don and Ted sat down and recounted their day. It was mid-afternoon.

"Ted, me old mate! That was one hell of a day! I think it's time to boil the billy and have a cuppa before we move on. After all of the excitement I think I need one. How about you?"
"By Jove, old chap. I do agree. A cup of tea would quite hit the spot," Ted replied.
They gathered a few sticks and lit a fire in the gutter near where the motor home had stood. The billy was on the fire in just a minute. Several minutes later it boiled and the two men were able to relax with a hot cuppa tea.

While Ted was drinking his tea, Don walked over to the ute and came back with the GPS, which Angelo had left with him.
"What do you have there old chap?" Ted asked.
"I'm not too sure what to think of it Ted. That Angelo bloke handed this to me and said, *"Keep this. The stored locations will be good for you. Keep out of the way of Mr Arnold. Don't tell the cops about it."*
"There are two locations listed. It shows a location just a few kays from here, so I think we should check that out first."
"It sure sounds intriguing, old chap. Why don't we head off to it as soon as we've finished here?"
"Yeah! I think we'll do just that." Don replied.

East of Warakurna, Great Central Road, Western Australia, 7th April

The tools and other gear, which had been used at the accident scene, had already been stored, so they were driving off after a few minutes.

Ted had Angelo's GPS on the map board and was directing Don to the location.
"There's a creek. The sign says Giles Creek."
Don came across a fresh vehicle track and followed this.
"That's the right heading, Don. Looks like about one hundred metres from here."
They could see where the other vehicle had turned around and some freshly disturbed ground with a couple of boulders on top. Don stopped the Ute alongside.
After double-checking the reading of the GPS, S 25° 6' 27", E 128° 33' 15", they took a shovel each from the trailer.

"Well it looks as though we'll need to dig here to have the mystery solved, Ted."
"Yes, old chap. We'll soon be able to get to the bottom of the mystery. I wonder if it is something to do with the gold which was taken from the Kalgoorlie bank."

They began digging.

It was easy going because the hole had only been filled a few hours earlier.
After digging down about thirty centimetres, their shovels made contact with the first wooden box.
Although it felt heavy they lifted it from the hole and when it was on the ground, they removed the top

section to reveal three bars of bright yellow, freshly minted gold.
Both men were astounded. They could not believe what they were looking at. They had seen plenty of gold before and knew at a glance that this was the real stuff.
"I now know what the police were talking about at the other ute, a while ago. It must have been carrying more boxes of gold in the back," Don exclaimed.
"How much gold was supposed to have been taken from the bank, do you remember, Don?" Ted asked.
"Well, I understand that it was about six point seven million dollars' worth. At three hundred and twenty dollars an ounce, that should make it about fifty or sixty bars," Don replied.
"We don't know how many boxes were on the ute but there might be more here! I think that it's worth continuing with the digging."

They took up their shovels and continued digging. After a half hours work they had seven boxes on the ground beside their Ute and an empty hole in the ground.

They rested their shovels aside on the ground and sat on the stack of boxes.

"Well, old chap. What do we do now? The gold is not ours!" exclaimed Ted.
"I'm at a loss as to know what to do, Ted. The gold obviously belongs to the mines, but their negligence led to its loss. I wonder who this *Mr. Arnold* is. Crime boss perhaps?"

East of Warakurna, Great Central Road, Western Australia, 7th April

"I would not like to run afoul of that sort of people. Would they know who we were?" Ted asked.
"Ted, they'd get that information from their contacts within the police. But whatever we do, we can't leave it here. Let's load it in the trailer while we work out the next step," Don paused. The he remembered the other location.
"Ted, there is another location on this GPS; I think we should check it out as well. What do you reckon?" Don asked.
"Alright, old chap. We are in this far now; we may as well know the entire story."
They moved some of the mining gear and made enough room for the seven boxes in the middle.
"Hey Ted, what if we just bury this lot again, at least we wouldn't get caught holding the stuff. We know where it is, even if we lose the GPS," Don suggested.
Ted thought about this for a while then replied, "By Jove, Don, I do believe that you're right again. It certainly would not do us any good to be found with that amount of gold in our possession without the necessary paperwork, so yes, I agree, we should do as you say and bury it again!"

After they had reburied the boxes, they drove back to the road again and headed for the other location.
Don came across a grove of Dessert Oak trees and the coordinates indicate a location just to the north.
Just then he came across fresh vehicle tracks so once again he followed these. The GPS was on a countdown as he followed the track. Presently they came to the area where the ground had been disturbed and came to a standstill.

Chapter 23

East of Warakurna, Great Central Road, Western Australia, 7th April

They repeated their previous procedure of digging and were very surprised to once again dig up a further seven boxes, all identical to the last lot.
By the time they buried this lot again, it was getting dark.

"I think we'll make camp here for the night. Let's sleep on the problem and in the morning we'll probably have the answer," Don suggested.

There was too much leaf litter on the ground so they decided not to have a fire but a cold meal. It was a fairly quiet camp that night as both men were deep in thought on the subject.

"Do you have any further thoughts about our current situation, Ted?" Don asked as they sat on the ground beside the vehicle.
"Well, old chap, it seems we have several options. We could just keep it, add it to the next gold pours from your mine and say nothing, or hand it back to the bank and get a small reward, or contact this Mr Arnold and get a reward from him or give it to the Warakurna Community through our proposed Lassiter's gold mine. That could be done and not traceable," Ted suggested.
"Yeah, I was thinking along similar lines. We have some time out here yet before we need to make our final decision. We should head off to where Billy-the-lid reckons Lassiter's mine is tomorrow and see how things pan out. Not a bad haul though, around eight million dollars' worth. I could do a lot with that. Retire even," quipped Don.

Chapter 23

East of Warakurna, Great Central Road, Western Australia, 7th April

As he had been away from home for a week, Don used his satellite telephone and called home. Macy answered in just a few seconds as she had just tucked the kids into bed but expecting his call tonight.
Don told her of the events without too much of the details and that they would probably get back to prospecting the next day.
She told him the she and kids were fine and looked forward to his next call.

They crawled into their sleeping bags but both men had some difficulty in getting to sleep because of the unusual activity of the day. But after an hour there came the breathing rhythm of those asleep.

East of Warakurna, Great Central Road, Western Australia, 8th April

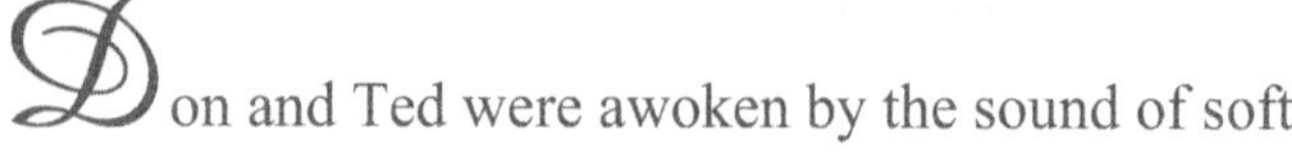

Don and Ted were awoken by the sound of soft footfalls on the dry leaves close by their camp. They both became instantly awake with the details of Angelo's message still keen in their minds.

"Ahoy the camp," came a loud call from close by. Don was the first out of his swag but was closely followed by Ted who seemed to get his foot tangled in the bedding of the swag. He hopped around on one foot until he got his balance back.
They were both standing near the back of the ute before Don answered.
"Ahoy yourself, who are you? Show yourself we can't see you!" Don yelled out.
"It's okay Ted and Don, it's Detective Sergeant Alec Webster and Senior Constable Richard Morrow, we're coming into your camp!" came the reply from behind the dessert oak trees.
They walked up to the two men and stood a few metres away.
"Good morning, chaps! I see you've had a comfortable night, which is more than I can say that the senior and I had." The policeman who had fired the shots yesterday followed in Alec's footsteps and stood beside him. "We only had a sleeping bag each and that ground is hard!"
"How can we help you blokes? Would you like a cuppa? We'll clear an area and get a fire going for you," Ted suggested.

"Sounds marvellous to me," replied Alec.

Ted raked the leaves and grass away from an area and began setting up to boil the billy. Don came back with a small armful of dried twigs. Soon the fire was going and the water in the billy was beginning to sing.

Nobody spoke for a while and there was some uneasiness in the camp as Don and Ted weren't sure what these two policemen had seen or wanted.
Don poured out the tea into four enamel mugs and they stood around drinking their tea.
"Don, I saw Angelo pass something to you yesterday and I noted your expression when he spoke to you. It seemed a bit suspicious to me, so as the others left the crash site, the senior and I back tracked and observed you from a distance," Alec began. He stopped to take a sip of tea before continuing. "We watched as you dug up some wooden boxes and then bury them again. We followed you at a distance to this site where you did the same thing. I didn't think that you would move out after dark so we set up camp a couple of hundred metres away for the night. Perhaps you'd like to fill in some details for me?" asked Alec.

Don and Ted were very uncomfortable with the knowledge that they had been observed, but as they realised it was better to be seen by the police and not this Mr Arnold's gang then they settled down and Don responded to the question.
"Mick Dunraven had a fight with Angelo; I found him on the ground, groggy and stopped to help him just as Dunraven took hold of Betty. He passed me the GPS and said *"Keep this. The stored locations will be good*

for you. Keep out of the way of Mr Arnold. Don't tell the cops about it. And don't ask any questions". I had no idea what he was talking about, so we checked out these two locations and now we have the answers," Don told them.
"Well, that's what we need to know Don! What are those answers?" asked Alec.

Don and Ted went on to tell them of their experiences at the crash site, what it was that they had found in the two caches and the reasons why the boxes were left buried.
"That's as much as I anticipated, Don. We called base on the satellite phone last night and got background checks on both of you blokes and we could see no reason to suspect you of being part of this gold robbery. We are satisfied that you just got caught up in the situation," Alec confirmed. He had finished his tea so he tossed the dregs into the bush and handed his mug back to Ted.
"So that leaves us with the dilemma of what to do next," Alec started thinking out loud but stopped before saying any more. He needed to confer with the senior constable and the boss before he told Don and Ted any more details of what was being planned.
"If you blokes will excuse us for a few minutes, we need to discuss our next move. It will involve you so don't bugger off on us, will you?" Alec told Don and Ted.
"Okay, we'll just pack our ute and wait here for you, Alec," Don said.

The two policemen, one in jeans and shirt and other in police overalls walked back to where their vehicle was

located. While they were walking, Alec began forming a plan and shared this with the senior.
"I think we can use this situation to our advantage, Richard. If we leak some information to the two robbers that are in custody that we have arrested Don and Ted but not found any further gold and stay in this area and monitor the situation, we might just find out about this Mr Arnold and what they intend to do next," Alec expressed his opinion to the senior constable.
"You know Alec, that just might work but don't you think that you might be putting these two blokes at risk if there's trouble?" Richard retorted.
"Yes there is always that to be considered, why don't we talk to the boss and see what he reckons," Alec replied just as they got to the vehicle.

He took the satellite phone and dialled up the station in Kalgoorlie. Connie answered.
"Hi Connie, Alec here, how are you this morning?" he asked in a polite manner.
"Fine as usual thanks Alec. How's the bush by the border?" she responded.
"Oh just dandy, the mattresses that they supply out here in this million star dormitory are soooo soft. Apart from that it's great," Alec paused then continued, "could you connect me to Collin please?"
"Sure thing, connecting yu now Alec."
"Detective Inspector Collin Watts," came the answer when the connection was made.
"Good Morning boss, Alec here. We have some new developments that I'd like to talk about if you've got the time right now."
"Sure thing, Alec. Your team arrived back about an hour ago; the two suspects have been processed and

are in the cells. Their vehicle is being taken apart by our forensic team. So what else is happening? Oh! By the way, good job at the border!"
"Yeah thanks for that. We've a good team here and I'm sure glad that our hunch of their direction of escape was right, otherwise we'd all look fools right now."
"You've got that right, Alec. So tell me what's happening?"
"Well we followed those other two, the prospectors, Don King and Ted Walsh. It's very interesting. At the crime scene yesterday, remember I told you last night, that I had seen something unusual between Don King and Angelo Botacelli, well it seems that Arnold's mob are heavily involved. That name came up when we researched Mick Dunraven. So I'm thinking that there is more evidence that the Sydney crime boss has planned this robbery. Angelo gave Don a GPS unit which has two locations locked in. Don and Ted found the two sites and you'd never guess as to what they dug up!"
"More gold in boxes?"
"Yes, you'd be right, in two stashes there are seven boxes in each. Each of these boxes with three bars of gold, stamped with the Middlemarch Gold Mine marking. So it seems that the haul was sixty bars," said Alec
"That agrees with the amount that NG Security claims, so that seems correct," replied Collin.
"After the two prospectors found out what was in the boxes they buried them again in the same holes. Then spread grass and leaves over the area to make it look like it's not been disturbed again," Alec told him. "So, I was thinking up this plan to apprehend the mob."

"I don't like the sound of it so far Alec but go on and I hope it gets better".
"Well so far it goes like this: We let the two that you have in custody know that we also have arrested the two prospectors with accessory to the robbery but have not recovered any gold. Then we stake out the area near where the two stashes are and nab the crooks when they come to retrieve it. How does that sound so far?"
"That sounds a bit more like it, Alec. I'll take care of this end and have the Sydney people help us by keeping tabs on the gang members most likely to make the collection and keep you informed. You and Richard stay on site and I'll send another half dozen reinforcements for you. They'll bring some tucker and a mattress for you too!"
"Great, now we are getting somewhere. There are two sites here which will need surveillance around the clock, so that number should suit. It would be best if the blokes that you send could come complete with video surveillance gear as well as a full set of riot gear, as this might get dirty."
"Okay, we can do that. But, I'll ask the question as I asked before, would you like some help on this?"
"Thanks for the offer boss, but after the experience of the last few days, I think that our blokes will be able to do the job. The smaller the number, the less chance of a leak of information too. Too many of us running around will only cause suspicion in the mob, so let's keep it simple."
"Okay then Alec, you have my full support and that of the whole team here. We'll inform only those who will be sent what's going on and keep our security tight in that matter. The two blokes in custody will have their

solicitor with them shortly so we'll get things rolling at this end."
"Thanks boss. Can we expect the team out here by tonight or tomorrow?"
"I'll see what I can do Alec but more likely tomorrow." Collin pauses for a second while he has another thought on that point. "No! That won't do! The sooner these blokes are out of here the better for all concerned. They will be with you tonight sometime, but we'll keep in touch by sat-phone."
"Thanks boss, I think that's a better solution. We'll have a hunt around here and locate the most suited sites for covert surveillance while we wait for the team. Don and Ted have plenty of tucker and water so we'll be right for the day. Talk to you soon."
"Fine Alec. Do take care."

Alec disconnected his sat-phone and puts it into his pocket. He tells Richard what the boss has planned. They drive their vehicle and park it beside Don and Ted's Landcruiser.
After having parked it Alec told Don and Ted of the plans as he had just discussed with Collin at Kalgoorlie.
"How long do you think you'll need to wait before these blokes would turn up?" Don asked of Alec.
"By now Angelo's solicitor will have informed Arnold's mob of what's going on and I think that they will want to get this gold recovered quickly before they lose it. I recon it would take them a day to get organised and two days to get here if they use a helicopter. Alternately they could fly on a commercial flight to Uluru and drive from there or take a commercial jet to Alice Springs and drive from there.

So there are several options. Still it'd be two or three days before we see them. In the mean time we need to work out our approach from here."
Don and Ted absorbed this information and Don replied, "What do you want us to do. We do have a mine to work just north of here. We could take off and work there and be available if you need us. I'm not comfortable getting any further involved in your police work and I don't think Ted is either, it sounds like it could get dangerous."
"I understand how you feel and I respect your suggestion but we will need you two to be here. I can see that you have far better bush skills than we do and in a fix like what may happen, your presence here when the brown stuff hits the fan could be just what tips the scales in our favour," Alec told them.
"Well I'm not going to commit myself to stay just yet but we'll stay here for a day or two just to help out. We'll reconsider our position at that time. That's the best I can offer at this stage," Don told them.
"Okay then, we'll leave it at that for the time and we'll talk more about your departure in a day or two. In the meantime, I'd like to make a camp around here somewhere where we have a concealed advantage to watch the roads from both directions. Can you blokes help us with that?" Alec asked them.
"Yes we can help with that. How far away from the two sites do you want to be? A couple of kays north and south? What if they come in by chopper?" Don put some questions to Alec and they sat down and talked for an hour while they devised a plan to watch the approaches to the two sites.

Chapter 24

East of Warakurna, Great Central Road, Western Australia, 8th April

By late morning they shifted camp, driving back near the second site of buried gold, close to Giles Creek, then across the road towards the hill to the south and set up a temporary camp by the creek bed well away from the road. Ted gathered wood and they made a good fire and lunch was cooked on the open fire. As the rest of the officers were to arrive just after dark, they had a nap after the meal. They would need to be on top of things, so that planning can be completed.

By mid-afternoon, Don and Ted had travelled with Alec and Richard in the police vehicle and could determine just one good vantage point from which the road could be viewed for about ten kays in each direction. It was on the northern end of Kathleen Range and the high peak gave a good view of the area. Unfortunately it was about five kays from the road but this could also work to their favour by helping to keep them out of sight of the road with greater ease. The powerful binoculars which they carried would help a lot too! This vantage point was unsuitable to camp at so they would have to have two camps. Alec will sort this out when the team arrives tonight.

The sun was beginning to dip as the end of the day approached, when Ted broke out four beers from his fridge. The four men sat around the camp and quietly sipped on their cold beer, enjoying every drop. It allowed then to relax perhaps for the first time since their ordeal the previous day. They watched the sun disappear behind the hills and sat with another beer each as they waited for the reinforcement team to announce their arrival. They were having a discussion about the local aboriginal mobs and their minds were so well occupied that they didn't notice that the time had slipped away.

Their peace was broken when Alec's phone came to life and belted out its ring tone. No one was prepared for it to happen and the sound broke the stillness of the peaceful occasion.
He took out the instrument from his pocket and yelled at it, "Alec Webster!"
The call had come from the other team and they were twenty kays from the camp. Alec gave them directions to find them. The four men waited after Alec had disconnected the call and presently two more police four wheel drives pulled into the area near the dry creek bed.
Six blokes got out of the vehicles and walked around stretching their arms and legs.

Alec introduced Don and Ted around so that everyone knew who was who. Alec told Don and Ted of some of the more outlandish exploits of several of the officers, some of whom had been in the police force for more than ten years.
The night was progressing and Alec said, "The best thing to do now is have a meal and get some sleep. We are all tired and I can see that you blokes are about stonkered too. We can start in the morning when we are all fresh, have a briefing session and set up this operation."

Ted took one of the officers and together they collected some firewood by torchlight to add to the fire. A flat steel plate was removed from one of the vehicles and set on rocks so it sat over the fire. Don added a little oil the placed about twenty prime lamb chops on the plate. During the evening he had made a damper mix and this was now cooking in the camp oven.

In a few minutes the meal was cooked and each one served themselves onto an enamel plate, sat down and began eating. It was the first time since their arrival that there was complete silence in the camp. The billy boiled and everyone had either tea or coffee to finish off the damper.
Presently, individuals began leaving the campfire and making their own way to where they would sleep. Most had swags but a couple of blokes put up small tents and slept on camp stretchers.

Just before midnight, the camp was quiet as everyone had succumbed to the fatigue which they all felt as it had been a long day for them.

Kalgoorlie, Western Australia, 8th April

Collin disconnected the call from Alec and then made another call to the New South Wales Police in Sydney and sorted out an arrangement with his contact. They agreed to watch the Arnold gang and let him know when something unusual happens.

Collin directed his team to organise a briefing for half an hour's time and then he visited the lockup. Angelo and Mick were in an interview room with their solicitor and he spoke to them all together.
"Well it seems that your other mates, the two prospectors, have been apprehended as well. They'll be joining you shortly in our nice comfortable holding cells. Probably this afternoon, even. Are you sure that all the gold that was taken from the bank vault was in the ute of yours? It seems that there should have been some more somewhere!" he told them. "That'll be all for now, just wanted you to know that you'll soon have company." After that he left them to talk amongst themselves. He stopped outside the room and although couldn't hear the words spoken he could understand that from the tone of their voices they were distressed. Shortly, the solicitor left the building.

Collin entered the briefing room as the team was assembling.
"Good morning all!" he started. "We have a very good result from the excursion to the Northern Territory Border last night. For the team members who participated, very well done. But now it's time for

them to get some rest and we have another flap on. I need another team of people for a special job. This is sensitive so I'll only give details of the job to those selected. The team that I'm looking for will be up to date with Tactical Response Procedures and have the appropriate training. Be excellent marksmen and good in the bush. Can I have eight people who can be away from home for a week?"
There were fifteen hands in the air immediately. Collin smiled as he surveyed his team, what an eager bunch of people, both men and women. Good at what they do too! Very pleasing to have a team like this.
"Thank you for your support, but I think that the nature of this operation, I have to keep it males only. Not that I don't think that you women could do the job, I have no doubts on that, it's just the situation calls for males only. I'm afraid I can't be more specific right now. So if everyone else could leave the room, I'd like to talk with the few."

After the rest of the shift moved out of the room the door was closed and Collin addressed the remaining eight officers.
"We have an operation to carry out that involves tight security, travel, camping out and catching crooks. I know that that seems to happen a lot out here in this district but this operation can also be more dangerous that you've been used to."
He now had the attention of everyone in the room, so he continued, "yesterday's operation has left us with a situation that if handled correctly and carefully, we can get the organisers of the gang who robbed the gold from our town. I have been on the sat-phone with Alec Webster who is still out at the site of the activities and

we have a plan of operation to work to. It seems that Angelo Botticelli gave Don King a GPS instrument which has the locations of two individual gold caches. Apparently on their way to the border they buried part of the load of gold in two dumps and recorded the location on the GPS. Don King and his mate Ted Walsh found these dumps, dug them up, found the gold and reburied them again. Alec and Richard watched this happen unbeknown to the two prospectors. This morning, after a night on the hard ground, Alec outlined his plan to me and we worked out the details. We need to send out two teams of three officers complete with video equipment to maintain surveillance on these two sites and then apprehend anyone who digs up the gold and tries to leave the area. It could take a week or more before anybody arrives but we certainly don't want to be caught napping, so the team will leave just as soon as it can get ready. If you're on the road by mid-morning you can be there just after dark. Each vehicle is to have one sat-phone and you talk only to me or Alec. I have made sure that the mob responsible understands that we haven't retrieved the gold but suspect two prospectors also. So we hope the trap is set. That's the reason for the special security. No one outside of this room must know of what we are about to do. So keep the chatter to a minimum and get yourselves organised. Are there any questions?"
"Yes sir, are the prospectors part of the robbery and going to be charged?" one officer asked.
"No! They are not part of the robbery but just happened to be in the wrong place at the wrong time. Alec is in close contact with them and they will probably assist in some way. That's up to Alec to sort

out," Collin concluded the briefing and the team dispersed to get themselves organised.

Just before ten o'clock two loaded, unmarked police Landcruisers left Kalgoorlie in the direction of Menzies. They headed for Leonora and then drove east past Laverton driving as fast as they could for the border.

East of Warakurna, Great Central Road, Western Australia, 9th April

The day started early with the team leaving their beds and swags just as the sun broke over the horizon. If their camp had been ten kilometres further east they wouldn't see the sun for another hour due to the range of hills which was there.

Don and Ted seemed to take on the role of camp captains and soon had bacon and eggs cooking for breakfast. The bacon was cooked in the camp oven and the eggs were fried in the flat cast iron pan. While this was happening the billy began to boil too.
The rest of the team lined up and Don forked bacon onto their plates while Ted lifted two eggs onto each plate which was held out for him by each team member. Tea was added to the billy and this was left to simmer by the fire. Everyone was busy with their food and by the lack of sound they were enjoying the taste of it as well. As the plates were returned to the washing up area which Ted had set up, the tea was poured into large enamel mugs for everyone. Just as well they all brought their own enamel ware and fighting gear or else the meal would have been drawn out.

Ted and Don began washing up as Alec called a briefing session with the team.

"Okay guys, this is how I see it happening at this point. Bear in mind always that as the situation changes so will this plan. It needs to be a living plan so we can be flexible enough to alter it as the situation alters." He paused for a while so every could focus their attention to him directly. "Yesterday we located a vantage point where we are going to set up the covert observation point." He pointed to the south where they could see a peak at the end of a range of hills. "I know it's a bit far off but just here it's the only high vantage point which we have that we can look at the road in both directions. You should be able to see seven or more kays in each way from up there. We'll have two people up there at all times of the day and night on a four hourly rotation. You'll have radios and both regular and night binoculars as well as the video monitors and camera. We need to obtain as much evidence as possible with these blokes. Every vehicle that uses this road will be photographed from a distance and if the occupants don't know they are being photographed, then that's even better. In fact that's essential." Alec paused to allow everyone to grasp that information before he continued, "Don and Ted have some good equipment in their outfit and have copied some fairly detailed maps of the area. There's one for everyone, so read it, understand it and memorise it because it shows where the two dumps are. Are there any questions so far?"

"Yes Alec," called one of the senior constables, "we have one vantage point and two dumps which are about ten kays apart by road. Don't you think that if we were to combine the two dumps or clear one out that we could put more resources to monitoring just the one?" he suggested.

"That's a valid point. But I think that if we are watching the road, we'll see anyone whose coming and going and if a vehicle leaves the road, you'll know immediately."
"Yes but we need to catch them in the act of loading the goods don't we? Or is it acceptable evidence if we catch them with it in their possession?"
"Okay, you have a good argument and I do agree to a certain extent! But we don't know which dump they'll head for first, so I feel it's much better to leave them be and monitor each site. I know it requires more manpower to monitor the two sites but don't forget, it's the evidence which is most important. We'll still nab these blokes."
Alec considers the alternatives for a while and the troops talk amongst themselves. The senior constable who spoke before spoke again and his experience in this type of operation became apparent.

"Alec we have a number of video cameras in our kit. Why don't we mount them close enough to each dump so that they can be turned on by their motion sensors when a vehicle approaches? That way we got them by the balls. If we conceal the cameras well enough they will never be seen. We've got transmitters for them too. We can transmit back to this base and set up the receiver and some video screens, where we can watch and record the action and be ready to jump them when we have the evidence."
"Yes I can see that working, too. Good idea, Bob," Alec said.

Chapter 26

East of Warakurna, Great Central Road, Western Australia, 9th April

Senior Constable Bob Goyder has been on many TRG ops and surveillance ops in his ten years on the force and has been team leader on many of those too.
Alec continues, “Okay Bob take a couple of blokes, the gear and carefully set up two cameras at each site. Being mindful, of course, that we don’t want to disturb the area any more than it already is. If we get this done right away, we should be able to keep ahead of them.”
“The next thing we need to do is set up a more permanent camp. We could be here for a few days and this is too close to one of the dumps. Don suggested we move over to the base of the Kathleen Range so then we’ll be closer to the vantage point lookout but still close enough to the dump sites. We’ll start moving camp now, before it gets too warm.” Alec broke up the briefing session and the men went about their job of breaking camp and leaving the site clean.

Don and Ted cleared out the fire; cleaned up the cooking gear and packed it all back onto the ute and trailer.

This camp is too close to where the gold robbers made their second dump so they moved the camp to the base of the hill and after about two hours or so they were set up and had the billy boiling for morning tea time.

Only half the team were able to indulge in smoko as the rest were off setting up the surveillance point at the peak of the hill or the video surveillance equipment at the dump points.

Bob Goyder’s group has brought with them some sophisticated video surveillance equipment and this is being set up in several of the trees close to each of the two dump points. There is sufficient elevation here to have their signals transmit to a receiver at the camp so the surveillance can be remotely monitored. They have monitors set up so the area is closely watched. The remotely operated cameras have a swing of 180 degrees but limited vertical movement but this will be enough to record activities in the area of the dumps.

They had a break at lunch time and by late afternoon the equipment at the dump sites was set up and they were running a series of tests when a motor vehicle was noticed driving on the Great Central Road. It was about ten kilometres away, travelling at speed, as most road users do in this part of the country, heading directly for their location at the base of the hill. The team with the binoculars at the peak of the hill were the first to notice the vehicle but they hadn't completed their concealment but as the vehicle did not deviate, they assumed that they were not spotted. The road has a bend in it about two kays before the base of the hill and the vehicle continued on the road, around the bend, past their camp and then continued heading east trailing its long plume of dust.

The surveillance team on the hill were able to get several long range photos of the vehicle but the video unit was not ready for this unexpected test. They worked on into the evening and did not stop until all was in readiness for the following day. Their video equipment was also transmitting to the receiver at the base camp.

Chapter 26

East of Warakurna, Great Central Road, Western Australia, 9th April

Don and Ted prepared another barbecue for the team and while they were eating, there was a lot of discussion about the surveillance project and the technicalities of how to best use the equipment and other assets for the duration.

The relief team replaced those on the hill top so they also could have a feed, which was waiting for them at the base camp. This took a little while as the track which they had made to reach the hill top was on the south side of the hill so that it was not visible from the road and its approaches.

While they were preparing things for the evening meal, Don's attention was caught by a very distant sound coming from the north.

When he turned around and looked he could see the thunderclouds in the sky. There was the occasional lightning and the sound which attracted his attention was that of thunder away in the distance.

"Hey look over there Ted!" he exclaimed, "looks like some rainfall out there to the north in that thunderstorm!"

"I say, old man, looks like quite a drop as well, I certainly hope that it dries out before we head out that way again," Ted replied.

"Yeah, I don't fancy digging this rig out of a bog," was Don's answer. "But I think it's a bit more to the east than the spot where Billy told us about. Where he reckons the reef is."

"I sure hope you're right, old man. Mud would be a bugger of a stuff to get out of, particularly in this country," Tec replied.

Chapter 26

East of Warakurna, Great Central Road, Western Australia, 9th April

The sun was dipping to the west and in the fading daylight the lightning became more spectacular. There was still enough light to see the hills to the north and it looked like the rain was to the north of them again. Don was quite certain that the storm was heading east so they would be okay for the night here at least. The sky overhead was clear as the clouds from the thunderstorm only covered about one third of the sky to the north.

"It'd make a spectacular sunset for someone over that way," Don said as he pointed to the north and faced Ted.

"That's what makes this country so incredible. The way it changes from dawn to dusk and then there are the stars at night. So bright! Almost enough light from them to read by," Ted replied.

"Yeah, we don't know how lucky we are," Alec said as he approached from behind them, "to have all of this! Sometimes it feels like we are so privileged to be able to be out here and watch these fantastic events which nature puts on for us."

Don and Ted turned to face Alec as he stands near them.
"I agree with that sentiment, old man," replied Ted.
"Yeah, it sure is great to see all this," was Don's response.
"How's everything going with your setting up, Alec?" Don asked him.
"I think it's all progressing very well so far, Don. We even had a vehicle through to do some testing on but

the video wasn't ready but all should be set up before meal time."

While they watched the lightning show, the rest of the team completed their tasks of setting up the equipment and began to move to the meals area.

The stew which Don had in the camp oven on the fire was nearly ready, so after cleaning up they sat around and enjoyed a cold beer while they were discussing the equipment and how it would all work and come together to make an effective surveillance system.

Night takes over from day very quickly at this time of year and soon they have to switch the camp light on so that they can see what they are doing while eating their meal.

The police officers were discussing their operation and talking about the many possibilities which may cause them to alter their plans. After an hour or so of this, they headed off to their swags for the night, leaving the two at the lookout keeping watch.

The next two would take over from them around ten o'clock tonight.

Don and Ted headed off to camp near their ute and Don said to Ted, "If things don't happen tomorrow, I think we might take off and get on with our job which we set out to do. This sitting around with these blokes and their problems of the operation is driving me nuts as I can't do anything but wait."

"Yes, old man, I can sympathise with you but that electronic equipment which they have set up is state of the art gear, don't you know?" Ted replied.

"Yeah, that's fine for you there's an interest to keep you occupied but all I seem to be doing is camp cook and I didn't come all this way just to do that," Don quipped. He was quiet for a few minutes then he said to Ted, "Well I'm off to my swag, Ted. I'll see you in the morning".

"Goodnight, old man. Don't let it get you down. Things will always look far better in the morning."

Yulara, Northern Territory, 10th April

Mick roused Castle from his sleep. He had been snoring for several hours, with the sound reverberating into Mick's adjoining resort room. As the window showed some light in from the new dawn, Mick thought that enough was enough. "It's time to wake this sleeping sound maker." He used the house phone to call his room to wake him up.

They had arrived several days before and had two ambulances meet them at the airport to collect the two victims of the road accident. They were both admitted to the hospital and when Mick phoned the ward nurse last evening they were both recovering well from their injuries.

Both Mick and Castle felt some responsibility to the two crash victims and would stay for a few days just to make sure everything was going well for them.

While Mick and Castle were walking through town yesterday they saw the red Mazda motorhome driving along. They hailed Gordon who was in the driver's seat and he pulled over to the curb and they had a talk for a few seconds. Mick suggested they park around the back where there as ample parking. Gordon shifted the vehicle and parked the vehicle behind the supermarket and they found a café where they sat and had a chat for a while as they enjoyed a cup of coffee. Gordon and Betty had recovered from the shock of their most unexpected unpleasant experience. Betty had a bad night the night of the event but seems to be well now.

Gordon told Mick that the vehicle needed repairs before they could get to Alice Springs and had a quote from the local mechanic. It was several thousand dollars which they had put away for their tour and would need to limit their travels so that they could get the vehicle repaired.

Mick said "Betty and Gordon, you both have done a marvellous job and have had a most unusual experience. Please let me pay for the repairs. It is something which I would get an enormous amount of pleasure in doing. I know of your plans for this trip, which you have been planning for all of those years and I really would love to be able to help just a little, so that you can continue to enjoy your travels."

Betty replied, "But Mick we can't take your money! I mean it is a fantastic offer but it was not your fault that we became involved in that situation back there on the Great Central Road."
"Yes I know but please let me help you with this. The money is not the issue and I do get such a buzz, helping people who have done well by themselves but are having a little tough spot. So, please allow me this opportunity to help," Mick countered.

Gordon and Betty were quiet for a short time and exchanged a look between them.

Gordon was the next to speak "Mick, thank you so much for the offer and we are very grateful for the assistance which you have already given to the victims and we will be graciously accepting your very kind offer."

Gordon stood up at the table and as Mick rose to his feet he clasped him by the hand and they exchanged a heartfelt handshake.
"Thank you so much, Mick! You've no idea just how happy we are to accept your very generous offer,' Betty said as the two men shook hands.
They seated themselves again and Mick said "Well that settles it then, we'll get this rig around to the mechanic in the morning and get him to start work on it immediately. Oh, by the way, while the repairs are being carried out, you'll have to stay in one of the rooms which I had booked for the two of us at the resort. It's already paid for so that's not a problem either. We'll head out in the helicopter tomorrow so that we can continue our project which became so interrupted when we met."

Gordon and Betty could not believe their luck. To find a person of the nature of Mick Jones, it just redeemed their faith in human nature. Both of them just sat in their chairs and their faces were covered with the broadest grins that they could manage.

"Well there you go Castle. That's all the thanks that I need. Somebody is happy and that makes me happy too!" Mick said as he turned to Castle, who was sitting in on this exchange but not wanting to break the magic of the moment.

They enjoyed another cup of coffee while they exchanged small talk about Ayres Rock and The Olgas and their plans once the motorhome was repaired.

"Well folks, please excuse me, I must be off now! I need to make some calls to the office in Sydney. Must keep the wheels turning, you know."
They all stood from the table and after Betty had kissed Mick and Castle on the cheek and Gordon had shaken their hand again they parted company.

That was yesterday, so now Mick packs up his clothes and laptop computer and other gear which they brought with them from the helicopter. A quick shower, breakfast and then call that taxi for the ride to the airport.
While Castle was showering, Mick called the aircraft engineers at the airport and arranged for the helicopter to be refuelled. He phoned the fuel depot at the Kaltukatjarra (Docker River) settlement and asked them to have 400 litres of Jet A1 fuel ready for him and that he would require 100 litres this morning and the rest over the next few days. Then he and Castle headed off to the dining room for their breakfast.

"Off to do some sightseeing are you Mr Jones?" asked the cab driver, who was the same driver who had transported Mick and Castle on each occasion that they required a taxi.
"No my friend, we have some special work to do over near the border, so we expect to be away for several days. Will you still be on shift when we get back?" Mick asked.

Chapter 27

Yulara, Northern Territory, 10th April

"Nah mate! I'm off for a few days as of tomorrow night. Got to go and see me mum in Adelaide," the cabbie replied.

As they drove through the security gate to the airport tarmac and were checked out by the security personnel, they noticed that there were a number of helicopters preparing for take-off, which were mostly operated by tour companies. The cabbie dropped them off to their white and red Bell 206. He took their bags from the boot of the taxi and put them on the ground for the two men. Mick paid off the cabbie and thanked him for his service. The cabbie drove out from the secure area and disappeared from view.
While Mick was stowing away the bags, several of the other helicopters were warming up or taking off, so there was ample noise around the tarmac.

While Mick was carrying out the pre-flight checks, Castle was again setting up the electronic equipment on the back section of the craft. It was all dismantled when they had the injured couple on board and stowed safely away but it wasn't too big a job to connect everything up again. The transponders on the support skids were left in place since their last flight, so this helped with the set up.

Castle strapped himself into the co-pilot's seat and when Mick had clearance from the control tower he fired up the turbine and they were soon in the air.

Mick took them on a short aerial tour of the town and then headed south to fly over Ayres Rock or Uluru as the indigenous locals refer to it. Soon they could see the Olgas to the west and after spending some time taking in the sights of "the rock", Mick changed course and they flew in a westerly direction, just to the south of The Olgas. The early morning sun on both of these incredibly ancient sights showed the profile of them as the shadows were deep and the east faces of both were bathed in the bright sunlight.

It was a clear day and the visibility was good, although they could see the remnants of last night's thunderstorm well to the north.

Mick flew just to the south of Great Central road which leads to Kaltukatjarra and onto the west. There were several vehicles on the road heading east showing their plumes of dust which was trailing them as they travelled along. They passed over several creeks and the numerous hills and gullies which they had flown over several days previously.

It was almost an hour since they had taken off from Yulara airport when Mick saw the settlement of Kaltukatjarra in the distance.

He touched Castle on the arm and pointed to the buildings which were becoming visible in the distance and said into his microphone, "That's Docker River settlement up ahead. We'll stop there and top up with fuel. It should only take us about twenty minutes then we'll be in the air again and you can boot up your system again and see if we can re-locate that area where you got those reading s from last time."

Chapter 27

Yulara, Northern Territory, 10th April

Mick traversed the helicopter over the creek which is called Docker River near where it cuts between the two hills, dissecting them like a knife in warm butter. He finds the intersection where the drum of fuel is waiting on the fuel agent's truck. The agent is standing alongside of the truck and waves Mick in as he approaches. There is a lot of dust as the chopper settles down. While the rotors are running down the agent begins moving in and soon has the pump running to transfer the fuel to the helicopter.

Mick alights from the chopper and talks to the operator and passes him the cheque for the fuel. "Thanks for your help! I'll give you a call on the satellite telephone when I can arrange to get back to take on the rest of that fuel." The operator waves to him and Mick climbs on board and in just twenty minutes after landing, they were in the air again, heading west to take up from where they left off the other day when they were distracted to the motor vehicle accident.

While they were on the ground Castle climbed into the back of the chopper and began booting up the equipment so that they can begin again as soon as they are in position.

Once they approach the crash site of the other day, Mick takes them at a slow rate of advance so that Castle can get more accurate readings.

"Mick, there's no response from that location! It's most unusual! Let me double check with the GPS location from the other day just to make sure," Castle said in a troubled tone.

"Okay, I'll just put her down over there on that flat ground where we were the other day while you get it sorted out," Mick replied as he banked sharply to the left and then descended the last 15 metres to make another soft landing.

Castle was loading the discs which contain the data from the other day into the computer and after a few minutes he finds the chart that he was searching for and calls Mick over to have a look.

"This is the spreadsheet which the program produced on the seventh of April. See, here is the location where we just were and by comparing both of these charts we can see that there was a massive return from the ground showing the presence of gold and now there is no sign of that gold! I just don't understand!"

Mick was indeed intrigued. "When we were here the other day, there were some vehicles around. Is it possible that we may have got an electronic bounce from one of them to cause a malfunction with the system?" Mick asked.

"I couldn't discount that possibility but I don't feel that is the right answer but it is truly baffling." After thinking about it for a while he carried on, "What is the possibility that one of those vehicles was carrying some gold?" Castle asked.

"Well anything is possible but I find that improbable," Mick responded. "When we left here with the accident victims, the police, the motorhome and the prospectors were still here." As an afterthought he added, "So was the Landcruiser with the brown tarp."

The two men continued their discussion for several minutes but could not come up with a feasible answer.

"Well, Castle, this is not getting us anywhere. I suggest that we proceed to the other location where you got another reading of heavy deposits and see what we can find from there. Do you have the GPS co-ordinates for me so we can go right there?" Mick suggested.
After sorting his data for a few seconds, Castle replied, "Yes sure Mick, here they are, I'll just write them down for you so we don't make any mistakes. It's S 25° 6' 27" and E 128° 33' 15", so that's only about 30 kilometres away from here." After a pause he continued, "That should only take a few minutes but I'll get things sorted out while you get us there."

"Okay then, Castle. This is certainly intriguing isn't it?" Mick pronounced. He climbed back into the pilot's seat and after bringing the turbine back to full power, took off again, heading west at about 50 knots. He watched as the GPS screen, which was mounted in front of him, counted down to the location which Castle had given him and he had entered into the GPS's memory. As he approached the site, he slowed their forward advance down to just a few metres per second so that Castle's equipment would be more efficient.

While they were travelling to this site, Castle was watching the monitor in a fixed gaze as he did not want to miss seeing anything. Details were being recorded on the hard-drive but he needed to see the data on the screen change as they traversed the country. The monitor was showing an amazing amount of mineralization but the atomic numbers for gold were not present on the screen. He was beginning to become despondent when he saw the indicators for the mineral of gold climb to amazing levels.

"Mick we have it." He yelled at the top of his voice into the microphone. The showing of gold on his monitor was extremely high and as he watched it he was able to give Mick directions so he could hover the helicopter over the area and get a positive fix on the site. He was amazed at such a small area for such a large reading of gold.

"Castle, I'll have to move about a hundred metres away so we can put the helicopter down. Then we can walk back to this site and have a scout around and see if we can find what out any more detail."

"Okay Mick, I'll just back up this data while you do that."

Castle did so and was ready to remove his safety harness just as soon as the craft touched down. Immediately the skids touched the ground, he jumped down and ran over to the area where he had pinpointed and just couldn't wait for Mick to follow.

"This ground around here has been disturbed by someone and look at those vehicle tracks. I think there is much more to this than we first thought Castle," Mick suggested as he surveyed the area.

"I thought that, from the way which the data was displayed on the screen was a bit odd! Very concentrated! Not the sort of indication I would have expected to find from a natural deposit. I wonder what it is that we have stumbled upon?" Castle commented deep in thought.

Meanwhile, several kilometres to the south, the police were watching the helicopter and the two men on the screen of their video surveillance monitor. They had heard a helicopter for some time, seen it moving around at low altitude and wondered what was going on. Some of the officers were speculating that perhaps the criminal sector from Sydney had travelled over by helicopter to collect the remainder of the gold.

Alec was looking at the two men on the screen and a thought crossed his mind.
"Those two blokes look somewhat familiar to me. Can you zoom into that helicopter? I'd like to have a look at the registration that is on the side."

The operator did just that and soon there was a full screen of helicopter and the registration details in full view. "VH MAX" said the operator, "Do you know who that might be?"

"That's Mick Jones and his offsider Ravin Goldcastle. They took those two MVA victims to the Yulara hospital, just the other day. Check out their details and get back to me as soon as possible. What the hell are they doing back here again and what are they doing at that exact spot?" Alec was full of questions and needed to find some answers. He just could not believe that they could be involved with this gold robbery but then sometimes you just don't know people and what they may be thinking or what stresses they are under.

He pointed to three other officers and said to them, "You blokes come with me in the Landcruiser. There are jackets and firearms in there so while I'm driving, you blokes get kitted out. We need to deal with this situation immediately to either apprehend these blokes or send them on their way. MOVE NOW!"
He ended up having to yell as they were astounded that things had happened so soon and were slow to move. They ran for the Landcruiser and in just a few seconds were on the way. It was seven kilometres to the site and in seven minutes they were approaching the dump site, the two men with the helicopter in the background.

The Landcruiser pulls up to a stop just twenty metres from the two men who were standing in amazement at having a police vehicle scream up to them out in the middle of the bush.
Who would have thought that!
Alec was out of the vehicle just behind the others who were approaching the two men at a run with their weapons drawn and pointing at the two men.

"Police, don't move!": "Police, don't move!": "Police, don't move!" Everybody yelled and continued to yell as they approached the two men.

"Get on the ground now with your legs and arms spread, do it now!" they all yelled as they ran forward.

Chapter 27

Yulara, Northern Territory, 10th April

The two men, who were absolutely astounded at the action which was happening, could do nothing else but comply with the police directions and were indeed flat on the ground with their legs and arms spread.

"All secure," one of the officers yelled to Alec who was coming up from the rear of the group.

"Okay let's have a look at who we have here," he said out loud.

"Oh! I see we have Mr. Mick Jones and Mr. Ravin Goldcastle and what do we owe the pleasure of your visit? And are they your real names? And who sent you to this location and what are you looking for?" he asked somewhat sarcastically.

Mick replied, "Hello Alec. Thank you for your kind introduction to your men. They are a credit to their training and your leadership. You certainly took us by surprise!"

"Flattery will get you nowhere Mr Jones but I think it's about time we had a little chat and for you to tell me all about your little excursion into this area and tell me of your reasons for being here."

"If you could let me sit up at least I'll give you all the details that you want, but this is a bit uncomfortable on the ground," Mick replied.

"Okay help Mr Jones to sit up but leave Mr Goldcastle where he is for the time being," Alec ordered.

As soon as Mick was more comfortable, he told Alec exactly what they were doing and after he explained some of Castle's equipment they were released from their handcuffs. They and Alec walked over to the helicopter where Castle showed Alec the equipment and what it could do. He produced a printout of the two locations and showed where the gold was indicated on their previous visit but is no longer. Alec was almost convinced that their story was correct but just not too sure yet.

While this discussion was going on, Alec's phone gave its ringtone and upon answering it, he was given the information that he was expecting.

"Well, we did some checking up on you two blokes and there are just a couple of questions that I need answers to before we can go any further. Who owns that helicopter for number one and who does Mr. Goldcastle work for?" Alec asked.

Mick replied, "Well that's very simple; the helicopter belongs to Macrodelphus Limited. This is the company which I started about twenty years ago from the garage at my home in Sydney. I am the CEO of that company and Mr. Goldcastle has been an employee of this company for five years. Does that give you the answers that you wanted?"

"That is what I needed to know, Thank you." Turning to the other police officers, Alec said, "Alright guys, you can stand down now, the situation has resolved itself and these two blokes are okay. Just not the blokes that we were looking for."

"And who is it that you are looking for? Those two prospectors?" asked Castle.

Alec replied, "No those blokes are okay but they left our camp this morning heading out to the north-west in the search of something which takes their fancy." He paused for a second or two before continuing, "remember Mick Dunraven and his mate Angelo who robbed the gold in Kalgoorlie? Well it seems there's more to their story than we first were aware of and we are waiting for their associates to show up. That's why we have surveillance on this area and you stumbled straight into it. I can't give you any more details at this time but I'd be happy to fill in some blanks for you in the near future, when this mess is all sorted out."

"Well it seems like you have your hands full with these blokes! So if you don't mind we'll depart from here and head off as well. We'll be out of your hair in a few minutes."

"That will be fine, but before you go, just leave me with your contact details as we might just need to contact you in the future. Now, make sure you don't breathe a word of this to anyone. Here's my card and if you need to contact me, all of the details are on there with the exception of this satellite phone number, so I'll scribble it on the back of the card," Alec told them.

Alec handed Mick his card with the notation on the back. There was hand shaking all around and then Mick and Castle walked over to the helicopter. In a few minutes it was in the air and moving away to the north. Once again Castle was in the back with his eye

glued to the monitor while Mick took them on a north-easterly course towards the range of hills which was rearing up in front of them. He kept this course until several hundred metres from the main parts of the hill then banked to the right and followed the edge of the hill flying over the gullies and rises as he tracked around the side of the hill. The south east edge of this hill brought them back close to the accident site. Although Castle was keeping a very close watch on the monitor there was a showing of multiple indications of minerals but the atomic number for gold was absent. He was beginning to become despondent. After thirty minutes of flying Castle called to Mick on the intercom, "Mick, we'll need to stop for a few minutes while I back up this data."
" Okay Castle, we'll land on top of this hill, on that flat area just to the north. We'll have a break for lunch and we'll have a bit of a look around before we take off again."

This sounded good to Castle as he was noticing the pangs of hunger biting. This also may have been due to the stress which they endured earlier on when the police made their presence known to them.

The helicopter settled on the top of the hill and when the rotors had run down Mick jumped down and had a walk around while Castle worked at the computer.

After they had eaten the lunch provided for them by the resort they both sat on the rocks for a break. Presently they walked around the helicopter and while Castle checked out the transponders fixings, Mick took a stroll on the top of the hill. It was mostly solid with

some stunted vegetation in some areas where soil had accumulated in the various depressions.
Mick enjoyed the tranquillity of the hill and when he mentioned this to Castle, he agreed and said that in spite of the disappointment of the lack of gold showing on his system, was developing a deep feeling for this country.

After being on the ground for about an hour they boarded the craft again and set off, following the north east edge of the hill. Mick slowed down a little and maintained an altitude of just 15 metres. Castle thinks that this speed and altitude will enable his system to give them the best results.

"That's better, Mick! There is the indication of some very low grade gold deposits. Can we overfly that area where we did prior to lunch? There might be something there which we missed?" Castle asked.
"Sounds like a good plan to me Castle," Mick responded and banked steeply to the left and backtracked over the area where they had flown for the last half an hour before they stopped for the lunch break.
Although Castle did have some indications of low grade gold on the monitor, it would not be in commercial quantities. Although this indication was disappointing, it also gave Castle some gratification too, because now he knew that the system was functioning correctly.

Mick had traversed the previous area and now headed to the north following the western edge of then hill. As they worked out a grid pattern, Mick noticed some fresh tyre tracks on the ground. A vehicle had passed this way previously and Mick wondered if this may have been the prospectors.

As they are heading in this northerly direction Castle was noticing some changes of the information on his monitor.

"Mick, there seems to be an increase in the amount of iron in this section of country. It is about the highest concentration of iron that we've had today."

"Castle, perhaps that may be an indication of an approaching gold deposit because there is a co-relation between gold and iron where they come into contact with quartz. Do you have any indication of quartz on the monitor?"

"No, Mick the quartz here is very low, but I'll set a parameter for that too and keep a closer watch on those three elements." Castle carried out a few key strokes on his keyboard and presently the system was grouping the atomic numbers for gold, iron and quartz at the top of his screen where he could monitor those more carefully.

The next leg of their grid pattern took them around the northern tip of the hill and Mick could see the creek which had flowed with water from the recent thunderstorm. Then he could see the tracks of the vehicle which he had noticed before and then they converged. Soon he came upon a vehicle which was bogged and two men were working at digging it out.

Chapter 27

Yulara, Northern Territory, 10th April

"Castle, it looks like we may have found the prospectors. You remember Don and Ted from the crash site? Well here they are and it looks like they may be in trouble themselves, so we'll put down here for a while. We can help them after you've backed up your data."
"Okay Mick. That's fine; I need to stretch my legs again anyway."

Mick landed the helicopter some fifty metres from where Don and Ted were working on their bogged vehicle. He was careful not to put it down where there may be soft ground and this looked suitable. After the engine was shut down Mick alighted and headed over to the vehicle. He could see that these men had experience with this sort of disaster. The bogged trailer was disconnected and the vehicle was jacked up and other side was sitting on some bog boards. They were working on the near side now as he approached them.

West of border, Great Central Road, Western Australia, 10th April

Both Don and Ted were up and about in the camp and had the breakfast almost ready for the police crew before any of them had roused.
"Wakey, wakey," Don called as he banged the spoon on the side of the skillet. "Time to get out of the sack! There's breakfast ready, the sun's shining, the birds are singing, it's a lovely day to be in the outback!"

It took them a few minutes to crawl out of their swags or tents. While they were putting on their boots, Don was adding the tea to the billy which had been boiling while he cooked the eggs and sausages.

"Sorry, no damper this morning, you blokes are out of flour and we'll need ours for the next few days," Don told them as they came to the cooking area to collect their breakfast.
It was the quiet time of the day and now with everyone moving around, that piece of magic had disappeared for Don. The sun was just peeking over the horizon between the hills to the east. There were only a few scattered clouds but the sun was causing these to show their pink morning colours with effect.

Ted moved alongside Don and asked him, "I say, old man, have you given any more thought to what we were discussing last evening just before bedtime?"

Chapter 28

West of border, Great Central Road, Western Australia, 10th April

Don sighed and after a few seconds replied, “Yeah Ted, I think it’s time for us to move out. I mean, we came out here for our own purposes and we’ve spent so much time doing everyone else’s things for them, I really do think it’s time we made the move and continued with our project. What do you think?”

“Oh, I whole heartedly agree, old man. There’s just so much a chap can take of this sort of thing. I’m not very good at this waiting for something to happen and then not being able to do anything anyway. I can’t really see any point in our being here any longer. So, if that is what you have in mind to do, then I’m right with you,” Ted answered.

Don moved over and sat down beside Alec and between mouthfuls of sausage and fried egg told Alec of their decision.
“When do you think you’ll likely to move out, Don?” Alec asked.

‘I think we’ll tidy up here after you blokes have finished with the breakfast things. The hotplate needs to cool, so it’ll take us about an hour then we’ll be out of here and leave you blokes to watch out and do your job.”

“Well, I’m sorry to have you blokes leave us, you’ve done so much to assist with the camp and sorting out our sites for the surveillance, we’ll miss that sort of help. Where are you heading?”

“You’re all big boys now and can fend for yourselves. Anyway Ted and I have some work that we’ve neglected for several days and it really is time for us to get back to that again. We'll head out to the north-west, there's something over there which we need to check out."

"Hey listen up everyone." Alec yelled as he stood up to get the attention of everyone in the camp, "Don and Ted are leaving us this morning to carry on with their own project, so we'll need to organise ourselves a bit better. More importantly I'd like to pass on our thanks to these two blokes who have helped us. If it wasn't for that accident, we'd never met. Not that I like motor vehicle accidents, but you never know what may come out of them. I recon we can all thank Don and Ted for their patience and help."
Everyone had put down their plates and a round of applause followed Alec's remarks.
There was some banter between themselves about who was to be the camp mother after these two blokes, the best camp captains that they had ever had the opportunity of meeting, had moved on.

The officers began washing their own dishes as they began the clean-up. Don and Ted sorted out the items around the camp putting aside those items which belonged to the police unit and taking their own gear to the ute or trailer. After the equipment was all sorted and cleaned up, it was fitted back into their storage areas. The hot plate being the last item, completed the loading.

Don started the engine of the ute and while it was warming up the officers approached and each of them shook hands with Don and Ted.

Chapter 28

West of border, Great Central Road, Western Australia, 10th April

"See ya soon," Don yelled out of his window as he drove off.

Soon they were back onto the Great Central Road heading out in an easterly direction.

Ted noticed this direction of travel and commented to Don, "I say, old man, you told to copper that you'd be heading out in a north-westerly direction and here we are driving east. What's up?"

"I didn't want to give them too much information; they've got enough on their plate. Besides, we need to get back to Sandy Blight Junction Road to get around the other side of that range of hills. That's where old Billy-the-Lid's map shows where Lasseter's gold is located."

"Now that makes more sense! By Jove, it's good to be back on the road again. It feels like we are doing something positive for a change."

They had travelled twenty kilometres along the road when they came to the place where the vehicles had crashed and everything went haywire several days ago. In another five kilometres they turned left onto Sandy Blight Junction Road and headed to the north.

With the hill on the left of the vehicle Don veered off the road and followed a pair of very faint racks that followed along the foot of the hill. The going was rough and they were forced to drive slowly. At times the vehicle was forced to slow right down to crawl

across some watercourses which had been washed out over the years. Luckily these were dry. After several hours, they stopped and with shovels made a particularly bad crossing more suitable for them to cross. After they had safely crossed they stopped and had a break and their lunch. The going had been tough and they were happy to stop and rest for a while.
After getting back onto the road again they had several more crossings to repair before they could cross but most of them were okay. Don had noticed that the last one they worked on was moist and wondered if that thunderstorm may have dumped some rain on this area yesterday. As they travelled further along, the ground now showed that rain had fallen recently but it had been fairly light and unlikely to cause them any concern.
It was mid-afternoon and as they crossed a watercourse, the ground gave way under the heavy vehicle and they became bogged.

Don tried to reverse but that only sent the trailer further down.
They unpacked a shovel each and began removing some of the damp soil from under the vehicle. The trailer was disconnected as they needed to get the ute un-bogged first. They would then hitch the rope onto the trailer to retrieve that.
With the kangaroo jack sitting on a plank and fitted into the socket at the side of the ute, one side was lifted clear of the ground. One of the other bog boards was then slid under each of the tyres and the vehicle was lowered down again.

Chapter 28

West of border, Great Central Road, Western Australia, 10th April

With the noise of their engine idling they did not hear the helicopter until it was close by. They stopped their work, stood up and looked at the helicopter.

"By Jove, old man! I do believe that we've seen that helicopter before and quite recently too!" Ted said as he recognised the markings on the side of the chopper.

"Yeah, I recon that's Mick Jones and his offsider, Castle in their Bell 206," Don replied, somewhat surprised that they could be found out here. "You never know who you might meet out here."
They waited for the helicopter to land close-by and they leaned on their shovels as they watched it land. Mick was the first one to alight and it looked like Castle was in the back doing something on a computer but he followed Mick in just a short time.
It had been several days since they last saw these blokes but their short time together had created something of a bond. The situation back at the crash site was stressful and they formed a strong respect for each other.
Both Don and Ted walked out to meet Mick and they shook hands as they came together. Shortly Castle was with them as well and it was just like old times. Well, times that may have been in different circumstances.

Don said as they approached Mick, "You never know who is looking at you out here do you? But it sure is good to see you blokes again."
"Well I never did!" Exclaimed Mick, "It is incredible just who you find when you wander around the scrub. Gee it's good to see you blokes. How have you been?"

"I'll say the same, Mick. But we're great thanks, apart from a little trouble with this track here. Fancy having you turn up, just as we're getting to the exciting part."
'Yes I can see that you've had a problem but have it well in hand. Is there something we can do to help," asked Mick as he looked over the situation of the ute and trailer."

Don explained what they were about to do and suggested that the newcomers could just watch at this stage and Don would get them to help when and if it was necessary. "There's no point in all of us getting covered in this mud, so we'll carry on and see how we go. Thanks for the offer, though."

Mick and Castle watched as Don worked the jack while Ted collected the other two planks from the trailer. These he slid under the tyres and the Don lowered the ute onto them. The planks sank a little but the tyres are now on top of the ground instead of below the crust. They set out some more timbers in front of the ute to make a path for it. Don got into the driver's seat and engaged low gear and drove the ute out of the bog and off the end of the planks and timbers. The ground here was firm enough for the ute without any further support. Now it was just a matter of dragging the trailer through. To do this they filled some dryer soil into the tracks left by the ute and covered this with timbers and planks. The trailer was jacked up and a plank put under the tyres, one side at a time. The tow hitch of the trailer was buried in the mud so they attached a rope to this and ran it out to the towbar of the ute and tied it off.

Chapter 28

West of border, Great Central Road, Western Australia, 10th April

Once again Don drove the ute forward and the rope took up the strain and then the trailer followed but fell off the timber track which they had so carefully laid out. Although this slowed the ute, it was still able to pull the trailer through without too much strain and soon it was on hard ground on the near side of the creek.

Mick turned to Castle, "That's how it's done, Castle. You can see we're in the presence of a couple of professionals who know how to do stuff."
"Yes I can see what you mean. When you do the preparation work correctly, the job works out well," Castle replied. "The same as any situation but to have the knowledge of this country and how survive in it would have to be the most important thing."

The front of the trailer was jacked up and then attached back onto the tow hitch of the ute. It was now just a matter of cleaning up and loading all the timber and planks back onto ute and trailer and they'd be ready carry on down the track.
In half an hour they had completed everything and the outfit was ready to move out again but by this time it was approaching late afternoon.
"I was wondering if we should call it a day or press on. What do you think Ted?" Don asked.
"Well, old man, this isn't a bad place to camp and we have some friends here too, so perhaps we could camp the night here and continue in the morning," Ted replied.
Don approached Mick and Castle, "Would you blokes like to share our camp tonight. We think we'll camp

here and move out in the morning again. We would appreciate your company if you're able."
"We'd be delighted to camp with you blokes, Don. We've got everything we need. Yes that would be good, thanks for the offer," Mick replied.

Just as Mick and castle moved off to collect what they needed for the night from the helicopter, Don's attention was caught by the sound of an engine. It was made by a vehicle approaching from the front of them and presently the Landcruiser wagon drove up to park beside the ute.
Don couldn't believe it. It was looking more like Geraldton's Marine Terrace Mall all the time. Way out here in the bush and we're inundated with vehicles of all sorts and people everywhere.
He began walking over to the vehicle and was astounded as the young aboriginal girl who they met at the Warburton Aboriginal Community got out of the driver's door. Don then had a closer look at the passenger who was also getting out of the vehicle.
"Hey Ted, look who we have with us now!" he called out over his shoulder.
"Well God bless my soul, if it isn't Millicent and Billy-the-lid from Warburton Community. Well I'll be blessed," Ted exclaimed as he too walked over to meet the new comers.

Old Billy-the-lid was having some difficulty in moving around but he hobbles over and shook hands with the two men.
"Be good seein' you fellas again," old Billy said.

Chapter 28

West of border, Great Central Road, Western Australia, 10th April

"I brung me grandfather out to see where you fellas are because we hadn't seen ya few a few days and wondered if ya was okay," Millie said.
"G'day Billy and Millie," Don said, "Yes we had a bit of a hold up, well quite literally really. We had to help some people who had a crash on the road and then there was an incident with some rough fellas and then the police but we are alright and just heading out to the spot which you marked on the map, Billy."
"Yeah I can see you've found out about the thunderstorm last night, Don. Been here long?" Billy asked.
"No Billy, just about two hours getting this outfit out of the creek. But now we are going to camp here for the night as some more of our friends have turned up. What are your plans?" Don asked.
"We came out here to see how you was goin' but couldn't find you blokes so we started look'n an look'n then we see that helicopter and see him landing and after that we see your motorcar and here we are too. Just concerned for you blokes, dat's all," Billy-the-lid said. His talking was becoming laboured and Don could see that his health was failing him. In fact he was much worse than when they met him just a few days ago.

Don could see that they had swags in the back of the Landcruiser, so he invited them to stay with them for the night. He would like to have a discussion about some of the details of what they talked about the other day. Bill said that yes they would stay. It would be good to talk things over.
Mick and Castle approached the group and were introduced.

Chapter 28

West of border, Great Central Road, Western Australia, 10th April

Mick said to Billy, "Do you remember me Billy? I was out this way about five years ago and we had a talk about some of the problems you were having and I sent out some people to help. Do you remember?"

"Well I'll be darned, Mick Jones. Yes I remember that very well. How bout dat? And yes that program we were able to put together was very good and now we have that drug problem under control. I never did get the chance to thank you personally, Mick but by gee, I'll do that right now." He turned to Millie, "you remember this bloke, Millie, he sent out those people who helped get the drugs out of our community."
"Yes granddad, I do. It make so much difference to everyone in the community, now it's a good place to live," Millie replied.
That was a relief for Don as he needed to talk to both of these people but about different things. Now it seems like it's all coming together.

While this was happening both Ted and Castle were scouting around collecting some wood so they could have a fire. It looked like it might get a bit colder in the night and a good fire just might help. In a few minutes it was alight and there was little smoke.
Don invited the others to follow him to the fire which was now blazing.
Castle was invited to meet Billy and Millie and presently there were several discussions going on at the same time.
Soon the conversation turned around to the subject of gold and there was a silence. No one know what the other was doing or thinking about gold.

Chapter 28

West of border, Great Central Road, Western Australia, 10th April

Don, who now knew more about the philanthropic activities of Mick Jones, broke the ice by telling Mick and Castle what the arrangement was about the location of Lasseter's gold and how it was to benefit the local community.

Mick was astounded that someone else was on the same path as himself, so he told his story of what they had been doing since flying out from Sydney.

When he completed the background of the story and told how the police had cornered them this morning everyone had a great laugh. At this time they could laugh about it but at the time of the incident it was very stressful and most unexpected.

Now that everyone was looking for the same thing and for the same reasons, they were able to have a meaningful discussion without holding back.

Millie and Ted put together a meal for everyone while this discussion was taking place and presently they were eating their meal while still talking excitedly about what had happened to them in the last few days.

While this discussion was in progress, Don was watching old Billy so he could gauge his response to the situation and was surprised to see him smiling the whole time and the gleam came back to his eyes. He seemed to be happy with things as they are turning out.

There were many questions to Castle about his electronic apparatus and how it was helping in this situation. He told them of the time when the flew over the ute with the brown cover and how the monitor looked to him and how he felt when they flew over the same place a few days later to get no signal. Now that he had all of the information he could understand the situation and even had a laugh at himself because of it.

Presently the talk turned around to the plans for the future and there were many suggestions which involved all of them.
They agreed that the local community was the one to benefit from the profits of the gold, all they had to do now was to locate the "reef", estimated its value and determine how to mine the gold so that the benefits could begin to flow.

"Well, when we visited Billy at the Community centre last week, he gave me his map of the area and he has marked on it where he remembers the gold reef is situated. I have it right here." Don spread out the map on the ground while Ted shone the torch on it. Don put his finger on their present location and drew a line from there to where Billy had marked. It was only fifteen kilometres from their present location.
"When we break camp in the morning we should all head out to that spot and see what we find," Don said.
Mick agreed with this plan and offered his helicopter to continue with what he and Castle were doing, to see if there are other gold deposits in the area as well.
"We'll give you all of the assistance we can in helping you to locate the reef but then leave you people to organise the arrangements as it seems like you have everything in hand for that purpose," Mick told them.

Everyone agreed that this was a good approach and soon everyone was heading off to their swags for the night.

Chapter 28

West of border, Great Central Road, Western Australia, 10th April

It had been an eventful day and the camp was quiet after a very short time.

East of Warakurna, Great Central Road, Western Australia, 11th April

The five other officers who were at the meal area for breakfast were starting to complain to Alec that they were getting tired of this stake-out.

They see about four vehicles a day on this road and with all of them taking their turn on the roster to man the surveillance point on the hill, they were getting tired of the job.

After the breakfast things had been cleared away Alec said to them "Well, I'll tell what we'll do. To break the boredom, we'll get some exercise. That will solve the problem."
As one voice, they complained "Aw Sarge!"
"No! This is what is going to happen. Two men at a time will run from here following the track up the hill to the top, relieve the two who are ready to be relieved anyway and have them return here on foot. I have a stopwatch here so, I'll time you and we'll see who is the fastest. I want to see your faces on that monitor so I can clock you off," Alec told them. Most of these blokes were fit so it should be quite a contest. "Who are going to be the first to go?"

Two of the fittest blokes volunteered to be the first ones to go. Alec set the stopwatch and away they went at a good pace. He reckons that it should take them only about eight or nine minutes to run that far, if they keep up that pace. In any case it'll take their minds off this inaction. The main concern with this plan was that he now was down to himself and four others at the base camp in case something happened. The other officers we either at the hill-top surveillance point, running up there, or running back from there. He hoped that something would happen before they were too tired.

His got a shout from the officer who was watching the monitor, “Hey Alec those first two guys have made it.” Alec checked his watch, that had taken them seven minutes and forty seconds, not bad, he thought.
“Okay the next two! GO!” He yelled as he pressed the button on the watch.
The second two did take a little longer but they still made good time.
They kept this activity up so that each of them had been to the top of the hill and returned twice. Several of them were showing signs of stress, so Alec called a halt while they had a cup of tea or coffee and relaxed for a few minutes.

The crew at the hill-top called on the radio. “*There's a vehicle approaching from the east*”. Alec checked the monitor and watched as the vehicle got closer and then as it slowed.
“Standby everyone, we could have some action here!” he said sharply to the team who was present. The entire team stopped what they were doing and congregated around the monitor. Their attention was set on the screen and they could see what was being recorded from the ridge-top vantage point.

Chapter 29

East of Warakurna, Great Central Road, Western Australia, 11th April

The vehicle came to a stop just where the road crosses Giles Creek. Next he had a closer look at the vehicle. He couldn't see it directly but the monitor showed a good clear image at about half a screen resolution. "Looks like a Landcruiser wagon with four blokes in it. Now, this could be interesting so let's keep a sharp eye on this one," saying the last comment into the radio.

The image on the monitor closed up and one of the officers carried out a screen capture and saved the image. This was immediately downloaded to the computer and after some face recognition had taken place could not get a name for the occupants.

"All that tells us is that they are from outside of WA," Alec told them. "Forward that image on the Federal Police and wait for their reply."

Before the vehicle had moved away from its position at Giles Creek a message came back from the Australian Federal Police. They have one of the occupant's details on file. He was a known associate of Mick Dunraven and frequents several of Arnold's clubs. Two of the others are familiar with the Feds but they did not have any details on them with the exception that they also frequent Arnold's nightclub. "Okay that's what we needed to know. Tell them thanks and we'll keep a watch on these blokes and also keep a sharp eye out to see if anything else is around," Alec told them.
Several of the officers began to make preparations to move the vehicles out should the need to apprehend these blokes arise.

Chapter 29

East of Warakurna, Great Central Road, Western Australia, 11th April

The vehicle which they had under surveillance, moved off and continued to travel along the Great Central Road heading west. It travelled for another ten kilometres to where the track turns from the road and leads to the first of the dumps of gold made by Dunraven and Botticelli. They do not have a very good view of it now as the distance is too great but they can still see where it goes to, should it turn from the road. The vehicle parks for about ten minutes and everybody is watching and waiting.

"A bit like the cat and mouse. Eh Sarge?" one of the officers commented, "they wait and we watch."
"Yeah, mate! That's what we are here for, the inevitable cat and mouse game. Just make sure that you bet on us being the cat, Eh?" Alec replied, "But I think these are more like rats than mice, so keep sharp!"
Those close by at the main camp had a cackle at this description of their job. It seemed to fit quite well, they thought.
After it had been parked for twelve minutes the vehicle they were watching drove off to the west at speed.
"Okay, so what is their game?" Alec wondered.
He called on the radio, "Keep those eyes peeled you blokes. In both directions, I have a feeling that things are changing and I want to be kept in the loop."

He could see on the monitor that the vehicle was now out of sight and would probably soon be at Warakurna Roadhouse, so he put in a call to the manager, who he had spoken to earlier on in the operation.

While he had the manager on the line he was told that the vehicle had pulled in and was refuelling. The call was disconnected.
About ten minutes later, the call came through again and it was the manager back again telling Alec what had happened. "They had refuelled and bought drinks and some fast food before asking about any backtracks to the east of here in the general direction of Alice Springs. We told them that the country was pretty rough and that it was advisable to stick to the main road, particularly as they didn't have a permit," the manager told him, "then they just took off back east on the road but I don't know how far they went but they should be back in your area soon."

All eyes were on the monitor which was still showing the place where that vehicle was when it went out of sight.
"There it is!" one of them exclaimed. "You can just see their dust about half way to the roadhouse. They should be visible in just a few minutes."
The vehicle was heading in their direction and at that speed the distance was decreasing rapidly. In five minutes the vehicle was just due north of the police position. Presently it turned from the main road and began heading directly towards the place where Don and Ted had uncovered the second dump of the crates of gold.
This was the area of the desert oak trees.
The vehicle disappeared into the forest of desert oaks but their dust could be seen on the monitor.
"Hey, Sarge! The tree camera has just picked up the Landcruiser." Came the call from the officer who was

monitoring that screen which was receiving from the tree camera.
Alec turned to that officer, "you stay here and keep a watch on that monitor, and keep me informed."
He turned to the rest of the crew who were nearby, "let's get mobile!"
They all gathered up their gear, piled into their Landcruiser and were heading out to intercept the other Landcruiser which is under surveillance at the first dump point at speed. As they left the main road on the side track towards the dump of gold they slowed down and proceeded at a crawl so as not to raise dust. About two hundred metres from the gold dump, they pulled up and after securing the vehicle, headed towards the area of the dump on foot. They were dressed in bullet proof vests and each of them carried an automatic weapon as well as their standard issue Glock nine millimetre automatic side arms.
The police were walking in single file at three metres intervals, crouching forward to present the smallest target.
Alec was the first to spot the vehicle and he signalled for the rest to stop. He could not see any activity at first but as he moved around the closest tree he could see that two of the four men were digging. There was no doubt in his mind as to their intentions. He was now very thankful of the resources which they had with them, as all of their activities would be recorded.
He called the base camp and was advised that indeed their activity was recorded on disk and that hard copy images were printed from time to time. Alec asked to be advised as soon as the first of the crates of gold bar was opened. At that stage they would move in.

Chapter 29

East of Warakurna, Great Central Road, Western Australia, 11th April

All of the officers were crouching down in the grass waiting for Alec to indicate for them to move forward. After a few minutes he received the call he was waiting for and he motioned for them to move forward. They did this very slowly and carefully so they could get as close to the men as possible before they became noticed and keeping to the cover of the trees and grass.
Alec and two others were approaching from behind the vehicle and stood behind it before they announced their presence.
When Alec could see that each of his team was in the best positions that they could find, he indicated for all of them to make their presence known.

"Police don't move! Police don't move! Police don't move!" they all yelled out at the same time.

The men who were digging as well as those who were taking gold bars from the crate were stunned into simply standing on the spot and frozen in movement. The look of absolute amazement on their faces was almost comical.
"This is the police! Stay where you are! Do not move! You are surrounded!" Then he added, "Put down the shovels and raise your hands in the air. Don't do anything stupid!"

Yeah you guessed it, they did something stupid.

The two men, who were handling the gold bars, dropped them, drew a handgun each and fired off in the general direction of Alec as he and his men dropped to the ground.

Chapter 29

East of Warakurna, Great Central Road, Western Australia, 11th April

Luckily Alec was standing behind the front wheel of the crook's Landcruiser which received one of the bullets which was fired. The other shot went overhead as the shooter didn't take any time to aim his weapon. The next shots went in the general direction of the officers but none of them were hit. Several trees were wounded in the fire-fight.

By the time the crooks had fired off several shots each, the police began returning fire. This fire was mainly over their heads as has been their training but Alec could see that something more definite needed to be done, so he returned fire and with a carefully aimed shot hit one of them in the shoulder. This bloke who was shot dropped his weapon and one of the blokes who was in the hole, digging, took it up and began shooting at the police as well. He was not very good at aiming his weapon either as he hit nothing more than the ground in the distance. As the magazine emptied and the gun stopped firing, he threw it onto the ground and sat down in the hole so he wouldn't get shot by the fire of the police officers.

One of the other officers could see Alec's point of aim and fired at the other of the crooks who was shooting at them. His aim was on target, as this man received a bullet in the hand which also knocked the gun from his grip. He let out a scream.

The two men who were in the hole threw the shovels onto the ground and lay flat on the bottom of the hole. It seemed to them that if they kept up this activity, they would get more than just a couple of flesh wounds as these blokes were specialists at using

firearms and the crooks just used them on the odd occasion.
With two of the crooks injured and none of them holding a weapon, the police began approaching cautiously, advising all the time that the men should "Get on the ground with your arms and legs spread and don't move."
With four heavily armed and battle dressed police officers approaching them, the four men succumbed without much resistance. They obviously didn't expect police opposition as heavy as this and could see no advantage in continuing with resistance.
After some scuffles between the officers and the crooks, the four men were secured and handcuffed.

After everyone had settled down and the crooks were handcuffed and seated near a tree, the wounds of the two injured men were being dressed and Alec began to ask a few questions.
"What made you blokes visit this site?"
There was no response from the group of men who seemed that they didn't want to answer any questions.
"We've had this area under surveillance for a couple of days and were just waiting for someone to drop in!" Alec continued.

No matter what he asked there were no answers from the men. They were very tight lipped. They would not even give their names until after ten minutes of continually being badgered and questioned.
Alec delivered the caution to them and told them they were under arrest for interfering in a police operation, unlawful discharge of firearms and carrying loaded weapons in public so as to cause havoc. He did not

want to allow them any more details at this time. That could come later when they were securely locked up.

A sat-phone call was placed back to Kalgoorlie and Alec was advised that the police heavy paddy wagon, an eight tonne air-conditioned eight seater truck, was at Warakurna and would be with them in a half hour. The local police were on their regular run which included this part of the district; the largest police district in Australia.
With the police Landcruisers brought up, the four men were distributed into the two vehicles and headed back to the main road to wait for the paddy wagon to arrive. The four men were transferred with no further incident and headed back to the Kalgoorlie station where they would be put into the cells for processing and further questioning.

Alec and his team were able to pack up all of their surveillance equipment and they too set off in the direction of Kalgoorlie.
They arrived the following day and after a debriefing headed off to their homes for a good night's rest.

The next day the newspapers all over Australia were commenting on how well the Western Australian police force was trained. The local newspapers took two full pages of description that had been leaked to them of the fire-fight that took place out in the bush by the desert oak trees.
"It sounds a bit like the last gun-fight at the OK Corral," commented several of the Kalgoorlie locals.

West of the border, Western Australia, 11th April

The entire group of people are standing around the fire before dawn this morning. Mostly they didn't sleep very well as they had such an anticipation of what this day would bring.

Some light low cloud to the east was providing them with a spectacular vision as the sun was trying to look over the tops of them. There were light pinks and gold which changed gradually to yellows and reds with some purples in the lower portions of the clouds which were closer to the horizon. A number of birds were calling in the early morning too.

With the hill to the back of them and facing east they had an excellent view of what nature was showing them this morning. The scene in front of them was so amazing that there was not even any talking. It was about the most spectacular sunrise that any of them had seen.

Presently the sun poked its head through a break in the clouds and they were bathed in the early morning sunshine.

"Well that would be the most spectacular sunrise that I have ever seen," said Mick. He had travelled around the world by helicopter, spent many hours in balloons and been on many mountains during his eventful life but was completely taken with this display of nature at its best.

Every one replied in their own words at the same time but they all meant the same thing, agreeing with Mick's description of the event.

Chapter 30

West of the border, Western Australia, 11th April

"Well," Don said as he turned to face everyone, "with a start to the day like that, let's hope it is an omen to what we expect to find today."
"Amen to that old man," Ted replied
Everyone agreed with Don.

Don and Millie began preparing some food for the start of the day. Soon there was bacon, eggs and sausages in the pans. The smell from this cooking had everyone collecting their plates and cutlery so that they could eat their food while it was hot and at its premium.
The billy was boiling and Ted added the tea and let the billy stand by the fire to keep it hot.
The meal was dished up and the talking between members of the group ceased as they all tucked into their meal and drank their tea.

As soon as everyone had finished, the plates and pans were washed and stowed and they began preparing for their day ahead.

Don said to Billy, "what do you want to do first Bill? At this stage we'll take your suggestions and go from there.
Billy-the-lid thought about this for a while and began by telling them "Millie an me'll head out to the north, back to where I remember I was with Lasseter all those years ago. I can recognise the place but it's also marked on that map which I gave to Don and Ted the last time we were together, back at Warburton. The map which they showed us all last night."

Everyone agreed that this would be a great way to start.

"Castle and I will continue with our aerial prospecting and follow along shortly. I am interested to see how the mineralisation changes as we approach the place which you have picked out Billy," Mick added.
"Sounds good to me," said Don. "So we'll tag along, following behind Millie, provided that she doesn't drive too fast." Millie just replied to Don with her big toothy smile.
"I don't drive fast!" she retorted, once again with that big toothy smile.

Soon they were all ready to leave the camp site. Millie was driving with old Billy in the passenger seat alongside her. Don and Ted followed in the ute with the trailer attached.
Mick and Castle were delayed for the few minutes it took Mick to carry out his pre-flight checks and fire up the turbine. The motor vehicles had been driving for about five minutes when they finally lifted off and followed along a similar path.

Castle had his eyes glued to the monitor once again just waiting for the time when the indication of the mineralisation would change. He did notice that there was less iron and quartz showing on the monitor, but silica and selenium had increased slightly. Not having a complete knowledge of geology and the relationship of the minerals with each other, he was not completely sure of the meaning of what he was seeing in front of him.

Chapter 30

West of the border, Western Australia, 11th April

While the vehicles were continuing on their basically north-westerly direction, Mick had the helicopter traversing to the left and right of their track by several hundred metres. He was slowly catching up to the other vehicles but by weaving left to right they were covering a lot more country. He was hoping that this would allow Castle to gain more data and his equipment could show a change as they approached the site which old Billy-the-lid was taking them to.

It was an hour before Millie stopped at the suggestion of old Billy. The track had been rough and they crossed several small creeks without incident. The track took them over several small rises and the vegetation was quite sparse. The long hill which they had camped by last night was stretched out to the left of them but now much further out in the distance.

To the north there were several low hills in the distance. Some desert oak trees were present in the distance but just here the ground has changed from a pale yellow colour of the dry grasses to a brownish colour. The most noticeable thing was that now there are a lot of quartz and ironstone rock strewn about. Like there has been a massive upheaval of the ground and the underlying layers of the earth had been pushed up to be exposed on the surface. There is a low hill with its ridge running north-west from this point and it looks so much different from the rest of the country. Almost like it doesn't belong there.

As Don and Ted were driving the last fifteen minutes of this section of the track, they had become more animated in their talking as the change of country is what they had been looking for. Up until now it didn't even look like gold bearing country. And with the experience which they have been able to accumulate over the years, they didn't think that this area was gold bearing at all but this change in the country has altered their outlook. That low hill out to the right was very rocky. The sharp edges of the rocks and boulders indicating the fracturing of the ground that made up the hill.

They all alighted from the vehicles and were standing around talking in a group when the helicopter landed just twenty metres away. As the rotors slowed down, Mick climbed into the back of the helicopter and Castle was pointing to the monitor in an excited way. In a short time they walked over and joined the others.

"Well it looks like our day is certainly getting better," Don told them. "This certainly looks much more like gold bearing country and I would recon that Billy's marker must be close by."
"Yes," old Billy said as he pointed a boulder on the ridge of the hill out to the right. "See dat boulder over dere? Well me marker is just to the udder side of dat. Dat's where we laid out Lasseter when he died. His diggin' for the yellow gold is right under 'im."

Castle piped up as he was having difficulty in restraining himself any longer. His excitement at what he had seen on his monitor was evident. "You should have seen what happened on my monitor as we approached this area. The silica and selenium dropped off and then the levels of iron and quartz increased. Just before we landed there was a massive spike to the

amount of gold. From what I see on the monitor this must be a very rich gold bearing deposit."
"Castle show us what this marvellous piece of electronic wizardry indicates," Don asked Castle, displaying his good natured grin. "It certainly sounds exciting."

Mick, Don and Ted followed Castle back to the helicopter and climbed into the rear section of the cabin. With Castle sitting at the keyboard of the computer terminal, they stood behind him and looked at the screen over his shoulder. He loaded the details of the last quarter of an hour and showed them what the program indicated on the screen. The different elements are listed in columns that show their description by their individual atomic numbers. They could see the listings under the headings of quartz and iron increase as the coordinates closed on their present location. At the same time they could see how those elements under the listings of silica and selenium drop away in numbers. At the last few seconds of the flight, they could see that under the heading of the atomic numbers for gold, it had risen from a figure that Castle pointed out was a trace to a much larger amount.

"Does this program determine the recoverable weight of gold per tonne of ore?" asked Don.
"That is something that we need to determine now. But you have the knowledge of gold mining, so perhaps with your input we can determine that," Castle answered.

"Well to do that we need to do some drilling and do some calculations the old fashioned way so that this program can be educated to show that recovery figure. That is the most important figure that we need to ascertain if this can be a profitable mining project," Don told them. "But from what I can see here from this country just here and with the amounts of accompanying minerals and elements, I think that this could be what we are looking for."

Ted spoke excitedly to Don, "Well, old man, it looks like we may have hit the jackpot with this one. Looks like there is going to be plenty to share around after all."

They all retuned to where Billy was standing with Millie and told him of the need to find out more detail of what lies beneath the low hill over to the right.

"Billy, I know that your map indicates the location, that you know so well, to be close by here. Could you please show us the place?" Don asked him.
"Yeah! It not far! Follow me," said Billy as he walked off towards the place where he had indicated his marker was and presently everyone else fell in step behind him. They climbed up and over the broken rock to the top and stopped beside the boulder where old Billy was standing.

"There it be," old Billy said as he rested his hand on a square slab of quartz rock which lay on a small mound of ironstone stones. "Dis is the grave of Lasseter and under his body is the diggin' he had done to find his yellow gold."

Chapter 30

West of the border, Western Australia, 11th April

The uneven ground was difficult to stand on, as the surfaces of the rocks were at all angles. The slab of quartz rock that Billy was resting his hand on was about half a metre square and about a third of a metre thick.

"Well, what a way to spend eternity," Mick said as he stood beside the others. "To be buried near the area which had made him famous, yet no-one would believe him." He turned to old Billy and said, "Thankyou Billy, for sharing these details with us. It certainly will go down in history now that Lasseter's reef of gold does in fact exist. What we need to determine now is the extent of the reef and see if that confirms Lasseter's notation of 11 kilometres long by 3.5 metre wide. By the looks of this hill, I would say its every bit that length and somewhat wider."

Don had brought with him his knapping tool and he spend several minutes with some of the quartz and ironstone rocks and after breaking one of these open had found a broad seam of gold in the fissure of the rock which he held in his hand.

"It certainly looks like it's high grade and if this sample is any indication of what the rest of this hill holds, then we may have one of the richest seams of gold in the history of the gold mining industry in Australia," Don said. Ted was standing beside him as Don passed the sample around. He pointed out to everyone the indications of gold as it appeared in the sample.

Chapter 30

West of the border, Western Australia, 11th April

"I say old man! That looks to me like it should yield about ten or fifteen ounces to the tonne, maybe even twenty," Ted said as he passed the sample to Mick who was beside him.

Don picked up several more ironstone and quartz rocks and after knapping at them with the hammer, found seams of gold in them as well. He continued doing this for ten minutes just to satisfy himself that they had found something that he could bet on. He needed to make absolutely certain of what they had found and while he was working on these samples and showing them around to everyone to look at he was formulating his plan.

Don addressed everyone, "Well there are two very important things which we must do straight away. One of those is to mark out a claim and lodge it with the mining registrar and the other is to determine the extent of the gold bearing area so we can make sure that the claim includes all of the gold bearing country."

Mick spoke up, "Well I can offer the services of my company lawyers to do what is necessary in the lodgement of that claim and I will also provide my helicopter to survey the area to do what is necessary, Don. Perhaps if you can tell me what needs to be done I can get things started."

"Thank you for your offer Mick but Macy, my wife and business partner, has lodged all of our claims in the past and is well versed on the requirements of lodging mining claims in Western Australia. So I think

she will continue to do a great job. I'll give her the details on the sat-phone when we have them," Don said and took a paused before continuing. "Firstly Mick, I think we should spend some time determining the extent of this gold bearing area. If I can fly with you and we can log the area using Castle's equipment, then I think we can do it very quickly. Once we have sufficient data, we can determine the co-ordinates and with the sat-phone organise the lodgement of the claim," Don said.
"That sounds like a plan to me Don, let's get under way now," Mick replied.

With Don's experience in the gold industry, everyone was looking to him for direction and he was rising to the occasion. He felt very comfortable with that situation, too.
Don continued, "While we are away doing this first survey, perhaps Ted if you can organise a camp where we can set up. I think just for several nights will do. Get Millie to help and let old Billy have a rest, he looks like he needs it right now. This excitement is getting to him and we don't need to have him collapsing on us out here."
"Yes, old man. Leave it to me. I'll get that organised for you and I'll spend a little time wandering around here with the knapping tool as well. It sure is exciting!" Ted said. He was excited and trying hard not to let it show on his face but he certainly did have a definite spring in his step.

Mick, Don and Castle walked over to and climbed into the helicopter. Mick was seated in the pilot's seat with Don beside him in the co-pilot's seat and Castle sat in the rear seat with his monitor in front of him. Everybody was fitted with headsets with microphones so that they could communicate with each other and in a few minutes they were airborne. Mick took them up to a thousand feet where they could get a good look at the topography and Don drew a rough sketch of the area showing the long narrow hill in the centre. Mick reduced altitude to five hundred feet and as they flew over the area, Castle was keeping them updated with the numbers of gold hits which showed up on the monitor and as the numbers diminished Castle advised Mick and then they swung around and flew on the opposing heading. Don was reading off the GPS screen in front of him and each time they reversed their direction he would write in the co-ordinates. After half an hour of flying in a ziz-zag pattern over the length of the hill, they had mapped out the area and set the co-ordinates for the extremities of the proposed lease. Soon after that Mick brought the aircraft back to land near the camp and after shutting down the engine, they had a look at the monitor which Castle had been watching so closely.

Because he now has so much data, he was able to produce a three dimensional computer image of the load of gold bearing ore. It was like a long sausage and only portions of it were exposed above the surface of the ground. Don was absolutely astounded at the detail and apparent accuracy of this system.

"Do you know that to do that same job which we have just completed in that hour, would have taken a team of drillers and geologist about three years to accomplish," Don said in amazement.

Chapter 30

West of the border, Western Australia, 11th April

"Yes thank you for that, Don. It has taken me years to perfect the system and if this can help these people out here, then I consider that an extreme benefit. What we can do at Macrodelphus now is to market a system which will assist in the development of the mining industry in this country and even around the world," Castle told them.

Don and Ted sorted out the information which they would need to lodge the application for the mining lease and called Macy with the details. They would have approval of the lease in the next few days provided there were no other mining leases on this piece of country.

Mick, Don and Castle joined the others at the camp which had been set up and in discussion with old Billy worked out how to set themselves up as a gold mining operation.

Don said, "I have a registered mining company and we can apply for the lease in that name and operated this lease as we discussed the other day. Once we have completed our assays of the various samples that we need to take we could organise a contractor who will get his machinery in here to carry out the physical work. That would be the quickest way to get started. We can transfer ownership at a later time if that is necessary or with the delay of a week or so we can register a new company. What do you think?"

Billy commented, "Don, I trust you an' Ted an' I tink that we should get this set up as your operation. You can just pay to our people the royalty that we talked of

the udder day. I would be happy to see it done dat way".
Both Ted and Don spoke at the same time, "yes that sounds good to me."
Ted and Don worked out the details and soon Don was on his satellite telephone organising the necessary details with Macy in Geraldton. After he had disconnected the call he joined the others again.

While Don was on the phone, Ted had begun organising to set up the diamond drill to get some core samples so that they could fine tune the data which Castle had provided for them with some old fashion rocks and samples. This machinery is attached to the rear of the ute and it was set up in just a few minutes and by mid-afternoon they had drilled down to 20 metres and had some very exciting samples. Don soon joined him and then the sample retrieving began. Once the samples were retrieved they were laid out on some half round trays attached to some planks on the ground so everyone could have a look at them. Don and Ted were showing the different aspects of the samples and where there were large high-grade deposits of gold in the samples. After some careful measuring of the cores, Ted took several samples and put them through his milling equipment and shortly had some results. His equipment was not as sophisticated as that of Castles but it worked well none the less. He determined that between zero and five metres there was gold at the rate ten ounces per tonne. From five metres to ten metres it assayed at seventeen ounces per tonne and from ten metres to twelve metres at showed thirty two ounces to the tonne. Then it reduced again with the twenty metre reading indicating gold at the rate of fourteen ounces per tonne.

From the profile of the three dimensional image from Castle's computer they carried out some measurements and estimations.
Mick was doing some calculations on his hand held computer and came up with the results.
"If we multiply the length of eleven thousand metres long by five metres wide and twenty metres deep we then assume that the total volume is four point four million tonnes of ore. Now if this averages at the twelve ounces that we've found so far, then we multiply that by the rate of six hundred dollars per ounce of gold in Australian dollars, then this body of ore will produce about thirty one billion, seven hundred million dollars."
Everybody was astounded at that value. It was so far beyond their expectations that it was an unbelievable value. The sum of the value of the gold had stunned everyone as they all just sat there with their mouths hanging open in absolute amazement.

That value was an unbelievable figure!

The atmosphere in the camp was electric as everyone was in excited shock at what they had found. Mick spent a few minutes to double check his figures and soon came back with a very similar answer. "Well folks, I have just checked those figures and still have the same answer, so I'm satisfied that with the information that we have on hand, that value can be expected," he said with a huge grin on his face.

Chapter 30

West of the border, Western Australia, 11th April

"Eureka!" yelled Ted in the famous yell of excited exclamation as he jumped up and down. "We have found it!"

Every one began jumping up and down and yelling about the find. They were slapping the backs of each other, showing their excitement. Castle even began doing a jig in front of everyone and soon they all joined in. This merriment continued on for some time before they sat down on the ground exhausted but so very pleased with themselves.

Even though old Billy didn't join in the dancing, he was in very high spirits as he could see how the community was going to benefit from the venture which was about to be undertaken. He would need to get back to the community to make sure that the new leaders are able to comprehend the value of what they have here and take the necessary steps to make sure that they have the correct controls in place so that there is positive benefit to the community. He could see that some careful planning was necessary but he could only advise the elders now that he had stepped down as the leader.

The day was coming to a close as the sun dipped to the west. Soon they would be in the shadow of the hill.

Ted took some photographs of the area, the camp and several more shots of Lasseter's last resting place, making sure that he had the piece of square quartz in the centre of the shot. These could be important when convincing some financiers and the contractors about their find.

Chapter 30

West of the border, Western Australia, 11th April

After he had stored the camera away he scouted around and collected some more wood. Millie was helping him and she was very excited and chatting away as though she had inherited the whole amount from the royalties of the gold.
Ted said to her, “Be very careful, Millie. Some people will take advantage of your people when they get to know about the wealth which is here. Some people are not very nice when there is a lot of money at stake. Of course be happy but be careful. I can see how this injection of capital can assist in the development of your community but I can also see many of the disadvantages. People new to great wealth must first learn how to manage the money so it will give them the best advantage from that wealth. Be careful and get some advice from some experts. I think Mick might be able to help out here again as he has in the past. Would you like me to talk to him for you?”

He could see that Millie could not grasp all of what he said but she did answer, “Thanks Ted, I would be happy to have Mick help with the money; he seems to be someone who would not take advantage of us like you said some people might do.”
“That’s fine Millie; I’ll take some time and speak to him tonight for you.”

Presently they returned to the camp with armfuls of wood each and the fire was soon roaring away. Millie went out again to collect some more and was singing and skipping as she went out.

Chapter 30

West of the border, Western Australia, 11th April

Don was preparing a damper; Castle was peeling some potatoes which he collected from the helicopter, while Mick was cutting up some beans.

Old Billy was sitting on a chair just gazing out in space. His mind had wandered back to the days when he was helping Lasseter out in this country that was so special to him. Working with the horses and camels and the men. How he had taught them to survive in his country but he also remembered some of the silly things the others had done that caused Lasseter to end his days out here. He was happy. He had waited all his life for this to happen and finally with these people around, he was happy that it had all turned out so well. Now his community would have the money they needed to progress and he hoped the new elders would be smart enough to handle this new wealth properly.

As they sat down to their meal, Don raised his can and said, “I'd like to propose a toast to Mr Lasseter. His years of work out here all that time ago, certainly has paid off. This find is absolutely remarkable.”

The others stood and raised their drinks as well and repeated the words, “Mr Lasseter”.

Mick responded by saying, “when you hear the stories from the time when he was out here, most people did think that the stories were a little farfetched and this was also borne out by the fact that no-one else could find the reef. Well we certainly have proved him right and them wrong. Cheers,” he concluded as he raised his glass in the air and then took a sip from it.

During the course of the evening, Ted approached Mick and passed on his concerns of the community with so much new wealth.

Mick replied, "Yes Ted, you're right of course, so leave it with me and I'll attend to the details."

Don and Ted spent some time talking excitedly about their find. This is the culmination of so many discussions between them and so many phone calls and emails over the last ten years. They had always wanted to fine Lasseter's "Reef of Gold" but were certainly not expecting the value that they had found. They continued talking quietly putting together some ideas of what they would be doing from this point forward.
For them it certainly is a dream-come-true.

Although it had been a very exciting day, everyone's spirits softened as they became tired from their activities and by midnight there wasn't a sound from the camp with the exception of the sounds of sleep.

Lasseter's reef has at last been found but its yield of gold is just so much greater than even he realised all those years ago.

The end.

Postscript

That story took place way back in 2002 and shows the value of the gold from those times at around $640 per ounce.

By the time the mine had reached full production in 2012, the value of gold had risen to a figure in excess of $1700.00 per ounce.

The profit from the mine had doubled in that time.

Don King and Ted Walsh have become very wealthy men and the local aboriginal community have also greatly prospered.

David Kentish

Glossary

ABC	Australian Broadcasting Corporation
Abo's	People of Aboriginal ancestry
Ansett	Australian airline that went broke
Big smoke	The city
Billy	A metal pannikin with a hinged handle on top used to make tea on a camp-fire
Bit sus	A situation that is slightly or greatly suspect
Bloke	Male person
Bog boards	Planks that go under a tyre to get out of boggy ground
Bonnet	The covering over the engine. Sometimes called a "hood"
Brahman	An Australian breed of robust cattle with a hump on the shoulders
Bush timber	Usually wood from the mallet or jam or mulga trees
Bushed	Tired
Camp	Collection of tents or apparatus for temporary living
Camp oven	A heavy cast-iron cooking pot
Claypans	Low depressions where clay collects as dust but become very slippery when they get wet
Cuppa	Usually a cup of tea
Damper	An unleavened bread made from flour
Dogg'n	Following and being a nuisance

Dolly	A frame on wheels that is used for carrying
Droughtmaster	An Australian breed of very robust cattle
Edgy	Nerves are on edge
EPIRB	Emergency position-indicating radio beacon similar to an ELT
Federation	The amalgamation of Australian states into the Commonwealth, 1901
G-day	Good day. A morning greeting
Gee-gees	Horses
Glock	Standard police issue 9 millimetre automatic hand gun
Gnamma holes	Naturally formed holes in flat rocks that collect rainwater
Homestead	The main house for the station owner or manager
Jackaroo	A male person who is learning to be a station hand
Jarrah	A Western Australian hardwood, very hard
Jillaroo	A female person who is learning to be a station hand
Kangaroo jack	A tall, strong jack that is used for lifting vehicles
Karri	A Western Australian hardwood with a long grain
Kays	Kilometres in distance
Keep the finger out	Maintain a fast rate of work
Knocked bark off her knees	Scraped a section of skin from her knees showing the pink epidermis

Murchison area	A district immediately east of Geraldton, Western Australia
Need-to-know	Only those persons with the authority to view certain restricted information.
Nod off	To sleep
Offsider	Companion or helper
Outback	Places of Australia outside of the various metropolitan areas.
Peckish	Hungry
Perth Mint	The Western Australian Government official gold repository.
Pick up the pace	Achieve a faster rate of work
Piss off	Gone! Go somewhere else. Don't be silly
Right away	Now
Road trains	Articulated trucks with up to 4 trailers following. These can be up to 55 metres in length.
Roadhouse	A place to purchase fuel and food
Roadkill	Animals that have been killed by collisions with motor vehicles
Sheila	Female person
Short-arsed-bloke	Man of short stature
Snaggers	Sausages
Snooze	Short sleep
Spinifex	A spiny green fodder plant found across Australia
Splash out	To spend money
Station	A large pastoral holding for raising cattle or sheep. Some Australian

	stations are larger than many European countries
Stuff-up	Mistake
Swag	A unit for sleeping in. It usually is a tube of heavy canvas on the outside with a sleeping bag inside. It keeps the user warm and dry.
Swig	Drink
Table drain	The depression beside the formed road that collects the run-off when it rains
Take a leak	Urinate
Top order	The best
Tucker	Food
Two pies and dead ‘orse	“Dead horse” rhymes with sauce and is spread over a meat pie
Ute	Ute is short for Utility Vehicle, similar to a pick-up truck
Wireless	Radio
Woolshed	The shed where the sheep are shorn to remove their wool
Ya mug	You idiot or clown
Yarns	Short stories of undetermined truth

The Author

David Kentish was raised on a dairy farm just south of Perth in Western Australia near the small settlement of Keysbrook.

Before the time of broadcast television, his father, J. Lance Kentish, spent time in the evenings inventing and telling stories about the bush animals, the talking red-gum tree and the magic carpet to his family.

David has continued in this same vein with the telling of stories of imaginary Australian bush animals and friends and the many predicaments that they find themselves involved in.

He has also completed two books of family history, *The Kentish's of Keysbrook* , which he has self-published and distributed around the family.

Another booklet, *Beside the Billabong* is a story of Warragul, who is a juvenile bunyip of Australian mythology and his animal friends who find the fun and adventures of living at a billabong.

David, with his wife Barbara, enjoys travelling with their 4x4 ute and caravan in and around the Australian outback and bush. This is where he gets most of his inspiration which has led to his collection of stories.

Paperback and E-book

Paperback and E-book

Paperback and E-book

Paperback and E-book

Paperback and E-book

Paperback and E-book

Paperback and E-book

Paperback and E-book

https://david-kentish.square.site

Scan the QR code for more stories to enjoy. Happy reading and enjoy everything that you do. Visit his website, https://david-kentish.square.site, to find the latest information.

www.ingramcontent.com/pod-product-compliance
Lightning Source LLC
Chambersburg PA
CBHW071142020726
47502CB00002B/233